Praise for Delores Fossen

"The perfect blend of sexy cowboys, humor and romance will rein you in from the first line."
—*New York Times* bestselling author B.J. Daniels

"From the shocking opening paragraph on, Fossen's tale just keeps getting better."
—*RT Book Reviews* on *Sawyer*, 4½ stars, Top Pick

"*Rustling Up Trouble* is action packed, but it's the relationship and emotional drama (and the sexy hero) that will reel readers in."
—*RT Book Reviews*, 4½ stars

"While not lacking in action or intrigue, it's the romance of two unlikely people that soars."
—*RT Book Reviews* on *Maverick Sheriff*, 4 stars

ISBN-13: 978-0-373-78961-0

Texas on My Mind

Copyright © 2016 by Delores Fossen

What Happens on the Ranch
Copyright © 2016 by Delores Fossen

This is a work of fiction. Names, characters, places and incidents are
either the product of the author's imagination or are used fictitiously,
and any resemblance to actual persons, living or dead, business
establishments, events or locales is entirely coincidental.

This edition published by arrangement with Harlequin Books S.A.

For questions and comments about the quality of this book,
please contact us at CustomerService@Harlequin.com.

® and TM are trademarks of Harlequin Enterprises Limited or its
corporate affiliates. Trademarks indicated with ® are registered in the
United States Patent and Trademark Office, the Canadian Intellectual
Property Office and in other countries.

www.HQNBooks.com

Printed in U.S.A.

DELORES FOSSEN

TEXAS ON MY MIND

CONTENTS

To my wonderful editor, Allison Lyons

TEXAS ON MY MIND

CHAPTER ONE

THERE WERE TWO women in Captain Riley McCord's bed. Women wearing cutoff shorts, skinny tops and flip-flops.

Riley blinked a couple of times to make sure they weren't by-products of his pain meds and bone-deep exhaustion. *Nope.* They were real enough because he could hear them breathing.

See them breathing, too.

The lamp on the nightstand was on, the milky-yellow light spilling over them. Their tops holding in those C-cups were doing plenty of moving with each breath they took.

He caught a glimpse of a nipple.

If he'd still been a teenager, Riley might have considered having two women in his bed a dream come true. Especially in this room. He'd grown up in this house, had had plenty of fantasies in that very bed. But he was thirty-one now, and with his shoulder throbbing like an abscessed tooth, taking on two women didn't fall into fantasy territory. More like suicide.

Besides, man-rule number two applied here: don't do anything half-assed. Anything he attempted right now would be significantly less than half and would make an ass out of him.

Who the hell were they?

And why were they there in his house, in his bed?

The place was supposed to be empty since he'd called ahead and given the cook and housekeeper the week off.

The sisters, Della and Stella, had pretty much run the house since Riley's folks had been killed in a car wreck thirteen years ago. Clearing out the pair hadn't been easy, but he'd used his captain's I'm-giving-the-orders-here voice.

For once it had worked.

His kid sister was away at college. His older brother Lucky was God knew where. Lucky's twin, Logan, was on a business trip and wouldn't be back for at least another week. Even when Logan returned, he'd be spending far more time running the family's cattle brokerage company than actually in the house. That lure of emptiness was the only reason Riley had decided to come here for some peace and quiet.

And so that nobody would see him wincing and grunting in pain.

Riley glanced around to try to figure out who the women were and why they were there. When he checked the family room, he saw a clue by the fireplace. A banner. Well, sort of. He flicked on the lights to get a better look. It was a ten-foot strip of white crepe paper.

Welcome Home, Riley, Our Hero, was written on it.

The black ink had bled, and the tape on one side had given way, and now it dangled and coiled like a soy-sauced ramen noodle.

There were bowls of chips, salsa and other food on the coffee table next to a picture of him in his uniform. Someone had tossed flag confetti all around the snacks, and some of the red, white and blue sparkles had landed on the floor and sofa. In the salsa, too.

Apparently, this was supposed to be the makings of a homecoming party for him.

Whoever had done this probably hadn't counted on his flight from the base in Germany being delayed nine hours. Riley hadn't counted on it, either. Now, it was three in the morning, and he darn sure didn't want to celebrate.

Or have women in his bed.

And he hoped it didn't lower his testosterone a couple of notches to have an unmanly thought like that.

Riley put his duffel bag on the floor. Not quietly, but the women didn't stir even an eyelash. He considered just waking them, but heck, that would require talking to them, and the only thing he wanted right now was another hit of pain meds and a place to collapse.

He went to the bedroom next to his. A guest room. No covers or pillows, which would mean a hunt to find some. That sent him to Lucky's room on the other side of the hall. Covers, yes, but there was another woman asleep facedown with her sleeve-tattooed arm dangling off the side. There was also a saddle on the foot of the bed. Thankfully, Riley's mind was too clouded to even want to consider why it was there.

Getting desperate now and feeling a little like Goldilocks in search of a "just right" place to crash, he went to Logan's suite, the only other bedroom downstairs. Definitely covers there. He didn't waste the energy to turn on the light to have a closer look; since this was Logan's space, it would no doubt be clean enough to pass a military inspection.

No saddles or women, thank God, and he wouldn't have to climb the stairs that he wasn't sure he could climb anyway.

Riley popped a couple of pain meds and dropped down on the bed, his eyes already closing before his head landed against something soft and crumbly. He considered investigating it. *Briefly* considered it. But when it didn't bite, shoot or scald him, he passed on the notion of an investigation.

Whatever was soft and crumbly would just have to wait.

RILEY JACKKNIFED IN Logan's bed, the pain knocking the breath right out of him. Without any kind of warning, the nightmare that he'd been having had morphed into a full-fledged flashback.

Sometimes he could catch the flashback just as it was bubbling to the surface, and he could stomp it back down with his mental steel-toed combat boots. Sometimes humming "Jingle Bells" helped.

Not this time, though. ·

The flashback had him by the throat before Riley could even get out a single note of that stupid song he hated. Why had his brain chosen that little Christmas ditty to blur out the images anyway?

The smell came first. Always the fucking smell. The dust and debris whipped up by the chopper. The Pave Hawk blades slicing through the dirt-colored smoke. But not drowning out the sounds.

He wasn't sure how sounds like that could make it through the thump of the blades, the shouts, screams and the chaos. But they did. The sounds always did.

Someone was calling for help in a dialect Riley barely understood. But you didn't need to know the words to hear the fear.

Or smell it.

The images came with a vengeance. Like a chopped-up snake crawling and coiling together to form a neat picture of hell. A handful of buildings on fire, others ripped apart from the explosion. Blood on the bleached-out sand. The screams for help. The kids.

Why the hell were there kids?

Riley had been trained to rescue military and civilians after the fight, after all hell had broken loose. Had been conditioned to deal with fires, blood, IEDs, gunfire, and being dropped into the middle of it so he could do his job and save lives.

But nobody had ever been able to tell him how to deal with the kids.

PTSD. Such a tidy little label. A dialect that civilians understood, or thought they did anyway. But it was just another label for shit. Shit that Riley didn't want in his head.

He grabbed his pain meds from the pocket of his uniform and shoved one, then another into his parched mouth. Soon, very soon, he could start stomping the images back into that little shoe box he'd built in his head.

Soon.

He closed his eyes, the words finally coming that he needed to hear.

"Jingle bells, jingle bells…"

He really did need to come up with a more manly sounding song to kick some flashback ass.

CHAPTER TWO

"HI DA TOOKIE," someone whispered.

Riley was sure he was still dreaming. At least, he was sure of it until someone poked him on the cheek.

Hell. What now?

"Hi da tookie," the voice repeated. Again in a whisper.

Obviously this was some kind of code or foreign language, but Riley's head was too foggy to process it. He groaned—and, yeah, it was a groan of pain—and forced his eyelids open so he could try to figure out what the heck was going on.

Eyeballs stared back at him.

Eyeballs that were really close. Like, just an inch from his.

That jolted him fully awake, and Riley automatically reached for his weapon. Which wasn't there, of course. He wasn't on assignment in hostile territory. He was in his own family's home. And the eyes so close to his didn't belong to the enemy.

They belonged to a kid.

A kid with brown eyes and dark brown hair. Maybe two or three years old, and he had a smear of something on his cheek.

"Hi da tookie," the kid said again. He didn't wait for Riley to respond, however. He jammed something beneath the pillow.

A cookie, aka tookie.

And it had an identical smell to the one Riley had just been dreaming about. Except it was no dream. Riley realized that when he lifted his head and the crumbs fell onto the collar of his uniform. *Hell's Texas bells.* He'd slept on a chocolate-chip cookie. But why the devil was it there in Logan's bed?

Like the women in his own bed and the gibberish-talking kid, an answer for that might have to wait a second or two because Riley had a more pressing question.

"Who are you?" he asked the kid.

"E-tan," the boy readily answered.

That didn't explain much, and Riley wasn't sure how much a kid that age could explain anyway.

"Tookie," the boy repeated. He took one of the crumbs from Riley's collar and ate it.

All right, so maybe that did explain why he'd slept on a cookie-laced pillow. This kid was responsible. But who was responsible for the kid? He didn't get a chance to find out because the little boy took off running out of the room.

Riley got up. More groaning. Some grimacing, too. The damage to his shoulder and knee weren't permanent, but at the moment it sure as hell felt like it.

The docs at the base in Ramstein, Germany, had told him he needed at least three more weeks to recover from the surgery to repair the damage done by the shrapnel when it'd slashed into his right shoulder and chest. After that, he'd start some physical therapy for both the shoulder and his wrenched knee. And after that, there would be a medical board to decide if he could continue being the only thing he'd ever wanted to be.

An AF CRO. Short for Air Force Combat Rescue Officer.

It twisted his gut to think that it could all be taken

away. That whole "life turning on a dime" sucked donkey dicks, and he could go from being part of an elite special ops force to someone he was darn sure he didn't want to be.

That was a violation of man-rule number one: don't be ordinary.

Frustrated with that thought, with the pain and with the whole world in general, Riley headed into the adjoining bathroom. When he came out, the kid was still nowhere in sight.

Brushing away some more cookie crumbs from his uniform, Riley went into the family room to look around. No sign of E-tan there. Someone had cleaned up the party remains, so Riley headed to his own bedroom. *Good gravy.* The two women were still there, still asleep. Riley was about to wake them, to tell them about the cookie-hiding toddler, but then he caught a whiff of something else.

Coffee. The miracle drug.

And he heard someone moving around in the kitchen. Since Della and her sister, Stella, had sworn on John Wayne's soul and their mama's Bible that they would follow Riley's orders and stay far away from the place, there shouldn't be any sounds or smells coming from anywhere in the house. Still, if this was a break-in, at least the burglar had made coffee. He might just give up everything of value to get a single cup.

Once Riley hobbled his way to the kitchen, he saw that E-tan had already crawled into a chair at the table. Like the rest of the house, the kitchen was sprawling, and even though they had two other dining rooms, Riley had eaten a lot of his meals in this room. In fact, he'd sat in that very chair where the kid was sitting now.

Riley immediately located the cookie source. There

was a plate of about a dozen or so of them on the kitchen table. He spotted the source of the moving-around sounds, too.

Another woman.

A blonde this time. Her hair was cut short and choppy and fell against her neck.

This one was very much awake. She was at the stove, her back to him, and she was stirring something in a skillet. Her body swayed a little with each stir, and despite the F-5 tornado in his head, Riley noticed. Hard not to notice since she was wearing denim shorts that hugged a very nice ass.

An ass that was strangely familiar.

She turned slightly to the side when she reached for the saltshaker, and Riley got a look at her face. Familiar all right.

Claire.

A real blast from the past. Calling Claire Davidson a childhood friend was a little like saying the ocean had a bit of water in it. Once they'd been as thick as thieves, but he'd pretty much lost touch with her after he graduated from college.

Riley took a moment to savor the moment. There was always something about Claire that reminded him of home. Of the things he'd left behind. Not that she'd been his to leave, but it always felt a little like that whenever he thought of her. Now he didn't have to conjure up a memory. She was right there in front of him.

Wearing those nice-fitting shorts.

Riley went to her, slipped his arm around her waist to give her a friendly hug.

And Claire screamed as if he'd just gutted her with a machete.

Along with slapping him upside the head with an egg-coated spatula.

She made some garbled sounds. Hit him again. This time on his already throbbing shoulder. She took aim at him once more, but her common sense must have kicked in, and she looked at his face.

"Riley, my God, you scared the life out of me!"

"Really? I hadn't noticed." He didn't mean to sound grouchy, but hell in a handbasket, that spatula had hit the wrong spot.

Claire's face flushed red. Then she smiled. And despite his eyes watering in pain, he had no trouble seeing it. That smile always lit up the room, and it gave him a sucker punch of attraction. But as Riley had done since about the time he'd first sprouted chest hair, he stepped back. For the past fifteen years or so, Claire had been hands-off.

Not that she'd ever actually been hands-on.

Evidently she didn't have the same rules about the hands-off part. She put her arms around him, pulled him really, really close to her for a hug. He wasn't able to bite back a grunt of pain so the hug was short and sweet.

"I'm so sorry." Claire grabbed a tea towel, began to wipe the egg off his face. "I heard about your injury, of course."

Judging from the noodle banner, so had everyone in town. "I'll be fine. I just need a few weeks to recover."

At best, that was wishful thinking. At worst, an out-and-out lie. It was a sad day when a man lied to himself, but right now Riley needed anything that would get him through this.

Lies and oxycodone.

She stared at him, made a sound as if she hadn't fully

bought his answer. Her smile faded. "Should I ask how much you're hurting right now?"

This was easy. "No."

Claire nodded, maybe even looked relieved. *Good.* Because if she was uncomfortable talking about it, then maybe it wouldn't come up again.

"About an hour ago someone dropped off an Angus bull that Logan bought," she said as if this were a normal conversation. It wasn't, but he guessed this was her way of chit-chatting about anything but his injury. "It must have been worth a fortune the way they were treating it. The men wore white gloves when they touched it. Don't worry. One of the guys took care of the paperwork and such."

By *guys,* she probably meant one of Logan's assistants from the office in town. Or maybe a ranch hand who tended the horses and cattle that came and went through the stables and grounds on the property. Other than a couple of riding horses for their personal use, none of the livestock stayed too long, just enough for Logan to make whatever amount of money he intended to make off the deal. As a broker, Logan usually dealt in bulk purchases.

Since Riley hadn't been home in nearly six months, he wasn't sure exactly who was on his brother's payroll for McCord Cattle Brokers or for managing the livestock on the grounds. *His* payroll, too.

Technically.

But while the house would always be Riley's home, it was Logan's heart and soul in the family business. Logan had been as happy to stay put, and buy and sell cattle as Riley had been to head out for more exciting pastures.

He looked out the back bay window at the sprawl of green grass, streaked with white fences and dotted with a dozen barns, corrals, the hands' quarters and outbuildings. Everything looked exactly the same as it always had down to the yellow Lab sleeping under one of the shade trees. Both a blessing and a curse as far as Riley was concerned.

"How'd you get from the San Antonio airport?" she asked.

"Taxi."

That earned him a raised eyebrow because Claire likely filled in the blanks. Riley hadn't called anyone to come and get him because he didn't want to see anyone. And he hadn't rented a car because he was in too much pain to drive. It'd been worth every penny of the hundred-dollar cab fare to get a driver who hadn't asked him a single question.

"Logan called the house phone earlier to check and make sure you got in all right," Claire went on after lowering that eyebrow. "He said he didn't want to call your cell and risk waking you. Oh, and no one's been able to get in touch with Lucky yet."

That was all right. He didn't want to deal with Lucky. Or Logan for that matter. They were his big brothers, and he loved them—most days anyway—but Riley wanted to go the less-is-better route with his recovery. Actually, he wanted the none-is-best route.

"Why are you here?" he asked Claire, and since it was probably all related, he added two other questions. "Why are there women in my bed?" No sense asking about the one in Lucky's because that was often the case. "And who is he?"

Riley tipped his head to the kid, who was now out of the chair and eating the bits of scrambled egg that'd fallen off the spatula and onto the floor.

"Ethan, no. That's yucky," Claire scolded, sticking out her tongue and making a face.

She scooped up the little boy, wiping that smear off his cheek. It was chocolate. And in the same motion she eased him back into the chair. A chair with a makeshift booster seat of old phone books.

"Don't wiggle around, or you'll fall," Claire told the kid. "I'll get you some eggs when they've cooled a little. The women in your bed are Wilbert Starkley's twin granddaughters," she added to Riley without missing a beat. "The one in Lucky's room is their sister."

After she moved the skillet from the burner to the back of the stove, Claire got busy cleaning up the egg mess on the floor. Cleaning off Riley, too.

"Wilbert Starkley's granddaughters?" Riley repeated. Wilbert owned the town's grocery store and was some-one Riley had known his whole life, which was pretty much the norm for Spring Hill. "No way are those his granddaughters. They're just kids. The two in my bed are grown women."

With boobs that jiggled when they breathed.

Claire smiled as if she knew exactly what he was thinking. "Not kids. They're nineteen and home from college for the summer. Their sister is twenty-one and works for their dad. Wilbert dropped them off last night, and they fell asleep waiting for you to get in."

He listened, still didn't hear them stirring around. "Are they deaf? Or drugged? They slept through your blood-curdling scream."

"I guess they're just deep sleepers. Anyway, when they heard you were coming home to recover and that Della and Stella were on vacation, they wanted to help."

Claire lifted her eyebrow again on the vacation part of that explanation. With reason. Della and Stella didn't normally take vacations and never at the same time. One of them was always around to take care of the place and the McCord clan.

"I *wanted* Della and Stella on vacation. I'm the one who told them to go. And how are those other women supposed to help?" Riley located the biggest cup he could find and filled it to the brim with coffee. Judging from the size of the headache he was going to have to cure, he'd need at least six more cups.

"They want to help by doing things for you so that you can get all the rest you need. That's why I'm here. To fix you breakfast."

It wasn't as if Riley didn't appreciate Claire's efforts. He did. However, it didn't help his confusion that was growing with every new bit of this conversation. "But why are you here? As in *here* in Spring Hill? Did you move back?"

Claire nodded. "I came back about six months ago when Gran got sick. I still have my apartment in San Antonio, though. I'm still working as a wedding photographer, too. But I'm staying on awhile longer here to clean out Gran's house so I can get it ready to sell."

Yeah, that. He had no trouble hearing the grief in her voice. "I was sorry to hear she passed away."

Claire didn't even try to dismiss his sympathy. Probably because she couldn't. She'd been close to her grandmother, and it didn't matter that the woman was old and had lived a full if not somewhat eccentric life. Claire obviously hadn't been ready to let her go.

Still multitasking, Claire took out two plates from the cabinet, scooped some of the eggs onto both of them and set the plates on the table. Apparently one of them was for him because Claire motioned for Riley to sit. The other plate was for the kid.

"And who's the kid?" Riley pressed.

"That's Ethan, my son. He's two years old." She smiled, this time one that only a mother could manage. Ethan gave her a toothy grin right back.

Riley's attention went straight to her left hand. No ring.

Claire followed his gaze. "I'm not married."

"Oh." And because Riley didn't know what else to say, he went with another "oh."

Man, he was way out of the gossip loop. His sister, Anna, had told him about Claire's grandmother dying two months ago but not about Claire being a mom. Better yet, Anna hadn't said a word about who had made Claire a mom.

Probably Daniel Larson.

Except Ethan didn't look a thing like Daniel. Ethan had dark brown hair more like the color of Riley's own. Daniel could have passed for a Swedish male model with his blond hair and pale blue eyes. Maybe that meant Claire had met someone else. Someone who looked like him.

But Riley rethought that.

Of course it was Daniel. The kid just got his looks from some past ancestor with that coloring. Because Claire was with Daniel. Daniel had captured her heart and just about every other part of her their sophomore year in high school, and Claire had chosen him.

Over Riley.

It hadn't been a particularly hard decision for her, either. And Riley knew that because she'd left her binder behind in chemistry class, and he had seen her list of why she should pick one over the other. Fifteen years later, Riley could remember that list in perfect detail.

Beneath Daniel's name, Claire had written, "Cute, reliable, good listener, likes cats, no plans to move off and join the military." Beneath Riley's name, she'd written only one word.

"Hot."

Hot had stroked his ego for a minute or two, but he definitely hadn't stacked up against the cute, cat-loving Daniel. And while Daniel and Riley had once been close friends, it'd been nearly four years since Riley had seen him. That was plenty enough time to make a two-year-old.

Now Claire was a mother.

He supposed that was the norm seeing she was thirty-one, the same age as he was. People did that. They made babies. Stayed in one place for more than a year. Didn't get shot at as a general rule. They had lives that Riley had always made sure to avoid.

Claire dodged Riley's stare, looking at the plate of cookies instead. Then she huffed, put her hands on her hips. "Ethan, you took another one of those cookies, didn't you? Where'd you hide it this time?"

"Logan's bed," Riley answered when Ethan didn't say anything.

But, man, Riley wished he hadn't ratted him out. The kid looked at him with wide-eyed bewilderment and betrayal. Ethan's bottom lip even quivered. Riley felt as if he had violated a major man-pact.

"So, that's what's in your hair." Claire plucked some crumbs from Riley's head. "I'm sorry. Ethan knows he's not allowed to have sweets without asking. He took at least two cookies last night when we were over here before you got home. He ate one, hid the other and now he's taken another one." She pointed her index finger at him. "No computer games for you today, young man."

The kid's look of betrayal intensified significantly.

"Sorry, buddy," Riley said.

Claire put some toast on the table, poured Riley a glass

of OJ from the fridge, topped off his coffee. She clearly hadn't forgotten the waitressing skills she'd learned from her afternoon job at the Fork and Spoon Café in high school.

"Eat up, Ethan," she told her boy. "We've got to get going soon. The next shift should be here any minute."

Riley looked at her midbite. "Shift?"

Claire nodded, started washing the skillet she'd used to cook the eggs. "Misty Reagan and Trisha Weller. They're coming to help you get dressed and then will fix your lunch."

Both women were familiar to him. *Intimately* familiar. He'd had sex with only two girls in high school.

And it was those two.

"Misty's divorced, no kids," Claire went on. "That brings the total to nine divorced couples in town now in case you're keeping count."

He wasn't, but divorce was a rare occurrence in Spring Hill—less than 1 percent of the marriages had failed. It was the cool springwater, some said. Most folks just fell in love, got hitched and stayed that way. Riley thought it didn't have as much to do with the water as it did with lack of options. Little pond. Not many fish.

"Trisha never married. Oh, except for that time she married you, of course." Another smile tugged at Claire's mouth. This one didn't so much light up the room as yank his chain.

"Trisha and I were six years old," Riley said in his defense. "And she had brownies."

That perked up Ethan. "Boun-knees." Obviously, the kid had a serious sweet tooth, something else he had in common with Riley.

"Well, I guess a home-baked dessert is a good reason for marriage," Claire remarked.

It sure seemed that way at the time. "It was Trisha's version of put a ring on it. No marriage, no brownies."

"And you did put a ring on it." Claire dried the skillet, put it away and dropped the spatula in the dishwasher after she rinsed it. "I seem to remember something gold with a red stone in it."

"Fake, and it fell apart after a few hours. Just like our fake marriage."

That eyebrow of hers went to work again. "I think she'd like to make that marriage the real deal."

Riley frowned. "Trisha said that?"

"Not with words, but she's a lawyer in Austin and cleared her schedule for the next two weeks just so she could be here. I'd say she really, really wants to be here *with you.*"

Well, hell. Riley liked Trisha enough, but he hadn't wanted anyone hanging around, including a woman who was looking for more than a plastic ring from a vending machine.

"Call them," Riley insisted. "Tell them not to come, that I don't need or want any help. I really just need to get some rest—that's all. That's why I told Della and Stella to take the week off."

The words had hardly left his mouth when Riley heard the sound of car engines. Ethan raced to the window in the living room with Riley and Claire trailing along right behind him. Sure enough two cars had pulled into the circular driveway that fronted the house.

Wearing a short blue skirt and snug top, Misty got out first from a bright yellow Mustang, and she snagged two shopping bags off the passenger's seat. She'd been a cheerleader in high school and still had some zip to her steps. Was still a looker, too, with her dark brown hair that she'd pulled up in a ponytail.

She might be trouble.

After all, she'd lost her virginity to Riley when she was seventeen after they'd dated for about four months. That tended to create a bond for women. Maybe Misty would be looking to *bond* again.

Then there was Trisha.

Riley had lost his virginity to her. And there'd been that wedding in first grade, possibly creating another problem with that whole bonding thing.

When Trisha stepped out of a silver BMW, she immediately looked up, her gaze snagging his in the window. She smiled. No chain yanking or "light up the room" smile, either. All Riley saw were lips and teeth, two things Trisha had used quite well on the night of his de-virgining.

"Oh, look," Claire said. "Trisha brought you a plate of brownies."

Yeah, she had.

And other things were familiar about Trisha, too. Like those curves that had stirred every man's zipper in town. Now all those curves were hugged up in a devil-red dress. She still looked hungry, as if she were ready to gobble up something. And judging from the smile she gave Riley, she wanted him to be the gobblee.

Another time, another place, Riley might have considered a good gobbling. Or at least some innocent flirting. But there was that part about people seeing him in pain. Plus, there was always the threat of a flashback. No way did he want anyone around to witness that little treat.

"Come on, Ethan," Claire said, scooping him up. "It's time for us to go."

"So soon?" Riley wanted to ask her to stay, but that would just sound wussy. His testosterone had already dropped enough for one day.

"So soon," Claire verified. She waggled her fingers in a goodbye wave and headed for the door. "Enjoy those brownies."

She probably would have just waltzed out, but Claire stopped in her tracks when their gazes met. She didn't ask what was going on in his head, and the chain-yanking expression was gone.

Hell.

He hadn't wanted her to see what was behind his eyes. Hadn't wanted anyone to see it. But Riley was as certain as he was of his boot size that Claire knew.

"Finish your breakfast," Claire instructed. Her voice was a little unsteady now. "I'll deal with them. I can't guarantee they won't come back, but you'll have a few hours at least. Is that enough time?"

Riley lied with a nod.

He used actual words for his next lie. "You don't have to worry about me, Claire. Soon I'll be as good as new."

CHAPTER THREE

"PAY DOUGH!" ETHAN squealed when Claire held up the picture of the painting.

Claire checked to make sure she was showing him the right one. Yes, it was van Gogh's *Starry Night*, but there was no Play-Doh on it.

"That's really close, sweetie, and the artist's name does sort of rhyme with Play-Doh," Claire encouraged.

"Pay dough!" he repeated, speeding up the words a little.

She tried not to look disappointed. The directions on the "Making Your Toddler a Little Genius" packet had said to make this activity fun. Or rather *FUN!!!!* Claire only hoped that the creators of this product had raised at least one semigenius child and that they hadn't just tossed some crap activities together to milk her out of her $89.95, plus shipping.

"Try again," she prompted, waving the picture at Ethan to get his already wandering attention. "You got this right yesterday." And, according to the rules, she wasn't supposed to move on to the next picture until he'd gotten this one right three days in a row. They'd been working on it for two weeks now with no end in sight.

Ethan studied the picture and grinned. "Money!"

Claire was certain she didn't contain her disappointment that time. "No. Not *Monet*." That'd been last month's lesson.

She snagged one of his toy vehicles. A van. And she held it up with the painting while trying to make a running/going motion with her index and middle fingers. Her nails nearly tore a hole in one of the star blobs. Evidently, $89.95 wasn't enough to buy higher-quality paper, and her example was obviously too abstract.

"Ri-wee!" Ethan squealed with more excitement than money or Play-Doh.

Frowning, Claire put aside the picture and the van. "No, not Riley." Or rather Ri-wee. "Why don't we work on this later? You can go ahead and play."

You would have thought she'd just announced he could have an entire toy store and unlimited chocolate-chip cookies for life. Ethan scooted across the floor and went back to his cars. The auto crashes started immediately.

"Ri-wee!" he repeated like some kind of tribal shout with each new collision.

Even though he didn't have the pronunciation down pat, Claire knew her son was only repeating what he'd heard her mumble for the past two days—Riley. For some reason, Riley's name kept popping into her head and then continued to randomly pop out of her mouth.

And there was no good reason for it.

A few bad reasons, though.

Riley was an attractive man. Still hot. No denying that. He was also very much hands-off since he wouldn't be around for long, as usual. Maybe her brain would figure that out soon enough and stop sending these ridiculous impulses to the rest of her body.

Claire stayed on the floor next to Ethan but grabbed her laptop from the sofa. Since she had struck out in creating a baby genius, she might as well get some work done, and she downloaded the last photo she needed to edit. When she finished, it would almost be bittersweet because it was also the last of her work in the queue.

More photo shoots would follow. They always did. But it was best if she didn't have any free time on her hands right now.

Of course, she could fill that free time, easily, by sorting through more of her gran's things. However, that was more bitter than sweet, and it was also the main reason she kept procrastinating. And overeating. She'd put on six pounds since the sorting had started. Soon, she'd either have to pay for therapy or Weight Watchers.

Her phone buzzed, and Claire saw Livvy Larimer's name on the screen. Her best friend and co-owner of their business, Dearly Beloved.

"Well?" Livvy started.

No greeting. Which meant she expected Claire to dish up something exciting. And the dishing up that Livvy wanted was about Riley. Best just to give her a summary and hope it didn't lead to too many other questions.

"Riley finally made it home day before yesterday after his flight was delayed. I fixed him breakfast, and I came back to Gran's to get some work done on the Herrington-Anderson engagement photos." An engagement that Livvy knew all about because she was the wedding planner for the event.

"That's it?" Livvy asked.

Here come the questions. But Claire made Livvy work for the answers. "What else were you expecting?"

"Fudging details. Specifically, fudging you did with Riley."

Fudging was the compromise they'd worked out instead of using the *F* word, one of Livvy's many favorites. They also used *sugar* for *shit* and *bubble gum* for *blow job*, something that came up surprisingly often in her conversations with Livvy.

They were still working on one for *asshole*.

Ethan's little ears picked up on anything Claire didn't want him to hear while selectively shutting out van Gogh, and since Livvy cursed like a meth dealer in an R-rated movie, they'd resorted to acceptable substitutions.

"No fudging," Claire explained. She was finally able to keep a straight face when she said it. "I only fixed Riley breakfast and ran interference from some unwanted visitors."

Livvy made a *yeah-right* sound. "And you've fawned over him for the past decade."

"Fawned over? What the heck does that even mean? Is that a new compromise word?"

"Yes, it means you dream of fudging and bubblegumming Riley."

Claire huffed. "Does any woman actually dream of bubblegumming a man? I don't. It's more of something that just sort of evolves during foreplay."

"Foreplay," Ethan said with perfect clarity. Great, they needed a compromise word for that now.

"Sugar yeah, you dreamed of fudging him," Livvy went on. "You pointed out his pictures in your high school yearbook. You've talked about him. And then there's Ethan—"

"Riley and I were friends in high school. *Friends*," Claire emphasized.

"You can fawn over friends. And fudge them, too. I've seen pictures of Riley, and he'd make a great fudge."

"Riley has never fudged me." Claire paused. "He's hurt, Livvy."

That reminder flicked away the annoyance she was feeling about Livvy's interrogation. But Claire replaced the flicked-away emotion with one she'd been trying to keep out of her head.

Worry.

"Is it bad?" Livvy asked.

"Maybe." *Probably*, Claire silently amended.

"God, I just can't imagine doing what he does. Ever googled *Combat Rescue Officer* and looked at some of those pictures?"

Once. It had been enough.

Livvy made a shuddering sound. "And to think, he's been doing that job for a long time."

Nine years. Since he graduated from college and joined the Air Force. Riley had been on six deployments, and even though Claire didn't know the exact locations, she was betting there'd been plenty of other times when he could have been wounded or killed.

Ethan grumbled something, clearly not pleased about his car-bashing game. Claire glanced over to make sure all was well. It wasn't. One of the cars had broken. Again. Thank heavens it wasn't one of his favorites so his re-action was mild. The Terrible Twos wasn't just a cliché when it came to her baby boy. He often aimed high to live up to that particular label.

She needed to find a toddler genius kit to help her with that.

"You think Riley's got PTSD or something?" Livvy went on.

This was even less comfortable than the fudge ques-tion. "If he does, I'm sure there's help for that at the base in San Antonio. From what he told his sister, he'll be starting physical therapy there soon."

The military would patch him up, both physically and mentally if needed, and Riley would go right back out there on deployment again. To someplace dangerous.

Because that's what he did. What he'd always wanted since middle school.

"You haven't asked me about the hot date," Livvy said a moment later.

"Date-date, or are we talking fruit now?" And Claire was serious. Livvy had a thing for trying new foods and men. Lots of men. She had been married three times and was always on the lookout for ex number four. Thankfully, she didn't live in Spring Hill or she would have single-handedly skewed their divorce stats.

"Date-date. You know, the guy I met from the dating site. I told you, didn't I?"

"I don't think so." She'd been living vicariously—sexually anyway—through Livvy since having Ethan. "How'd it go?"

"Sugar hot," Livvy declared. "His name is Alejandro just like the Lady Gaga song. He's an albino drummer in a heavy metal band." She giggled like a schoolgirl. "I predict lots of fudging in my future."

Since Livvy seemed excited about his name/career/pigment/fudging combo, Claire was happy for her. Or rather cautiously optimistic. "Is he nice?"

"Of course. I wouldn't go out with a grouchy asshole again. Sorry, we'll work on that word. Anyway, other than his pinkeye, he's perfect."

"Uh, I don't know a lot about albinos, but I think pink eyes are normal for them."

"Not pink *eyes*," Livvy quickly corrected. "Pink*eye*. He's using drops for it, though, so it should clear up soon. You really should use this dating site, Claire. It's the best one yet."

She'd rather have pinkeye. "I'm on hiatus from dating. Until I get Ethan potty trained." Of course, there was no correlation. None. But thankfully it was an argument that always worked with Livvy.

"So, making any progress getting the house ready to sell?" Livvy asked.

Claire wanted to say a hallelujah for the change of topic. "Some. Gran wasn't a hoarder exactly, but she didn't throw away much. I'll keep at it until a new job comes in."

"Already got two. Wedding announcement photos. I'll email you the dates and details."

There were clearly more procrastination possibilities on the horizon. It was probably depression over Gran's death, but Claire felt stuck in Neutral.

"Oh, and Daniel called the office, looking for you," Livvy added. "Said his fudging phone died after a software update, and he lost all his sugar, including your phone number."

The timing was odd. What with Riley's arrival back in Spring Hill. Like her, Daniel no longer lived there, but that didn't mean a gossip or two hadn't called him in San Antonio with news of Riley's homecoming.

Rather than come out and ask that, Claire took the roundabout route. "Did Daniel want anything specific?"

"Well, I'm guessing he wanted *you*. I gave him your number, so I figure you'll get a call from him soon."

"Good." And Claire would be happy to hear from Daniel. Almost. "Gotta go," she said when Ethan yawned and stomped on one of the cars. "I'll send you these engagement pictures as soon as I'm done."

The moment she ended the call, Claire hit the save button on her files and picked up Ethan. He started to fuss right away. In part because he knew nap time was coming. Also in part because he needed a nap.

She changed his diaper. Not an easy feat now that the

grumpy boy had emerged. Still, she loved grumpy boy just as much as the other boys that materialized throughout the day. Ethan had her heart. And the little sugar knew it.

"No getting up," she warned him when she put him in his crib.

He was quickly outgrowing it. Outgrowing naps, too. And it wouldn't be long before he really would be ready for potty training.

Her baby was growing up so fast.

Not that she would miss the whole diapering thing and having him test his aiming skills by trying to pee in her eye. She'd convinced herself that it was a labor of love. But it was also time when she had Ethan close and he wasn't running away from her.

Plus, she'd lose that excuse she kept giving to Livvy about not dating.

Since Ethan might or might not obey that no-getting-up part and since he might try to climb out of the crib again, Claire knew she'd need to spend at least fifteen minutes with him while he fell asleep. No use wasting that time, so she went into the hall to bring one of the cardboard boxes into the makeshift nursery with her. She had plenty of boxes to choose from. At least thirty that she'd already dragged down from the attic or found in the back of her gran's closet.

There'd been spiders involved.

Something that made her shiver just thinking about it.

The various cousins had already gone through the house and taken items of furniture and such that they'd wanted. Which wasn't nearly enough to clear out the place. Every room, every corner was still crammed with bits and pieces that reminded Claire of the woman who'd raised her. The woman she'd loved.

Damn it.

The tears came. They always did whenever she thought of Gran.

God, she missed her.

Opening the box wouldn't help, either, but going through whatever was inside was the next step to getting the house ready to go on the market. Claire wasn't exactly strapped for cash. Yet. But her savings had dwindled considerably what with all the time she'd taken off to be with Ethan.

She didn't regret that time off, not for a second, but she didn't have the comfortable financial pad that she needed. Since Gran had left her the house free and clear, anything Claire got from the sale would be hers to keep.

She put the box on the floor, glanced over at Ethan. Still not asleep, but his eyelids were getting droopy.

The tape holding the box was so old that it gave way with a gentle tug, and Claire opened the flap. Checked for spiders.

Nothing scurried out at her.

So she began the sorting. She'd set aside another area at the end of the hall to deal with the contents of each box. One pile for stuff to keep. Another for items to be donated. A final one for trash.

She'd yet to put anything in the trash pile.

Not a good sign.

Of course, it was probably wishful thinking on her part that a charity group would want copies of old magazines and newspapers, panties with shot elastic and mismatched socks. This box was pretty much the same. Magazines from the 1980s. More newspapers. A Gerber baby food jar filled with buttons. Another had sequins. There were some Mardi Gras beads, though Claire couldn't recall Gran ever mentioning a trip to New Orleans.

And then Claire saw the old photo of Riley's parents—Betsy and Sherman.

More bittersweetness.

Claire had been in the car with them the night they'd died. Still had both the physical and emotional scars from it. It'd been pouring rain, and they'd given her a ride from the high school basketball game where the Spring Hill Mavericks had won by eleven points. Daniel was away visiting his sick aunt and had missed the game. Riley had stayed behind to be with Misty. Anna was home studying. Logan was on a date. And Lucky was at a rodeo.

She remembered all those little details. Every last one of them. The knock-knock joke that Mr. McCord had told just before the crash. Mrs. McCord's laughter at the lame punch line. The Alan Jackson song playing on the radio. The way her band uniform was scratching against her skin. But Claire couldn't remember the accident itself.

Sometimes she would recall a blur of motion from the red car that'd plowed into them. But Claire was thankful that it stayed just a blur.

She put the picture aside—definitely a keeper—and moved on to the next items in the box. Desk calendars. At least a dozen of them stacked together. They were freebies that an insurance company had sent Gran, but there was a handwritten note on the first one she looked at. January 5.

Enroll Claire in school.

She checked the year, not that she didn't already know. Claire had been five years old. And two days earlier her mother had left her at Gran's house. Dumped her, really, not even taking the time to say goodbye. If her mother had known it would be a real goodbye, that in a year she'd be dead, maybe she would have said a proper farewell.

At least that's what Claire liked to tell herself.

The ache came. The one that crushed her heart and had her eyes burning with tears that she refused to cry. Never had, never would shed a tear over her worthless excuse for a mother. Claire pushed it all aside. Not her bridge, not her water. Not anymore. And she wouldn't repeat the mistakes her mother had made. She'd be the best mom ever to her son.

She flipped through the calendar and saw another note. "Bennie" with a heart drawn around it and the time 7:00 p.m. No doubt a date. Claire had vague memories of the man. He'd worked for Riley's family and had been seeing Gran around the time Claire moved in.

Claire did the math. Her grandmother had been in her late forties then, a youngish widow, and had no trouble attracting men. Apparently, she didn't have trouble unattracting them, either, because six weeks later, Bennie's name had a huge X through it, their date obviously off.

Beneath the X, Gran had scrawled, "Pigs do fly if you kick them hard enough in the ass."

Ouch.

Claire moved on to the next calendar. There were more notes about doctor's appointments, parent-teacher meetings and more dates with men who'd initially gotten their names enclosed with hearts. Then, had been X'ed out.

She hadn't remembered her grandmother having an appointment book, and the woman didn't use a computer, so this must have been her way of keeping track. A good thing, too, since there were a lot of date-dates to keep track of. Claire read each one, savoring the little tidbits Gran had left behind.

Get cash to pay McCord boys.

That was an entry for the September when Claire
had been ten. There were two more for the same month.
Events Claire remembered because she'd been close to
the same age as the McCord boys and had begged to help
Riley and Logan move the woodpile and do some other
yard chores. However, Gran had insisted it wasn't work
for a girl and that she would pay Riley and Logan despite
their having volunteered.

More entries. All of them brought back smiles and
childhood memories. Until she landed on October 14 of
that same year.

Give Claire the letter.

Claire frowned. *What letter?* It'd been a long time,
twenty-one years, but she was pretty sure she would have
remembered Gran giving her a letter. And who was it
from?

Hoping she would find it, Claire had a closer look in
the box. Not the careful, piece-by-piece way she'd been
taking out the other things. She dumped the contents on
the floor and riffled through them.

Nothing.

But there was a book. Judging from the battered blue
hardback cover, it was old. She opened it, flipped through
it, hoping the letter was tucked inside. But no letter. However, it wasn't just an ordinary book.

It was a journal.

Her mother's journal.

Her mother had scrolled her own name complete with
hearts and flowers on the inside cover. Then Claire's at-

tention landed on two other words centered in the first page. Her mother had drawn a rectangle around it.

Fucking kid.

Claire slammed it shut and couldn't toss it fast enough back into the box. She definitely hadn't wanted to see that. She wanted to erase it from her head.

She didn't want to cry.

Where the heck was that letter? It'd get her mind off those two words that were now burning like fire in her gut. She stood to get another box but didn't make it but a few steps when her phone buzzed.

Riley.

And this time, the name didn't just pop into her head. It actually popped onto her phone screen. She checked on Ethan. Asleep, finally, so she eased the nursery door shut and went into the living room to take the call.

She also took a minute to steady her nerves. No way did she want Riley to hear she was shaken up by two words written by a woman who'd abandoned her.

"Claire?" Riley greeted her.

Just the sound of his voice calmed her. It excited her in a different way, too, but for now, she'd take it. Claire needed something that wasn't dark and heart crushing.

She scowled when she felt the little flutter in her stomach at the mere sound of his voice. "Eat any good brownies lately?" she asked.

"Very funny. You might have run off Misty and Trisha, but you still left me here with three women barely old enough to be classified as women. And Trisha and Misty didn't stay away. They returned and didn't leave until the swing shift arrived." He cursed, and he didn't use any of the compromise words. "At least I haven't been involved with any of them."

Not that batch. These were women from the historical society. Nobody under sixty in the bunch. Of course, it was possible one or two of them had the hots for Riley. He seemed to bring that out in women of all ages.

"They won't be coming back," Riley continued. "Neither will the twins, their sister or the midmorning shift."

"Really? Trisha will be so disappointed." But for reasons Claire didn't want to explore, she actually felt good about disappointing Trisha. Probably because Trisha had used her 36-Ds to seduce Riley in high school.

Seriously, who had boobs that big in the tenth grade?

"Not sure *disappointed* is the right word for it," Riley went on, "but she seemed upset that I didn't want her here. Like I said, it's nothing personal. I just need some peace and quiet."

"But not peace and quiet right now? Or are you calling to tell me I'm off breakfast duty tomorrow?"

He huffed. "The peace and quiet doesn't apply to you right now. And, yeah, you're off breakfast duty."

Good grief. That stung. What she should feel was relief. Being around Riley wasn't good for her. He was a forbidden-fruit kind of thing, and she didn't need any more choices of fruit, fudge or bubblegum in her life.

"All right. If you're sure," she said. "If you change your mind, though, just give me a call." Claire was about to say goodbye, but she thought of that note. "By any chance, when we were about ten years old, did Gran ever say anything to you about giving me a letter?"

"Letter?" Claire couldn't be sure, but she thought maybe he hesitated. "What kind of letter?"

"Don't know. It was something she'd marked on her

calendar, and I thought maybe you remembered it since you did some yard work for her around that same time."

Of course, it sounded stupid now that she'd said it aloud. At ten years old, Riley would have been less interested in some letter than in finishing the duties that Logan had no doubt volunteered him to do.

"Sorry, I can't help you." Riley paused. Mumbled something she didn't catch. Paused again. "But maybe you can help me. Is it my imagination or do some of those women who came over think I'm Ethan's father?"

Claire was so glad he wasn't there to see her expression. She was certain she'd gone a little pale. "Uh, do they?"

"Yeah. I heard some whispers about Ethan having my smile. As if anyone's seen my smile since I got back. Has anyone come out and asked you if I'm his father?"

Several dozen times. "Once or twice," she settled for saying. "I denied it, but I don't think they believed me."

"Even when you told them we've never had sex?"

"Well, I didn't really tell them that. I sort of hoped they would infer it when I said you're not his father."

"They're not inferring it right. They think the kid's mine because he looks like me."

"Does he?" No way in hell on a good day would Claire confirm or deny that, and she could practically hear the next question that was about to come out of Riley's mouth.

Since I know I'm not Ethan's father, who is?

Claire decided to put an end to it before it started. "Get some rest, Riley. I'll call you soon." And before Riley could utter another word, or ask another question, she hung up.

CHAPTER FOUR

RILEY WAS SURE someone was watching him. Since this was downtown Spring Hill and not hostile territory, he wasn't overly alarmed, but he could sense that someone had him under surveillance.

He glanced around Main Street at the line of shops and buildings, including the Fork and Spoon Café, the bank and the pharmacy where Riley had just picked up a refill of his oxycodone. The biggest building, however, was the two-story Victorian inn that Logan had converted into headquarters for the family business. Logan had added a new sign in the past six months. *McCord Cattle Brokers* was emblazed on a copper-and-brass background.

Classy.

But then Riley hadn't expected anything less from Logan. His brother was a ball-busting Renaissance man in a four-hundred-dollar cowboy hat.

Since it was close to dinnertime, Riley hadn't expected to see so many people milling around Main Street. None was especially looking at him, though he did get a friendly wave from Bert Starkley who was in the doorway of the café he owned.

He got a not-so-friendly look, however, from Misty. The woman was coming out of the bank, but when Misty laid eyes on him, she whirled around and went back in. Clearly he'd ruffled some feathers by refusing her help, but he preferred that to some of the TLC that was being offered.

Hell, Trisha had wanted to run his bath for him, and he didn't think it was his imagination that she would have joined him in the sudsy oasis if he'd been agreeable. She'd also eyed that saddle on Lucky's bed. Riley wasn't in any shape for suds, saddles or Trisha.

"Want a cold glass of sweet tea?" Bert called out to Riley. "It's on the house for our local military hero."

"Thanks. If the offer's still good tomorrow, I'll take you up on it then," Riley answered.

Maybe.

Riley made sure to smile. Hoped it didn't look as forced and creepy as it felt, but it was something he was working on.

He still wasn't in a socializing kind of mood, but he had needed a flat surface to walk so he could get in some exercise. Only every other step hurt now. Well, all of them hurt, but only one out of two made him see gigantic stars. Riley figured that was a good sign. What wasn't a good sign was that he still needed lots of pain meds to get through every minute of every hour.

And then there were the flashbacks.

Since the bad one two nights ago, he'd kept them from trying to claw their way to the surface. "Jingle Bells" and a good mental boot stomping had worked. Temporarily. But he needed another weapon in his arsenal. Sex, maybe. Lately, he'd been thinking a lot about sex.

And Claire.

Too bad he'd been thinking about them at the same time.

When he got the niggling feeling again that he was being followed, Riley glanced quickly behind him and spotted the twins. Not exactly being stealth-like because he heard them giggling before they darted into their grandfather's store. He hoped they'd stay there. He didn't want to see any glimmer of a nipple.

"Just admiring the view," one of them called out. And giggled again.

The view being his butt. Now, normally he would have been flattered by something like that, but if Wilbert found out that his backside was the object of his young granddaughters' attention, then Riley would have one more riled citizen on his hands. He'd get that sweet tea all right—dumped on his head.

Riley picked up the pace in case the twins came in pursuit, and he ducked down the side street just as his phone rang. It was his sister, Anna, the one person he did want to have a talk with, and that's why he'd already left her two messages. If she hadn't been all the way over in Florida where she was attending college near her military fiancé, Riley would have gone after her for a face-to-face chat.

"Don't you know I have certain skills that make it dangerous to piss me off?" Riley said when he answered.

"And how did I piss you off?" Anna didn't pause, didn't miss a beat, which meant she'd no doubt been expecting his surly protest.

"When I got home, I found two women in my bed."

"Okay. And I guess you want to thank me for that?" she teased.

"No. They're young women. Too young. And you sent a team of women to my house to babysit me."

"I heard about you giving Della and Stella time off. I knew Logan would be busy because he's, well, Logan, and Lucky is, well, Lucky. I couldn't be there with you, so I made a few calls to let people know you'd be at the house. *Alone.* While recovering from an injury that could have killed you."

Oh, man. Anna's voice trembled on that last handful of words, and Riley felt the tremble tug right at his gut. "I'm okay."

"Yes, because you got lucky. Don't bullshit me. That shrapnel was just an inch from your heart."

"Shrapnel I got because I was trying to rescue a kid from a very bad situation." And that's all he could and would say about it.

Jingle bells... Jingle bells...

Anna didn't argue. Wouldn't. But she wouldn't just accept this, either, because she was his kid sister, and it was in her job description to worry about him and nag him. "Look, I'm not asking you to give up what you do. You love it. You're good at it. And it's you. I'm just asking for you to accept their help so you can recover."

"I did accept help. *Some.* Those women stocked the fridge, brought over even more food. And Claire fixed me breakfast." Which reminded him of something else he wanted to ask. "Claire's got a kid. Why didn't you tell me about that?"

"Because I thought it was something you'd eventually want to tell *me.* Ethan's your son, right?"

Riley found himself cursing again. "Jesus H. No, he's not. Why does everyone think that?"

Anna made a sound of mock contemplation. "Hmm. Maybe because it's true?"

"It's not. I've never had sex with Claire. She's Daniel's girl."

"Yes," Anna stretched that out a few syllables. "In high school, she was. I just figured you two had hooked up since then."

"I can't move in on a best friend's girl even when

the girl becomes an ex. That's man-rule number three—never take anything that's not yours."

"Even when the relationship happened in high school?" No teasing tone this time. Just lots and lots of skepticism.

"Even then. It's a *forever and ever amen* thing."

"Sheez. Who makes up these stupid rules?" she asked.

"Men. *Real* men. Including me. Besides, Daniel might not be her ex. I'm thinking they're back together and that he's the kid's father."

"Did you ask Claire about that?"

Well, he hadn't gotten a chance because she'd hung up on him. "It's none of my business."

More of those hmm-ing sounds. "But you're curious or you wouldn't have just asked me to gossip about it."

"Man-rule again. It's not gossip if the dirt comes from a sibling. Especially a sibling who owes her brother because said sibling unleashed a horde of horny females on him."

"I'm not speculating about Claire, her sexual partners or her exes. But I'm scratching my head over that so-called rule and code. Men are idiots," she concluded.

Perhaps in a woman's mind, but it still made sense to Riley. Rules kept him grounded and marked his territory. Marked others' territories, too. "You're engaged to a man. One who no doubt has some codes and rules since he wears a uniform just like me. How's Heath by the way?"

Even though he couldn't see her face, he figured that got her to smile. "He's enjoying me."

Riley winced. "I don't want to know that. You're my kid sister, and as far as I'm concerned, you're an eternal virgin."

"Thank God you're wrong about that. Heath's enjoying me a lot. Oh, and his new instructor job. Surprised?"

Yeah, about the new job. But then maybe not. Since

Heath Moore and Anna had gotten engaged, Heath had settled down some. That restless streak in him wasn't so restless, and last Riley had spoken to Heath, he was talking about the possibility of them having a wedding as soon as Anna finished law school.

Riley wasn't sure how a Combat Rescue Officer went from heart-stopping, life-on-the-line missions to being a fiancé with a desk job, but it had worked for Heath. Riley was thankful for it, too, since the happiness of both his sister, and future nieces and nephews was at stake.

"Tell Heath hello for me," Riley said, ending the call, and he was still in the process of putting his phone away when he practically ran into the woman who was coming out of the side entrance of the What's Old Is New antiques shop.

Trisha.

No brownies with her today. Nor was that a gobbling smile. Trisha gave him a cool glance instead. Still riled, apparently.

"Going to Claire's?" she asked, also cool-ish.

"Huh?" Riley looked up, to see exactly where he was, and, yep, he was only about a half block from Claire's place.

It wasn't intentional. It was just the way the town was laid out. All roads here didn't lead to Rome but rather to Claire's grandmother's old house.

"I've heard rumors," Trisha said before he could say anything else. "I heard Claire isn't really going to sell her grandmother's house, that she's too attached to it."

All right. So not a rumor about his alleged fatherhood. And Riley had heard that same rumor about the house, as well, from the swing shift crew before he'd dismissed them.

"Understandable, I suppose," Trisha went on, examin-

ing her nails. Then his crotch. "Claire loved her grandmother and was happy living there with her. I mean, after
her mother dumped her and all."

Yes, *and all* was a good way to sum up the emotional
shit Claire had likely gone through. Not that she'd ever
shared that with him. Claire wasn't the shit-sharing type.

"I'm not sure how Daniel will feel about Claire staying
here, though," Trisha added. "He'd probably rather see
her back at her place in San Antonio since it's so close
to where he lives."

It seemed like a good time for Riley to answer with
"Oh." It was a noncommittal answer, didn't really en-
courage gossip, but hearing anything about Daniel did
pique his interest.

Trisha fluttered her perfectly manicured fingers toward the small shop across the street. Over the years, it'd
been a bakery, a florist and a bookstore. All had come
and gone, but there was no sign on the front now.

"That's Daniel's office," she supplied. "He only uses
it a couple of times a month when he's showing property in the area, but he's been using it a lot more since
Claire returned."

"So, they're back together." Riley hadn't actually
planned on saying that aloud, but he sort of had to say
something when Trisha stopped talking.

"I'm not sure what's going on between them. What
does Claire say about it?"

"Not much." Not to him anyway.

"What about you? Are you seeing anyone?" she asked.
Another glance at his crotch.

Normally he wouldn't have minded glances like that,
but Riley nodded since those glances and her question
seemed like the start of an invitation he didn't want to
get and wasn't in any shape to accept.

"Yes, I'm seeing someone. Her name is Jodi." It was an on-again, off-again relationship.

Mostly off.

Heck, who was he kidding?

It wasn't *on* with Jodi even when they were together. She was a friend he had sex with. A no-strings-attached kind of friend, which suited them both just fine. Not that he was totally opposed to strings and rings, but in his experience most women didn't want to get into a long relationship with a man whose job description included deployments into direct combat.

"Jodi's a photographer," Riley added just because he felt he should be adding something.

"A photographer, like Claire?" Trisha made a weird little sound that made this seem like a big coincidence.

Or no coincidence at all.

Nope, they weren't going there. Plenty of people knew he'd been hung up on Claire, but that didn't mean he chose facsimiles of her to take to bed.

"Jodi does combat photos for a couple of big magazines and newspapers." The opposite of Claire, who shot wedding and engagement pictures. In fact, the only thing Jodi and Claire had in common was the general overall label of photographer. And the blond hair.

Yeah, the green eyes, too. But other than that, they were nothing alike.

Trisha blinked. "Oh."

That had a liar-liar-pants-on-fire ring to it. One that Riley didn't like much. Of course, there wasn't much about this conversation he did like. "I thought you'd be back in Austin by now," he threw out there.

"Not yet. I decided to take some time off to catch up with friends and make sure you're doing as well as you claim. Besides, I can do most of my work from here anyway." She moved an inch closer. "Riley, you know if you ever need my help or whatever, all you have to do is ask?"

He did know. He also knew what that *whatever* entailed, too. "Thanks, but I'm fine."

Liar-liar-pants-on-fire came in the form of a frown this time. "The offer stands." The frown was still on her mouth when she checked her phone. "I should be going. Enjoy your visit with Claire."

Since Trisha didn't move and since she appeared to be waiting for him to head in Claire's direction, that's what Riley did after they exchanged cheek kisses, goodbyes and one final crotch glance.

Great day. Next time he needed to walk in the pastures. Or buy a treadmill. A ten-minute conversation with Trisha, and he'd spilled more than he should. He'd asked about Claire, and he was betting it wouldn't take that long to hit the gossip mill. Riley was convinced that telepathy was involved, considering the staggering speed with which news got around Spring Hill.

And that was the reason he wasn't going to stop by Claire's.

If anyone saw him, and they would, it'd get back to Daniel, who'd think Riley was horning in on his woman and son.

Riley picked up the pace, intending to limp his way past Claire's house, but when he was still within fifty feet, he heard a sound that had him slowing down so he could see what was going on.

Someone was crying.

The kid.

And not just ordinary crying—he was wailing as if he'd been hurt or something. That got Riley moving faster, and he hurried through the gate and into the front yard. Ethan was sitting on the porch of the old Craftsman-style house, and Claire had stooped down in front of him and was trying to console him.

"Is he hurt?" Riley shouted. He stomped down the flashback. *Not now.* "Jingle Bells" had to get the mojo working and fast.

Claire snapped toward him, clearly not expecting the sound of his voice or his presence in her yard. She didn't scream this time, but Riley could tell he'd given her another jolt.

Well, she'd given him a bit of one, too. Sadly, just the sight of her could do that to him. Maybe she was the cure for flashbacks.

"No. Ethan's not hurt," Claire answered. "He broke his favorite car, that's all."

Sheez Louise, that was a lot of loud crying for a car, especially since there were about fifty others on the porch. But Riley soon saw why this particular one had caused tears. It was a vintage red Corvette. Even as a toy, it had plenty of sentimental value, and Ethan seemed to get that even though he was just a kid.

With a part sigh, part huff coming from her mouth, Claire stooped even lower so she could give Ethan a kiss on the cheek. No shorts for her today. Instead, she was wearing a denim skirt and a top. Barefoot. And with the way she was stooping, he could see her pink panties.

Trisha wasn't the only one whose gaze wandered in the wrong direction.

Riley reacted all right. He felt that stirring behind his zipper. Felt his testosterone soar past normal levels.

He glanced around, mainly because he needed to get his attention off her underwear, and he pretended to look at the house. It was in serious need of a paint job, and the white picket fence needed repairs, but the place had always had good bones. However, something was missing.

"No cats?" Riley asked. There'd been at least a half dozen around when her grandmother was alive.

"Gran gave them away when she got sick."

Too bad because Claire had always loved them, and apparently it'd been one of the tipping points for her choosing Daniel.

"Ix it, peas," Ethan said, holding out the car to Riley.

It took Riley a moment to work out the translation: fix it, please. The car was in three pieces, and Riley took them with all the reverence that a vintage car like that deserved.

"You don't need to trouble yourself," Claire insisted. "Just sit down and relax. You look exhausted."

Judging from the cardboard box and its contents scattered on the porch, she had been going through her grandmother's things, and she pushed some of the items aside to make room for Riley.

"I can get Ethan another car like that the next time I go to the store," she added.

But the fat tears rolling down Ethan's cheeks let Riley know the kid didn't want a new one. Riley eased down onto the porch next to him and tried to remember how he'd repaired his own toy cars after he'd given them a good bashing. After all, what else was a kid to do with toy cars other than create a perpetual stream of wrecks, increasing the gore of those wrecks with each new play session?

"Got any superglue?" Riley asked her.

Claire nodded, moved as if to go inside, but then stopped. "Really, you don't have to do this."

Riley couldn't be positive, but he thought maybe this had something to do with his walking-wounded status. Something that automatically put his teeth on edge. "Just get the glue."

Hard for his teeth to stay on edge though when she ran inside, leaving him alone with the kid. Ethan looked up at him. "Ix it?"

"I'll sure try." Riley glanced around at the other cars, but he soon spotted what had likely caused the damage. Several big-assed action figures. He wasn't certain who or what they were supposed to be, but they looked like a mix of the Grim Reaper, Cyclops and Mick Jagger. With big-assed lips and wings.

"Here you go," Claire said when she came racing back out.

Riley took the glue and tipped his head to the action figures. "Your idea?" Because they darn sure didn't seem like something Claire would buy.

"No. Livvy, my business partner, is responsible. She took Ethan to the toy store for his second birthday and told him he could pick out anything he wanted. He wanted those. They're supposed to be some kind of protectors of the universe."

Riley nodded. "Good choice."

Ethan grinned. The man-pact was back on, and the kid seemed to have forgiven him or at least forgotten about the hidden cookie caper.

"Why are you out here anyway?" Claire asked.

"Walking is part of my physical therapy." Riley squirted the first dollop of glue to get the rear axle back in place. "I just saw Trisha by the antiques shop. She said Daniel's got an office here in town."

Riley wasn't going to win any awards for being subtle, but he figured it wouldn't take more than a minute or two for the car repairs, and then he wouldn't have any reason to stay. Any good reason anyway.

"Yes, he does," Claire answered.

Clearly not chatty today. Riley went in a slightly different direction. "I guess Daniel did that so he could see you. And Ethan."

She didn't huff, but that's exactly what she looked as if she wanted to do. "You know how you don't want to talk about your injury or the pain? Well, I don't want to talk about Daniel. Deal?"

Since she was as testy as he was, it was best to let it drop. Besides, it really wasn't his business, only idle curiosity as to why the kid looked more like Riley than any real kid of his probably would.

Best to move on to a different conversation thread. "How's the box sorting going?"

The sigh that left her mouth was one of frustration. So, testy, nontalkative and frustrated. Oh, yeah, this was a good visit, but at least the car repairs were going well.

"I'm still looking for the letter Gran mentioned on the calendar. I have no idea what was in it or even if it was from her."

Riley glanced at the stack of letters that'd been tied together with white ribbon. "It's not one of those?"

Another sigh. Man, he was picking at scabs today. "No. Those are from various men," Claire said, her forehead bunching up. "Gran was obviously, um, popular. It's strange to learn she had so many things going on in her life that I never knew about."

Apparently that was a pattern Claire was continuing to follow when it came to her son's paternity. Riley frowned. He really needed to get his mind on something else. Heck, the memory of her pink panties flash was better than this.

"I brought down more boxes from the attic, and I've got at least twenty others to go through," she went on. "Maybe I'll find the letter in one of them."

"Maybe she decided not to give it to you," Riley suggested. "Or she could have lost it."

He'd dropped in that last idea only because the first one sounded kind of sinister, as if the letter might be so god-awful that her grandmother had decided Claire shouldn't see it after all.

"I think it might have been from my mother." Claire didn't look at him. She suddenly got very interested in picking at the nonexistent lint on her skirt. "Or my father."

From her mother, yes, he could understand that. The woman had ditched Claire and then had died a while later. Not in a clean, it's-your-time kind of way, either. She'd gotten drunk, thrown up and had choked to death on her own vomit. But Claire's father was a different matter.

"Do you even know who your father is?" Riley asked.

She shook her head. Didn't add anything else. Apparently, any talk involving fatherhood was off the table. In this case, that wasn't a bad thing.

From what Riley had heard, her father had never been in her life and had left her mother before Claire was even born. That made the man lower than pig shit, and as a kid Riley had often thought about what it would be like to punch the idiot for doing that.

His own parents had disappeared from his life when he was a teenager, but that's because they'd been killed by a drunk driver—an accident that Claire knew about all too well since she'd been in the vehicle.

And was the sole survivor.

Being in the backseat had saved her from dying in the head-on collision. The drunk driver had died on impact. His parents, shortly thereafter.

It had hardly been his parents' choice to leave. And despite the fact he'd been planning to go out of state for college, Riley hadn't left, either. He'd stayed at home with Logan to help raise his then fourteen-year-old sister and Lucky. Though Lucky had been Logan's age, only younger by a few minutes, he had still required some raising.

Along with occasional bail money.

Heck, Lucky still required occasional bail money.

Riley had wanted nothing more than to get out of town fast and find his destiny, but instead he'd gone to college in nearby San Antonio to be closer to Anna until she turned eighteen and headed off to her own college choice. Logan had taken it a step further and even dropped out of the University of Texas to be home. It was just something family would do for family.

Unlike Claire's scummy parents.

Riley added the last bit of glue to put the car's hood back in place and blew on it so it would dry. It didn't take long, and he examined his repair job before he handed it to Ethan. However, Ethan reached for it first and missed, and his hard little hand bashed right into Riley's shoulder.

Riley bit back the thousand really bad curse words that bubbled up in this throat. The pain exploded in his head, and it was a good thing he was sitting, or it would have brought him to his knees.

"Sor-wee," Ethan blurted out.

Riley wanted to lie and say it was okay. No sense making the kid feel bad for an accident, but he was having trouble gathering enough breath to speak. However, he did manage to utter a "shit."

"Sugar," Claire corrected. She scrambled toward him, and before Riley could stop her, she started unbuttoning his shirt. "Here, let me take a look."

"Are you qualified to do that?" he grumbled.

"Sure. I've been *looking* all my life."

Riley appreciated the smartass-ness, but he knew it wouldn't last. And it didn't. When Claire eased back the bandage on his shoulder, the color drained from her face. Every last rosy drop. He didn't have to see the raw, angry gash to know that she was about to lose her lunch.

"God, Riley," she said on a rise of breath. A breath that landed right against his neck.

Apparently, there was a semicure for blistering pain after all, and it was Claire's breathing. Of course, it helped that her mouth was now plenty close to his. Close enough to kiss…if he'd been in any state to kiss her, that was.

He wasn't.

Did that make the desire go away? *Nope.* Which meant this situation with Claire could turn out to be trouble.

"Sugar," she said. And then she added other words. *Fudge* and *divinity.* Substitutions for the kid's sake probably. "I didn't know you were hurt this bad."

Even though every movement throbbed like hell, Riley jerked his shirt back together and even managed to do some of the buttons. "We agreed not to talk about this, remember?"

"Yes." Claire cleared her throat. "I'm not sure I can hear it anyway. It hurts too much to think about it."

And he couldn't take that look on her face. Pity. Something he divinity sure didn't want.

"I'm all right," he told Ethan. Riley forced a smile that possibly looked even creepier than his earlier one since the muscles in his face were stretched tight. "My shoulder just needed some fixing like your car, but it's better now."

No way did the kid believe that. No way could Riley take the time to convince him, either. Not with the pain still shooting through him. Plus, he felt a flashback coming on, and he didn't want to have one of those in front of the kid.

Not in front of anybody.

He fished through his pocket, grabbed the new bottle

of meds and downed a couple of them, somehow managing to get to his feet in the process. "Better go. These knock me out pretty fast."

Still pale, still looking at him as if he were the most pitiful creature on earth, Claire stood. "You want me to drive you home? It's nearly a half mile, and that's too far for you to walk—"

"No, thanks." Riley was already off the porch and into the yard when he heard the footsteps hurrying after him. Not Claire. But Ethan.

"Sor-wee," Ethan repeated and he held up one of the winged action figures. He took Riley's hand and put the toy in it. "For you."

Well, that was far more touching than Riley had ever thought it would be. The kid had a good heart. "It's okay. I'll be fine. You don't have to give me your toy."

But Riley was talking to himself because Ethan gave him a little wave and raced back toward the porch.

Riley felt a tug of a different kind. Something akin to the same feelings he'd had with his kid sister when he'd helped raise her. A stupid tug in this case because Ethan wasn't his to raise.

Even if everyone in town thought he was.

Yeah, the whole situation with Claire was definitely trouble. So much so that even "Jingle Bells" might not work on this one.

CHAPTER FIVE

CLAIRE WISHED SHE could go back in time and stop her grandmother from purchasing a single roll of wallpaper. Or better yet, use that going-back-in-time superpower to stop wallpaper from ever being invented.

She held the steamer over the wallpaper, following the instructions to a tee. She waited, then scraped. Like the three million other steam, wait and scrape sequences, she didn't get a lot for her efforts. A postage-stamp-size piece of the paper came off. Only to reveal another layer of wallpaper beneath that one.

There was enough of it to create a quarantine facility to contain an outbreak of Ebola.

That's the way it had been for the bathroom and the kitchen. Layer after layer and layer. It was entirely possible there weren't even any walls left, that the entire house was held together with varying colors of floral wallpaper—each layer seemingly more butt ugly and more steam resistant than the last one.

Steam, keep steaming, scrape.

She got off another piece and tried to hold on to the reminder that one day this would all look as if it weren't stuck in the seventies. One day she'd be able to finish off the walls and the floors, and clear out the boxes so that she could see a sign she wanted to see.

For Sale.

Steam, keep steaming, scrape.

But on the scrape segment of this particular square inch of space, Claire heard something that had her climbing off the step ladder. It wasn't Ethan, either, because she could see him. He was sitting nearby creating a toy-car postapocalyptic scene on the floor.

Claire stepped around Ethan and looked out the screen portion of the front door. She'd left the actual front door open to catch the semicool breeze.

Uh-oh.

This was an unholy alliance if ever Claire had seen one.

Livvy, Daniel and Trisha.

All three of them had just exited their vehicles and were strolling toward the front porch. Claire was sure there was a joke in there somewhere: a blond Realtor, a brunette lawyer and a redheaded wedding planner all walk into a house…

But she couldn't quite come up with a punch line that would ease the sudden knot in her stomach.

Claire had known Livvy was on her way because Livvy had called to say she'd be there sometime that afternoon. But the other two certainly hadn't given her a heads-up. Too bad or she would have been somewhere else. *Anywhere* else.

If Claire had still been in third grade, such wimpiness would have earned her the chicken-dookie label, but it was a label she would proudly bear if she could have just delayed this meeting with Daniel.

Thankfully, Livvy had brought wine with her.

Claire put her steamer and scraper aside, opened the screen door and steeled herself for this visit.

Livvy went ahead of the other two, teetering up the limestone walk on sparkly silver heels so thin she could have picked her teeth with them. They matched her sparkly silver pants and top stretched around her latest boob job. Like with her husbands, Livvy liked to trade up in bra sizes every couple of years.

Claire wasn't sure exactly what Livvy's natural hair color was. That, too, had changed frequently over the past eight years since they'd bought Dearly Beloved together. Today it was *I Love Lucy* red with threads of acid green and was piled on top of her head like a volcanic eruption.

Somehow, Livvy made it all work.

"Vee!" Ethan squealed, and he rushed out to greet Livvy. She scooped him up, spun him around and made piggy snorting sounds while she kissed his neck.

Ethan laughed like a loon, and Claire lapsed into a smile despite that abdominal knot. Yes, Livvy always made it work not just with her son and hair but also with everything else. Livvy created magic.

"I've got something for my favorite boy," Livvy announced. She set him back down on the porch and plucked a silver toy car from her cleavage.

Another squeal from Ethan. Another laugh. God, he was such an easy kid to please. Despite the car stash he already had on the porch and in the house, he obviously thought this one was special.

"And this is for you, Claire. I stopped at the grocery store for this." Livvy held up a bottle of wine, the sweet, cheap stuff they both favored. She gathered Claire into her arms, smacked a kiss on her cheek and added in a whisper, "These two saw me in town, and I wasn't able to shake them."

Of course, Livvy didn't actually whisper it softly enough for Daniel and Trisha not to hear her. Which was probably Livvy's intent all along. She played a little passive-aggressive with people she didn't like.

"Claire," Trisha said, obviously taking Livvy's cue and hugged Claire, too. She looked as if she were about to head off to a photo shoot for Chanel number whatever. Smelled like it, too. "We came to check on you. To make sure you weren't wallowing in your grief."

"No wallowing," Claire assured her, sounding as genuine in her response as Trisha had been with the comment.

No genuineness whatsoever.

Daniel stayed back, waiting his turn, and when Trisha stepped away, he moved in for his own hug. "Good to see you, baby," he said in a real whisper, and he went in for a kiss. Not a cheek smacker like Livvy, but the real thing.

Claire felt her muscles go stiff. Felt that knot in her stomach tighten. *Nerves*, she assured herself. *Not repulsion.*

Daniel stepped back, taking in everything with a sweeping glance. Her shorts and top. Bare feet. Ethan's car menagerie. The boxes she'd been sorting through. The bits of wallpaper stuck to her hair and face.

"I thought you'd be further along in clearing out this stuff," he commented.

Daniel started a lot of sentences with those three words, including the contraction—*I thought you'd.* Anything that came after that would almost certainly be a drawled dressing-down that he would then punctuate with a smile.

Right on cue, he smiled.

Livvy wasn't the only one who liked to play the passive-aggressive game.

"I'm making progress," she assured him though it didn't look like it at the moment.

This latest round of boxes was mostly paper—more calendars, magazines and old bills. Claire had put some rocks and terracotta pots with dead plants on top of the various piles to keep the wind from blowing anything away.

"Did you find the letter?" Livvy asked. She had plopped herself down on the porch with Ethan and the cars and didn't seem to notice the way her question snagged Trisha's and Daniel's attention.

"What letter?" the pair asked in unison.

Claire had to shrug. "It was just something Gran mentioned on a calendar. But she never gave me a letter." She waited to see if either of them knew anything about it, but Trisha had moved on to checking her phone and Daniel was more interested in observing her half-up, half-down ponytail.

"I thought you'd have called me by now," he said. The smile came just as the *now* was slipping from his mouth.

The mess on her porch actually came in handy. "I've been busy."

He made a sound that could have meant anything and picked up the folder beneath the pot holding a dead spider plant.

"How's Ethan doing with the Little Genius kits?" Since Daniel had been the one to recommend them, he clearly had an interest in them.

Claire made a so-so motion with her hand.

"Maybe I can give it a try. Sometimes boys respond better to a man's voice."

She would have liked to challenge that, but Daniel did do a lot of reading about child development. More than she did.

Daniel took the picture on top, van Gogh's *Starry Night*, and he held it up. "Ethan?" Of course, he had to repeat it because Ethan was bashing his new car into the old ones. By the time he'd said Ethan's name four times, Daniel's voice was more of a bark.

"Remember the *FUN!* part of this," Claire mumbled to herself.

Ethan finally realized he was being summoned and looked at the picture. "Money!" he yelled.

"He means Monet," Claire translated.

"No." Daniel drew that out a few syllables, probably not nearly as frustrated with Ethan as he was with not proving the point about that whole male-voice thing. "Try again."

"Riley!" Ethan shouted. And no Ri-wee, either. This was very, very clear.

Trisha and Daniel turned to her so fast that Claire heard necks pop. "Riley's been working with him on these?" Daniel's question sounded a lot like a jealous accusation.

Which it probably was.

"Of course not," Claire answered. "Riley's recovering from his injury. He doesn't have time to play with Ethan."

Daniel looked at her as if he expected her nose to start growing. But it wasn't a lie. It'd been three days since Riley's visit, and he certainly hadn't played with Ethan then. Riley had fixed Ethan's car and then left looking as if he was about to collapse from the pain.

"Give me that." Livvy craned her long, lithe body up enough to snatch the picture from Daniel. She didn't even have to say Ethan's name to get his attention. "Okay, see this." She held up the toy van.

Claire nearly confessed that she'd already tried that, but she decided to watch and see how this played out.

Livvy tugged off one of her shoes, wiggled her toes and put the van right next to all that wiggling.

"Van Gogh!" Ethan squealed.

Claire laughed.

But Daniel huffed. "How does that help him, giving him a clue like that?"

"Seriously? It helped because he got it right." Livvy put her shoe back on, plucked another car from her cleavage—a candy-apple-red Mustang—and gave it to Ethan. "Here's your prize for guessing right." That brought on more squeals of delight, more giggling.

More huffing from Daniel.

And a bitchy look from Trisha. "What else do you have in there?" Trisha tipped her head to Livvy's boobs.

"A picnic basket." Livvy stood and patted Trisha's arm, and Claire could almost feel the condescension coming. Livvy looked at Trisha's breasts, which were impressively sized but looked more like fried eggs when compared with Livvy's. "Maybe you can try growth cream on them or something. Then you'll have a place for a Lunchable or maybe just some Goldfish crackers."

Time for some interference since Trisha was no doubt gearing up her bitchy-response generator. Claire looped her arm around Livvy's waist. "Livvy and I will get some iced tea."

Trisha must have taken that as a call to arms because she followed them, leaving Daniel and Ethan on the porch.

"Are you falling for Riley again?" Trisha asked the moment they were out of Daniel's earshot.

Claire kept moving toward the kitchen. "That's an are-you-still-beating-your-wife question. Because you're assuming I've fallen for Riley before."

Claire had, but that wouldn't help her win this argument, and if she started losing too much ground, Livvy would step in and try to win the argument for her. It could turn into a catfight. Not an actual one, but there'd be some name-calling and shouting. Something that Claire didn't want Ethan to hear.

"Riley won't be as good with Ethan as Daniel," Trisha added as if it were gospel.

And, of course, if Riley was indeed with Ethan and her, then he wouldn't be with Trisha. That's really what this was all about, but Trisha skittered out of there before Claire could remind her of that. Trisha probably hurried so she could tell Daniel he needed to watch his back, that he had some competition.

Livvy unscrewed the wine bottle, dumped a generous portion into a glass measuring cup that she took from the drying rack in the sink. "You want a side of backbone to go with that slice of milquetoast?"

Claire didn't have to ask for clarification. Livvy was talking about Daniel's and Claire's reactions, or Claire's lack of reaction, to each other.

"I can't imagine you ever having sex with that guy," Livvy added.

Claire skipped a glass and drank right out of the bottle. "Daniel's really good-looking."

"So is that painting by van Gogh. Doesn't mean it'd be great in bed." Livvy downed half a glass of the wine in one long swig. "Was he ever a *great*?"

"Of course." Claire had more wine. Figured she'd regret what she was about to say but said it anyway. "If I grade it on a curve."

Livvy leaned in and lowered her voice to a real whisper. "Never grade a fuck on a curve, Claire. Never."

And with that screensaver-worthy advice, Livvy gave a satisfied nod.

Probably because Livvy knew she was right. Still, there were other things more important than sex. Like being with a man who hadn't had a hole blown in his shoulder. A man who would go back for another hole-blowing as soon as he could.

Gosh, that was a dismal thought. One that ate away at that safety net she'd spent too long building around herself.

Since it seemed as if Livvy was about to dole out more advice, Claire went on the offensive. "How are things with the albino? Did his pinkeye clear up?"

Livvy had more wine before she answered. "It didn't work out. He said my tits were hard as rocks."

"They are." Claire went to the fridge, took out the pitcher of iced tea, a juice box for Ethan and some glasses. "Hugging you comes with risks. I think you inverted one of my nipples once."

"Ha-ha. I'm not arguing with you, but he said my tits bruise his chest when I'm on top."

That wasn't an image Claire wanted in her head. Too late. It was already there. "So, you're not going to see him again?"

"Nope. I have another date next week. I'll call you afterwards and tell you all about it. Come on. Give them their tea so they'll get the hell out of here and we can have a good visit."

Livvy helped her with the glasses, and they made their way back to the porch. Trisha and Daniel were having a whispered conversation, but they broke away as if they'd just been caught picking their noses.

"Is there a problem?" Claire asked.

Daniel cleared his throat. "I thought you'd want me to correct Ethan. I told him not to keep crashing the cars." He paused, gently put his hand on her shoulder. "Because it might bring up old memories for you."

Maybe it was the rush of sugary wine to her head, but it took Claire a moment to make the connection. He was talking about the accident that'd killed Riley's parents. "Uh, I know the difference between a toy car crash and a real one."

And thankfully Ethan seemed to get that, too, because he kept playing his crashing game, which pretty much shot that theory about boys listening better to men.

Maybe that's what put Daniel in such a sour mood, but Claire was betting it had to do with the gossip floating around about Riley's visit to her place. And the other five-hundred-pound elephant on the porch—gossip about why Ethan looked so much like the man whose name her son loved to squeal. Whatever it was, it caused Daniel to slip his hand in Claire's and maneuver her to the other end of the porch. Away from the metaphorical elephant. Away from Livvy and Trisha, too.

Of course, since Livvy and Trisha weren't actually talking to each other, and the porch was only about ten feet wide, this likely wasn't going to be a private conversation.

Or one that she especially wanted to have.

"Look, Daniel, Riley will be going back soon, so there's really no need for us to discuss him." There. She'd gotten that order of backbone after all, and it felt good.

"I don't want to talk about Riley. I know you're not interested in him and haven't been since high school."

Oh, if only that were true.

Claire didn't mention that, though.

"Besides," Daniel went on, "if he was Ethan's father, he would have manned up and told me that he'd stabbed me in the back by sleeping with you. Riley's got a lot of faults, but lying isn't one of them."

And he stood there, clearly waiting. Claire didn't have to guess what he was waiting for. This was the part where he wanted her to tell him who Ethan's father was. One way or another, it came up every single time they were together. After a dozen or so interrogations in which she hadn't confessed, Daniel had let her know that he forgave her for being with another man. Since, after all, they'd been in an off phase at the time it'd happened.

Claire didn't confess today, either.

She wouldn't.

Because a confession would only lead to a second confession and an admission that Daniel was not going to want to hear.

"I thought you'd have made up your mind about us before now," Daniel went on. Of course, he smiled, but it was brief and strained. "I mean, you know how I feel about you and know I'd love Ethan as my own. I'm good for you. I know what you need."

God. Not another proposal, and she didn't have time to stop it. Daniel took a box from his pocket and dropped it into her hand.

A box just the right size for an engagement ring. And the right color, too, since it was Tiffany blue. She didn't have to look at it to know that it would be big and budget breaking.

"Don't say anything right now." Daniel made sure she didn't by kissing her again.

"Fudge," Livvy mumbled.

Trisha squealed.

Claire wanted to throw up. That knot in her stomach was now making its way to her throat, and it didn't ease up even when Daniel broke the kiss and stepped back.

"I thought you'd have made up your mind by now," Daniel repeated, "but since you haven't, I'm giving you one week."

Daniel waved to Trisha and Ethan and delivered the rest of his proposal from over his shoulder as he walked away. "Or else."

CHAPTER SIX

Get the hell out now!

The words roared through Riley's head, but he couldn't listen to that warning even if he knew gut deep that it was more than just a warning. The only thing that mattered right now was time.

He had one minute left, and those seconds were ticking off.

Riley couldn't see shit. The wall of sand had rolled in, swallowing him up and had erased everything within view at the rescue site.

Everything but the sounds.

He could hear the thump of the Pave Hawk's blades behind him. Could hear the cry for help just ahead.

His extractions.

An airman and a kid, injured from an IED. Riley knew why the airman had been there. He'd been doing his job, but Riley didn't want to guess about the kid. Didn't want to think about the kid, either.

Focus.

A quick in and out.

Forty-five seconds left.

Riley trudged forward. Fast but cautious steps toward those sounds. His crew was around him, nearby, and every now and then he caught a glimpse of one of them from the corner of his eye before the sand curtained them again.

His heartbeat was drumming in his ears. His pulse too fast like those seconds that were ticking away. He'd done rescues like this nearly a hundred times but never with that warning punching him in the gut.

Get the hell out now!

"I got a visual," one of the crew said. Not a shout but loud enough for Riley and the others to hear. "McCord, your one o'clock."

Riley automatically adjusted, moving slightly to the right, and he spotted the extractions. Both down. Both injured. He knew after just a glimpse that the airman wouldn't make it, not with the blood spurting from his femoral like that. The kid was fifty-fifty.

Sixty-forty if Riley went in even faster and got him back to the Pave Hawk in under thirty seconds.

So that's what he did.

Riley pushed forward, his boots bogging down in the sand, and made it to the kid. He scooped him up, knowing someone would be right behind him to take the airman. Riley focused on the kid. He would save him and get the rest of his crew and the airman back on the Pave Hawk.

But that didn't happen.

The sounds stopped. Everything stopped. Like that split second of watching and waiting for a pin to drop onto a tile floor.

This was no pin, though.

The pressure exploded in his head. And the pain came, cutting off the air to his lungs. Strangling him. Riley couldn't move, couldn't run, but he could feel the blood, all warm and thick. His blood.

Get the hell out now!

"Riley?"

The sound of someone calling out his name gave him a jolt. Riley's eyes flew open, but since the nightmare was still with him, it took him a moment to realize this wasn't one of his extractions.

It was Claire.

And she was leaning over him, her mouth so close to his that he nearly kissed her. She was a welcome sight, all right. A lot more welcome than the flashbacks. But she was sporting a very concerned look on her face.

"You were dreaming," she said.

Yeah, that was a good word for it. Better than the brain-fuck label that Riley had slapped on it. Because it hadn't been just a dream. All of that, and more, had happened in the blink of an eye.

Since Claire's mouth and therefore that kiss was still within striking range, he waited until she backed away a little before Riley sat up in the porch swing. He only grunted once. Only felt the blinding pain twice.

She looked amazing. Since this was Claire, looking amazing was a given. Her face was a little shiny with sweat. Her top, a little clingy—also from the sweat. But she didn't smell like sweat. She smelled like roses. Except he soon realized that smell wasn't coming from her. She really did have some roses in her hand.

"I wouldn't have woken you up," Claire added, "but you were talking and thrashing around. I was afraid you'd hurt yourself. Do you need your pain meds?"

He did, and needed them badly, but Riley shook his head. "I'm off the oxy, and the new stuff makes me drowsy."

Which explained why he'd fallen asleep in his uniform in the porch swing. It was spring, but in Texas that meant it was already hotter than hell. Of course, that pretty much described three and a half of their four seasons.

Riley put his feet on the porch but didn't risk standing just yet. The porch was swirling beneath him. However, there was maybe something he could do to get that look of pity off Claire's face.

"I nearly kissed you," he admitted.

As expected, the pity vanished, and she looked about as shocked as if he really had kissed her. "When? Wait, that wasn't part of the dream, was it?"

Uh, no. "I nearly kissed you just now when you were leaning over me."

Since he had never kissed her, this would have been the time when most women would have asked why he'd nearly done that. Or at least continued on the subject a bit until she got some more info. Claire didn't. She dropped back another step.

"What happened to the kid?" she asked. She hooked her fingers around the neck strap that was holding a camera. "The kid in the nightmare you were having?"

Ah, hell. How much had he said? Apparently, too damn much. Since that was the last thing he wanted to discuss with her, with anyone, Riley went on the offensive.

"I heard about Daniel's proposal. Including the *or else*." He wouldn't give her his opinion about that.

She nodded. "Trisha blabbed." That was it. Her complete response on the matter before Claire suddenly got very interested in looking at her fingernails.

"Do you think we can find a subject that we both will actually discuss?" he asked. "If not, this is going to be a very short visit." And while he was at it, Riley added something else that was sure to get her mind off what he had said or hadn't said while napping. "Why are you visiting anyway? Did you bring me flowers?"

His tone alone should have put her off since it wasn't very welcoming, but Claire didn't huff or look insulted. She sank down on the seat next to him. "I'm just taking a break from stripping wallpaper and sorting boxes.

And, no, the roses are for your mother's grave. They're the first batch from Gran's garden, and I thought your mom would like them."

That put an instant lump in his throat. He wasn't usually so lump prone when it came to the mention of his mother, but those flashbacks had left him raw, as if some of his skin had been stripped away. It made it too easy for the feelings to get in.

"Mom would like them," Riley settled for saying.

Claire nodded, smiled, put the flowers on the railing. "I'll swing by the cemetery on the way home, but Ethan wanted to play with Crazy Dog first. I brought my camera so I could get some pictures. He's growing up so fast that I'm trying to hang on to the minutes by making sure I get at least one new picture of him every week."

Since Riley hadn't heard a peep from Ethan, he looked at the yellow Lab's usual resting spot, and as predicted Crazy Dog was there, sleeping, and Ethan was tugging on his ears, trying to get the dog to move.

Good luck with that.

"Crazy Dog's not so crazy anymore," Riley remarked. And he hadn't been for the past six years or so.

But before that, he'd been worthy of the name that Lucky had given him. Well, actually the name had been Bat-Shit Crazy Dog, but that hadn't gone over well with Della and Stella. Neither had Ol' Yeller—Riley's suggestion. Logan hadn't offered any name options, but he had been the one to call a dog obedience instructor.

For the most part, Crazy Dog slept under that particular tree during the day, though there was a doggy door for the house so he could come and go as he pleased. The only time he went inside was to eat and do more sleeping. The vet had assured them that the dog wasn't sick;

all the tests had been done to rule that out. Apparently, Crazy Dog was more Lazy Dog now.

"You're wearing your uniform," Claire commented.

Riley hadn't forgotten he had it on, of course, but he glanced down at it. "I was at the base getting physical therapy and a checkup first thing this morning. I'm healing," he added so that she wouldn't ask.

Nor would he explain that wearing the uniform to the appointment hadn't been necessary. Riley just felt better when he had it on. Not like the ordinary Riley with the head-exploding pain. In the uniform he was Captain McCord, CRO. People saluted him, called him sir and there was the awe factor of being special ops.

Since his comments about the dog and his physical therapy hadn't generated any safe conversation, Riley went back to an unsafe subject. "What are you going to do about Daniel's proposal?"

Her lips tightened as if she might tell him it was none of his business, but it was a sigh rather than a huff that left her mouth—which he was still thinking about kissing.

"I don't know." She leaned back in the swing, sighed again.

All right, so maybe she had come here to talk this over. It made more sense than Ethan playing with Crazy Dog since there was zero playing going on.

"What would you do?" she asked.

"I wouldn't marry him, but then I'm straight." He flashed her a smile that had her rolling her eyes. Riley waited until the eye roll was done before he continued. And here was the six-million-dollar question. "Do you love him?"

"Some." She screwed up her face and shook her head. "I know, I know. Livvy said I shouldn't grade love...or sex on a curve."

Livvy was obviously a font of wisdom. "You shouldn't." And, no, that didn't have anything to do with Daniel himself. Or Claire. "Why would you have to grade sex on a curve anyway?"

"Clearly, you've never had mediocre sex. But then you're a guy. Lucky told me once that for guys, no sex is actually bad. Some times are just better than others."

Riley was sure he screwed up his face, too. "When the hell did my brother tell you that?"

"Oh, I guess I was about nineteen or so and home from college. We ran into each other at Calhoun's Pub." She dismissed it with the flip of her hand.

Riley sure as heck didn't dismiss it, and the next time he saw his brother, he'd rip off Lucky's ears—maybe his dick, too.

Sheez. Was nothing sacred with Lucky? Because his brother had obviously been hitting on Claire if he'd broached the subject of sex with her. Of course, Lucky hit on every woman within breathing range, but even Lucky should have had enough brain cells to know that Claire was off-limits.

And Riley really didn't want to think about why Lucky would know that. He just would.

Claire thankfully missed his little mental implosion because she groaned, scrubbed her hand over her face. "What am I going to do, Riley? There are only three days left on Daniel's *or else* deadline."

Shoot, he might rip off Daniel's dick, too. "I should probably stay quiet on the subject, but why would you let him give you an ultimatum like that, especially when you only love him *some*?"

Claire's attention drifted to Ethan who was now using Crazy Dog's back as a track for two toy cars.

Oh.

Claire's drifted attention gave Riley a reminder that he'd been trying to forget. That Daniel was almost certainly Ethan's father.

Well, shit.

That explained Daniel's ultimatum. If Ethan was Riley's kid, he would have wanted to raise him, too. He was an all right kid. Creative, too, since he used the folds on Crazy Dog's neck to hide one of the cars, and Ethan was doing it gently enough so that Riley knew the boy cared.

"I've been with Daniel a long time," she finally said. "It feels a little like an investment, you know?"

Riley didn't have a clue, and that only riled him even more, but he nodded anyway.

"Sometimes, I just think…" She paused. "Well, sometimes I wonder if my slogan is just a pile of sugar."

All right, he really, really didn't have a clue. "Huh?"

"I say sugar instead of shit because I don't want Ethan to curse," she clarified in a whisper. "And I meant my sugary slogan—Making Fantasies Come True. That's the slogan Livvy and I picked for our business, but…"

"Daniel's not doing it for you, fantasy-wise?" Oh, he so should have given that some thought before it came out of his mouth. Too bad the new pain meds hadn't made him comatose instead of just dizzy and drowsy.

A teeny-tiny smile crossed her lips and then vanished. "Do you really want to talk about me and Daniel having sex?"

Yeah, right after he slid down a mile-long stretch of razor blades. Riley hoped his silence, and possibly his wincing, let her know that it was not something on the discussion table.

"Are you sleeping better?" she asked.

Not exactly a safe subject, but they were running out of topics here. "Some."

And that led him to something else he'd been thinking about lately. He tipped his head to the flowers she'd brought. "How did you deal with the memories of what happened to my mom and dad?"

Claire gave him a long look. "I don't have a lot of memories. It's more like little bits and pieces, you know?"

This time, he did know, but bits and pieces could still come together for an ugly picture.

"And the bits and pieces aren't all of the accident itself. Your father told a joke," Claire went on. "Your mother laughed. Then the crash happened."

He knew all of that. It'd been a knock-knock joke.

His dad: Knock knock.

His mom: Who's there?

Dad: Boo

Mom: Boo who?

Dad: Ah, don't cry, honey.

Riley hadn't been there, but Claire had filled him in over the years. Those last moments of their lives were as clear in his head as if he had witnessed every second of it. *Heck.* He wished he had. Then he could have had the chance to say goodbye.

He looked at her, hoping that her eyes weren't burning like his. Because if Claire lost it, Riley would have to pull her into his arms. It wasn't a good time for that to happen. Not with all this nervous energy zinging between them.

But no tears. She smiled when she glanced at the roses.

"You have nightmares about it?" he asked her.

She drew in a long breath. "Not very often. Why are you asking? Are you having a lot of nightmares? Is that what was happening when I woke you?" Thankfully, she didn't wait for him to answer. Or for him to flub around with an explanation. "Because what helped me was a picture of you."

Riley had to go back through that to make sure he'd heard her right. "Me?"

She nodded. "You just seemed to be holding things together a lot better than I was. So when I'd have bad dreams and sad thoughts, I'd look at your picture in the yearbook—the one with you in your football uniform— and I'd remind myself that if you could do it, then so could I."

He definitely hadn't been holding it together. But Logan had. He'd swooped in and taken care of all the funeral arrangements, the business stuff. Even Anna. Riley had put on a front, but it was just that—a front. It'd been good practice, though, for the front he was putting on now.

"I still look at your picture sometimes," she went on. "Because every now and then the dreams come back."

"And looking at my picture actually helps?" Riley wished he hadn't sounded so astonished, but he was.

"Sure. Well, for the nightmares but not for thunderstorms. You don't work for me in thunderstorms."

Yeah, Claire had a thing about storms, spiders and zombie movies. But Riley hadn't had a clue she'd even attempted to use his picture or anything about him to help her get through it.

"Riley!" Ethan called out. The kid had obviously noticed he was awake and sounded excited to see him. Riley was mildly surprised that he was excited to see Ethan, too.

Ethan had given up on his Crazy Dog playdate, and he barreled up the steps toward them. But he didn't just come onto the porch. He crawled into the porch swing, wriggling his pint-size body in between Claire and him.

He had a toy car in each hand. Several were crammed in his pockets, and the ones in his left pocket dug into the outside of Riley's thigh. Since that was his sore leg, the pain nudged Riley a bit, but he didn't move. Riley wanted to hang on to this closeness for a little while.

"Angel," Ethan said, and he pointed to the Combat Rescue Officer badge on Riley's uniform. The kid climbed into Riley's lap to get a better look at it.

"No." Claire immediately reached for her son, probably because she thought it would hurt Riley.

And it did. More than just a nudge this time, but Riley stopped her from whisking him up. Instead, Riley fished out his phone and maneuvered Claire closer so that her head was right against Ethan's.

"Smile. It's a picture for Anna," he said, snapping the shot. "She wanted to see how big Ethan's getting."

That was such a huge lie that Riley thought it might spur even Crazy Dog to action. Claire gave him that look, the one that let him know that she knew he was lying, but the look also told him that she really wasn't sure she wanted to know what was simmering beneath the lie.

Good.

Because Riley turned the phone and snapped a picture of just her. She was caught with her mouth slightly puckered, as if she was waiting for that kiss he'd been considering.

Hell. He just might have a cure for those flashbacks after all.

CHAPTER SEVEN

THE MIGRAINE WAS chasing Logan McCord, and it was winning.

The blind spots were already there. The little swirly bright dots, too. He figured he had less than a half hour before he would have to pretend he was so exhausted that he needed a morning nap.

At least Della and Stella wouldn't be around to try to mother him because they wouldn't be back until tomorrow from their forced vacation. Riley wouldn't be there, either, since he was at physical therapy. Lucky was still off doing things that Logan didn't want to think about.

But the reporter and photographer were a different story.

The reporter, Andrea-something, came up the steps behind him, her heels sounding like a persistent woodpecker. She was persistent about getting this story, too, and if Logan hadn't wanted this article to promote his new business venture, he would have sent her and those heels clacking.

The photographer, whose name Logan didn't bother to catch, lagged along behind her while he adjusted his camera. Occasionally, the photographer scratched his balls, too. Logan wasn't opposed to ball scratching, but even that sound was amplified so it seemed as if the guy was scratching a hundred chalkboards.

"We'll just need a few more pictures," Andrea said in between the clacking-heel sounds.

She was a reporter for one of the San Antonio newspapers, and even though she'd already interviewed Logan at the office, she had insisted on snapping a few pictures here at the ranch.

"One picture," Logan said. He used the tone that he knew would set her teeth on edge. He knew all the tricks for doing that because people with their teeth on edge didn't stay in his face pestering him.

Trying to make as little noise as possible so he could buy himself some time with the migraine, Logan opened the front door.

And the first thing he saw was the naked woman.

"Ta-da!" she said, and then a split second later she shrieked louder than a horde of banshees with bullhorns.

Trisha.

Even with the blind spots and aura speckles, Logan could make out her face. Though he had to admit her face wasn't the first thing that'd caught his attention. It was her huge breasts and the tiny patch of shiny red fabric that he supposed was meant to be panties. An eye patch would have more fabric than that little thing.

Trisha shrieked again, and she scurried to the sofa to grab a dress that she held up in front of her like a shield. A piss-poor shield because it didn't cover her left boob or that panty swatch.

The photographer snapped a few pictures of her.

Logan shot him a look to let him know that he was going to delete each one he'd just taken. A hard look wasn't that difficult to manage since Trisha's shrieks had caused the migraine to close in on him.

"Logan, what are you doing here?" Trisha asked.

"That was the question I planned to ask you."

"I was waiting for Riley," she said as if that explained everything.

And maybe it did.

Logan hadn't heard any rumors about Riley and Trisha getting back together, but maybe his little brother had found a new way to relieve pain.

Logan closed the door, leaving the reporter and the ball-scratcher on the porch. "Riley's at PT in San Antonio," he told Trisha.

"I know." She huffed, blew at a strand of her hair that'd fallen onto her cheek. "I called one of the ranch hands, and he said Riley should be back by now. I, uh, wanted to surprise him. Please, Logan," she repeated. "You can't tell anyone about this."

He wouldn't, but the photographer would. Probably the reporter, too. By noon it would be all over town, possibly posted on the internet, and the gossips would add that Logan had stepped behind closed doors with her. That meant Logan needed to call his girlfriend, Helene Langford, and let her know what had happened. Since Helene and he had been together for years, she would believe he hadn't cheated on her with Trisha, but he didn't want Helene blindsided by the bullshit.

Trisha started to wiggle into the dress. It was a testament to how much pain he was in that he hoped she would hurry.

"What are you doing here anyway?" Trisha asked. "You were supposed to be on a two-week business trip and shouldn't be back for three more days."

"I wrapped up things early—" He would have continued his own questions if Trisha hadn't interrupted.

"But you rarely stay here anymore. I didn't figure you'd be coming home."

So the gossips had picked up on that, too. And it wasn't

just gossip. Logan had indeed converted the third floor of his office building to a loft apartment, and with the hours he worked, it was easier just to sleep there. Besides, it wasn't as if he had family here now that Anna had moved off to Florida.

But Logan had no intentions of getting into that with Trisha.

"Where's your car?" he asked, hoping he didn't have to drive her anywhere.

She hitched her thumb toward the back. "I parked behind the house. I was going for an element of surprise."

"Element accomplished."

Logan went to the door to tell the reporter and photographer to take a hike, but it wasn't only them on the other side. It was Riley, too. And he practically punched Logan in the gut because he was reaching for the doorknob.

"Go," Logan growled to the news crew. He glared at the photographer. "And if those photos or anything else about this situation show up anywhere, you'll deal with me."

Logan didn't wait for their reaction. The blind spots were getting even spottier. From the looks of it, Riley wasn't faring much better in the pain department.

Riley stepped in right before Logan shut the door, and his brother volleyed glances between Trisha and him. It didn't help that the front of Trisha's dress was still hiked up, and he could see that sad excuse for panties.

"Trisha wanted to surprise you," Logan summarized. Some people probably would have just let this all play out, but he wanted to hurry things along. "I'll take a nap while you two have fun."

"Thank you," Trisha said at the exact moment Riley said, "I can't. I need to talk to you, Logan," Riley added.

Shit on a stick. That didn't seem like an end to a conversation but rather the beginning of one Logan didn't want to have.

Riley turned to Trisha. "I haven't seen Logan in months. We need to get some family things settled."

Translation: Riley didn't want what Trisha was offering behind those red panties.

"Plus, I'm in pain. It was a rough session of PT today." Riley rotated his shoulder and winced. Probably not fake, either, like that family-things comment.

Riley never wanted to discuss family things.

"I'll call you," Riley told Trisha when she didn't budge.

Maybe the last bit of her dignity kicked in because the woman finally scurried to gather the rest of her things. Of course, she had on woodpecker heels, too, and they hammered against the hardwood floor. Trisha turned, heading toward the back of the house, but then she stopped.

"I just thought…" she said to Riley. "Well, I just thought I could cheer you up. I mean, I thought you might be feeling a little blue what with Claire marrying Daniel and all."

Translation: pity sex.

And judging from the way Riley's expression soured, he might just be in need of pity something. That wasn't the expression of a man who'd just learned a *friend* was getting married. No. But then, Riley had always had a thing for Claire.

"Call me," Trisha reminded Riley. She dropped a kiss on his cheek. Paused. As if waiting for Riley to do something more than make it a cheek kiss. When he didn't, Trisha finally left.

"Sorry about that," Riley mumbled. He was wearing his uniform, and with the exception of that weary, pained expression, he looked every bit the part of a military superstar. Which from all accounts, he was.

Logan considered repeating that part about needing a nap, but instead he found himself sinking down on the chair across from Riley. "Want to talk about it?"

Riley dropped the back of his head against the sofa and let out a long breath. "Which part—Trisha or the PT?"

"Both. Or neither," Logan amended. "Or you can talk—*briefly*—about Claire and Daniel."

Riley lifted his head and made eye contact with him, and for a moment Logan thought Riley would question that *briefly* part. To the best of his knowledge, Riley didn't know about the migraines, and Logan wanted to keep it that way. Besides, his little brother no doubt had him beat a thousandfold in the pain department.

"Claire hasn't decided if she's marrying Daniel, but he did propose again, and he gave her a week to decide. There's only one day left on his deadline. Trisha wants a repeat of what we did in high school. The PT's going nowhere."

Logan dismissed the first two topics, went with the last one. "How much time do you have left on your medical leave?"

"A month, maybe less." He aimed his eyes at the ceiling, avoiding eye contact. "If I can't pass a physical, I might be given a medical discharge."

Riley said it in the same tone as someone would admit they were dying from cancer or some other horrible disease. But he wasn't dying. He just wouldn't be able to lead the life he wanted more than being near family.

"Are you still having flashbacks?" Logan asked.

That got his eyes away from the ceiling, and Logan earned a glare for his question. "Who said I was having them in the first place? Hell. Claire told you?"

"No. One of the ranch hands heard you when you

were sleeping on the back porch, but if Claire knows, at least you're talking to someone about it."

"I'm not talking to her about it. Not talking to you about it, either."

Logan decided it was a good time to listen. Besides, it was easier to deal with the spots if he didn't have the sound of his own voice echoing in his head.

"I can't get kicked out of the Air Force," Riley snarled. He motioned toward his uniform. "This isn't just what I do. It's who I am. I help people. I rescue them. I save them from dying. Most of the time," he added.

Logan nodded. This wasn't anything new. "Man-rule number two—don't be ordinary."

"It's man-rule number one," Riley snapped.

Right. The headache must have fuzzed his memory up a little. As often as Logan had heard those rules, he should have remembered. "I don't need to know the number of the rule to know what it means, Riley. You left home because you wanted something more than this place could offer."

Logan's strong suit wasn't being warm and fuzzy, and clearly he missed the boat this time, too.

"You stayed because you chose to stay," Riley reminded him.

Ah, hell. That was not the thing to say right now. It wasn't the first time it'd come up, and sometimes Logan just walked away from it.

Not today, though.

"I stayed to make sure the business that Dad started didn't go under," he reminded Riley. "I'm the one who made it what it is today. The one who went to parent–teacher meetings for Anna—"

"You stepped up to do that."

"Yeah. But Lucky and you could have stepped up,

too. You didn't, and neither did he. When you say you don't want to be here because it's ordinary, just remember you're calling my life and everything that I've worked for ordinary, too."

Logan stood and said the rest of what he wanted to say while he was walking away. "I need that nap now."

The migraine, and this conversation, had caught up with him and was already kicking him in the nuts.

CLAIRE OPENED HER back door to take out the trash, and that's when she saw it. A creature was just sitting there on the steps. It was in the shape of a ball, with gray fur sticking out in every direction.

And it had one eye.

She shrieked, scrambled away from it, banging her hip against the kitchen counter, but all the commotion didn't stop it from coming closer. It just ambled in the house as if she'd given it an invitation.

"Whoa," Ethan said. He scooted down from his booster seat where he was eating his lunch. "Cat." Or rather "tat."

Claire had already picked up the broom to try to shoo it out, but she gave it another look. Maybe it was a cat. It squalled, a sound that a cat might make, so maybe Ethan was right.

"Don't get too close, Ethan," she warned her son. If she could catch it, she'd take it into the vet to make sure he or she was okay and wasn't the survivor of some radiation experiments.

But Ethan didn't listen. He immediately offered the critter a bite of his PB&J sandwich. There was some sniffing involved on both the cat's and Ethan's parts before the animal took a bite. Clearly, it was starving if it would go after that.

With the broom still in her hand and while keeping an eye on their visitor, Claire poured some milk in a saucer, sloshing it all over her and the floor before she managed to put it in front of the animal. It took a lap but went back for another taste of the PB&J.

"Whoa," Ethan said again, giggling.

Well, Whoa was certainly a good name for it, but she hoped this wasn't an omen. A bad one. Of course, she'd been looking for omens and signs all day since the deadline for Daniel's marriage proposal was only hours away.

"Don't get too attached," she told Ethan. "We can't keep it."

Claire used the PB&J and the saucer of milk to lure the cat back out onto the porch, and shut the screen door before it could get back in. Ethan sat down on the floor to watch, and she saw something in his eyes that she instantly recognized.

Love.

Apparently, pet fever ran in the family, and while this was no cute fur ball, Ethan didn't seem to mind. Too bad she couldn't explain that it was a stray and this might be the one and only time they saw him.

She gathered up the stuff to make Ethan another sandwich, but she heard the *NSYNC ringtone, and it sent her heart banging against her chest. *Sheez.* She braced herself for the conversation she was going to need to have with Daniel, but she saw a name on the screen that she hadn't expected to see.

Logan.

She tried to hit the button so fast that she nearly dropped her phone. "Is everything okay?" she asked.

What she really wanted to know—was Riley okay? Logan must not have picked up on that subtext, but judging from the sound he made, he was a little taken aback by her frantic tone.

"I've got a big favor to ask you," he said. "I have to take another business trip, and I need you to check on Riley for me."

No frantic tone for him. It was cool and terse, which pretty much described the man himself. Of course, like the rest of the McCord men, he was hot and gorgeous. Alarmingly handsome. So hot that Claire wasn't immune to getting a little tongue-tied around him. She suspected that Logan used those good looks to coerce women, like her, into doing favors, like this, for him.

"But you just got back from a business trip yesterday," she said, stalling so she could come up with a good answer.

"Yeah, but something came up, and I need to leave right now. Will you do it? Will you make sure Riley's okay?" he pressed. "Now?"

"Uh, you're sure he wants me to check on him? It's all over town that he's not happy about women visiting him."

"It's all over town about Trisha," he corrected. "And you're right. He's not happy about that, but I want you to see to him anyway. He had a nightmare last night. Loud enough to wake me, and when I went in to see if he was okay, he was looking at a picture on his phone. A picture of you. He said it steadied his nerves."

So, he hadn't sent the photo to Anna after all. Claire had known something was up with that.

"Did it? Steady Riley's nerves, I mean?" she asked.

"I'm not sure. He wasn't fully awake, and he said something about it maybe not working in thunderstorms."

She smiled. Then undid that smile. "Look, Logan. I'm in a weird place right now—"

"Because of Daniel's proposal. Your *or else* answer is

due today. And, yes, that's all over town, too. But Daniel shouldn't mind if you visit a friend."

Wanna bet? Daniel was the green-eyed monster when it came to Riley. And for no good reason. Riley had kept his hands off her during the entire time he'd been back in Spring Hill. The entire time before that, too.

"You'll do this for me, right?" Logan asked.

Oh, well. At least Logan hadn't tried to play the daddy card—he hadn't insinuated that since Riley might or might not be Ethan's father that the paternity obligated her in some way to check on him.

And give him a picture to scare off nightmares.

"Yes, I'll check on him." She was in the middle of saying goodbye when Logan rattled off a thanks and hung up.

Claire stared at the phone a moment, wondering if she should call him back and say no. Or at least attempt to. Riley was a temptation she didn't need right now. However, her ringtone went off again before she could finish the debate she was having with herself. And this time it wasn't Logan.

It was Daniel.

She got another slam of her heart and made a quick check of the time. Even though she still had a couple of hours left on Daniel's proposal-ultimatum, this was a pee-or-get-off-the-pot kind of moment.

*NSYNC just kept on singing "This I Promise You."

The *pee* was a natural thing, she reminded herself. Marriage to a longtime partner was what women her age did all the time. And getting off the pot could mean there were zero chances of getting a shot at making those fantasies come true.

More *NSYNC. More debate. Until the singing finally

stopped, and the call went to voice mail. She'd have to give Daniel an answer, of course.

First, though, she needed to prove to herself that Riley wasn't a reason for her to get off the pot.

CHAPTER EIGHT

She was only doing what Logan had asked. At least that's what Claire kept telling herself on the walk over to the McCord Ranch. Riley had apparently had another nightmare, one so serious that it'd troubled Logan. And serious enough for him to ask her to check on him.

What Logan hadn't asked her to do was kiss Riley.

But that's exactly what she intended to do.

Kiss him. Right on the mouth.

Claire kept going over how her response to Daniel's proposal would play out. If she said yes, she might regret it down the road. And the reason for that regret was something that was hard for her to admit.

She might not have gotten Riley out of her system.

The best way to determine that was to kiss him. If she felt something, then she'd tell Daniel no, that she couldn't marry him when she might have feelings for another man. Of course, that other man might not have feelings for her, and even if Riley did, it didn't mean they would ever have a future together. Still, she needed to test this. For her own sake.

She huffed. *All right.* Maybe she just wanted to kiss him, and it didn't have diddly piddly to do with the proposal. She just wanted to know if there was something more to feel than only the lukewarm heat she did with Daniel.

God, she hoped so.

Ten minutes into the walk, and Claire was sorry she hadn't driven over instead. The April sun was bearing down on her, and by the time she made it to the ranch, she was hot and itchy. That didn't go away when she spotted Riley.

Her mouth went dry.

She hadn't expected to see him out of the house or off the porch, but there he was—in a corral with two other men and some horses. He wasn't wearing his uniform today but was instead dressed in jeans and a button-up, and the sun was hitting him just right to spotlight that face. That hair.

Yes, he was still hot.

And, yes, she was going to kiss him.

"Horses," Ethan squealed.

Riley looked up, smiled when he saw them and started toward them. He looked like his usual self. No limp, no signs of pain. Not until he got closer, that was.

He opened the corral gate, his grip on the metal latch turning his fingers white. Now that she could see him better, he looked ready to pitch face-first onto the ground. Claire tried not to seem so obvious, but she hurried to him, slipped her arm around his waist.

"Thanks," he whispered. Riley glanced back at the ranch hands, thanked them.

Ah. She got it then. Riley didn't want them to know he was in pain. Of course, he didn't like anyone knowing that, but it would probably break one of his man-rules if he showed any signs of weakness to the hands.

"Horses!" Ethan squealed again.

Riley nodded, eked out a smile. "Cutting horses. Logan's new project," he added to Claire. "He arranged to have them delivered today, and he needed me to sign for them. Logan's sneaky like that. He leaves for a trip, knowing I'll have to get involved."

Yes, Logan was sneaky. After all, here she was.

"Let me guess," Riley continued. "Logan asked you to check on me."

"He did," she readily admitted. "But I came here to…"

Heck, she just went for it. Claire came up on her toes to plant one on his mouth. At that exact moment, though, the stars aligned against her. Riley grimaced, turned his head, and her lips landed on his cheek instead.

He froze. Turned. Looked down at her. "Was that meant to be a real kiss or was it an accident?" he asked.

Good question. Claire nearly wimped out, but hey, this was her test, her rules. "Real," she admitted.

Riley kept staring at her. And staring. Specifically, he looked at her mouth, and the muscles in his jaw stirred like crazy. Then, his gaze drifted to Ethan—who was also staring at them.

"Tell you what," Riley said, his voice all low and doused with eighty-three gallons of testosterone. "We'll make it real but not in front of the kid. And after you've turned down Daniel's proposal."

"Man-rule?" she grumbled under what little breath she had left. Being near all that testosterone had tightened her throat and chest along with making her nether regions do some whining and begging.

"Man-rule number three," Riley confirmed. "Don't take anything that's not mine."

So, there it was. Her entire debate rolled up into one ball. Or rather two—the testosterone thing was really stuck in her head. She could toss away a fifteen-year relationship that came with a marriage proposal, or she could kiss Riley. Even though that kiss might not lead to anything.

Claire was still leaning toward the kiss.

She didn't spell that out to Riley, though. Didn't have to. His sly little smile told her that he knew what she knew—that the kiss was probably going to happen even if it meant it could be the start of a good heart crushing for her.

"Questions?" he asked.

Yes, but it was best to change the subject. To one that would make Riley as uncomfortable as the kissing topic had made her.

"I heard about Trisha's visit." She got them moving toward the porch. "Were her panties really as small as the gossips are saying?"

Claire whispered *panties* just in case Ethan was paying attention. But he wasn't. He spotted Crazy Dog asleep in his usual shady place and started running toward him.

"They were that small," Riley admitted. "By the way, I saw your pink panties. On the porch the other day when I was at your place."

Now it was her turn to freeze.

"I just thought you should know," he added.

"Uh, why?" Had he been thinking about her panties?

He shrugged with his good shoulder. "It's just something I remembered when the subject of panties came up." Riley looked at her, and the moment seemed to freeze, too.

Oh, those eyes. That mouth.

She wondered if she could call Daniel right now and nix the proposal, but that would seem sort of desperate. As if she couldn't wait to get her mouth on Riley.

Thankfully, she got another reminder of why that kiss couldn't happen now. Ethan squealed and clapped when Crazy Dog lifted his ears. It only lasted a few seconds, but the signs of life clearly pleased her son and caused Riley to chuckle.

"So, is motherhood everything you thought it would be?" he asked. He was hobbling a bit now as he made his way over toward Ethan and Crazy Dog.

"Almost."

He made a sound of pain, which he tried to muffle; then he followed it with a grunt of confusion. And, yes, she could tell the difference. "Almost?" he repeated.

Another hard question. "Well, you know how it is the first time you had sex? It hurt and was great all at the same time. That's how motherhood is." Too bad she hadn't come up with a different analogy.

"I don't remember the hurt part."

Because he was a guy, he wouldn't. And since his first time—according to the gossips anyway—had been with Trisha, Claire hated the analogy even more. "I mean, when Ethan gets hurt, I hurt probably more than he does. His smile turns me to goo. But then he can frustrate me."

"Like with the cookie thievery and the Baby Genius packets. Gossip," he added when she looked surprised with his packet knowledge. "Why would you make him do those anyway?"

He stopped beneath the shade tree, several feet from Ethan.

"Don't you remember?" she prompted. "I was barely a B student in school. I want more for Ethan, and the Baby Genius kits aren't just supposed to help with IQ. They're supposed to help with discipline, potty training and such."

Riley's left eyebrow lifted. Skepticism. Something she couldn't argue with because she was skeptical, too.

"I'm working on the discipline," she continued. Unfortunately, she got a reminder of one of the big discipline concerns. Ethan stomped on a clump of grass for no reason. Then he hurried to another clump to stomp it, too. "Like that."

"Huh?"

"He likes to stomp on things," she clarified.

"Well, that's an easy fix, and you don't need a Baby Genius kit for it. Give him something suitable to stomp on. Like bubble wrap or some ants. Lucky used to pee on things. Anything. My dad gave him a peeing tree, and that all stopped."

Pee. That word sort of killed the mood.

Sort of.

Riley pointed out the tree that was only about ten feet from them. It was by far the smallest live oak in the yard, and she wondered if all that pee had somehow stunted its growth.

"Lucky potty trained me the same way," Riley added.

She thought of Lucky. Logan's equally hot twin brother with the reputation for the quickest zipper in town. It didn't go with the peeing image. "Lucky potty trained you?"

"There was some pressure involved. He was two years older than me, four at the time, and he apparently didn't like tripping over my little potty seat in the bathroom that we shared." He looked at her. Looked at her mouth. "Maybe you should think about making that call to Daniel?"

"Now?" she asked, sounding way too dreamy and schoolgirlish. Actually, she sounded aroused. And was.

"Now," he verified. "Then we can test that kiss."

She nodded and reached for her phone but then stopped when she heard the splashing sound. Except it wasn't a splash exactly. It was Ethan, and he had hiked down his elastic waist jeans and diaper and was peeing on the pee tree. He looked back at them, grinning, and finished his first out-of-diaper toileting experience by hosing down the lawn.

Ethan giggled. Claire did, too. And somehow in all their laughter and jumping around, she ended up in Riley's arms. The giggling and jumping immediately stopped. Claire thought maybe her heart had, too.

Yes, her answer to Daniel would definitely be no.

"Am I interrupting anything?" someone called out.

Claire looked in the back door and spotted a woman coming onto the porch. She was tall, blonde and was wearing a sand-colored outfit. But she didn't stay on the porch. With a wide smile on her face and her attention fixed on Riley, she hurried down the steps and made a beeline toward them.

"You know her?" Claire asked. She intended to whisper it, but she obviously failed because the woman heard her.

"Of course Riley knows me," she answered.

Judging from the way he grunted, he did indeed know her. And Claire got more proof of that.

The blonde made her way to Riley, practically elbowing Claire out of the way, and hooked her arm around Riley's neck.

"I'm his girlfriend," the woman purred.

Girlfriend? Claire coughed, not a normal-sounding one, either. It sounded, well, guilty or something. Probably because it was. After all, she'd just been lusting after this woman's boyfriend.

Of course, Claire had heard the gossip about Riley being involved with someone, but since the gossip had come from Trisha, Claire had blown it off—figuring that it was something Riley had told Trisha to show he wasn't interested.

The woman smiled, all her attention on Riley. The pee on the tree held more interest for her than Claire did.

And the smiling, purring woman took things one step further. She pulled Riley to her for a kiss that should have been Claire's. At least it would have been if Claire had gotten a chance to make that call to Daniel.

Sheez.

It was French. Who the heck French-kissed in front of a toddler? Apparently this woman and Riley, that's who.

"Uh, I should be going," Claire said, trying to tear her gaze away from them.

Thankfully, Riley did some tearing, too. He took his mouth from the woman's, wiped his lips with the back of his hand. He also made some of those *uh* sounds of his own.

"Claire, this is—"

"Jodi Kingston," the woman interrupted. "Like I said, I'm Riley's girlfriend." She thrust out her hand for Claire to shake. Claire did. Then she winced at Jodi's lumberjack grip.

Show-off.

All right, that was too catty for someone she didn't even know because after all, Riley hadn't put a stop to that French kiss. He'd let it go on and on and on.

"And you are?" the woman asked. She slid her arm around Riley again.

"Claire Davidson." She didn't add a label like old friend. Old flame. Or the woman who'd nearly kissed your boyfriend. "And that's my son, Ethan."

Of course, Ethan had turned, facing them, and was doing a full monty since he hadn't mastered the art of pulling back up his diaper and jeans. Claire hurried over to fix that.

"Surprised to see me?" Jodi asked Riley.

Claire hadn't planned to eavesdrop, but Jodi didn't exactly whisper the question.

"Definitely surprised," Riley answered. Unlike Jodi, he was volleying his attention between Claire and her. "I thought you were in Kandahar."

"I was. I finished up early. Hitched a ride on a C-130 to get to Ramstein. Then bummed another ride with some Turkish guy on a motorcycle. He got me to the airport, and I caught the first plane out of there so I could come see you."

Riley nodded. Nodded again. "Jodi's a civilian combat photographer for a couple of the big newsmagazines," Riley explained to Claire. "We run into each other sometimes in the field."

Jodi laughed as if that were some sexy inside joke. Riley didn't crack a smile, though, probably because he felt uncomfortable. He hadn't exactly gotten caught with his hand in the cookie jar, but Claire didn't think it was her imagination that he'd been thinking about putting his hand in the jar.

Or maybe that was wishful thinking on her part.

What wasn't in dispute was that Jodi looked a lot like her. Same hair and eye color. Similar build. Of course, that's where the similarities ended. Jodi was obviously into adventure.

Like Riley.

Which explained why Jodi was his girlfriend.

"Kandahar was wild this time," Jodi went on. "Ended up about thirty miles from there and got some great shots of an extraction by some PJs after an IED shit-bath."

"Sugar," Riley corrected, hitching his thumb to Ethan. "Little pitcher, big ears."

"Oh, right. The kid." Jodi said *kid* in the same tone

one might refer to a persistent toenail fungus. "You know me. Not one to watch my language."

Or her hands. They were all over Riley again, and that really was Claire's cue to get the heck out of there. She scooped up Ethan in her arms.

"Nice to meet you, Jodi." She nearly choked on the words, but it was a testament to her upbringing that Claire managed to make it sound genuine.

"Nice to meet you, too, Candy."

"Claire," she corrected, though she figured it wasn't actually necessary.

Either Jodi was playing fifth-grade games with her or she was so genuinely disinterested in Claire that she hadn't bothered to commit to memory anything except the first letter of her name.

"Enjoy your visit," Claire said to no one in particular. She turned, and, with Ethan on her hip, she walked away.

Riley didn't say a word to her. Not even a goodbye.

Claire got a really bad feeling in the pit of her stomach. The feeling she'd gotten when she had lost her lunch money or broken something she really liked. Except this feeling was a thousand times worse than that.

It was the feeling that she'd lost something important.

And that she was never going to get it back.

CHAPTER NINE

RILEY WATCHED CLAIRE walk away. Was it his imagination or were her shoulders slumping? Of course, it could be just the fact she was carrying Ethan so she could lightning-bolt out of there.

He couldn't blame her.

Jodi had done everything except pee on him to mark her territory. Which was strange because Riley hadn't been aware there was territory to mark. Things had always been so casual with Jodi. Or at least the sex had been. But that clearly wasn't a casual look she was giving him now.

"Let's go inside and catch up," Jodi said. She snuggled up to him and got him moving toward the back porch.

She snuggled in just the wrong place against his shoulder, though, and Riley wasn't able to bite back the groan in time. He didn't want to show his pain in front of anyone, including Jodi, but for once the pain worked in his favor. Jodi moved off him.

"Man, you really are hurt," she said as if it was some kind of revelation.

"I'm on medical leave," he reminded her.

"Yeah, but I didn't think you'd actually be in pain. I mean, I've never seen you in pain before." She laughed, nudged him. "Well, unless it was painful pleasure."

Right. "About that..."

But Riley didn't continue until they were inside the

kitchen. Considering that the ranch hands had ratted to Logan about his porch-swing nightmares, Riley didn't want them blabbing about how he'd handled this impromptu visit from a fuck buddy.

And that's exactly what Jodi was.

"I'm not in any shape for painful pleasures," he finished.

Jodi looked as if he'd slapped her, and she dropped back a couple of feet. Her gaze lowered to his shoulder and then went back to the window, where Claire was still in sight. She and Ethan were making their way along the back road that led to her house. It would be a half-mile walk for her, and Riley nearly went after her to see if she wanted a ride. She wouldn't, though, of course. Not after what she'd just endured with Jodi.

"I see," Jodi said in that tone that only she and a third-grade teacher could have managed after listening to a student explain why she'd just caught them cheating.

Of course, Riley hadn't cheated. Not in body anyway. But for some moments there, he'd wished... Well, it didn't matter what he wished. The way Claire had hightailed it out of there, she was probably already on the phone, giving Daniel the answer he'd been waiting to hear for more than a decade.

Jodi cursed. And she didn't use *sugar* or any of those other goofy substitutions. "The kid is yours." It wasn't a question, either.

Now Riley cursed. "Why does everyone keep thinking that?"

"He's not?" Jodi inched back closer to him.

"No. I've never been with Claire like that."

Jodi gave him a bit of the stink eye. "You're sure? Because the kid looks just like you, Riley. Who is his father?"

Riley had to shake his head. "Claire won't say."

She coupled the stink eye with a *hmm*. "He's probably one of your brothers' kid then because…"

Jodi kept on talking, pointing out all the similar features between Ethan and him, but Riley had such a sudden roar in his head that he didn't exactly hear what she was saying. That's because he remembered the conversation that Claire had mentioned having. A conversation about sex.

With Lucky.

The sonofabitch.

Logan had enough boundaries and common sense to keep his hands off Claire, and Logan wouldn't have cheated on his longtime girlfriend. But Lucky wouldn't know a boundary if it kicked him in the ass. Which was exactly what Riley planned to do.

"Riley?" Jodi asked. "Are you in pain again? Your face is all red."

"Yeah, I'm in pain," he lied. "If you don't mind, I think I'll grab a shower and see if that helps." And it wasn't a total lie. He'd been handling those horses for hours, and he probably smelled. Plus, the pain would be there the moment he peeled off his shirt.

"Just help yourself to anything in the fridge," he offered and headed toward his bedroom. Riley stopped when he spotted her duffel bag by the front door.

Soon, very soon, he'd need to tell her if she was staying the night, it would have to be in one of the guest rooms. Because sex was out, and he wished he could put all the blame on his injury. But he couldn't. He just wasn't in the mood—or in any shape—to tangle with Jodi.

Riley went to his room, shut the door, and in the same motion he flipped through the numbers on his phone to call Lucky. He didn't have a clue what his brother's hours were these days. Didn't care, either. He stabbed the number as if he'd declared war on it.

"Yeah?" Lucky greeted when he answered. It was followed by a noisy yawn.

"Did you touch Claire?" Riley snapped.

"Excuse me?" Another yawn.

"Did you touch her?" Though it came out a little garbled with his jaw and teeth clenched.

A third yawn. Then a groan. "I'm sure I did at some point over the past thirty years. Are you talking about a good touch or a bad one?"

That was Lucky's usual brand of smart-assed humor, and Riley was so not in the mood for it. "I'm talking about you not keeping your dick zipped up. Is Claire's son yours?"

"What? No!" No yawn or groan that time. His response was really loud, and it appeared to wake up someone who was with Lucky because Riley heard a woman's voice. "No, I'm not talking to you, honey. Just my idiot brother. Why would you think something like that?"

It took Riley a moment to realize that Lucky's question was for him and that it wasn't part of the conversation Lucky was having with his current bedmate.

"Because Ethan looks like us," Riley growled.

More groaning. "According to the woman I'm with right now, so do a whole bunch of actors."

"Hot actors," his bedmate supplied.

"That doesn't mean I fathered any of them," Lucky went on, "and I sure as heck didn't father Ethan." He cursed some more, which was out of the ordinary for Lucky. Despite his hellion, bed-hopping reputation, Lucky usually kept his language fairly clean.

"What's this phone call really about?" Lucky barked

a moment later. "Why would you think I'd ever sleep with Claire?"

"You had that sex talk with her, the one where you told her for a guy there was no such thing as bad sex." The moment he heard the words come out of his mouth, Riley felt as if he were back in junior high.

"Say what?" Lucky questioned.

Of course Lucky wouldn't remember talking about sex to a woman since it was probably something he did on a daily basis. He was thirty-three now, which meant he'd had thousands of such conversations. Maybe millions.

"You shouldn't have talked to Claire about sex," Riley settled for saying, mainly because he didn't know what else to say.

"It's not like that between us. Yeah, we're friendly, but she's like a sister to me, Riley."

The fit of temper disappeared just as quickly as it had come, and it left Riley feeling as though he'd just earned the label of the idiot brother.

"It was just something someone said," Riley explained. "And Claire won't talk about it." He paused, figured since he'd already made an ass of himself that he might as well continue. "Has she said anything to you about the father of her son?"

Lucky made an *isn't-it-obvious* sound. "I always figured it was you."

Now it was Riley's turn to shout. "No!"

"Well, my bad, then. The kid does look like you, though."

Riley wanted to reach through the phone, rip off Lucky's dick and beat him senseless with it. Hell, he wanted to beat those hot actors senseless while he was at it.

"Ethan's not my son." Riley was in pain now, not from his shoulder but from his too-tight jaw.

"Too bad. I always figured… Well, never mind."

"Say it," Riley demanded. The temper was making a comeback.

"All right. I always figured that sooner or later Claire would do something to make you forget all about those stupid man-rules."

"They're not stupid." Sometimes they were constricting and frustrating, but they definitely weren't stupid.

"Right. Whatever. You know, for a hotshot special ops guy, you're a turd head. You just don't get it, do you?"

Riley didn't think they were talking about the man-rules just now. "Get what?"

Lucky cursed again before he answered. "That Claire's been in love with you for years."

His brother hung up, leaving Riley to stand there, staring at the phone. He felt a little as if a fully loaded Mack Truck had just slammed into him.

Claire was in love with him?

But wait. He shook off the question before an answer could even form in his mind. Of course she wasn't in love with him. Riley had to consider the source—Lucky—and his brother had never been a font of reliable information. Lucky probably just wanted to put an end to the conversation.

Which he'd managed to do.

Riley considered calling him right back and interrupting another round in Lucky's latest hookup, but the sound of someone talking stopped him. At first he thought maybe Jodi was on the phone, but it wasn't just her voice. He heard two people. And it wasn't a call on speaker, either.

Then he recognized who she was speaking with. Daniel.

Great day. He so didn't need this right now, but Riley

wasn't about to hide behind the pain or the frustration that he was suddenly feeling.

He took a minute, steadying his nerves. "Jingle Bells" didn't do squat for nerves, but he had something in his hand that helped. Right there on his phone's screen saver.

Claire's picture.

He'd caught the shot with her partway between a smile and a surprised look. Not exactly a soothing pose, but it had the intended effect.

How long that effect would last was anyone's guess, especially if Daniel had come there to invite him to Claire's and his wedding. Certainly Claire had had time to call him by now, and Daniel had probably scurried right over to tell Riley the *good* news.

Riley made his way back into the living room. There was definitely a celebratory vibe in the air. Jodi and Daniel were both smiling, and even though he didn't know the reason for it, something Daniel said caused her to erupt into a giggle.

They were so involved in their conversation that it took them a couple of seconds to hear Riley and turn in his direction. Jodi would be plenty pleased with the news of Claire's wedding, too, but that still didn't mean he was going to invite her into his bed.

"There you are," Jodi said.

She went to Riley, hooked her arm through his as if that was something they did all the time. It wasn't. Cuddling, romance and the lingering look she was giving him were things that just didn't happen.

Saying hello was Jodi's idea of foreplay.

"You two have met, I see?" Riley nearly groaned.

He couldn't have possibly sounded any more wussy if he'd been dosing up on wuss pills. But he didn't have much of an alternative. He needed to keep this visit pleasant—and short. Punching Daniel wouldn't accomplish that, but hell in a handbasket, he might burn off some of this restless energy if he punched something.

"Yes, we met." Daniel wasn't just smiling. He was grinning. An ear-to-ear kind of grin. "Didn't know you were involved with anyone."

If that was the truth, then Daniel clearly wasn't in the gossip loop. Riley was certain Trisha had spilled the handful of details that he'd given her about Jodi and then added some details of her own for embellishment. Like maybe Jodi being a substitute for Claire. Which she wasn't.

"Riley and I have been involved for a couple of years now," Jodi explained. "I had a week off before my next assignment, and I decided to nurse him back to health."

A week? Oh, man. He really needed to nip that in the bud. First, though, he had some bud nipping to do with Daniel.

"Was there something I could do for you?" Riley asked. It was better than barking out, *Why the hell are you here anyway?*

Daniel just kept on smiling. "I just dropped by to catch up. But I can see this is a bad time." He checked his watch. "I need to be at Claire's soon anyway."

"Claire?" That perked Jodi up even more. "You mean the woman who was here earlier, the one with the kid?"

That perked up Daniel, too, but not in the same way as Jodi. "Claire was here?" Daniel asked.

Riley nodded. "Logan's doing. He had to go out of town, and he asked her to check on me."

There went the rest of Daniel's smile. "Do you still need someone to check on you? I thought you'd be past all of that now."

"Still healing."

Daniel lifted his shoulder. "Well, it's not as if Claire has any nursing skills. And she stays so busy with Ethan these days and going through all that junk at her grandmother's place. I'm just surprised she had any free time to come over here."

Riley wouldn't dare mention the near kiss. But mercy, he was thinking about it right now. Thinking about that stupid thing Lucky had said, too, about Claire being in love with him.

"I met Claire," Jodi volunteered. "And her son. He was peeing on a tree in the backyard."

Daniel turned his head so fast that Riley was surprised he didn't dislocate his neck. "I hope you stopped him," he said to Riley.

"Wasn't really my place."

Daniel gave him that look, the one that implied he was waiting for Riley to confess what everyone else already knew. That Ethan was Riley's.

"Sometimes, Claire's too easy on him," Daniel finally continued. "Of course, I help her, but Ethan's strong willed. He's already behind other kids his age, and Claire's not making much progress with the Baby Genius packets."

"Ethan's as smart as a whip," Riley argued. "He potty trained himself in thirty seconds."

"By peeing on a tree." Daniel's look was flat. The run-over-twice-by-a-bulldozer kind of flat.

"It worked for Lucky." Which, of course, was a terrible argument. Lucky was as maladjusted as they came.

Daniel huffed. "You clearly don't know much about kids. But I'd have thought you would have at least read some books about it."

"And why would Riley have done that?" Jodi asked. For seven little words, her question was a powerful gauntlet. Daniel stared at him, waiting for an answer. Jodi stared at him, too. And Riley decided while it might not be very mature, he wouldn't be the one to answer Jodi's question.

Finally Daniel said, "Well, it doesn't matter who Ethan's father is. Even if it's you, I'm the one who's been there for him, and I'll continue to be there for him. And for Claire, of course."

Riley broke his stare when Jodi made a slight gasping sound. "You said the kid wasn't yours. Is he?"

It was the renewed anger over the question that caused Riley to pause and generally look pissed off. But Jodi—Daniel, too—apparently took that pause as a confession.

"Ethan's not my son," Riley finally said. But it was too late. It sounded like a lie.

"Well." Jodi flexed her eyebrows, said another *well*, then did more eyebrow flexing. "You know I have fun with you," Jodi said to Riley, "but this isn't fun. Jodi-rule number six—don't get involved with men who have kids."

Yeah, he knew about that rule. Ironically, it was ahead of the Jodi-rules about her not getting involved with a married man or convicted felons.

"Is there a hotel in town?" she asked Daniel, not him. "I need to get some pictures edited."

Daniel nodded. "There's an inn on Main Street, just up from my office. It's not that far, but you can follow behind me if you like. I'm headed in that general direction anyway."

Where he was headed was to Claire's.

Jodi grabbed her duffel bag and hoisted it up over her shoulder with all the efficiency of a lumberjack and his ax. Riley nearly stopped her. Nearly went on the offensive so he could try to dispel once and for all that he hadn't slept with Claire. But he'd just be wasting his breath.

Besides, he really didn't want Jodi hanging around for a week. The only time they could tolerate each other was when they were in bed, and no way was that happening.

"Be seeing you," Jodi said, patting Riley's cheek.

That was it. Apparently the only goodbye he was going to get after a two-year semirelationship. Of course, Riley wasn't feeling any tugs of his heartstrings, either.

Jodi went out the door and down the porch steps, but Daniel lingered in the doorway. "She might change her mind when she's had a chance to deal with the shock."

No. She wouldn't. But Riley decided not to prolong this conversation, so he nodded.

"I'll check on Jodi later," Daniel went on. "After I see Claire, of course. I'm pretty sure that in the next hour or two, I'll become an engaged man."

"Really? I thought Claire was still thinking about it."

Daniel smiled again. "I talked to her right before I came here, and the thinking is finally over. I'm ninety-nine point nine percent sure that this time Claire will say yes."

CHAPTER TEN

"NO," CLAIRE SAID.

She wasn't sure who was more surprised by the word that came out of her mouth—her or Daniel. She hadn't hesitated, hadn't blinked. She'd put on her big-girl panties and delivered the answer that she should have delivered years ago.

"No?" Daniel asked. He didn't look just thunderstruck. He looked as if he'd been hit with a sledgehammer.

"No," she repeated, and since she was ready for this moment, Claire took his hand and put the engagement ring in his palm. "I'm sorry, but I can't marry you."

His mouth didn't drop open exactly, but it was close. "I thought for sure you'd say yes. Claire, we're so good together, and you know how much I love you and Ethan."

"I know." She glanced at Ethan to see if he was hearing any of this, but he was sacked out on the sofa. Obviously the walk to and from Riley's had worn him out. The tree peeing, too, since he'd repeated that once they made it home.

"Then, if you know I love you, why don't you say yes? I even told people you'd say yes," he amended.

Great. So it was all over town, and it wouldn't be long before she'd start getting congratulatory calls. Calls where she would have to dodge questions about not only why she'd dumped her longtime boyfriend but also whether it had anything to do with Riley.

"Does this have to do with Riley?" Daniel snapped.

Obviously she'd have to deal with that question a little sooner than planned. "No." And that wasn't a lie, either.

Daniel clearly thought it was. "He has a girlfriend, you know?"

She nodded. "I met her." Claire considered adding something polite like that Jodi was lovely, but she couldn't even muster up the effort.

"Then you know they're right for each other," Daniel went on. "They're not like us. They're adrenaline junkies. They want to live their lives on the line. You should have heard the stories she was telling me about some of the missions she's been on with Riley."

Claire didn't want to hear. She saw the proof of one of those missions every time she looked at Riley's face. The pain was right there, and judging from the conversation she'd had with Logan, Riley was still having flashbacks. He might never get over those, and even if he did, Riley would just want to go back into situations where he could be hurt.

Or worse.

It crushed her heart to think of Riley dying. Crushed it even more to know there was nothing she could do to stop him.

"Are you listening to me?" Daniel snarled.

"Of course." Now, that was a lie.

For a moment she thought he might call her on it, but he finally huffed. "Even if Riley and Jodi don't agree on everything right now, they'll be together."

Claire was with him on all but one point. "Uh, what don't they agree on?"

Daniel promptly waved that off. "I don't want to talk about Jodi and Riley. I want to talk about us. Look, I'll give you an extension on the proposal. Take another week to think it over. Just know that this time, I'll expect the answer to be yes."

She took in a long, deep breath. Had Daniel always been like this? Persistent to the point of being a bully?

Maybe.

But she'd been so comforted by the notion that he had a safe job and safe expectations that she'd over-looked that particular aspect of his personality. Well, he'd obviously overlooked one of hers. Her need for a safe, white-picket-fence life didn't mean she was brain-less and spineless.

"I don't need a week," she assured him, "because my answer won't change. It'll still be no."

He huffed again, looked ready to gear up for what would be more of the same argument, but Claire took Daniel by the arm and led him to the front door. She hoped to usher him out and then have a huge glass of wine before Ethan woke up. But a quick ushering wasn't in the cards.

That's because Livvy and Riley—yes, Riley—were making their way up the porch steps.

Daniel spun toward her, the accusation all over his face. "What are they doing here?"

"I saw Riley walking this way, and I gave him a ride," Livvy volunteered. "Claire and I have some work to do."

Partially true. Livvy had called her about forty-five minutes earlier to say she had to see her, that they needed to talk. That was possibly work related, but Claire sus-pected Livvy had come over for what would have no doubt turned into some wine drinking and consoling.

But she didn't have a clue why Riley was there.

"I just need to talk to you," Riley said. That sounded a little ominous. Had he come to tell her he couldn't see her, not even as a friend, because of his relationship with Jodi?

Livvy pulled her into a hug and put her mouth right against Claire's ear. "Don't say anything until we've talked." Heck, that sounded ominous, too.

What was going on?

Daniel looked at all of them as if expecting an explanation. Riley shrugged. Livvy smiled. Claire stayed quiet, too afraid to talk after Livvy's warning. Daniel obviously didn't appreciate any of their responses.

"Claire, I'll expect your answer in a week." Daniel slapped the engagement-ring box on the table next to the door and stormed out.

"I thought you were going to tell him no," Livvy said.

"I did. I guess he didn't believe me." Claire looked at her friend, hoping for more clues about that warning, but Livvy headed toward a still-sleeping Ethan to give him some air kisses and air cuddles before she started for the bathroom.

"I'll give you two a couple of minutes to talk. Remember what I said, though."

Claire wanted to throw up her hands. She still had that blasted engagement ring in her house, which meant she would need to go another round with Daniel. And now here was Riley, no doubt ready to deliver news that she didn't want to hear.

"Did Lucky call you, by any chance?" Riley asked.

Okay. That wasn't the news Claire had been expecting. "No. Why? Is anything wrong?"

He shook his head. Looked relieved, or something. "I was just wondering." Riley wasn't actually fidgeting, but she thought he might start at any moment. "I, uh, wanted to apologize for what happened with Jodi. She can come on a little strong."

"That's okay." No, it wasn't, but Claire did want to be nice now. This was already going to end on a sour note, so there was no sense her adding yet more sourness to it. "I think she was just surprised to see me there with you."

"She was." He didn't exactly spew forth any details, but she wondered if Jodi had gotten jealous.

Even if Riley and Jodi don't agree on everything right now...

That's what Daniel had said, so maybe that meant he'd witnessed some of Jodi's displeasure.

"Anyway, Jodi's not staying at my house. She took a room at the Bluebonnet Inn." He rotated his shoulder a little, maybe silently telling her that he'd distanced himself from Jodi because he hadn't wanted to be tempted into having sex.

But Claire wasn't fond of this filling-in-the-blanks stuff. "So, Jodi's planning on staying in town?"

"For a day or two, I think. She's got some work to do. And so do you." He tipped his head to the bathroom, where Livvy was no doubt—*no doubt*—just on the other side, listening to their every word. Claire just hoped after her friend's piss-poor warning that she wasn't saying the wrong words.

"I'll be in touch," Riley said, and he headed out.

Claire shut the door, huffed, but before the huff was even out of her mouth, Livvy was out of the bathroom. She wasn't wearing mile-high heels today, but she teetered toward her as if she were, making Claire briefly wonder if Livvy had permanently altered her arches.

Livvy opened her mouth to say something but then glanced back at Ethan. She motioned for Claire to follow her into the kitchen. *Oh, no.* Since she figured Livvy wasn't there to delve into the juicy details of her latest date, privacy was needed for a different reason. A reason that went along with that cryptic warning.

"Uh, has Lucky McCord called you?" Livvy asked the moment they were in the kitchen.

Claire did throw her hands in the air. "Riley asked me the same thing. Why would Lucky call me?"

The way that Livvy screwed up her mouth, Claire knew this was something she wasn't going to like. "I ran into Lucky at a bar last night," Livvy explained. "And we sort of…"

Claire held up her hands for a different reason. "I don't need to hear the details of that. I don't want them in my head because Lucky's like a brother to me."

"Funny that you mentioned that because Lucky said you were like a sister to him." She went to the fridge, helped herself to some wine. From the bottle.

"How did you and Lucky get on the subject of me? And why did you tell me not to say a word?"

"Riley called him this morning, and I was still there." Livvy stopped, smiled. "Don't you think Lucky looks like one of those hot actors who stars in those action movies?"

Heck, she might as well keep her hands in the air. "What does that have to do with Riley calling him?"

"Nothing. It's just that it also came up in conversation."

"That must have been some morning chat. Lucky's sibling-esque feelings for me. His movie-star looks." Claire took the bottle from her and got in her face. "What aren't you telling me?"

"Well, Riley called because he was mad. He thought Lucky was Ethan's father."

"What?" Since she'd practically burst her own eardrums with that shout, Claire peeked into the living room to make sure she hadn't woken Ethan. Thankfully she hadn't. "Why would he think that?"

"I'm not sure. Maybe it came from Daniel?"

Probably. After all, Daniel had been over there because he'd met Jodi. "What did Lucky tell Riley?"

"That's where the sister part came in. He said he didn't think of you that way." Livvy took back the wine. "Has Riley asked you again about Ethan's father?"

"In a roundabout way. But I can tell he wants me to fess up."

"A lot of people want you to fess up. Don't you think it's time?"

"No." And that wasn't up for debate. "If I tell them... tell Riley," Claire corrected, "it won't make things easier between us. He's got a girlfriend, Livvy."

Livvy made a sound that could have meant a dozen different things, but since this was Livvy, it meant something important. "What else did Riley and Lucky talk about?"

"Well, Lucky didn't put the call on speaker, mind you, so I didn't hear everything." Which meant she'd heard enough.

"What?" Claire pressed.

Claire had never seen a clearer example of hemming and hawing. "Lucky called Riley a turd-head and told Riley that you were in love with him." Livvy said that last handful of words faster than some people ripped off bandages.

Despite the speed of Livvy's speech, Claire had no trouble hearing it. "Lucky said I was in love with him?"

"No, he said you were in love with Riley."

Holy moly. That required her to sit down. "It's not true," Claire managed to say.

But Riley wouldn't believe that. He would think she was in love with him, and that would send him running. That's what his visit had been about. He was putting some distance between them.

Livvy handed her the bottle. "Drink up. I'll get the ice cream from the freezer."

Wine and ice cream. Livvy was bringing out the big guns, and Claire wasn't sure it was at all necessary. "I'm not going to cry," she insisted, but her eyes seemed to have a different notion about that.

Livvy had made it back to her with two spoons and a quart of double-fudge rocky road before the first tear slid down Claire's cheek.

"This is so stupid." Claire fought those tears and sort of won the battle, but she didn't win the battle going on in her heart. "I mean, it's not as if Riley was mine to lose."

"Yeah, he was." Livvy handed Claire the spoon piled high with ice cream. "It doesn't have to make sense. Childhood crushes are like that. They'll always be yours."

"But that's just it. I chose Daniel. I had a list."

"A list you wrote when you were a child. That was then. This is now. You had no idea that Daniel would grow up to be a dickweed."

"He's not. That's just it. Despite his flaws, he loves me. I have no doubts about that."

"Ah, got it." Livvy talked around the ice cream in her mouth. "You're afraid no one else will ever love you." She didn't wait for Claire to consider it. And confirm it. "Daddy issues again. Your daddy did a Houdini, and now you want to reward Daniel because he wasn't like your dad. He stuck around, and he loves you. Still not a reason he can't have the dickweed label."

Maybe not. But Claire had never wanted to be an old maid. Heck, she'd really wanted that picket-fence life, and Daniel might have been her only shot at getting it.

Livvy nudged her with her elbow. "Want me to go into town, find Riley's girlfriend and start a fight with her or something?"

"No." And Claire couldn't say it fast enough. "You're staying away from her. So am I, and if Riley and she hook up again, then it's just something I have to accept. Besides, she could probably take us both in a bar fight."

Even though she was about the same size as Claire, Jodi looked a lot tougher.

There was a scratching sound at the back door, and Claire didn't have to guess who or what it was. The cat. Since she was running low on milk, she dumped some of the ice cream in a saucer.

"Got a new friend?" Livvy asked, following her to the door. "Whoa," Livvy shrieked when she saw the animal.

"That's what Ethan named her. It," she corrected since Claire still didn't know if it was male or female.

Livvy studied the cat for a couple of moments, actually cringed. "Well, Whoa looks as if he cooks meth. And he brought a friend."

Claire hadn't noticed the second cat until she put down the saucer, and the gray tabby came running toward it. This one was nothing like Whoa and actually looked and sounded like a real cat.

"I think it's Whoa's girlfriend," Livvy remarked.

The newcomer did indeed sidle up to Whoa, and just the sight of the pair caused Claire's eyes to water again.

"Oh, honey." Livvy dragged Claire into her arms for one of those nipple-bruising hugs. "You know what we need? A girls' night out. Let's plan that for tomorrow night. You get a sitter, and I'll swing by and pick you up."

Claire nodded, mainly because she didn't want to explain to Livvy that there was no way she wanted to go out and party. Her party meter was at zero. Plus, it was short notice for a sitter. In the morning she'd call Livvy and tell her that it was a no go.

"We should get to work," Claire said, moving away from her.

She took her laptop from the living room, and since Ethan was still sleeping, she led Livvy toward the make-shift nursery that Claire had been using as a makeshift office. They went well with her makeshift life.

Which was exactly the reminder she needed that no one liked a whiner.

"Uh, how's the box sorting going?" Livvy asked, the question prompted by the fact that she had to step around a half-dozen boxes to get in the room. There was another half dozen inside.

"I think the boxes are breeding. I found more in the attic behind an old chest of drawers. There were other small boxes inside the drawers."

Livvy sank down next to one, pulling up her long legs in a lotus position, and she started rummaging through the nearest box. "Any sign of that letter yet?"

"None. I'm beginning to think Gran threw it away. Still, I'll keep looking. It might be in one of these boxes or somewhere else in the house."

"Maybe it's in this." Livvy dragged a book from the bottom of the box. "Bet there are some naughty details in there. Always did love your gran's sense of adventure."

Claire's heart and stomach dropped. She snatched the book from Livvy.

"No. It's my mother's journal," Claire managed to say.

"She left a journal? Have you read it? Oh, God. You've read it, haven't you?"

"Just two words." Claire opened to the first page so Livvy could see those two words, and then she turned that very page back so she could see it again for herself.

The two words were indeed still there.

Fucking kid.

The next words weren't any better. Words like *miserable, swollen. Hell.*

"Fudge." Livvy again. "You're sure you actually want to read that?"

Claire wasn't sure at all, but she couldn't stop herself from doing just that. The entry on the first page was dated, and Claire quickly did the math. Her mother would have been eighteen, and after just a few lines, she realized this wasn't the journal of a normal teenager.

"'The baby moved today,'" Claire read aloud. She looked at Livvy. "She wrote this when she was pregnant with me."

"You're sure you want to read that?" Livvy repeated.

It had become a moth-to-flame moment, and Claire frantically skimmed through the next passage.

Rocky broke up with me. The bastard. He didn't even tell me to my face. He just disappeared. What kind of sick bastard does that? Here, I'm carrying his brat kid and he leaves me here in this shit-hole.

Rocky. That was the first time Claire had ever heard her father's name. And it might just be a nickname. It was stupid, but she latched onto that little piece of information as if it were gold.

Rocky-somebody was her father.

"Claire," Livvy tried again. "You're crying. Girl, you need to put that away."

Claire intended to do just that, but she read the next line before she could stop herself.

Tomorrow, I'm getting rid of this kid.

Oh. God. Oh, God. Oh, God.

Claire slammed the journal shut and tossed it into the box marked Trash. She was already feeling raw and bruised, and nothing written on those pages would help. They certainly wouldn't help her understand why her mother had run out on her.

Or why those words still crushed her heart after all this time.

Her mother clearly hadn't ended the pregnancy, but the fact that she'd even considered it nearly brought Claire to her knees.

"Still up for that girls' night out?" Claire asked.

Livvy nodded. "You bet. Set up a babysitter for Ethan, and I'll pick you up tomorrow night. And wear something slutty." She hooked her arm around Claire. "You, my friend, are having sex with the hottest cowboy we can find."

insulted. She would have been far more than insulted if she'd seen the mess he had for a shoulder.

She would have been worried.

Stella, too. And that's the reason Riley had demanded they stay away for a while. They still had to see him in pain, but he was getting some home-cooked meals as a trade-off.

Riley followed the sounds of their voices as he made his way to the kitchen. They were gossiping about Trisha and a bad waxing experience she'd had at a salon up in Austin while Johnny Cash and June Carter blared out a duet about pepper sprouts on the radio.

He didn't want to ask about Trisha, especially didn't want to ask what she'd had waxed, but Riley hoped that meant she was back in Austin for good. He didn't want her unveiling that new wax job for him with another surprise visit.

While he was hoping, he added that maybe Jodi had left, too. After the way things had played out, she probably wouldn't have stopped by the house to say goodbye. Heck, she was probably already off on another adventure.

Riley only had one pang that he wasn't on an adventure, too. All right, there were two pangs, but they were slightly overshadowed by the smell of heaven.

Chocolate-chip cookies.

Or rather tookies.

Riley laughed at the reminder of Ethan. Then he cursed himself for the way the kid, and the kid's mom, just kept popping into his head.

"Well, lookie here," Della said when Riley strolled into the kitchen. She stopped stirring whatever she was cooking and made a show of ogling him. "Did a movie star just come walking in the kitchen?"

It wasn't party clothes, but Riley had managed to but-

CHAPTER ELEVEN

RILEY ACTUALLY FELT HUMAN. Well, close to human anyway. If he discounted the constant throb in his shoulder, the twinges in his knee, the continuing flashbacks and the crappy feeling he had about how he'd left things with Claire the day before.

So, maybe not that human after all, now that he'd taken inventory.

But at least he had showered, and there were some muscles aching that should be aching. The kind of muscles that got worked by herding horses from the corral to one of the pastures. He hadn't done any heavy lifting—none had been required, and it wasn't possible yet anyway. However, he had twisted and turned more in the saddle than was probably good for his shoulder.

Tomorrow morning he would probably have to take that human feeling down yet another notch when those aching muscles turned stiff. Still, he'd done the job and hadn't violated a man-rule by doing it half-assed.

Not bad for someone who hadn't done real ranch work in more than a decade.

He heard the women, Della and Stella. They weren't quiet women and were even louder since they'd gotten back from their forced vacation. The extra volume was probably to teach him a lesson for trying to make a go of his recovery on his own. Neither had been pleased about that, and Della had let him know that she'd been flat-out ton up his shirt, tuck it in and put on a belt, all with minimal grunting and wincing. The cowboy boots, however, had required some grunts. They took more tugging and pulling than the combat boots he'd been living in.

"He's joining the other movie star," Stella remarked.

Riley wasn't sure what she was making, but she was punching a basketball-size wad of dough with her fists. She could have knocked out Mike Tyson with the force she was putting behind those wallops.

Riley glanced around to see what Stella meant by that other-movie-star comment, and he spotted Logan at the table. A rare sighting indeed, and he was using the kitchen table to do some paperwork on the horse shipment they'd just received. But heck, Logan did sort of look like a movie star in his Texas tuxedo. He'd probably just come from a meeting or was headed to one.

Della plucked a cookie right from the baking sheet that she'd just taken out of the oven and handed it to Riley on the down low as if trying to hide it from her sister and Logan. One bite of it, and it was like being transported back to his childhood. Suddenly, he was six years old again, not a care in the world, and with Della sneaking him cookies while Stella and his mom pretended not to notice.

The sisters weren't gray haired then, and they'd been young, only in their late thirties, but at the time Riley had thought they were old. The first cookie Della had sneaked him was as good as this last one.

Ethan would have loved every bite.

The thought just jumped in his head, causing the childhood memories to vanish. Riley was back to being thirty-one again, feeling partly human, but he still had his cookie. It was warm, gooey and perfect.

"Are you going somewhere?" Logan asked, glancing up from his paperwork.

Riley shrugged, finished off the cookie. "Thought I might go to Calhoun's Pub."

The three froze, looked at him as if he'd just announced a solo expedition to Antarctica.

"You're sure you're up to that?" Della asked. "You looked tuckered out when you came in from dealing with those new horses."

"I *am* tuckered out." Though he hated using that word, *tuckered.* "But I thought I could use a cold beer, maybe see some old friends."

Again more of those stares.

"I'm not really asking permission," Riley finally said when the staring continued and then the concerned looks kicked in. But he stopped. Maybe he didn't need to ask for permission, but he sure needed some information. And some keys. "I need to use a vehicle. What's in the garage?"

Logan got to his feet. "I'll drive you. Wouldn't mind having a beer myself."

Now Riley was the one who stared. "I don't need a babysitter, Logan."

"Good. Because I wasn't offering. You can buy. I'll have one beer—then I'll go to the office and clear out some of this paperwork. When you're done at Calhoun's, you can walk over or give me a call, and I'll drive you home. Consider me your designated driver."

Logan apparently assumed that offer was a done deal because he gathered up his papers and headed to the side door, which led to where he'd parked. Riley considered arguing but realized he'd be doing it just for argument's sake—a constant problem for him when dealing

with Logan—but he really did want to just get out and
maybe clear his head.

Of Ethan.

Of Claire.

Especially Claire.

"Dinner's ready, but if you're in a hurry to take off,
I'll hold some for both of you in the microwave," Della
called out to them.

"No need," Logan answered at the same time Riley
said, "Thanks. I appreciate it." Maybe she'd leave him
some more of those cookies, too.

Riley followed Logan outside to a big silver truck with
the McCord Cattle Brokers copper logo painted on the
door. On both doors, Riley realized when he went to
get in.

"Thanks for helping today," Logan said.

Riley didn't wait for more praise because with Logan
that was about as good as it would get. But Riley didn't
need his praise anyway. Hadn't in a long time. He hadn't
done the work today for Logan but rather for the family.
And for himself.

"I called Lucky earlier," Logan went on as he pulled
out of the driveway. "I asked him to come home to help
you with the cutting horses. The new trainer gets here
tomorrow, and Lucky and you can get him settled. Plus,
I need the two of you to go look at some other horses I'd
like to add to the inventory."

There was so much wrong with that handful of sentences that Riley didn't know where to start. "You really
think Lucky will come home?"

"He should. This is his business, too."

Which wasn't an answer at all, but Riley knew how
things would likely go. Or rather not go. Lucky wouldn't
be there because he was off doing some rodeo promo-

tion. Riley didn't know a lot of the details because Lucky didn't make it home often enough to share what was going on in his life, but Lucky wouldn't just drop everything—or *anything* for that matter—to attend to family business.

Especially when his twin brother had ordered him home.

But that wasn't the only thing wrong with Logan's decree. "I don't know how much longer I'll be able to help, either," Riley said. "The Air Force should be scheduling my physical soon, and once I'm cleared for duty, I'll be leaving."

Now, normally that gave Riley a nice kick of adrenaline, but tonight it made his stomach feel a little acidy. He'd probably downed that cookie too fast.

"You're sure you'll be cleared?" Logan asked.

"Of course." That was perhaps the biggest lie he'd ever told, but it was a lie that Riley had to hang on to. He couldn't fail at this. He had to go back on active duty.

"What about the flashbacks? Are you still having them?" Logan pressed.

Thankfully Riley didn't have to lie and say no because Logan's phone beeped. A simple little sound to indicate he had a phone call. Judging by what Riley could hear of the conversation, it was about those horses Logan had just mentioned, and the deal apparently wasn't going well, if Logan's terse, one- and two-word replies were any indication.

Too much. Renegotiate. Now.

He said *now* a lot.

Logan was still growling out those replies when he pulled into the parking lot of Calhoun's Pub. He motioned for Riley to go ahead in, which suited him just fine. If he waited around with Logan much longer, his brother would try to rope him into doing something else that Riley was reasonably sure he wouldn't want to do.

It was only a short walk from the parking lot to the entrance, but by the time Riley made it, the sweat was already making his back and neck sticky. Inside wasn't a whole lot better. The place was a converted nineteenth-century barn, and even though it had AC and dozens of ceiling fans, it wasn't cooling off the place much.

Riley figured that was the owner Donnie Calhoun's way of getting people to buy more cold beers.

Since it was a Saturday night, the pub was packed. He'd forgotten how it could be and that it was the only place where folks could unwind at the end of a work-week. Not exactly a quiet place to have a beer with the jukebox blaring, the customers trying to be heard over the music and even the crunch of the peanut shells beneath him. One step, and Riley felt his boots shift a little. Just enough.

As they'd done that day in the sand.

The fan blades whipped through the air above him, somehow cutting through the other sounds but not the heat, and they stirred up the dust. Smothering him. Someone, a man, shouted out something. Maybe his name. But it was just an echo in Riley's head. A cry for help.

Shit.

The sensations all hit him at once, and Riley felt himself being yanked back into the middle of the flashback. *No.* This couldn't happen. Not here in front of everybody.

Jingle bells. Jingle bells.

That didn't work, so he pulled out his phone to look at Claire's picture. Maybe it was the poor lighting or maybe he just hadn't caught it in time, but the picture didn't work. He was going down fast.

Because he could hear the kid.

He could feel the warm blood snaking down his body. *Get the hell out now!*

But he couldn't run. The sand was pulling him down, and the pain. *Fuck, the pain. Too much.* And the kid wasn't moving.

Sixty-forty chance if he got him moving, but Riley couldn't lift his feet.

It'd been a huge mistake coming here, and he turned to try to leave—fast—when he saw something. The woman pushing her way through the crowd. Or maybe she was a mirage.

Because it was Claire.

Not a picture on his phone, either. She was wearing jeans and a snug little red top and had a beer in her hand. She was making her way toward him.

"Riley," she said, obviously aware that all hell had broken loose inside his head. Probably because she'd seen him like this on the porch that day. But that was a picnic compared with the roar going on inside him right now.

Livvy was with her, right by her side, but unlike Claire, she didn't seem to notice what was going on because she was smiling in between swigs of a beer.

"Now, there's the hot cowboy Claire's been looking for," Livvy declared.

And Livvy pushed Claire right into his arms.

Oh, no. This wasn't good. Claire knew that look, knew that Riley was about to lose it.

"Come on," Claire said. She slipped her arm around Riley's waist and got him moving toward the back exit. "I'll get you out of here."

Livvy clapped her hands. "Now, that's what I'm talking about."

She no doubt thought Claire was finally taking the

initiative with Riley and was hauling him off for a good make-out session. But making out was the last thing on Claire's mind as she worked to get Riley away from the crowd and thought of ways to help him fight these demons that were bearing down on him.

If that was even possible.

Claire had been doing some reading about PTSD and combat flashbacks, and while the websites had given her some useful information, all of that went out the window when it was happening right in front of her. Especially since it was happening to Riley.

"Just put one foot ahead of the other," she instructed, though she had to yell it to be heard over the music. She considered dropping her beer, but that would only cause unwanted attention.

"The sand," he said.

"I'll get you through it." Both the sand in his head and the stuff just out the back door of the pub.

Donnie Calhoun had added several inches of sand to the back so the smokers would have a place to squash out their cigarette butts, but that meant Riley and she were trudging through it while dodging any questions from the gaggle of smokers out there.

Claire had a solution to avoid those questions. It wasn't a good solution, but desperation took over. She knew above all else that Riley wouldn't want anyone to know what he was going through. So she put her mouth on his neck and pulled down his head so that it looked as if they were kissing.

It worked.

They didn't get a single flashback/PTSD/what's-wrong-with-you? question from the dozen or so smokers. Though Riley did get some cheers and dirty suggestions.

Maybe it was the neck nuzzling or those dirty suggestions, but it seemed to get Riley to pick up some speed.

"Sixty-forty if I hurry," he said.

He was still in the nightmare, still clearly fighting it, judging from his steel-hard muscles and the sweat that had beaded on his face. Claire figured that ratio had something to do with his chance of succeeding on a mission. Not ideal odds considering he was probably talking about his life.

"Gotta get the kid out," he said. Each word seemed to be a battle in itself.

One he was losing.

Claire went with something drastic. She poured her beer over his head.

Riley stopped in his tracks, gasping for breath. The kind of gasp someone might make if they'd been underwater too long. And he looked at her, the beer trickling from his hair and down his face.

"You poured your beer on me." His words weren't so shaky now, but Riley did look at her as if she'd lost her mind.

Since they were still in view of the smokers, the beer ploy had gotten their attention, too, and the questions came.

Can't handle her, Riley?

Does the flyboy need some help locating his target?

The questions were punctuated with laughter, some jeering, and Claire shot them nasty glares before she pulled Riley to the side of the old barn. Thankfully, there was no one else here, and there was still enough light coming from the front of the building so she could make sure she wasn't maneuvering them into a fire-ant bed.

"You poured your beer on me," Riley repeated.

She nodded. "All the websites I read said I shouldn't

tell you to snap out of it, offer advice or minimize what you've been through, but none of the sites said I couldn't pour a beer on you."

He stared at her. Laughed. It wasn't a 100 percent kind of a laugh. More like that sixty-forty ratio he'd mentioned earlier, and it was short, but at least she could see Riley coming back to her.

"Logan," Riley said, leaning the back of his head against the wall. "He's in his truck in the parking lot."

"You want me to get him?"

"Hell, no."

All right. "I can text him and tell him that I'll make sure you get home." Claire put the empty beer bottle on the ground and fired off a message to Logan. He answered right away, saying that he'd skipped Calhoun's and was at his office.

Good.

Riley definitely wouldn't have wanted to face Logan with his head smelling like beer and the semi-shell-shocked look still on his face. She showed Riley the text response, then put her phone back into her pocket and debated what to do next. Anything she did could cause Riley's walls to go up again, but she wouldn't be much of a friend if she blew this off.

"Now, according to the websites, this is when I should ask you if you want to talk about it?" she tossed out there.

He had his head tipped up to the sky as if seeking some kind of divine assistance. And maybe he was. The websites had suggested that as an option, too. Then, by degrees his chin came back down until they made eye contact.

"I'm getting help," he said. "At the base. I've only been to one session, but there are, well, exercises and stuff. Nothing about beer pouring though. Or neck kissing. But

I have to say, that worked pretty well. The kissing, not the beer." He licked some of it from the corner of his mouth.

Now she laughed. "That was my attempt at a distraction. And I didn't actually kiss you. I just wanted to avoid the jerks in that smoking crowd."

"Does the flyboy need some help locating his target?" Riley repeated. "And Jake Banchini offered to lend me a condom if he could join us."

Claire hadn't heard that, but she'd deal with Jake the next time she saw him. Maybe she'd dump a beer on Jake's head, too. For very different reasons.

"You know the gossips will get wind of this," she reminded him.

"Yeah." Definitely no trace of that laughter now, and she hated that she'd even brought it up. "I'm sorry about that."

Claire shrugged. "Either way, we would have given them gossip fodder, but the talk will die down when folks see you with Jodi."

It was such a stupid thing to say, and the trouble was, Claire didn't want to take back the comment.

"Jodi's probably gone by now," he said.

"Oh. Well. How do you feel about that?"

She got the look, the one to let her know that this subject was off-limits. The old, normal Riley was back, not a trace of the flashbacks anywhere on his face. "I don't have my car, Livvy drove me, but I can walk you home if you like," she suggested. It was more than a mile from this part of town, and it was a scorcher of a night, but she didn't want to leave him alone just yet. "Or I can have Livvy take you."

A taxi wasn't an option because the sole taxi driver in the town, Walter Meekins, was home with a gout flare-up. For once, the gossip mill had actually given her some relevant information so she wouldn't bother wasting time calling him.

Riley shook his head. "Let's just stay here a little longer. Then I can walk home."

And she would follow him to make sure he didn't have another episode on the way there.

He wiped his face with his shirtsleeve. "I'm not sure how much of this is sweat and how much is beer. It's hot enough to catch malaria out here."

It was, but he didn't budge. Riley didn't talk, either. He just stood there, looking up at the sky. Claire looked, too. Or rather she tried, but her attention just kept going back to him. Even with the beer-head and wet shirt, he still managed to look, well, mouthwatering.

"This might be the malaria talking, but you're hot." *Uh-oh.* She hadn't exactly intended to say that out loud, and it got Riley's attention all right.

Not 60 percent of it, either.

All of it.

"Want to do something we'll probably regret?" he asked. But he didn't give her a chance to answer.

Riley slipped his hand around the back of her neck, lowered his head and kissed her.

CHAPTER TWELVE

AS REGRETS WENT, it was a damn good one.

Riley had always figured that Claire would taste like something sweet, but he hadn't known just how sweet that sweet could be. Of course, her taste was mixed with some of the beer she'd had before rescuing him, some of the beer on his own mouth, too, but that only added another memory to the one he was making.

It'd be a short memory, though.

Or so he'd thought when he first touched his lips to hers.

He'd thought she would immediately come to her senses and put a stop to this fire-playing game. But Claire upped the memory-making a thousandfold by making a little sound. Barely audible over Garth Brooks, who was now belting out "Friends in Low Places" on the jukebox. But it was audible enough for Riley's ears to catch it.

And have that sound slide right through his whole body.

Not a purr, exactly. More like surprise mixed with a whole lot of heat. Yeah, maybe the malaria had kicked in after all. Or maybe he'd just lost what little of his mind he had left, but that didn't get him to back away.

Riley continued kissing her until lack of oxygen became a serious issue. They broke the mouth-to-mouth just seconds before they certainly would have passed out.

"Oh," she said, the single word muttered as she gulped in some air.

That was it. Nothing else. And Riley was still trying to gather enough breath to say something even marginally PG-rated or relevant. "Me, man. You, woman" probably wouldn't do it.

She looked up at him as if waiting to see what he would do next. She was still breathing through her mouth, and her warm breath was hitting against his face. Her breath smelled good, too. Again, beer with a whole lot of heat that was zinging between them.

Since Claire clearly wasn't going to do any moving away, Riley figured he should be the one to do it. Really. As in right now. Before he crushed what was left of their friendship.

But that didn't happen.

He was obviously weak and mindless when it came to Claire, and that really stupid part of him behind the zipper of his jeans was encouraging him to go in for another round.

So, that's what he did.

"I didn't regret that nearly enough," he said, right before he kissed her again.

Claire didn't stay passive this time, either. Her hands went to his waist, and she leaned in, not exactly deepening the kiss, but rather deepening something even better.

Her belly landed against the beginnings of his hard-on.

Now, that was something she noticed, and she did pull back. She slid her tongue over her lips, dropped a glance at the front of his jeans, at the intruder that had just popped up between them.

All right. So, that was the end of the kissing.

Or so he thought.

But Claire cursed, caught on to him again and kissed

him the right way. She made it French. Made it hard and long—mirroring what was happening in his jeans.

Riley turned her, putting her back against the wall so he could add some more of that body pressure without ramming his shoulder into her. Nothing would kill the mood faster than if he had to howl in pain.

They grappled for position, not breaking the kiss, and generally acting as if they were starved for each other. This time, it was Riley who stopped, but only because he didn't want to start dragging her to the ground.

"Ouch," Claire grumbled.

It took him a moment to realize she wasn't saying that because of the kiss. She was rubbing her butt, and he hadn't kissed or touched her there.

Not yet anyway.

"I think I got a splinter," she said.

Of all the things Riley had thought she might say, that wasn't one of them. "Where?"

She looked behind her where just seconds earlier her backside had been firmly planted against the wall. "You think it's some kind of sign to get us to stop?"

"I think it's just a splinter."

But that was his hard-on talking, and Riley knew from experience that when his dick was in that particular state, wise words never came out of his mouth. Often, unwise actions followed, too.

The splinter, whether a sign or not, did the trick of getting her out of his arms. Claire signaled the end of this regret-testing/make-out session by putting a couple of inches distance between them.

His hard-on reminded him that a couple of inches was nothing and that it could still reach pay dirt and complete that whole "Me, man. You, woman" thing. But this was Claire, and he really did need to consider the consequences here. For one thing, Daniel's proposal was still on the table.

Literally.

Della had heard that the guy who'd gone to Claire's to collect some stuff for Goodwill had seen the engagement-ring box still on the table in her foyer.

Violate the man-rule.

Of course, that was his hard-on talking again, but Riley still had a brain. Well, for the most part. Plus, there was the other thing to consider here. He wouldn't be in Spring Hill or even Texas much longer. A few more weeks at most. And then he'd have to leave and go wherever the Air Force sent him.

Probably to another deployment.

That wouldn't sit well with Claire's safe-flying ways, and it would drive her crazy knowing he was there, doing the stuff that had given him these nightmares and flashbacks.

"Arguing with yourself?" she asked.

"Yeah," he admitted.

"Who's winning?" She glanced at the front of his jeans again.

"Right now, it's a draw." Not even close. Brainless was still in the lead. "Are *you* arguing with yourself?"

"Not really. I think we both know this can't work out." She paused, shrugged. "But the kiss was, well, really, really, really good."

Riley smiled. He'd gotten a triple really. From Claire.

"Don't grin like that." She hit him on his good arm. "You know we just made things a lot harder on ourselves." Another gaze drop to his jeans. "And I'm not just talking about *that*."

Yes, he did know. But that didn't stop him from wanting to make things a lot more complicated.

"It's not just us," she went on. "I've got Ethan to consider. If I get close to you, *closer*," Claire amended, "I have to think about how that'll affect him."

No effect whatsoever. Again, not Riley's brain talking because he knew what she meant. If he insinuated himself into Claire's life, he was also including Ethan in certain parts of that insinuation. Riley didn't know much about kids, but he knew Ethan well enough now to know that when Riley just up and disappeared, Ethan would notice. Might even be confused or hurt.

Riley would rather punch himself in his bad shoulder than let that happen.

"And there's one more thing," Claire went on. She actually touched the front of his jeans this time. "I know what's going on there." Then she touched his head. "But I don't know what's happening in there. I don't know if you're even in a place to think about kissing me again."

Oh, he was in the right place for that, but he heard the logic of what she was saying. He cursed the fucking logic, too.

"You want to know what's going on in my head?" he asked.

She nodded.

All right. Not exactly a shout for more, but Riley would give her what he could.

"I'm scared," he confessed. "And if you don't think it took a lot to admit that to you, think again."

She nodded. "I know it took a lot. Thank you."

Riley figured this could be the jumping-off point for a long conversation. One that he wasn't ready to have with her yet, and if they stayed out here against the barn wall, he'd just end up kissing her again. Besides, he thought he might have softened up enough now so he could walk.

He decided to go with the safer option.

"Come on." He slipped his arm around her waist and got her moving. "Let's go inside. I'm ready for another cold beer. This time, I'm going to drink it."

WELL, CLAIRE WASN'T ready for a beer. After that kissing session, she was ready to haul Riley off to bed. Her body was itching for more, more, more.

But the beer was a much safer option.

She hadn't been just doling out lip service when she'd spelled out her concerns. About Ethan. About Riley's mental health. About their polar-opposite lifestyles. He would be leaving soon, and she would be staying if not in Spring Hill, close enough to still call it home. And she wanted to call it home as much as Riley wanted to eye the town and his family's ranch in his rearview mirror as he sped away.

In his uniform.

Headed right back into situations where he could be killed.

Those were all major deal breakers, and still she had to force herself away from him and start the trek back into Calhoun's.

There was a fresh group of smokers at the back now. A small blessing. And they were in the middle of a heated discussion about the high school basketball team, so they barely noticed when she and Riley slipped past them inside.

"You're sure this is okay?" she asked. The crowd seemed even louder and rowdier than earlier.

Riley nodded. No verbal answer. Was that because he didn't want her to hear the lie in his voice? Just in case, Claire decided to stay close to him. However, she hadn't realized just how close that close would be when they started to worm their way through the crowd toward the bar.

Calhoun's wasn't exactly a dance hall, but that never stopped people from doing just that. The dancing started in the center and spread out, sometimes with couples bumping into tables and sloshing drinks. Which was exactly what happened to Riley and her.

Terrence Joe O'Malley and Misty were doing their own version of a boot-scootin' boogie, and they collided with Riley and her. They, in turn, collided with a table filled with pitchers of beer and the Nederland brothers. All three of them. No necks, bear-size shoulders. Low IQs. Beered up.

Never a good combination.

If Riley had been any other man in the place, with the exception of Logan, a fight would have quickly followed, but one of the Nederlands—she didn't know which one because they were like snowflakes, and she couldn't tell them apart—gave Riley a wobbly salute and snapped his fingers to the harried waitress to order another pitcher.

Since there were no open tables for Riley and her to do a finger snap of their own, the bar trek continued. More collisions. Claire got groped. Riley, too. And she prayed the groping didn't extend to his shoulder. He seemed to be making progress with the physical healing, and she didn't want him to have a setback, all because he insisted on having a beer.

"Well?" Livvy said from behind her.

She wasn't sure how her friend had gotten through the crowd at that angle, but Livvy even managed to crook her arm around Claire and yank her closer.

"How was it?" Livvy asked. Of course, she had to shout it.

There was no way Claire could answer that in this

place. Probably no way to answer it even when Livvy and she were alone, so Claire just smiled and nodded.

But Livvy wasn't exactly smiling. Even in the filmy light, Claire could see something was wrong. Livvy got Riley's attention by tapping him on the back of the head, and then she motioned for Claire and him to follow her.

Away from the bar.

Too bad because Claire had worked up a thirst, and she needed something to cool her off.

It was impossible to ask Livvy why they were making the detour, and the detour wasn't any faster than their trek to the bar would have been. Livvy kept herding them through the crowd, all the way to the front entrance. It was marginally quieter there but much farther away from the beer.

"Your girlfriend's here," Livvy announced. She pointed toward the bar. Actually, she pointed *on* the bar. And Claire saw the woman dancing there. It took her another moment to realize that it was indeed Riley's girlfriend.

Jodi.

Well, that was a quick reminder for Claire of why she shouldn't have been kissing Riley outside.

"She's been asking for you," Livvy added. Not looking at Riley but rather Claire.

"Me?" Claire asked.

"Her?" Riley asked. "Why?"

"It was hard to hear the details, but I think Jodi believes you stole her man."

Well, good grief. And it wasn't exactly something that Claire could jump to deny. Except she could. The kissing hadn't gone beyond kissing. And an erection. But the erection had been Riley's reaction, of course, not hers.

Riley mumbled some profanity. "Jodi's drunk. She

never makes sense when she's drunk. I'll handle this," he insisted and would have started toward the bar if Livvy hadn't stopped him.

"There's more," Livvy said, still looking at Riley now. "Daniel's here, too, and he's accusing you of stealing his girlfriend."

Claire wanted to scream, but instead she blurted out, "Balderdash." A word she'd never used in her life, but it beat screaming and the real profanity she wanted to use instead.

"My advice?" Livvy went on. "Why don't we just go over to the Tip Top and have a drink?"

The Tip Top was the only other drinking place in town, and there'd be no noise or bar dancing there. That was because it was a vegan, organic wine bar, and the only people who ever went there were people over seventy or the occasional drunkard who'd been kicked out of Calhoun's.

If Livvy had had her way, she would have pulled them right out of the pub, but before she could do that, Claire heard a shout. One that was very audible even over the crowd.

"Cindy!" Jodi shouted. "Don't you ignore me!"

And Claire knew the woman was referring to her. "I'll handle this," Riley repeated, and he started toward the bar with Claire and Livvy trailing along behind him.

"Remember Daniel's up there somewhere," Livvy yelled.

In the meantime, Jodi continued to yell, too. "That's right. Come on, Candy." She was facing Claire now and waggling her fingers. "We'll settle this woman to woman."

"You should stay back," Riley warned her.

Of course Claire ignored that. Yes, she was a mother,

but that didn't mean she was just going to tuck tail and run. And there was an even bigger issue here if she didn't stand up to this loudmouth. In addition to the gossips blabbing about Riley and her smooching outside Calhoun's, there'd be new gossip now about Jodi besting her in a showdown. Claire didn't especially want a showdown, but maybe, just maybe, they could get Jodi out of there so they could have a civil conversation.

"Claire," she heard when she got closer to the bar. Not Jodi—the woman wouldn't have gotten her name right—but Daniel. He fell in step alongside her as Riley continued to lead the way.

"You're really here with Riley?" Daniel asked. "I thought that was just a rumor."

"No. I came with Livvy, and Riley and I ran into each other." That was the sanitized version anyway. He'd hear the rest soon enough. Maybe then he'd want his ring back and would stop proposing to her.

They kept moving, and Claire noticed something strange going on. Something more strange than Jodi's slurred, staggering attempts to call her names.

Chloe was her latest attempt.

But the other thing going on was that people were moving out of the way for Riley, Livvy, Daniel and Claire. She had no idea where the people were actually going because there was no room to create the path they were creating. But there it was.

And the now-open path led straight to the bar.

"Carrie!" Jodi shouted, pointing at Claire again. It was much easier for Jodi to see her now that only Riley was in the way. And the woman's glare zoomed right over Riley to Claire.

"She's been drinking," Mr. Obvious—aka Daniel—said. "I should get you out of here."

But Claire held her ground.

Unfortunately Jodi didn't.

She brought back her hand to do another finger point, probably more name-calling, too, but the sudden motion must have thrown her off balance. Jodi let out a loud shriek and fell face forward. If Riley hadn't rushed to grab her, she would have splatted right on the peanut-covered floor.

Riley howled. But his howl was one of pain. No doubt because the rescue had hurt his shoulder. Claire wanted to throttle Jodi for that alone. Jodi must have had throttling on the mind, too, because without any concern whatsoever about Riley, Jodi shrieked out some curse words and launched herself at Claire.

Someone got in the way.

At the exact moment of Jodi's launch, one of the Nederland sisters moved to the bar. Moved into Jodi's path, too. And the fist that Jodi had apparently meant for Claire slammed into the Nederland sister's face.

Oh no.

She didn't know which Nederland sister this was—Claire couldn't tell them apart, either—but there were three of them, all built like their linebacker-size brothers. The sister who'd gotten hit, hit back, and her sisters hurried to join the fray. The brothers, too.

Claire couldn't see much after that. Fists started flying. Chairs, too. A beer bottle went zinging past her, and it smacked her on the head. She would have gotten smacked with a second one if Riley hadn't gotten her out of the way.

"Get Claire out of here," Daniel told Riley. "I'll take care of Jodi."

Riley was still grimacing in pain, but Claire saw the

debate he was waging with himself. He didn't want to leave Jodi in the middle of this.

More flying beer—this time in a pitcher—must have ended the debate for him because he caught on to Livvy with one hand, Claire with the other, and began to plow through the chaos.

They were still much too far away from the front door when Claire heard a sound that stopped everyone and everything. Including her heart.

Sirens.

And the Spring Hill Police Department cruiser squealed to a stop right in front of them.

CHAPTER THIRTEEN

WELL, THIS WAS not what Riley had in mind when he'd decided to go to Calhoun's for a beer. Here he was at the Spring Hill Police Department, hauled in for questioning in what had become a full-fledged brawl. Riley wasn't under arrest.

But Claire was.

And so were Daniel and Jodi.

Even though Riley had tried to explain that Claire didn't have any part in starting or finishing the fight, it didn't matter. Whoever had called the cops—apparently before blood was even drawn—had said that Claire and "Riley's crazy-assed girlfriend" were fighting. The cops had gone to Calhoun's looking specifically to break up that fight and had stormed in after Jodi and Claire just as Daniel threw a punch at one of the Nederland brothers. Or maybe it was one of their sisters.

Now there they were. And even though Riley wasn't behind bars with them, he'd decided to stay as close as possible and was sitting on the floor across from the side-by-side cells.

Claire's expression said it all. She was not pleased about any of this. Maybe because she was not only behind bars but was also pacing while holding an ice pack to her head where she'd gotten hit with a beer bottle.

She wasn't alone in that cell, either.

The Spring Hill Police Department only had two holding cells, and the Nederland siblings were in one of them. Riley was convinced all six siblings had glandular issues to make them the size of tree trunks, and when they were drunk—which they were—it wasn't safe to put anyone else in there with them. That's how Daniel, Claire and Jodi had ended up together in the other cell.

"This is all your fault," Daniel growled for the umpteenth time, and his growled words were meant for Riley.

Riley had given up on the notion of defending himself. Besides, it was his fault in a roundabout way. He should have insisted that Jodi leave Spring Hill. She probably wouldn't have listened—Jodi wasn't exactly one to do what people asked of her—but at least he could have tried. Now, here they were in this mess.

"It's her fault," Jodi argued, hitching her thumb in Claire's direction. Jodi winced, probably because she'd bruised her hand when she was trading punches with one of the Nederlands.

Claire gave Jodi a look that could have instantly frozen a vat of boiling water.

"It's your fault," one of the Nederland sisters said to no one in particular. The clan was all stewing but mainly because they hadn't gotten to finish their pitchers of beer before being hauled in.

Livvy stuck her head around the corner and motioned for Riley to get up. "This cop wants you to sign some papers."

That brought Claire to her feet, too. "Does that mean we're getting out?"

"I sure hope so." And Riley did hope that.

The minutes had crawled into hours, and he wanted Claire out of there and home. Daniel and Jodi, too, only because he thought he owed them that much. After that, Riley could go home, as well, and take some pain meds.

His shoulder had gone past the throbbing stage and was now screaming at him.

He followed Livvy into the squad room. Such that it was. Crime wasn't a big problem in Spring Hill, so there was only the chief of police, Luke Mercer, two deputies and an admin assistant. Only the chief and one of the deputies were there tonight, and it was Deputy Davy Divine—his real name—who was sitting at the front desk with some papers neatly arranged in front of him.

"It's for their bail," Davy explained. He was a wormy-looking guy who'd never had a date or even a single look from a girl in school, but he'd found his forte with that badge. If Mayberry's Barney Fife and a zombie had managed to have a kid, it would have looked a lot like Davy.

"How much and who do I pay?" Riley asked.

"Five hundred apiece, and you pay here. We take check, debit or credit."

Riley whipped out his MasterCard. "But do you really think Claire and Daniel are flight risks?" He didn't include Jodi in that because she certainly could and would hightail it out of there just for the thrill of it.

"Doesn't matter what I think. The law's the law. Are you paying for the Nederlands, too?" Davy asked.

"No." And Riley couldn't say that fast enough. He needed to get a head start on them in case they renewed their disagreement with Jodi. "Just Claire, Daniel and Jodi." He signed the papers, and Davy took the credit card.

"I'll have to make sure the card is good." Davy examined it as if it were the norm for people in Spring Hill to give him fake credit cards. "Might take a while since our computer's down, and I'll have to call. You can sit back in there with your...friends or wait out here."

"Great. More waiting," Livvy mumbled.

Maybe this time it wouldn't take as long as it had to get the paperwork done. Holding on to that hope, Riley sank down in the chair across from Davy's desk to wait.

"Is Jodi usually like this?" Livvy asked.

"Sometimes. I've never been with her in a bar fight, but she tends to live life on the edge."

Which was exactly what had attracted him to her in the first place. Of course, she was drawn to his desire to live life on the edge, too, but Riley had never mixed that particular side of him with a dose of crazy.

"Claire was supposed to have hot sex tonight," Livvy said, sitting next to him. "Did she?"

It took him a moment to shift gears and absorb what Livvy said. Another moment to decide if he was going to answer at all. "No. Sadly, the closest she came was getting a splinter in her butt." Realizing just how that sounded, Riley gave her a warning glare. "And if you tell anyone that, I will hunt you down."

Livvy held up her hands in mock defense. "No threat needed. I'm not into gossip, and besides, any details I hear, I'd rather get from Claire."

Riley wondered exactly how Claire would catalogue this night. First, she'd had to coax him out of the flashback, then they'd kissed, then she'd gotten arrested. He figured the kiss was going to get lost in all that other mess. But it wasn't lost for him.

Nope.

He stood no chance whatsoever of forgetting exactly how Claire had felt in his arms. How she'd tasted. That sound she'd made. Now, that was a sound and a flashback he actually wanted to experience. With the way Davy was dragging his feet—he'd struck up a conversation with the chief now about whose turn it was to descale the coffeepot—there might be time for a flashback or two.

Riley was still thinking about that kiss when something else popped into his head. "What about Ethan? Who's with him?"

"Claire got a sitter." Livvy checked the time. "If Claire's not out in the next hour, I'll go to her house so the sitter can get home. I figured I'd be spending the night there anyway. Well, unless you're staying."

"I won't be staying."

Riley was certain of that. He was going to need a big dose of the painkillers, and they made him drowsy. They also made him talk in his sleep. Claire had been through enough without hearing about shit he didn't want her to hear about.

He was so caught up in his pain and thoughts that it took him a second to realize that Livvy's tone had changed on her next-to-last sentence.

"Why did you figure you needed to spend the night at Claire's?" he asked.

As Riley had done earlier, Livvy paused, maybe debating if she would answer. Or rather *how* to answer. "When Claire was sorting through a box, she found her mother's journal."

Hell. Riley didn't have to ask what was in it. He knew that if it had anything to do with her mother, it couldn't be good.

"She's torn up about what she read in it, Riley," Livvy added.

Of course she was. Her mother had been dead since she was a kid, and yet she could still put knots in Claire's stomach. "I don't guess Claire burned it?"

Livvy shook her head. "No such luck. She put it in one of the trash boxes, but she's been sorting for weeks, and not one trash box has left the house."

And this one wouldn't go out, either. Claire would

end up reading every painful word in it. "Any idea what her mother wrote?"

"I only saw two words, fudging kid, except she used the real *F* word."

Great. He wondered if he could somehow talk Claire into putting it in a real trash bin. One that contained stuff she'd never see again. But he had to be honest with himself. He'd likely lost a lot of clout with Claire tonight. Ironic since they'd had their first kiss.

Second one, too.

But those might be the only kisses they'd ever have. She was probably ready to wash her hands of him and his crazy girlfriend. A girlfriend who would soon become an ex if Jodi didn't know that already. And that was an ex in a forever-and-ever kind of way, too.

Riley heard some movement in the holding cell, and he got up to make sure Claire was okay. Thankfully Jodi was asleep and snoring like a hibernating buffalo. Even Daniel had closed his eyes, and the Nederlands were all knocked out. The movement had come from an ice cube falling out of the plastic bag that Claire had been holding against her head.

"It won't be long now," Riley told her, something he'd been telling her since they arrived.

Even though it was against Deputy Davy's rules, Riley sank down on the floor right next to the cell, instead of across from it.

"You think we tempted fate or something?" she asked. She was still pacing. Not that she could go far. Six steps forward, six steps back. There were definitely no remnants of the heat that'd been between them at Calhoun's, and Riley didn't think the chill in the room was all from the AC.

"I think we just got unlucky," Riley answered.

"Hey, did somebody say my name?" a male voice called out.

Riley recognized the voice, of course, but he was hoping it was some kind of trick brought on by the pain and fatigue.

It wasn't.

With his arms outstretched and that cocky grin on his face, his brother Lucky walked in.

LUCKY HADN'T EXPECTED to see party faces, but this was one notch below the gloom-and-doom stage. It had a whole vibe of one of Dante's levels of hell.

And speaking of hell, Riley brought up the subject right away.

"What the hell are you doing here?" Riley asked, getting to his feet.

"I brought bail money. *Cash*. It'll take Deputy Dweeb out there all night to process a credit card, but he knows how to count money, provided you give him big enough bills so he doesn't have too many of them." Lucky had a little experience with that. "He's getting the keys now to unlock the cell."

Maybe it was the mention of being sprung, but thankfully Claire had a warmer reaction to Lucky than Riley had. She smiled, but that smile didn't win him any brotherly awards with Riley because it only deepened his scowl. That scowl was probably about that phone conversation they'd had a couple of nights ago. The one where Riley grilled him about the sex talk Lucky had had with Claire ages ago.

Riley just liked to hang on to things.

Like beer, apparently.

Lucky got a strong whiff of it when he walked closer. "Jeez, what'd you do? Pour a beer over your head?"

Riley could have sent small children and animals running with that glare. "That look doesn't work on big brothers," Lucky let him know.

Lucky pushed past him to get to Claire and he gave her a cheek kiss through the cell bars. Like his experience with bail money, it wasn't his first through-the-bars kiss. "Are you okay?"

She gave him a flat look, too, but then added another smile. A really small one. Of course, the new smile didn't sit well with little brother, and Lucky wondered if Riley knew it was jealousy driving all these intense feelings. Probably not. Jealousy wasn't covered by one of Riley's man-rules.

"How'd you know we were here?" Claire asked.

Lucky held up his phone and showed her the flurry of calls, texts and voice mails he'd gotten in the past hour. It was the norm for the Nederlands to land in jail, but it was the story of the decade, maybe the century, for Claire to get locked up. Folks just couldn't wait to tell him that Riley had been at the scene of the crime, too.

It was a funny, tenuous thing being a McCord. Having money generated as much admiration as it did sour grapes, and people were always happy to see a McCord come down a notch.

That was one of the reasons Lucky liked to provide such entertainment to the townsfolk. Even though he'd never get any thanks for being labeled the family screwup, it took pressure off Riley, Anna and Logan.

Deputy Dweeb finally arrived with a ring of keys that clanged and rattled as he went through them, searching for the right one. Since there weren't that many doors in the entire town, Lucky had a theory that Davy had scrounged up the extra keys just to make himself look more important. It didn't work. Davy could have had the keys to every door in the world, and he'd still be a dweeb.

The moment the cell door was open, Claire rushed out. She hugged him and then made a beeline for Livvy.

Ah, Livvy.

No gloom and doom for her. Well, not when Lucky had first come in anyway, but it was obvious the woman was ready to get Claire out of there.

Daniel got up, too, and he shook the snoring woman on the cot. This was Jodi, no doubt. Riley's girlfriend and the reason for Claire's incarceration.

Lucky would take that up with his brother later.

"You got one more paper you have to sign," the deputy told Claire.

With Daniel still trying to rouse Jodi, Riley, Claire, Livvy and Lucky all went back into the squad room. And, yes, there was a paper to be signed. Of course, Davy had to find it first. Then he'd have to find a working pen.

Lucky wasn't sure how Davy even made it out of the house by himself.

The wait gave Riley more chances to sling that ugly look at Lucky. "Why are you here in Spring Hill?"

Lucky shrugged. "Logan called and asked me to come home."

No glare this time. Riley looked at him as if he'd sprouted an extra ear. "Logan calls you all the time and asks you to come home. You never do."

"I like being unpredictable." That was his answer, and he was sticking to it. Of course, Riley would soon figure it out. Unlike Deputy Dweeb, his brother had a functioning brain. And when Riley did figure it out, he wasn't going to like it.

This was going to be like the potty training all over

again except this time it was going to require more than pissing on a tree.

"Ouch," Claire grumbled, getting all their attention.

Lucky hadn't seen what had prompted her ouch, but in the aftermath he noticed she was looking at her backside. He made it to her ahead of Riley, turned her and quickly spotted the problem.

"You got splinters." He plucked the ones he could see from her jeans. "That happened to me once. Got it when I was making out with Wendy Lee Keller against the wall outside Calhoun's Pub."

And the silence rolled in like London fog.

So, hell. That's what had happened. Riley and Claire had made out. Maybe even more. Lucky glanced at them, assessing.

No. Not more.

They would have been more content, or uneasy, if they'd had sex.

But the making out had been enough. Maybe Jodi had gotten jealous. Daniel, too. Or as Lucky liked to call Daniel, Dweeb Two. The Nederlands had likely just been the rocket fuel that fed all this.

On general principle Lucky wasn't opposed to Riley and Claire making out. But—and this was a huge *but*—he didn't want Riley doing that unless he'd come to his senses and realized that playing with Claire's heart was the same thing as giving it a good ass-whipping.

If Riley didn't use his more than half a brain to figure that out, Lucky intended to spell it out for him.

"I need to sleep," Jodi grumbled from behind them. Daniel had managed to get her on her feet, barely, and he had finally gotten her out of the cell. Daniel looked at Riley as if he expected him to take things from there.

Riley didn't budge.

That half brain was doing its job. Lucky didn't know this Jodi, but she had bad news written all over her. And Lucky should know. He was an expert at picking out bad girls. She was far more his type that GI Riley's.

Deputy Dweeb finally made it back with the paperwork, and Lucky provided the pen. One that he'd taken from the dweeb's desk right after he came into the police station. Dealing with the deputy was a little like getting stuck in the movie *Groundhog Day*, and Lucky had learned some shortcuts to speed things up. Like bringing cash and stealing pens. In case it had been needed, he also had some advice on how to descale a coffeepot.

Claire hurried to sign the paper.

"I just got a call from Wilma over at the newspaper," the deputy said. "I think you should know they're running a story on the pub brawl in the morning. There'll be pictures."

"How'd the newspaper get pictures?" Daniel howled. He was apparently the only one in the room who didn't know the answer.

"Cell phones," each of them answered, adding varying verbs and adjectives. Jodi even added a knowing grunt. Anyone who wasn't falling-down drunk would have wanted to snap shots of something like that. It wasn't as if brawls happened in the pub on a daily basis.

More like monthly.

Claire didn't even read the paper Davy gave her. She just signed it and glanced at Lucky. "Thanks for the bail money. I'll pay you back." Then she turned to Livvy. "Please take me home now. I have to get some rest, and makeup concealer, before I do that photo shoot in the morning."

For a moment Lucky thought she was just going to

waltz out of there and not even say goodbye. And she did sort of do just that.

"Next time I want a beer, I'll have it at home," Claire grumbled.

Livvy winked at Lucky, gave him the call-me sign with her pinkie and thumb, and slipped her arm around Claire to get them moving. Claire did look back, though. At Riley this time, and Lucky tried to figure out how to describe the look she gave him. Definitely no Mona Lisa smile moment. More like Munch's *The Scream*. There was no call-me gesture involved.

"She's just tired and upset," Lucky said. And he nudged Riley, as well, and moved him to the big glass window so they could watch Claire and Livvy leave. "But you gotta admit, this proves exactly what I was saying to you the last time we talked."

Riley looked at him as if he'd sprouted another nose to go with that extra ear. "What the hell are you talking about?"

"That." Lucky motioned toward Claire. "That's the face of a woman who's in love with you."

Even though they were in the police station and Lucky knew it would hurt like hell, he let Riley ball up his fist and punch him.

CHAPTER FOURTEEN

CLAIRE FIGURED THAT was the worst photo shoot she'd ever done, but at least she had managed to finish it. Not easy with her head still hurting from the beer and lack of sleep.

Especially the lack of sleep.

After getting home from the bar brawl/arrest ordeal, she had been so wound up that she hadn't slept a wink. She'd finally given up, left Ethan with Livvy and had gotten some pictures edited before leaving hours earlier than necessary for the photo shoot. Now that it was done, she was going to have to face a cold, hard reality.

She had kissed Riley, and she'd liked it. Too much. So much so that it was driving her crazy. And it was just the tip of the frosty little iceberg that was now her life.

She had a police record.

Her face was plastered in the town newspaper.

And, yes, it was there because she hadn't been able to resist glancing at it in the stand when she'd driven past the grocery store. On the front page was a picture of one of the Nederlands flinging Jodi at her. It looked a lot worse than it'd been, which, of course, was exactly why it had gone on the front page. Claire had no doubts, *none*, that by now every copy had already sold out.

Balancing her camera equipment, Claire let herself into the house, expecting to see Summer Starkley, one of the twins, there with Ethan. But it wasn't Summer or her sister, Savannah. It was Livvy. She and Ethan were at the kitchen table, and judging from the volume of cookies and ice cream in front of them, they were either on a quest to become diabetic or celebrating something.

Claire figured it wasn't the latter because there was nothing to celebrate.

"Summer had car trouble, couldn't come," Livvy said, not addressing the treats. "So Ethan got me as a sitter today."

Both Ethan and Livvy seemed pretty happy about that, but the happiness could have been just a sugar high.

"Thanks for staying with him," she told Livvy.

"No prob. And hey, you did a great job covering up the bruise on your face. I can hardly see it."

That was a very bad lie. The couple that Claire had photographed had noticed it first thing. So had the attendant at the gas station where she'd filled up. And now so did Ethan.

"Boo-boo," he said, pointing right to it.

He'd been asleep when Claire had gotten home from jail—now, that was something she thought she'd never say about herself. *Home from jail.* Anyway, Ethan had still been asleep when she'd left for work, so this was his first chance to see the proof of the bad decisions she'd made the night before.

"Mommy's fine," Claire assured him, and she kissed his cheek. She hugged him, too, despite the fact he was holding a spoon dripping with ice cream. "What's with all the sugar?"

The confused look on Livvy's face let Claire know she needed to clarify. "Sugar-sugar." Not shit.

"Oh, this," Livvy said in the tone of something not even worth mentioning. "Riley dropped by earlier and brought it. Oh, and Ethan peed on the tree in your backyard. Is that okay?"

No, it wasn't. She was trying to redirect his bodily functions in the direction of a real toilet, but since his diaper usage had been cut by half, it was hard for Claire to dispute the temporary potty-training method. However, that wasn't what had her attention now.

"Riley was here?" Claire asked.

"Riley!" Ethan squealed, and he clapped his hand against the drippy spoon.

Livvy nodded. "He brought ice cream, cookies and a new wallpaper scraper for you." She pointed to the scraper on the counter. "He said word around town was you'd broken your other one."

She had but was miffed about how something so mundane had made the gossip factory when there were so many other juicy things for people to discuss.

"Did Riley, uh, say anything else?" Claire asked.

"Sor-ree," Ethan supplied.

"Yes, sorry. Riley did say that a lot," Livvy continued, talking around the egg-size bite of ice cream she'd just stuffed into her mouth. "He really is sorry for what happened at Calhoun's. I think all this was his idea of a peace offering. A sugar-hot peace offering if you ask me."

Yes, it was, but Claire would have liked to have been there for his visit. Or maybe not, she quickly amended. She was embarrassed and not at all sure what to say to him, so maybe it was a good thing she'd been at work.

"Don't worry," Livvy went on. "I had Ethan eat some healthy stuff before he got dessert."

"Ickin, tarrots," Ethan attempted. "Bocci." Chicken, carrots and broccoli. The first two were his favorites, the broccoli not so much, but her son must have known there was sugar and lots of it at the end of the proverbial veggie tunnel.

"Did Riley say anything else?" Claire pressed. The

first time she'd asked it, Livvy had barely spared her a glance. But she stared at Claire now.

"He didn't bring up j-a-i-l, and neither did I. Didn't bring up the k-i-s-s-y stuff, either."

Ethan stared at her, too. "K-i-spell-y?"

Livvy cackled with laughter, causing Ethan to laugh, too, and while it normally would have gotten a smile or chuckle from Claire, her funny bone was broken today. She'd left it and her dignity on the floor of Calhoun's Pub.

Riley hadn't mentioned something as huge as jail and the kiss? Of course, Claire hadn't wanted him to talk to Livvy about either of those, but she'd figured he would have mentioned it in a roundabout way. Ditto for the roundabout approach to the kiss since he might have figured that she had already discussed it with Livvy.

She hadn't. Not in detail anyway.

Despite Livvy's best attempts to get her to bare her soul, Claire had only acknowledged the kiss and nothing more. Since Livvy had been the one to get out the final splinter, Claire had decided that baring her butt to her friend was plenty enough for one night.

"There was so much ice cream. Three half gallons," Livvy went on, still eating. "I put some in the freezer for later, and we gave Whoa a scoop of the vanilla."

Sure enough Claire could see the cat through the glass door on the back porch, and he/she and his/her companion were licking away. It probably wasn't good for a cat to have that much sugar, either, but considering this was Whoa, she doubted anything would do much more harm. He didn't just look as if he'd been cooking meth, more as though he had been using it frequently.

"If you want to go over to Riley's and thank him," Livvy added, "I can watch Ethan a little longer."

Claire didn't even consider it. She looked like hell, felt even worse. What she really needed was a bath and a nap.

After some ice cream, of course.

Claire was about to sit down and see if she could start her own journey toward type 2 diabetes when her phone rang. For one heartbeat-skipping moment she thought it might be Riley, and she had to fight back the panic of what or what not to say to him. But it was a different McCord.

Anna.

Oh, no. Had the gossip managed to reach Riley's sister even though she was miles and miles away in Florida? In case it had, Claire stepped into the living room to take the call. She didn't want to have to explain j-a-i-l in front of Ethan.

"I hate to bother you," Anna greeted, "but I wondered if you'd heard from Riley?"

That was such a loaded question that Claire went with one of her own. "What's this about?"

Anna made a sound of frustration. "I just got a call from Lucky, who said Riley had gotten news from the military base. He has to show up tomorrow morning first thing for a meeting with the brass."

"This is the first I'm hearing about it." Claire tried not to be alarmed. However, Anna clearly was. "What's the meeting about?"

"Well, Riley didn't get into a lot of details. He just said it was a meeting about his medical review. Lucky said Riley's expecting good news, that he'll soon be returning to active duty. God, Claire. Is he ready for that? I mean, has his shoulder healed? Has *Riley* healed?"

"He's *healing*," she settled for saying. But it'd been less than twenty-four hours since he'd had a flashback. How would he deal with those if he was right back in a situation that had caused those flashbacks in the first place?

"And Riley thought this meeting would actually put him back in uniform?" Claire asked.

"That's what Lucky was pretty sure he heard, and he said Riley went straight to his room and started packing. Listen, Claire, if you hear from him, let me know. I've tried calling, but it goes straight to voice mail."

Oh, God.

Claire felt stunned. Then furious. Riley could teach her son to pee on a tree, he could bring over a mountain of ice cream, but he couldn't tell her something as important as this?

Then the sickening feeling came. And the heart-crushing ache.

So, maybe the ice cream and cookies hadn't been an apology after all. Maybe that had been Riley's way of saying goodbye.

"CAPTAIN McCORD," the first lieutenant greeted him when Riley walked into the office.

According to his name tag, his last name was Silverman. Riley didn't know him, but he was probably the colonel's exec, which was the military's equivalent of an assistant. Riley hoped this would be the last time he'd ever see him.

Because Riley wanted to walk out of this building with an assurance that he'd be returning to duty, immediately, as a Combat Rescue Officer.

"Colonel Becker will call you back when he's ready." The lieutenant motioned toward some chairs. "You can sit there and wait...with your guest."

Riley certainly hadn't forgotten about his *guest*. Lucky. Apparently, the lieutenant hadn't, either, because he eyed Lucky, who'd not only already sat down but was in his usual lounging pose, slumped in the seat, arms folded over his chest, his jeans-clad legs stretched out in front of him. He was wearing a shiny silver rodeo buckle the size of a child's head. If this wait went on very long, Lucky would probably pull down the brim of his Stetson and take a nap.

Lucky wasn't the ideal person to bring along for moral support, but his shoulder was still giving him trouble when driving in the city traffic during rush hour, and the base was situated right in San Antonio. That's the reason he'd scheduled his PT and doctor's appointments at hours when the traffic wouldn't be so bad. But he hadn't had control of the timing for this meeting.

Riley hadn't wanted to risk showing up while on pain meds, especially since he was weaning himself off them.

"This reminds me of the Spring Hill jail," Lucky remarked.

It would look like that to Lucky. Anything resembling structure and rules would make him feel hemmed in. But when Riley looked at it, he saw the polished tiled floors. The tasteful, patriotic artwork on the walls. The lieutenant's neatly organized desk. Everything was in its place. All the expectations spelled out in black-and-white in the regulations.

Unlike life in Spring Hill.

He was never sure what Logan expected or wanted from him. Claire, either, for that matter. Especially her. He needed to call her soon. Maybe after this meeting was over and things were settled. He owed her a face-to-face apology.

That mentally stopped him.

Was that all he owed her?

After all, he had gotten close to her over the past

month. And he'd kissed her. Plus, she'd gotten him through the bad flashback at Calhoun's even if it had taken him a half hour of showering to get the smell of beer off him.

"You're doing some deep thinking." Lucky rubbed his jaw where Riley had punched him. "You're not thinking about hitting me again, are you?"

"No." At least not here. "And you deserved that, by the way."

Lucky didn't argue, which meant he likely knew it was true.

"Claire's not in love with me," Riley mumbled.

Lucky didn't argue with that, either, but damn it, his silence felt like an argument anyway. Or maybe he was just losing it. He needed to get his mind on something else.

"Thanks for driving me," Riley told him. "I didn't think you'd come."

Lucky shrugged. "Didn't think you'd want me to come."

"I didn't," he admitted. "But thanks anyway. I didn't want to have to ask Logan."

"Logan," Lucky repeated. "On the drive over he would have talked you into doing some work for the family business. Not that he needs you specifically to do it. Or me. He's got people who know that business better than I know my own toenails. I've got a theory, though, that Logan wants us involved because it gives him validation."

Riley wasn't following him. "Validation for what?"

"That he did the right thing by staying behind and building the company." Lucky shifted in the seat so he could face him. "You see, part of my theory is that he'd like to be off doing things we're doing."

Riley never considered Lucky the model for human

logic, but he might be on to something. Either that or Logan just wanted McCord Cattle Brokers to grow, grow and keep on growing. Sometimes, it was a uniform—or a silver rodeo buckle—that fueled people, but maybe at the root of it, all three of them were just running from being ordinary. And in their own varying ways, they had succeeded.

At least Logan and he had. Riley wasn't sure about Lucky.

"Logan will still try to suck you back in before you manage to run for the sandy places where you rescue people," Lucky continued. "My advice—don't let him bully you into doing anything you don't want to do."

Bully was sure a harsh word. Logan had more of the make-'em-feel-guilty approach. "He bullied you into coming back," Riley reminded him.

"No. I didn't come back because he asked me. I came back for *you*."

Riley turned toward him so quickly that it caused the lieutenant to look up from a file he was reading.

"For me?" Riley shook his head. "How'd you figure that?"

"I knew Logan would be coming at you with guns loaded. That's a metaphor," Lucky added, glancing at the lieutenant in case he was still listening. "I thought you could use somebody on your side to make sure you get to live the life you want to live. When it's time for you to go, just go. I'll deal with these horse trainers that Logan keeps pissing off. Will deal with the horses, too. Heck, he pisses them off, as well. I get along with horses, women and trainers just fine."

"Does that mean you're moving back home?"

"Heck, no." Lucky didn't hesitate, either. "But Logan's

not the only one with sneaky skills. I've got a rodeo up in Abilene in a week, and I'll be there."

Riley didn't doubt it, but all this talk made him realize he really didn't know much about Lucky's life. Or Logan's for that matter. Logan had a longtime girlfriend— perfect, of course. Helene.

Well, perfect for him anyway.

Beautiful, polished, business savvy. She'd look good on those magazine covers Logan was always appearing on. Riley figured one day they'd get married and be the perfect couple together, on and off the magazine covers.

But Lucky was a different story, and Riley had his own theory about Lucky's future. Definitely not picture-perfect by most people's standards.

Of the four McCord kids, Lucky had been the closest to their mom. Losing her and their dad had been hard on all of them, but that's when Lucky had started to pull away from the family. And the pulling away had only caused Logan to try to herd them all back together. Logan had stayed and been the responsible one. Lucky had joined the rodeo, which was a Texan's version of running off to join the circus.

"Are you happy?" Riley asked his brother. It wasn't something guys usually asked each other, but he figured this might be as close to a heart-to-heart as he'd ever get with Lucky.

"Sure." But it took Lucky too long to answer. "Don't know how much longer I'll be able to bull ride though. There's only so much ball-busting a man can take before the balls start to protest."

Lucky didn't change his expression, but Riley heard it in his brother's voice. The fear of losing what made him Lucky McCord. Yeah, Riley got that. His uniform was like that rodeo buckle that Lucky was always trying to win.

Before Riley could ask more about that sneaky skill set, a skill set Riley might want to learn, the colonel's door opened, and he motioned for Riley to go inside his office.

Unlike the lieutenant, this was an officer that Riley did know. Colonel Becker had visited the base during Riley's second deployment, and Riley had escorted him into a classified area for a briefing. The colonel hadn't changed much in those couple of years. A little more gray at his temples. Maybe an extra wrinkle or two, but he was someone Riley trusted to give it to him straight.

Riley only hoped that *straight* was good news.

However, judging from the colonel's expression, maybe it wasn't as good as Riley had hoped for.

Riley reported in by saluting. "Captain McCord reporting as ordered." He held the salute until the colonel saluted him back and then lowered his hand. With the formalities over, Riley took a seat when the colonel gestured for him to sit.

"You didn't pass your physical," he told Riley right off.

Riley nodded. Not exactly a news flash. "But the shoulder's improving, and I should be able to pass the next one. The physical therapist said I could up my home exercises to three hours a day."

Colonel Becker looked him straight in the eyes. "Can you pass a physical in two weeks?"

"Sure."

Riley didn't have a clue if that was true or not. But it was something that was partially in his control. He was doing all the physical therapy exercises and then some. He was up to five hours a day with what he was doing at

PT and at home. And convincing the mental health folks was doable, as well.

If he didn't mention the flashbacks, that is.

However, it was possible the exercises still wouldn't be enough to get him through the physical. His shoulder simply might not be able to take the weight that he'd be required to lift.

That didn't mean he wouldn't try. Hell, yes. He'd try. That's why he'd gone ahead and packed because when he got orders, he wanted to be ready to go.

"The flight surgeon doesn't think you can pass the physical," the colonel went on. "Not even in a month, much less in half that time. He thinks your injury will give you limitations—permanent ones. Ones that you can't have and still be a Combat Rescue Officer."

Riley sure hoped he didn't look as bad as he suddenly felt. Each word was like a punch from a fist.

"You personally talked to the flight surgeon?" Riley asked.

The colonel nodded.

Good. Riley continued, "And did he or she give you odds as to whether or not I could pass that physical in two weeks?"

Colonel Becker blew out a long breath. What he didn't do was answer.

"Was it fifty-fifty?" Riley pressed. "Because I can win if it's fifty-fifty."

"Maybe when it comes to extractions in the desert, but this isn't a fifty-fifty kind of situation."

"Then what is it?" Riley insisted.

"Twenty-eighty at best."

Oh, hell. Yeah, that was bad, but he'd won with odds that bad before, too. *Once.* But if he had been able to do it then, he could do it again.

The colonel put his elbows on his desk, leaned closer. "Look, you know how this works, Captain. A Combat Rescue Officer has to be a hundred percent. If not, you put your whole team, your extractions and the mission at risk."

"I know that." Riley hadn't intended to snap while talking to a superior officer, but he did. "But I have to be a CRO. There's no other choice."

The colonel made a sound to indicate otherwise. "If you fail the physical, you'll either have to retrain into a different career field, one less physically demanding—"

"I don't want a different career field." And yeah, he snapped again.

"Then you'd have to resign your commission."

To a civilian, those words might not mean much, but they sure as heck meant something to Riley. Resigning his commission would mean getting out of the Air Force.

He'd be ordinary again.

"I'm telling you all of this because you should prepare yourself for the worst," the colonel added. "I'll see you in two weeks."

Riley went on autopilot, standing, then saluting the colonel before he did an about-face and walked out of the room. It felt as if his entire world had come crashing down on him.

Lucky stood when he saw his face, and his brother mumbled something Riley didn't catch. Lucky went to him and gave him a pat on the back.

"Come on," Lucky said. "I think you need some therapy. Not that kind of therapy," he corrected when Riley just stared at him. "My version of therapy. In a couple of hours, I promise you that things are going to look a whole lot brighter."

CHAPTER FIFTEEN

THINGS DIDN'T LOOK brighter at all, but Riley had to admit that things weren't feeling as shitty as they had. The shots of tequila had helped with that, but underneath the tequila haze, Riley knew this was a temporary lull. Tomorrow, he'd have to face a cold, hard reality.

But that was tomorrow.

Tonight, he was back at Calhoun's Pub, drinking his troubles away.

Lucky had brought him here after they'd gotten back from the base. They'd made a quick trip to the house just so Riley could change out of his uniform. Lucky had said something about not wanting to disgrace it, and Riley had agreed.

He figured he'd get a full glass of disgracing tonight.

With several of the Nederlands cheering him on, Riley bit into the lime, took a shot of tequila and finished the ritual by licking the salt. At first all of this had felt very frat-party-ish, but after multiple bites, shots and licks, Riley wasn't sure he cared. Neither did the Nederlands, who were doing two shots for Riley's every one.

Of course, they were double his size, so it probably took that much tequila for them to get the same buzz that was going on in Riley's head.

There'd be no brawls tonight—mainly because he was now drinking with the brawlers. Plus, there really wasn't anyone to start any trouble. Other than the now-

friendly Nederlands, there was just Lucky, him, the bar-
tender and the petite blonde waitress who was flirting
with Lucky. Naturally, Lucky was flirting back. Except
it had moved past the flirting stage, Riley realized, when
Lucky kissed her.

Seeing that kiss brought it all back. Not the flashback,
thank God, but what had happened with Claire outside
this very building. *Oh, man.* He could still taste her.
Could still remember everything about those moments.

And he wanted more.

Of course, the tequila could be playing into that desire, but Riley didn't think so. He didn't need alcohol to
make him want Claire. Plus, he did owe her that apology.

"Think I'll go for a walk," Riley said to no one in
particular.

Lucky tore himself away from his flirting/kissing with
the cocktail waitress and looked at him. "You want me
to drive you?"

"No. I'll be fine."

Lucky tore himself away even more. "You're not driving, are you?"

Not a chance. He was well past his limit, and he wasn't
stupid.

"Nope. It's a nice night for a walk." Maybe it was.
Riley didn't have a clue. But he didn't want Lucky driving him to Claire's. That would feel more like junior high
than a frat party.

Besides, Claire's place wasn't far, and he could get
there, apologize. Maybe kiss her good-night. And then
head on home. If there ended up being more than one
good-night kiss, even better.

Seven would be ideal. That would equal the amount
of tequila shots he'd taken.

It turned out, though, that it really wasn't a good night

for a walk. It was still hot, and he'd drank so much that he was sweating tequila by the time he made it the handful of blocks to her place. When he saw her lights were still on, Riley took that as a good sign, especially since he'd forgotten to check the time. It could have been anywhere between eight at night and three in the morning.

He made it up the steps of her porch, knocked and did a breath test by blowing against his palm. On the first attempt, he missed his palm and had to do it again. Too bad he didn't have a mint or something, but maybe the lime would mask the tequila.

Or not.

Claire opened the door, cautiously, as if she expected Jack the Ripper to be on her porch. She took one look at him. One whiff, too. "You're drunk?"

It was possible that it wasn't even a question, but Riley chose to put a question mark at the end of what she'd just said.

"Tequila shots with Lucky," he explained.

"Of course," she said as if this were a normal occurrence. She glanced behind him. "How'd you get here?"

Now, that was a question. "Walked from Calhoun's." Was he slurring? *Hell.* Yeah, he was. "I wanted to say I was sorry."

She folded her arms over her chest and that's when Riley realized she was wearing just a T-shirt and nothing else. It was a longish T-shirt that hit her midthigh, but the arm folding hiked it up a bit.

"You packed your clothes. Are you here to tell me goodbye?" she asked. Now, that was a real question.

Because his head was suddenly whirling, it took him a moment to wrap his mind around what she was saying. "No. I'm here to apologize and to kiss you seven times."

The last part was something he shouldn't have said aloud. "Sorry. That was the tequila talking."

"Obviously." She huffed, unfolded her arms so she could put her hand on his waist and led him inside.

No kiss, though, and Riley was so dizzy, he wasn't even sure if he could locate her mouth. Any attempt at this point might result in an ear kiss.

"Is Ethan up?" he asked.

"No. It's ten thirty. He's been in bed for hours."

Ten thirty didn't sound that late to him, but he'd forgotten that Claire's schedule probably included turning in early so she could then get up early with Ethan. Did that mean he'd woken her? Maybe. But there were some boxes in the living room so maybe she'd been doing more sorting.

He wondered if she'd tossed the journal. Wondered, too, if he was sober enough to work that into the conversation.

No, Riley decided. He wasn't sober enough for that.

She led him to the sofa, had him sit. She disappeared into the kitchen and came back with a bottle of water. "What happened? Did you have another flashback?"

"No. I was at the base, got some...news."

"Bad news?"

"Twenty-eighty." Riley didn't expect her to get that, and maybe she didn't, but she made a sound that could have been one of understanding.

"You can stay in the guest room," she said, motioning for him to follow her. "And I can drive you home in the morning. Logan's at your house, and I doubt you want to run into him tonight. Not like this anyway."

Riley didn't. He didn't want to know the things he'd say to his big brother while under the influence of Jose Cuervo. "How did you know Logan was there?"

"He called earlier to find out if I knew where you and Lucky were. He mentioned he was at the house and that he'd be spending the night because another shipment of horses is scheduled to arrive in the morning." She paused. "What's he doing with all those horses anyway?"

"Making money, I'm sure. And setting a trap to snare Lucky and me into adding a cutting-horse empire to the cattle empire he already runs."

Of course there was more to it than that. Their father had always wanted to bring in cutting horses, and maybe that's what was fueling Logan. Maybe he wanted to keep being Daddy's good boy. It was hard to know since Logan wasn't the feeling-sharing type.

One thing for certain—Logan was the money-sharing type. Even though he ran the business, he split the profits four ways. Riley had never touched his portion. It was in his accounts being invested and reinvested by Logan's financial gurus. But Riley always figured if he touched it that it would obligate him to do a lot more than he wanted to do—like stay in Spring Hill.

Riley knew where the guest room was. He'd helped Claire's grandmother haul some old furniture out of there when he'd been about sixteen or so. Despite the other changes in the house—stripped wallpaper and some fresh paint—the room hadn't changed in all that time. Even with the tequila messing with his head, he thought maybe that was the same quilted bedspread. And because the tequila was messing with his head, Riley had no choice but to drop down on it.

Claire didn't drop down, though. She pulled back the covers for him on the other side of the bed and started helping with this boots. Good thing, too, because Riley wasn't sure he could see his boots, much less take them off.

He made a mental note to avoid all forms of bite, drink

and lick in the future. Tomorrow, he probably wouldn't remember that mental note, but he was certain his head would remind him.

Certain that Claire would, too.

"I don't suppose Lucky or you will fall in to this trap Logan is setting?" she asked.

"Not a chance." He chuckled but quit when he saw that it wasn't funny to her. Just the opposite.

"Anna said you packed your things when you heard about the meeting at the base," Claire tossed out there.

Hell's bells. "Anna called you, too?"

Claire nodded, pulled off the second boot. "She's worried about you. Everyone's worried about you."

"Does that include you?" he asked.

"I thought I made that pretty clear when I said *everyone*." And she didn't sound at all happy about that.

This sure wasn't going the way Riley had thought it would. A shame. Since Claire looked darn amazing in that old *NSYNC T-shirt. And that wasn't the tequila talking. She always looked amazing.

Always looked kissable, too.

"Sleep," she insisted. "We'll talk in the morning." Then she did something else amazing.

Claire kissed him.

Not on the cheek, either. It was full on the mouth.

Well, he got the good-night kiss after all, but Riley wasn't in any shape to do anything about it. Nor did Claire wait around for him to do anything about it. She pulled the covers over him, turned off the lights and walked out.

"TOOKIE?"

The word seemed to come out of nowhere, and it forced its way into Riley's dream. Not a nightmare. He was dreaming about Claire. Specifically, Claire kissing him, and he wanted to hang on to that dream as long as possible.

The jab to his cheek put an end to it, though.

Riley forced open his eyes, caught a glimpse of Ethan and was so glad he was able to bite back the profanity that was trying to leap out of his mouth. The pain shot through his head. Not the other kinds of pain he'd been feeling, either. This was fresh, new and raw. Really raw. Added to that his mouth felt as if skunks had nested in it.

In short, he had a hangover.

And Ethan was there, holding a cookie under Riley's nose.

It took Riley a couple of seconds to realize that Ethan and the cookie weren't part of the dream. They were real. And so was the bed he was sleeping in. Claire's bed. Or rather the bed in Claire's guest room. It all came rushing back to him then in perfect detail. He'd gotten drunk, shown up at her house and she'd put him to bed to sleep it off.

"Tookie?" Ethan offered him again. He had two, both half-eaten, and he was offering Riley one of the halves.

"Ethan, you'd better not be into those cookies again," Claire called out.

For a kid who didn't talk much, Ethan certainly had no trouble communicating. His eyes widened, and he knew he was in a boatload of trouble. Probably because Claire didn't want her son to eat cookies for breakfast.

Or rather lunch.

Riley checked his watch and nearly bolted from the bed. Hell, it was almost noon. He hadn't slept that late since he'd gone in the military. He was usually an up-before-the-sun kind of guy. That only reinforced his vow never to touch tequila again—and never to go drinking with Lucky.

"Ethan?" Claire said, the sound of her footsteps headed right toward the guest room. It was probably a violation of some parenting rule, but Riley took both cookie halves from Ethan and started eating the evidence.

His stomach protested right off, but he kept eating. However, he wasn't finished when Claire poked her head around the doorjamb. She didn't have to say words, either, for her expression to scold Ethan.

"He brought me some cookies for lunch," Riley volunteered.

Claire looked skeptical. Ethan looked skeptical, too, probably knowing that his mom wouldn't buy the little white lie that Riley had told. But Claire didn't address the white lying. That's because she was hopping around, trying to put on her shoes. No more *NSYNC T-shirt or mussed bedtime hair. She was wearing a slim blue skirt and top. Makeup, too.

"An engagement photo shoot had to be moved to today," she said, "and I have to head out like—" she did a watch check, as well "—now. The sitter can't be here for another half hour so I was wondering if you could watch Ethan until she arrives?"

Ethan looked as skeptical as Riley felt. Instead of expressing that, he said to Claire, "Of course. No problem."

"You're sure? I wouldn't want to interfere with the PT exercises you've been doing."

Even with the fuzzy head, Riley knew what that meant. One of his siblings had no doubt told her about the hours of exercises he'd been doing each day. If it had been Anna doing the telling, she would have gotten her info from Della or Stella, and the sisters would have told his own sister that he was overdoing it.

"I'll have time," he assured her. Later, he'd call each of his siblings and tell them to quit blabbing to Claire.

"Good. Thanks so much for this. If you need to go to the bathroom, you should do that now while I'm still here."

She was talking to him, Riley realized. And he hobbled off to do as she suggested. When he got back, Claire scooped up Ethan, kissed him. "Be a good boy for Riley."

Ethan rattled off something that Riley didn't catch, and ran out of the room. That was Riley's cue to get moving, too. But he didn't exactly move with the same speed and enthusiasm as Ethan. Riley finally caught up with them in the living room.

"Ethan's had his lunch," Claire said, hurrying to the front door. "No more treats, though. I think those cookies you two shared are more than enough dessert."

So, Riley had been right about the cookie eating not fooling anyone. He'd upset his stomach for nothing.

"Plus, if Ethan has too much sugar," Claire went on, snatching up her purse, camera bag and keys, "you'll have to peel him off the ceiling. Oh, you already have my cell number, but I left the number of where I'll be. The sitter's and Livvy's, too, along with the contact info for Ethan's pediatrician on the table by the door. There's a cup of coffee for you, too."

With that, Claire blew a kiss—Riley decided to claim that one for himself—and hurried out. Riley went straight for the coffee. It wouldn't cure his hangover, but it might stop the woodpecker that had set up shop in his head. It also might wash out that family of skunks in his mouth.

Ethan looked at him as if sizing up not only him but this situation. "Tookie?" Ethan asked.

"Sorry, buddy. That ceiling's too high for me to reach

to peel you off it." But then, what did you do with a two-year-old other than dose him up on sugar?

Ethan solved that problem for him. He dumped out a huge basket of cars in the middle of the living room floor. Riley had seen Ethan play with cars before, and as expected, the crashes started almost immediately. Normally, a few toy crashes wouldn't have caused him to lift an eyebrow, but with the other things going on in his head, Riley's brain must have thought it was an okay time for a flashback.

No.

Not this, not now.

But it didn't come in that dark, sandy wave like it usually did. This was just a flash of the kid.

The *other* kid.

The extraction. Riley got just a glimmer of him, and his trick-playing mind decided to impose that glimmer right over Ethan's face.

Ethan laughed, snapping Riley back, and Riley realized he was humming "Jingle Bells." However, he didn't think it was the song that'd worked for him that time but rather Ethan's laughter. Maybe he could record that laughter to take with him when he went back on duty. He refused to put an *if* anywhere in that. He would get back in uniform as a CRO.

Some movement on the coffee table caught Riley's eye. It was the slideshow screen saver on the laptop that Claire had left there. Pictures of Ethan scrolled by, and when it got to the beginning, he saw Ethan as a newborn. Claire was in a hospital bed, Ethan bundled in her arms, and she was smiling. The kind of smile that made him smile, too. Riley went closer for a better look, and he sank down on the floor next to the coffee table.

"Me," Ethan announced pointing to the picture.

The next photo popped on the screen. Ethan, still a newborn, this time asleep in a bassinet. "Me," Ethan said, and the *me* continued with each photo.

Riley remembered Claire saying she took at least a photo a week of her son, and it was all here, scrolling for him to see. Ethan crawling. Ethan walking. Even Ethan playing with Crazy Dog at the ranch. Claire was in a few of the shots, Livvy, as well. There was even one of Riley in the background of the Crazy Dog picture. But there was definitely someone missing.

Ethan's father.

Other than Riley, there wasn't a man in any of the shots. Not even Daniel. Of course, Daniel had already said he wasn't Ethan's father, and Riley's mind latched onto that now. Where was the man responsible for Ethan?

And then Riley got a thought that turned his stomach far more than wolfing down the cookies had.

Had the jerk abandoned Claire the way her own father had? That had to be it. No way would Claire want everyone to know she had a broken heart, but if Riley ever got his hands on the turd, he was going to have a word or two with him. Seriously, how could a man abandon a kid like Ethan and a woman like Claire?

Except that was sort of what he was doing.

But Riley's situation was different. Ethan wasn't his son. Claire wasn't his lover. And he'd made a commitment to himself and the uniform.

With those thoughts still stewing in his mind, Riley's phone beeped, indicating he had a call, and he fished it from his pocket.

Logan's name popped up on the screen.

Riley hadn't had nearly enough coffee yet to deal with his big brother so he let it go to voice mail. That's when he saw the other voice mails. Some from Anna and more from Logan. He'd missed those while in his tequila-induced stupor, but when Logan immediately called him back, Riley had a bad feeling. Had there been some kind of family emergency?

"Are you okay?" Logan asked when he answered. "Della said you didn't come home last night. She was worried about you."

All right, so no family emergency after all. Riley didn't want to tell Logan that he was at Claire's, though the news would probably reach the gossips before too long, depending on who the sitter was. The sitter would see Riley there and perhaps start blabbing. But Riley wasn't interested in explaining to his big brother what had gone on the night before.

"I was worried, too," Logan added a moment later.

There was something in Logan's voice, something he wasn't saying, but something that Riley heard loud and clear. "Lucky told you about what happened at the meeting at the base?"

"No. I guessed something didn't go your way. If it had, you would have cleared out by now."

True. Riley had left his packed duffel bag on the bed. "It'll all work out," Riley assured him. "I'll make it work out."

Twenty-eighty was still a shot.

Ethan must have gotten bored with the pictures of himself and saying "Me," and went back to playing with his cars. Since Riley's leg was now in the traffic pattern, Ethan used it as a hill.

"By any chance have you heard from Lucky?" Logan asked.

"No, not since last night. But he did mention something about registering for a rodeo in Lubbock that's tomorrow and then he'd be going straight from there to the one in Abilene."

"Of course, he did."

There it was again, something in Logan's voice, but Riley didn't think this had to do with him. "Anything wrong?" Riley asked.

"Yes. It's the negotiation for some cutting horses I want to add to the program. Things aren't going well. The owner is a retired military guy. Army, I think. And I thought maybe you could talk to him."

Sneaky for Logan to mention the Army part. He probably thought it would hook Riley's attention. "I've got a lot of physical therapy—"

"This wouldn't take long. Maybe just a single phone conversation."

Yeah, or maybe sixteen conversations, some visits and formal mediation with lawyers. Riley huffed. Still, he needed to do something in between the physical therapy and this weight pressing down on his mind, and it was probably a safer alternative than lusting after Claire.

Of course, he'd probably still lust after her, but this would give him something to distract him from the lust.

"When do you want me to call him?" Riley asked.

"Tomorrow if possible. I'll email you the file with all the info. Thanks." And Logan hung up.

Riley didn't have time to decide if he'd just made a mistake because there was a knock on the door, and a second later it opened. The sitter. One of the big-busted Starkley girls.

"Riley," she said, letting herself in. "Claire mentioned you'd be here. Sorry I missed you the night of your home-coming."

Well, Riley wasn't sorry about that at all. He hadn't been in much of a visiting mood that night. Still wasn't.

And he didn't like that his time with Ethan was about to end.

"Mind if I hang around a while longer and spend some time with Ethan?" Riley asked her.

"Of course not." She held up a thick book that prompted Ethan to say his version of "book" and then go running out of the living room. "I've got a chem test tomorrow and an art project due, and I need to study."

"Then, study away."

Riley got up, not easily, and with his coffee cup in his hand, he went in search of Ethan. He didn't want the kid getting into those cookies, but Ethan wasn't in the kitchen. He was in the room that Claire was using as a nursery, and the kid was pulling out a blue book from one of the boxes.

"Book," Ethan announced handing it to him. Maybe it was a homemade storybook that Claire had read to him.

Except it wasn't.

According to the name inside, it was her mother's journal. Riley didn't mean to read the first page, but his attention went there anyway. Then to the next page.

Ethan lost interest in the book, thank God. Even though he wasn't anywhere close to being able to read, Riley didn't want him near this piece of toxic shit. Too bad Livvy hadn't been able to talk Claire into burning it or putting it in the trash.

Riley sat back down on the floor, unable to stop himself from turning the page.

Tomorrow, I'm getting rid of this kid.

Mercy, it hurt to read that, and if Claire had read it, too, it must have crushed her. He went to the next page, then the next. When he was about ten pages in, something slipped out.

Some kind of dried flower.

And he could tell from the way the image was pressed into the page that it hadn't been opened in a long time. That probably meant Claire hadn't made it this far. *Good.* Livvy had said Claire was shaken up about it, so maybe she'd just quit reading.

Riley, however, didn't.

Yeah, it was a violation of privacy, but Claire's mother was long dead, and her privacy didn't matter to Riley anyway. The only thing that mattered now was how this would affect Claire.

He found a comment about the flower. It was just something she'd picked that reminded her of the prom corsage she'd always wanted. A prom she hadn't been able to attend because she'd been pregnant with Claire.

Her mom definitely wasn't happy about that.

Riley kept reading, wanting enough fodder to convince her to destroy this particular family heirloom.

And he soon found it.

Shit.

Riley had to slam the journal shut. There was no way he was going to let Claire read *that*.

CHAPTER SIXTEEN

CLAIRE HATED THAT she was going to miss seeing Ethan before bedtime, but she was so late that there was no way he'd still be up. Or if he was, he'd be so grumpy that Claire would wish that he was asleep. Still, she'd be able to sneak in a kiss or two before collapsing into her own bed.

Most engagement shoots were fun, being with the happy couple and trying to capture that love and happiness in the photos. Not this one, though. Both sets of parents had been there. It had involved four different locations, including an abandoned drive-in movie theater where one set of the parents had met. Claire was sunburned and had a few fire-ant bites, and she knew without a doubt that she hadn't captured much happiness in those shots.

She definitely hadn't made any fantasies come true today.

Claire unlocked the front door and froze. No sitter. But Riley was still there. He was asleep on the floor, Ethan asleep next to him. There was a junkyard of cars and toys scattered all around them.

What the heck had happened here?

And where was Summer?

There was a car parked in the back part of the driveway, and Claire had assumed it was Summer's vehicle. Claire soon figured out what was going on when she saw the note on the table next to all the phone numbers she'd left.

Riley said he'd stay with Ethan, so I cut out early to study. Riley paid me. Summer

Claire didn't groan, but that's what she wanted to do. She wasn't sure she had the energy to deal with Riley. But then his eyes opened, he lifted his head and he gave her a lazy, half-asleep smile that made her nether regions go warm.

So maybe she did have the energy to deal with him after all. But that didn't mean she should.

She repeated that to herself.

Riley stood, scooping up Ethan in his arms and tiptoeing—yes, tiptoeing because he was barefoot—to the nursery. He eased Ethan into his crib as if he'd done it a thousand times. After Claire kissed her son, whispered a good-night, Riley motioned for her to go back into the living room with him.

"Why did you stay?" she asked, also in a whisper.

He shrugged. "After I did my workout at home and showered, I decided to come back. Summer has a chemistry test and an art project due tomorrow."

All right, that was a good reason, she supposed, but then he dodged her gaze, and Claire knew something other than her nether regions were up to something funny.

"Ethan brought me your mother's journal." Riley pointed to the blue book he'd put on the mantel.

That was all he needed to say before it felt as if the world had dropped out beneath her feet. Riley was right there to take hold of her, and as gently as he'd handled Ethan, he had her sit on the sofa.

"You read it?" she asked.

"Some. How much did you read?"

"Some," Claire settled for saying. "But I want to read more. I want to know if it got any better for her."

"You don't need to read more. There's stuff in there that you don't want to know, trust me."

"Stuff? What do you mean?" There were plenty of bad things on those pages, but Riley seemed to be referring to something specific.

But he didn't go the specific route. "Just crap stuff. You need to burn the damn thing and put this behind you."

She knew that. Knew now, too, that there was something worse than what she'd already read. God, something worse.

The tears came. She cursed them, blinked them back, but they came anyway. "I can't put it behind me. Maybe if I read it all, I'll either be at peace or else be so fed up with all this old baggage that I'll toss it once and for all."

Because the tears were already there, the razor-sharp emotions, too, Claire got up, snatched the journal from the mantel, and before he could stop her, she opened it to the page that she'd already read.

Tomorrow, i'm getting rid of this kid.

"Obviously, she changed her mind," Claire said.

"Yeah." Riley didn't look anywhere near tears, but the anger was there. He pulled her beside him, still treating her with kid gloves, and he turned the page. "If you're going to do this, read with me here. Then I can hold you, kiss you, sleep with you or whatever hell else it takes to help you get through it."

Whatever was in there must be pretty bad for him to offer to sleep with her. Did that stop her? No. Neither did her tear-filled eyes. Claire read the page he'd opened.

Didn't go to the clinic after all. Call me chicken-shit, but I guess I'll carry this kid after all. Mom says she'll help, of course, but she's bat-shit on a good day. Besides, I know she doesn't want to get stuck with another kid either.

Riley stabbed the last sentence with his index finger. "That's not true. Your grandmother loved you."

"I know." Still, it made her breath so thin for her mother to say something so horrible. Her grandmother had indeed loved her, and she'd loved Claire's mother, too.

Riley cursed. "I didn't want you to see that. I didn't want it in your head."

She looked at him, met his gaze. "Everything on these pages is already in my head, Riley. I don't have to read it to imagine it or even something much worse. After all, I know how this ends. My mother left me."

Claire doubted she'd convinced him, but she went to the next entry. It was dated a week after the last one.

The kids at school know I'm knocked up. It's all over town. Bitches spread gossip. Mom says I should go back, that I can graduate in just three months, but in three months I'll be as big as a whale. Once this kid is out of me, I'm out of this shit town for good.

"Sometimes I forget just how young she was," Claire said.

Too young. Claire had been twenty-nine when she was pregnant with Ethan, and she couldn't have imagined doing that at eighteen. No wonder her mother had been so angry, and the anger was there all over the other pages.

Especially the next one.

A shit-hole of a day. I wish Mom and this kid was
dead. I made a mistake keeping this brat.

Dead. There it was. More of the little knives slicing
away at her. Her mother was obviously on an emotional
roller coaster, and now Claire was, too, because she was
reliving this.

"I didn't want you to see that," Riley said, his voice
strained.

She hadn't wanted to see it, either, but she couldn't
stop herself from continuing, either. With Riley right
next to her, Claire kept reading, and she prayed that it
would get better.

Rocky isn't coming back. I know that now, and
even if he did, I would kick his sorry excuse for
an ass. What kind of man just knocks up a girl and
then runs out on her?

Yes, what kind of man did that?

"Do you feel that way about Ethan's father?" Riley
asked, but he waved it off just as quickly as it left his
mouth.

"No," she answered. It wasn't a lie, but judging from
his expression, Riley didn't believe her.

"I'm sorry," he said.

She wasn't sure exactly what the apology was for.
Claire wasn't sure of much at the moment except that
she was going to have to take him up on that kissing and
holding he'd offered.

But he beat her to it.

Riley hauled her to him, pulling her onto his lap, and
he kissed her first.

RILEY WAS CERTAIN he'd lost his mind. With all the energy zinging between them, the last thing he should be doing was kissing Claire. But it was the only thing that made sense to him right now.

Not much sense, though.

But enough that it didn't stop him.

He'd already known how she tasted, but this was even better than the kisses outside Calhoun's Pub. Maybe because there wasn't sweat and beer running down his face, and they weren't plastered against a splintery wall. They were on a soft couch, behind closed doors.

And Ethan was asleep.

This was as dangerous of a situation as going into enemy territory, but knowing that still didn't stop him. He deepened the kiss, dragging Claire closer and closer.

"Your shoulder," she mumbled.

At least that's what he thought she said, but his shoulder wasn't the problem here. The problem was that in just a matter of seconds, the kiss had already gotten hotter than wildfire and was spreading just as fast. This certainly wasn't the holding/kissing comfort session she'd likely been expecting. Nor was it what she needed.

That stopped him.

Riley pulled back. "We might need to rethink this."

"I'm tired of thinking." And she went right back into the kiss.

Obviously, that meant she was no longer considering Daniel's proposal. This was the part where a smart man might have made sure she was telling the truth, or that it wasn't just the lust or hurt talking, but apparently he was no longer a smart man.

Riley kept kissing her, and he added some more trouble to this brew by slipping his hand beneath her top. His fingers brushed across bare skin, and that was all it took for his body to go into serious overdrive.

Man, he wanted her.

And since wanting her would almost certainly involve getting naked, he scooped her up and headed to her bedroom. There was a baby monitor in there. He'd already spotted it earlier, and this way if Ethan woke up, they'd hear him. Yes, it was a miracle that he could consider such a thing at a time like this, but Riley was used to considering many factors when it came to a mission.

And what a mission it was.

He closed the bedroom door behind them and placed Claire on her bed; the feather mattress swelled around her, giving way to her weight when her body landed against it. Her top slid up a little, exposing the part of her he'd just touched.

So, Riley touched some more.

With his mouth this time.

It was a much better experience, not just for him but apparently for Claire, too, because she lifted her hips and made that hot little sound of pleasure.

Riley figured the grunt he made wasn't nearly as sweet sounding, but he didn't make it for long. He kept kissing her, sliding up the top to reveal more and more that he kissed, too. Soon though, that wasn't enough, and he pulled the top off her and went after her bra.

How many times he'd dreamed of doing this. Too many. Claire had been a steady source of dream fantasies for years, and now here she was in front of him.

He unclipped her bra, taking her breasts into his hands so he could kiss them. The only thing that would have made it more pleasurable was for him to have two mouths, but Claire seemed to be happy with his one-mouthed attempt.

She fisted her hand in his hair, dragging him closer. Not that he could get much closer, mind you, and they grappled, kissed and generally drove each other crazy until something had to be done.

Riley went after her skirt next.

He skimmed it off her, not intending to remove the panties just yet, but he did. And with a toss of her clothes, he had a naked Claire on the bed in front of him.

Oh, mercy.

He'd been working up an erection since the first touch of her mouth to his, but now he went rock hard. He was ready to take her and fulfill all those fantasies that'd been in his dreams, both the sleeping and the waking ones. But first he wanted more kissing. On her belly.

Her thighs.

The inside of her thighs.

Then the center.

That got a really good reaction from her. She bucked beneath him and fought to drag him back to her so she could start a war with his shirt. She wasn't winning, mainly because she was trying to kiss him while she undid the buttons. Riley stopped his kisses to help her.

There was no longer a bandage on his shoulder, and for a moment he considered that Claire would freak when she saw the scar. She didn't. She kissed it, too, a lot more gently than he'd kissed her thigh region.

That got him much hotter than he thought it would, but it was lukewarm compared with her going after his zipper. He had to help her again so she could remove his jeans, making sure he didn't bang his shoulder in the process. No sense working themselves up to this point if he couldn't finish it.

It was the thought of finishing this that had everything inside him freezing.

And Claire noticed. She levered herself up on her elbows, her attention on his shoulder. "What's wrong?"

Riley really hated to have to tell her this. "I don't have a condom. Do you?"

No freezing for her. Claire groaned and dropped back down onto the mattress. "No. And I'm not on the pill, either."

Riley wasn't ready to give up just yet, and it was desperation that made him ask the next question. "You don't think your grandmother left any condoms?"

All right, it was a horrible question and a way to kill the mood. Almost. The mood was definitely still there with him, pressing against the fabric of his boxers.

Riley decided to look at this as a different kind of mission. Things went wrong all the time, and he often had to improvise. He could go to the pharmacy and get some condoms. Except it was closed by now.

That left the gas station/convenience store on the edge of town. It'd be open, might even have condoms, but if he hurried in there, it would be all over town that Claire and he had done the dirty—especially when coupled with any gossip Summer would spill about Riley spending most of the day with Ethan. After the pub brawl/jail incident, Claire didn't need that kind of talk going around.

Claire shook her head and moved as if to get off the bed. "Maybe this is fate—"

Riley didn't let her finish that. He stopped her with a kiss. Stopped her from moving off the bed, too. No way was this fate. It was just bad preparations on his part. He should have stuck a condom in his wallet. Of course, when he'd decided to spend the day with Ethan, he hadn't exactly had Claire and condoms on his mind.

And now he needed to improvise.

"We're finishing this," he insisted. Which was more or less the truth. He would finish Claire anyway.

Riley started a trail of kisses that went from her mouth to the exact spot where he could finish her. Not with his hard-on, which was begging to get in on this. Nope. He used his mouth, and he kissed her, kissed her and kissed her until Claire *finished*.

She wasn't a screamer but rather a moaner. Good thing because the sound wouldn't wake up Ethan, and her soft moans went with the ones Riley was making. Both pleasure and pain, as life so often was. His erection was throbbing, but the throbbing that Claire was doing was certainly pleasurable to watch.

As backup plans went, it wasn't ideal, but at least one of them would sleep better tonight. And it wouldn't be him. Claire pulled him down to her, the glow of the orgasm all over her face. She was happy, smiling, and he'd already noticed the glowing part.

All in all, it was amazing to see. Just as he'd thought it would be if he ever got to do anything remotely sexual with her.

But when the glow had run its course and the morning came, Riley didn't have to guess what the percentage was for this complicating the hell out of both his and Claire's lives.

This would fuck things up between them 100 percent.

CHAPTER SEVENTEEN

RILEY'S ALARM CLOCK—the one in his head—went off at 6:00 a.m. Not that he'd actually needed it to wake him. He hadn't done much sleeping with a naked Claire beside him in bed. He was probably in pain, too, but it was hard to tell because his body was giving him some mixed signals.

On the one hand, he was feeling slack and sated after a couple of rounds of oral sex with Claire. Riley had been on both the receiving and giving ends, and he wasn't sure which one he liked better. All right, he was sure, but both had been mind-blowing.

And terrifying.

Because with her in his arms like this, it only reminded him that he had crossed a bridge that he would soon have to leave behind. Yeah, it was a bad metaphor, but when the lust had been clouding his head and judgment, he hadn't thought to see this to its possible conclusion.

Claire could get hurt.

That was the very thing Lucky had warned him about, and even though Riley never thought he would hear himself say this, for once Lucky had given him good relationship advice. Ironic since the advice had come from a man who'd never had a relationship last more than a week.

Riley eased out of the bed, trying not to wake Claire, but just the slight shift of the mattress caused her to open her eyes. She smiled at him, kissed him and then went back to sleep. *Good.* Conversation was best left for when they both had clearer heads. Of course, after her head cleared, she might be ready to throttle him.

Claire had been at a seriously low point after reading that asinine journal. Riley had known that. He'd seen the tears in her eyes, and he figured those tears had played into her decision to kiss him.

All over his body.

In a way, it was as if he'd taken advantage of a drunk woman. Something he never did. Well, not before last night anyway.

He made another attempt to get out of bed, and this time she didn't wake up. Riley dressed. Not easily. There was pain now, and while he wouldn't medicate it, he would need to start his exercises to get rid of some of the stiffness. Too bad the exercises wouldn't take care of the stiffness of the brainless part of him in his boxers. No, the best cure for that was to quit looking at a naked Claire and get the heck out of her bedroom before Ethan woke up.

Riley tiptoed out of the room, checked on Ethan. The kid was still sacked out. He went to the living room to put on his boots. Claire's note was still there, the one with the phone numbers, so Riley added his own note to it.

"I'll call you later," he wrote.

He considered adding something else, but anything he could come up with would only complicate things. Definitely no "love, Riley" at the end of it. And no hearts or some other doodling to trivialize what'd happened.

Besides, he wasn't even sure what had happened.

Was this an oral fling? Or was Claire expecting a whole lot more?

With those questions on his mind, Riley put on his

boots and slipped out the front door. He locked it behind him and made his way to the car he'd parked on the side of her house. He rounded the corner and immediately had an ah-shit moment.

Because Daniel was there.

Leaning against Riley's car.

Riley so didn't want to deal with Daniel this morning, but since Daniel was right against the driver's-side door, he was going to have to speak at least one word to him.

Move was the first word that came to mind.

"We have to talk," Daniel insisted.

Daniel took a drag off a cigarette—Riley didn't even know the man smoked—and he flicked the cigarette butt on the ground, crushing it with his shoe. That's when Riley noticed there were multiple butts there. At least a dozen. Which meant Daniel had been out there most of the night.

Riley didn't think Daniel was perverse enough to peek through Claire's bedroom window, but he wouldn't have actually needed to peek. Given the hour and after one look at Riley's walk-of-shame wrinkled clothes, Daniel had likely guessed what had gone on.

Or rather what he thought had gone on.

"You broke your own man-rule," Daniel tossed right out there.

Yeah, and it didn't matter that it hadn't been fully broken. Riley wasn't going to mention anything about a condom holding him back because the intent of man-rule number three had indeed been violated.

Don't take anything that wasn't his.

While he didn't believe that Claire was Daniel's girl, not anymore, Riley also knew she wasn't his for the taking.

"Are you happy with yourself now?" Daniel snarled, and there was no doubt about it—it was indeed a snarl.

Riley huffed. Certain parts of him were happy, but he wasn't giving those parts a vote in this. "None of this was planned."

Which, of course, was the worst excuse of all worst excuses.

"So, what happens now?" Daniel lit up another cigarette, his right eye squinting from the coil of smoke. "You leave town to go do your military thing, and Claire is stuck here to pick up the pieces."

As much as he hated the way Daniel had put it, that pretty much summed it up. It wouldn't do any good to repeat to him, or Claire, that this hadn't been planned. Though it hadn't been. Still, there were consequences, and Riley had to accept that things would never be the same.

He might even lose Claire's friendship.

"I don't want her hurt," Riley said. Yet another stupid comment, but he meant it. It wasn't nearly enough, though.

Daniel cursed. "You should have thought about that before you slept with her." He cursed some more and used the cigarette to point at Riley. "I'm going to try to fix this. I'll help her put the pieces back together. You do know that she still has my engagement ring, right?"

Riley did know that, and he hadn't been worried about it until now. "She told you no, that she wouldn't marry you."

"She's still thinking it over. Why else would she have kept the ring?"

Riley certainly couldn't think of a reason. Not a good one anyway.

Well, hell. For Claire to have been with him like that while still mulling over Daniel's proposal meant she hadn't been thinking straight. As in not one tiny bit of thinking straight. That journal must have shaken Claire even more than Riley had realized—and it had shaken her a lot.

Of course, he was hearing this from Daniel, and it was possible, likely even, that Claire's answer to the proposal was still going to be no.

But it should have been no before she ever got into bed with Riley.

"I love her," Daniel went on. "I want to stay in Texas and marry her. That's all Claire's ever wanted—a man who would be here for her and not run off like her father did."

It was indeed what she wanted. And it was something Riley had always known he couldn't give her, not with those Texas-deep roots of hers. Heck, Riley didn't even doubt that Daniel loved her.

"I don't want you taking any of this out on her," Riley insisted. "Everything that happened was my fault."

Daniel made a face as if thoroughly insulted by that. "I wouldn't take anything out on her, and I'll forgive her. That's what I'll tell her, that I love and forgive her, and that I'll be here as long as she needs me."

As mission statements went, it was a powerful one. Daniel was like the Texas heat. He would always be around. And that's exactly what Claire and Ethan needed. Even if it made Riley feel like shit.

"I'm sorry," Riley said, and that encompassed a lot of things.

"I sure hope so." Daniel ground out the cigarette he tossed. "Because now I've got to go in there and clean up this mess."

Daniel didn't exactly ask permission, and Riley wasn't in a position to stop him. Heck, he didn't know what his position was, but Claire certainly didn't have an engagement ring from Riley in her house.

Riley got in his car and drove off. As he did, he made the mistake of checking the rearview mirror, and saw something that he was sorry he'd seen. Claire had opened the door to Daniel and was letting him inside her house.

CLAIRE KNEW THERE would be a price to pay for what she'd done with Riley, but she just hadn't expected to start paying so soon. The only reason she'd opened her door when she heard the knock was because she thought it was Riley, that maybe he'd forgotten something.

Like a kiss goodbye.

But no Riley. It was Daniel. He was sporting a scowl, a scowl that deepened when he looked over his shoulder at Riley driving away.

Oh, no.

She was betting that hadn't been a friendly conversation. Nor was the one she was about to have with Daniel. That's why Claire had him come inside. Best to air her dirty laundry behind closed doors.

"What did you say to Riley?" she demanded.

Better yet, what had Riley said to him? Because Riley certainly hadn't said much in the note he'd left her.

Since Daniel wasn't battered and bruised, there probably hadn't been any punches thrown. Daniel wasn't the punch-throwing type anyway. But she was betting there had been a man-pissing contest with their war of words.

"Where's Ethan?" Daniel asked, looking at the car and toy mess on the floor.

"Still asleep, but since he'll be waking up any minute, let's finish this conversation before he does. What did you say to Riley?" she repeated, expecting an answer this time.

Daniel eyed her the same way he'd eyed the toy clutter. She'd put on some clothes, but she probably still looked as if she'd just climbed out of bed with a man. Plus, she hadn't showered yet and had Riley's scent all over her.

"Riley and I talked," Daniel finally said. "I made him understand that what he did with you was wrong."

"What?" she practically shouted, probably waking Ethan. "You had no right to do that. None." And Riley didn't have to listen to any of it.

When Ethan called out for her, Claire went to him before he tried to climb out of his crib.

Daniel followed right behind her.

"Of course I had a right," Daniel argued. "I love you. I want to marry you."

Despite her suddenly surly mood, Claire managed to scrounge up a smile and a kiss for Ethan, but he was the grumpy boy this morning, and he gave her a scowl that matched Daniel's. Or maybe Ethan was actually scowling at Daniel. It was hard to tell anything other than obviously her son didn't want to be awake yet.

"For what it's worth," Daniel went on while she changed Ethan's diaper, "Riley agreed with me. He's not going to be in town much longer. We all know that. And you don't need him playing with your heartstrings."

Well, it hadn't been her heartstrings that Riley had played with, but she wasn't getting into that with Daniel. She finished the diapering, and while still smiling at Ethan and pretending nothing was wrong, she carried him into the kitchen.

Daniel followed her there, too.

"Also for what it's worth," he repeated, "it didn't take much to convince Riley to leave this morning."

She tried not to let that sting. But it did. Because it was likely the cold, hard truth. The night before she and Riley had been caught up in the heat of the moment, but now that the heat had been satiated, he might be seeing a lot clearer than she was.

Yes, Riley was leaving.

But Claire still wanted him.

That heat had satiated much for her, but it might be the only taste she ever got of Riley McCord. After all, they'd never gotten around to discussing how his meeting at the military base had gone. It was possible he'd spent that day with Ethan, and that night with her, as a way of saying goodbye.

She put Ethan in his high chair, poured some Cheerios right on the tray and fixed him a sippy cup of milk. All of that while her heart felt as if someone were stomping on it. If Ethan noticed the tension in the room, he didn't react. He dove right into the cereal.

"I reminded Riley you still have my engagement ring," Daniel added.

Claire had been about to put some fresh blueberries on Ethan's tray, but Daniel's words stopped her. "You told him that?"

"Of course. Because it's true."

"It's only true because you wouldn't take it back." Claire certainly hadn't meant to yell, but even a hard-of-hearing person would have labeled it as a shout.

Ethan stopped munching and started watching them. It was for her son and her son alone that she forced herself to calm down. If Ethan hadn't been there, she would have let Daniel see, and hear, just how upset she really was.

Damn.

Now Riley probably thought she'd done all those things with him in the bedroom while she was still keeping Daniel on the hook. Well, Daniel was about to get dropped from that hook right now.

She hurried into the living room, took out the ring

that she'd shoved into the foyer table drawer. Thankfully, this time Daniel didn't follow her, and when Claire returned to the kitchen, he was standing there, the look on his face indicating he'd just stepped in something he was going to regret.

Claire took his hand, slapped the box in his palm. "If you try to leave it again, I'll flush it down the toilet. Understand?" She didn't give him a chance to answer. "And there won't be any more proposals or any more conversations with Riley about me. Got that?"

Daniel looked at the ring. Then at her. "You'll never find another man who loves you as much as I do."

"I know." And that broke her heart.

The first tear made it down Claire's cheek before he even walked out the door.

RILEY HAD DONE something to get his mind off Claire. And it had actually worked better than he'd thought it would.

Of course, nothing was going to erase Claire from his mind. She was in every corner of it. However, for a couple of hours he'd felt as if he had done something that he hadn't screwed up.

"Well done," the text from Logan had said.

High praise coming from Logan, and Riley knew it hadn't been just lip service. Riley had negotiated a much better deal for the new cutting horses—championship lines, at that—than even Logan had anticipated. And Riley had played the military card to help him do it.

The owner of the horses, Frank Doolittle, had been Army all right. A Ranger, which made him special ops just like Riley. The first hour of their conversation had been about missions, and they'd discovered that Riley's first mission and Frank's last one had overlapped. They'd been in the same area, assisting with the same situation.

Small world.

That small world had bulldozed through some barriers that Logan had put up with his less than warm-and-fuzzy demeanor. Riley hadn't been exactly warm and fuzzy, but the shared camaraderie of being with a fellow serviceman had no doubt played into Frank giving a sweet deal to McCord Cattle Brokers. With this deal, Logan just might have to change the name to Cattle and Horse Brokers.

The next step would be for Riley to interview some new cutters, the slang term for the cutting horse trainers. Frank had given him a few leads on that. Good thing, too, because the last couple that Logan had hired had already quit. Lucky had managed to talk one into staying before his brother took off, but with this new group of horses Riley had just bought, they'd need at least three more cutters.

Riley would work on hiring those cutters after his usual hours of PT. Between the work and the PT, he might actually be able to deal with the hurricane of thoughts and worries over Claire and his upcoming physical. He had to reduce those twenty-eighty odds.

For the physical anyway.

He wasn't sure there were any odds when it came to Claire.

Riley would give her a few more hours and then call and… Well, he wasn't sure what he would say to her yet. But maybe the right words would come to him during a long, sweaty workout.

Riley turned into the driveway that fronted his house, and he cursed when he saw a familiar car—Trisha's. *Oh, man.* He hoped she hadn't shown up half-naked again. But if she had, then she'd probably given Della and Stella an eyeful since they were home, too.

Steeling himself, Riley parked, went inside, but he was

the one who got a shock. It was Trisha all right. Fully clothed, thank goodness. But she wasn't alone. She was in the living room, sitting on the sofa and chatting with Jodi.

Both women stood and looked about as uneasy as Riley felt.

"Walter Meekins is still out with a gout flare-up," Trisha said. "So I gave Jodi a ride."

Yes, Riley knew all about Walter and his medical problems, but that didn't explain why the women were here.

"Trisha was kind enough to drive me," Jodi continued. "Daniel introduced us."

That still didn't explain much. Of course, Daniel had driven Jodi to the inn. Maybe to Calhoun's, too, and since Trisha was clearly still in town, maybe they'd run into each other. And then proceeded to come to his living room together.

"I'll wait outside," Trisha added.

Uh-oh. There was only one reason for her to do that. Because she knew Jodi wanted to talk about things that Riley wasn't sure he wanted to hear. Still, after all the time he and Jodi had spent together, he owed her a least a listening session.

Jodi didn't say a word until Trisha was out the door. "Trisha said you've been spending time with Claire."

Well, that put a quick end to the listening session. Riley groaned. "Is that really why you're here—to ask me if I'm seeing Claire?" He hoped not because he didn't know the answer to that himself.

But thankfully Jodi shook her head. "No, that was my attempt at small talk. I'm here to apologize for the bar brawl. For getting Claire and Daniel arrested, too." She drew in a long breath. "I was just blowing off steam and some frustration over not getting to spend time with you."

He groaned again but didn't get to elaborate on that

groan because Jodi continued. "No, it's not like that. I'm not hung up on you or anything. Not my style. But I'm going to be around town a couple more days. I sublet my condo in DC, don't have any other travel plans and I need to get some work done. I decided Spring Hill was just as good of a place to do that as anywhere else."

No, it wasn't, and his expression must have conveyed that because Jodi chuckled, patted his cheek. "This isn't about you, Riley. I just wanted you to know that I'd be around in case we ran into each other. But only for a couple of days. Then I'll be out of your hair for good."

Riley figured after all this time, he should feel something. This was confirmation of their breakup. All he felt was regret that it hadn't ended better between them, but what he couldn't do was be sad that it was over.

"Be safe," Jodi whispered to him, kissing him on the cheek. "And if you can't be safe, then it means you're probably having fun."

Always the party girl. She dropped another kiss on his cheek, her mouth lingering there a moment as if to see if he was going to do something about her mouth being so close to his.

Riley didn't.

"Goodbye, Jodi," he said.

She flexed her eyebrows, looked disappointed for a couple of seconds and left. "Ready to hit Calhoun's now?" she asked Trisha on the way out.

Apparently, Jodi had found a new friend. *Good.* Riley wished her only the best.

Feeling as if he'd lost some of the happy air he'd walked in with, Riley headed to his room to get his workout clothes. However, he didn't make it far when his phone buzzed, and he saw the name on the screen.

Claire.

Part of him felt that tug in his stomach. A happy tug. But another part of him didn't know what to say to her. Still, he wasn't going to dodge her.

"Don't say anything," Claire said the moment he answered the call.

Well, good. That worked in his favor.

"I'm calling to invite you to dinner tomorrow night," she continued. "Around seven. Can you come?"

That seemed like a trick question. Or one that could make this situation even messier than it was. For that reason alone, Riley knew he should say no.

He didn't.

"I'll be there," he said.

And maybe by then he'd know what the hell he was going to do.

CHAPTER EIGHTEEN

CLAIRE DIDN'T REMEMBER being this nervous before her first date. And this wasn't even a date-date. It was dinner with Riley. But she couldn't stop herself from shaking. Couldn't keep the nerves at bay.

It was possible she was going to throw up.

She'd already gone over all her lists. Not just the ones for the dinner itself and what to wear but also her conversation list. She needed to tell Riley that she no longer had Daniel's ring. Nor was his proposal still on the table. She'd ended things with Daniel with absolutely no hope whatsoever that it meant anything for Riley and her.

Well, other than it meant she hadn't gotten into bed with Riley while still in a semirelationship with Daniel. She didn't need to have a woman-rule about that. It was just something she wouldn't have done, but Riley perhaps thought she had.

She checked the roast again. The temp was right where it should be and would be ready to take out at six-fifty. Ten minutes from now, which meant there were still twenty minutes before Riley was due to arrive.

Too much fidgeting time.

She paced to the bathroom to check her hair again and feel for razor stubble on her legs. It was something she'd been obsessing about all day, though she doubted Riley would get his hand within touching distance of her legs. Still, it was something she would allow her slight OCD tendencies.

The knock at the door nearly caused her to shriek, but it wasn't Riley. She looked through the glass side-light window and saw someone she certainly hadn't expected to see tonight.

Lucky.

"Did Riley send you?" Claire asked the second she threw open the door.

Lucky gave her a look for a second or two before he shook his head and pulled something from his shirt. A ball of yellow fur. "I brought something for you. This house just isn't the same without a cat."

Claire gave him a look, too, and it lasted for more than a second or two. "I'm already feeding a stray." Which was a reminder that she'd have to figure out what to do with Whoa before she sold the place. "And my condo in San Antonio is pretty small."

"The kitten's pretty small, too, and I sort of saved her. She was on kitty death row at the pound."

Claire was horrified that something so fluffy, tiny and…yes, cute, could have been on death row. But then, this was Lucky, and he had a silver tongue when it came to putting a spin on things.

"All right, I confess." He put the fur ball in her hands. "I went there to chat with a friend, saw this little girl and thought she'd be perfect for Ethan. You can show her to him when he gets back from Livvy's tomorrow morning."

"How'd you know Ethan was at Livvy's?" But she huffed to dismiss that question. Livvy and Lucky had slept together, and maybe they'd extended their one-night stand for another time or two.

"I might not be able to keep her," Claire said, but Lucky was already bringing in something off the porch.

A litter box, food, bowls and treats. He'd even included a scooper.

"Give her a trial run," he suggested. "Keep her a couple of days, and if it doesn't work out, call me, and I'll see if my partner can take her."

Claire knew his partner in the rodeo-promotion business. Dixie Mae Weatherall. A very colorful woman who dressed like Dolly Parton. She was built like her, too, but doled out profanity like a sailor's cursing coach. Dixie Mae was originally from Spring Hill and had returned to town a time or two to visit her granddaughter who'd gone to Spring Hill High School. While Claire didn't know the woman personally, Dixie Mae didn't look like the cat-cuddling type.

"So, why would you think Riley had sent me?" Lucky sniffed the air. "He's coming over, isn't he? And you made him roast beef, those little baby potatoes, a salad and some key lime pie."

"You can't smell the salad." She gave him the stink eye not just for the kitten that she couldn't resist but because he'd likely heard all about the menu from Livvy. Though Claire couldn't imagine that would make good pillow talk.

"Well, I just figured you'd serve some kind of green vegetable," he answered, "and since I didn't smell one, I guessed."

Her timer went off, and she put the kitten on the floor so she could hurry to wash her hands and take out the roast.

"Don't ask me about Riley," she added. Best to cut him off at the pass. "Don't ask why he's coming over, either."

He paused, watched her fuss with the roast, basting, rebasting, poking at it with a fork. "How about Daniel?" Lucky went on. "Can I ask about him?"

"No," Claire answered.

Lucky made a sound as if everything was suddenly very clear, and then he went back into the living room and glanced out the window. No doubt checking for Riley. So did Claire.

"Riley and I had a chance to talk when I was driving him to and from his appointment at the base," Lucky threw out there.

This was tricky territory. If she asked if Riley had talked about her, that would be opening up the conversation for her to talk about Riley. And she didn't want to do that. For a man, Lucky was perceptive—she figured that was why he was so good with women. But she wasn't ready to bare her heart just yet, so she just waited for him to continue.

"When he came out of that meeting with the colonel, Riley was pretty messed up. It took me a while to get it out of him, but he's got two weeks to get his body and head together. If he can't pass a physical then, they'll give him some kind of review board. He didn't explain what that was exactly, but judging from his expression, it's the medical version of a firing squad."

Oh. She'd known the meeting hadn't gone well because Riley had ended up at her house. Drunk, no less.

"Two weeks," she repeated.

Not much time at all, although it was better than she'd thought after Anna had called. After talking to Riley's sister, Claire had thought Riley was already on his way out the door.

Instead of just being partially out.

"Of course, Riley's all geared up to pass that physical," Lucky continued. "He's pushing himself."

"Too much?" she asked.

Lucky shrugged. "It'd be the pot calling the kettle

black if I said it was too much. After all, for fun I climb on the back of a seventeen-hundred-pound bull with an attitude problem and let him sling the crap out of me. Not literally," he added with a wink.

Lucky had already moved from shrugging to winking and smiling, which meant he was trying to soften the news he'd given her.

Two weeks.

And Riley would do whatever it took—even if it would sling the crap out of him—to make sure he passed that physical.

Lucky still had a half smile when he reached out, rubbed her arm. "I'm worried about you if he passes whatever tests the Air Force will give him. Worried about him if he doesn't. Picking up pieces isn't my strong suit, but…"

He didn't finish, didn't have to. Someone was going to get hurt in this. Probably her. In fact, she wanted it to be her. She could heal from a broken heart. After a while, at least. But for Riley, failing this physical would crush him.

"I'm not sure picking up pieces is my strong suit, either," she said.

"Yeah, but you've got a huge advantage. You can make things better just by being around him. For Riley, I mean. Not for you. Just know that no matter how this all shakes out, you can call me."

No wonder the women flocked to him. Claire didn't have an ounce of attraction in her body for Lucky, but he wasn't just a charmer; he was a good listener and someone who cared more than he liked to let people know.

He also brought stupid gifts.

The kitten had stopped its sniffing and exploring and was now jetting around the living room at supersonic speed. No way could she keep it, but if she did, Bullet would be a good name for it.

When Lucky moved his hand from her arm, his attention landed on the mantel. And the journal. Judging from his suddenly tight mouth, Livvy had told Lucky about that, too.

Sheez, it was a wonder they had time for sex with all this talk about her.

What they wouldn't have been able to talk about was the almost sex that she'd had with Riley. That's because Claire hadn't told Livvy. And Livvy had given her the full-court press, too, to get details in not one but three phone calls. If Claire had spilled and then pinkie-sworn Livvy to secrecy, Livvy would have taken it to the grave. But Claire hadn't wanted to share any of it.

When things crashed and burned between Riley and her, Claire didn't want to have to explain why she'd done something as stupid as inviting him to her bed.

"What are you going to do about that?" Lucky asked, tipping his head to the journal.

"I don't want to burn it." Not yet anyway, but it did bring her to something she wanted to ask him. "Did you ever hear anyone mention a man named Rocky?"

It didn't take him but a couple of seconds to piece together why she had mentioned that particular name. "That's your father?"

She nodded. Shrugged. "I think he could be. If my mother was telling the truth in the journal."

"You want me to ask around and find out if anyone's ever heard of him?"

Did she? It suddenly seemed like a huge can of worms to open, and her heart was already on shaky ground. Still, Claire nodded again.

"All right," he agreed. "I'll ask but will be discreet. I'll say it's someone Dixie Mae used to know."

That was the good thing about Lucky; he usually got it without having to be told. With the exception of kittens, that is. His boundaries were a little less defined when it came to totally inappropriate gifts like that.

He glanced out the window again. "I need to get out of here because Riley's coming."

Sure enough Riley was driving up.

Her heart thudded against her chest.

"I don't want to spoil the mood," Lucky said. "So, I'll just head out back." He took something from his pocket, put it in the drawer of the foyer table and hurried out the back before she could see what it was.

A cat toy probably.

She pulled open the drawer and looked. No cat toy.

It was a condom in a pretty gold foil wrapper.

Claire didn't know whether to go after Lucky and throttle him or tell him that he was a couple of days late with this particular gift. But she didn't have time for either because Riley knocked on the door. She slammed the drawer, catching her thumb. Cursed. Danced around while she tried not to curse some more. But she was sure her face was still a little screwed up when she opened the door.

However, Riley wasn't looking at her. He was admiring the new paint job on the exterior of the house. "It looks great."

So did Riley. Of course, he always looked great so that was nothing new, but what was new was that she'd seen just how great he looked naked. Those memories came back to her now. All warm and glowing.

Exactly the feeling she got whenever she thought of

what Riley had done to her in the bed. He'd given new meaning to a memorable kiss.

"You're really whipping this into shape," he said.

Because her mind was on that special kissing, it took her a moment to switch gears. "Thanks." At least she had that part of her life under control. The rest of her was suspect, along with being warm and glowing.

"I thought about bringing you flowers," he said, "but, well, that didn't feel right. But I did bring you this." He took something from his pocket. A picture.

Of a kitten.

It was yellow and fluffy and looked exactly like the one that came running through the living room and nearly collided with the wall.

"It was a gift," she said but then immediately realized that Riley might think the gift had been from Daniel. "Lucky brought her, him, it." Claire scooped up the kitten, had a look at its bottom. "Her," she amended.

Judging from the way Riley stared at her, he wanted a bit more of an explanation than that.

"Lucky said he rescued her from the pound, that she was on kitty death row." Claire set the kitten back down, and it took off again.

Riley frowned. "There's a wait list for the kittens. Lucky must have sweet-talked Mary Alice into giving him one." He took back the picture. "Well, I reserved one for Ethan, but I didn't want to just bring it without asking you first."

That was the difference between Riley and Lucky. Impulse control.

"I'm not sure I can keep this one," Claire explained. "But thanks for thinking of Ethan."

Riley slid the picture back in his pocket and came in, eyeing the cat and the interior paint job. No more blue floral wallpaper. It was now a tasteful shade of beige, a good color for prospective home buyers. Or so Daniel had told her. Which was a reminder that she'd need to find a different real estate agent when it went on the market.

"So, when was Lucky here?" Riley asked.

"Earlier."

Another stare, another silent request for more info. "He's worried about you," Claire settled for saying. "How's the PT going?"

"Great. And I closed on a horse sale for Logan."

She'd already heard about that from the clerk at the bank and the cashier at the grocery store. It was the buzz of Spring Hill, and the consensus was that it was Riley's last hurrah and a way of appeasing Logan before he headed back out.

Riley did more glancing around. "Where's Ethan?"

"With Livvy. Once a month he spends the night at her place." That was almost the truth. Ethan's sleepover with Livvy wasn't due for another two weeks, but Claire had moved it up.

"So, it's just us?" he clarified.

She couldn't tell if he was happy about that or if, like her, he wanted to fidget. Claire resisted, but the only way she managed it was to do some controlled fidgeting. She led him into the kitchen so she could check the food that in no way needed checking, and she poured them each a glass of wine.

"Smells good in here. Looks good, too." His gaze skirted over the roast, the potatoes and the pie.

And then settled on her.

Oh, my. Those bedroom eyes of his were in full force tonight, or maybe that was just the way her body was interpreting it. Riley used those bedroom eyes to stare at her as if he were about to tell her something important, but there was something important she had to tell him, too.

"I broke things off with Daniel. Gave him back his ring and told him there'd be no more proposals. We're finished."

She didn't think it was her imagination that he looked relieved. Or maybe that was wishful thinking.

"I saw Jodi yesterday," he said.

God. Had her heart skipped a beat? Claire tried not to jump to conclusions. She failed. Had Jodi managed to lure Riley back into her arms—and into her other places? Claire was too afraid to ask.

"Things are over between me and her," he added.

Her heart skipped even more beats. Much more of this and she'd end up in the ER on an EKG machine. Claire just took some deep breaths and waited for Riley to continue.

"But Jodi will still be around town for a while so she can get some work done," he added. "I thought you should know in case you ran into her."

"I won't be going to Calhoun's." Or into town for that matter. Claire wasn't opposed to a confrontation, but after what'd happened with those special kisses, Claire was certain she wouldn't be able to keep a straight face around the woman. One look at her, and Jodi would know.

And worse, Claire would want her to know.

It wasn't a neener-neener kind of thing, either. All right, maybe it was. A little. But Claire had always had a thing for Riley, and that thing had just gone to another level. The question now was just how far did she want those levels to keep going?

Far, she decided.

She hadn't known what decision she would make, but

looking at him now, she realized she knew exactly what she wanted to do with Riley.

"Do you want to have sex?" Claire asked.

IT WAS ONLY pure blind luck that Riley didn't choke on his wine. Definitely not the reaction he wanted to have. But then neither was the instant hard-on he got from Claire just asking that question.

Asking a man if he wanted to have sex was akin to asking if he wanted that air he was breathing. Air that suddenly seemed a little thin right now.

Of course he wanted sex. This was Claire, and he'd wanted to have sex with her since about the time he'd gotten his first hard-on. In fact, she'd been the cause of that first one. But then Riley had pushed his feelings and hard-ons for her aside because she'd chosen Daniel.

However, she seemed to be choosing *him* right now, and while Riley wanted to jump on that, jump on her, too, he needed to take a step back. "Well, do you?" Claire pressed.

Her breath was thin, as well, judging from the way she was sucking it in, and it was coming too fast. Not exactly an erotic come-on. More like the beginnings of hyperventilation.

Riley took hold of her arm and had her sit at the table. He sat, too. Not easily. But he managed it. "Of course I would."

He'd barely gotten out the words when she came out of the chair and kissed him. Now, that was a nice slam of heat. Of course, he didn't need that slam because it messed with his head. Other parts, too. And even though it pained him to admit it, they should talk about this first.

Then jump into bed.

Maybe he could make it a short talk.

"I just want to make sure—" he started, but his question ground to a halt when she kissed him again.

"I'm sure," Claire insisted. And judging from the way she'd bit his lip at the end of that kiss, she was.

Well, Riley was as sure as that and then some, but he needed to hang on to that clear head a little longer.

"Did, uh, anything happen to make you decide to do this?" he asked.

Was that a blank look she gave him? Well, if it was, it only lasted a couple of seconds before she huffed. The lip biting was gone but not the scalding attraction that was still heating up the kitchen. Riley didn't think it was leftover heat from the oven, either.

"Look, I know you'll be leaving soon," she said. "Lucky told me about the physical you needed to pass, and since I know you, I also know you'll pass it."

Twenty-eighty flashed in his head. But with all the exercises he'd been doing, he had to be up to twenty-two–seventy-eight by now. And while he wanted to believe with all his heart that those odds would improve in his favor, Claire clearly had more faith in him than he did.

However, this was more than faith.

"Then, you know I'll be leaving," he said though Riley knew she hadn't forgotten that part.

She nodded.

Okay, he'd expected a bit more of an explanation than just a nod. Preferably, a short explanation that actually made sense.

Claire was a sensible woman, and he seriously doubted she was the fling-having type. Even after what'd happened between them two nights ago. They'd been caught up in the heat of the moment then, no time to give it much thought. She'd clearly given it some thought since, though.

"All right, let's just say we do this," Riley speculated. "Then what? I leave and you just accept that?"

"More or less."

Riley frowned. She wasn't totally killing the mood, not much could do that, but he wanted to know more about that less.

"I don't want you to get hurt," he clarified.

She drew in another of those quick breaths. "I won't. I've been doing a lot of soul-searching about this, and I'm not offering you a white picket fence at the end of these two weeks. I'm offering you sex with no strings attached."

Soul-searching, huh? Riley was reasonably sure this was the first time those words about sex with no strings attached had ever come out of her mouth, but she didn't give him a chance to remind her of that.

"Making fantasies come true," she blurted out. "That's the motto of my and Livvy's business, and it's what I want from you. Starting tonight."

Oh, she looked so hot. Sounded so confident. But Riley could see the nerves just below the surface. They were simmering there with all that heat.

"Tonight? I didn't bring a condom with me."

That was a lie. He had one in his wallet. All right, he had two. But he hadn't exactly felt good about putting them there. It had seemed, well, calculated, as if he were doing something that would lead Claire down the path to a broken heart.

Unless…

Maybe her feelings for him didn't go past this attraction. Oh, and friendship. But maybe that was it, and who was he to argue with a woman who seemed to know her own mind? One who had done some actual soul-searching. Clearly, she was set on doing this.

The little voice in his head, though, wasn't convinced. "You're sure?" he asked one more time.

She nodded. "And it doesn't have to happen tonight. I'll give you a day or two to think it over, and—"

Claire was possibly going to say something important, but Riley made the decision that this was going to happen no matter what else she had to say. He kissed her.

CHAPTER NINETEEN

EVEN AFTER PRACTICALLY throwing herself at Riley, she still hadn't seen the kiss coming, but Claire sure felt it. *Oh, my.* Riley was so good at this, and despite all that oral foreplay the night before last, her body was aching for a real fix.

Claire refused to think about if this was a mistake or not. She'd already been doing too much thinking, and she was tired of waffling, whining and especially aching. Even if this turned out to put an end to Riley's and her friendship, then so be it. For tonight, she was getting that fantasy.

With just a few of Riley's kisses, the memories of their other encounter came washing over her. Of course, the fire was there, that was a given, but this felt like so much more. Good thing they hadn't become lovers in high school or they might not have ever gotten anything accomplished—including graduation—because Claire suddenly felt as if she'd missed something incredibly good.

Livvy was right about not grading sex on a curve.

Never again.

Of course, that might mean she'd never have sex again, either, but that was a bridge she would cross when she came to it. For now, she just wanted Riley. And she got him. His mouth, his hands, pretty much the rest of him when they landed body to body.

She was mostly responsible for that because Claire hooked her arms around him and kept pulling him closer until she had him where she wanted him. He didn't put up any resistance to that maneuvering, but it was clear he was more interested in the kissing than he was the jockeying for position.

Claire was interested in both.

Taking a step back, she took Riley with her, heading toward the bedroom where she'd stashed the condoms she'd bought. Of course, the one Lucky had given her was closer, so if they didn't actually make it to the bed, she could use that as a backup.

Which she might have to do.

That became clear with the next step when she landed against the freshly stripped and painted wall. It was all smooth and cool now, and Riley pressed her back against it when he took her mouth as if it were his for the taking. He certainly wasn't having any second thoughts about this, thank goodness. For a moment, she wondered if he would, but that thought flew right out of her head when he shoved up her top and kissed her breasts.

Mercy.

The man had a magic mouth.

She'd worn a pink lacy bra, and she thought maybe the grunt he made was one of approval. Yes, approval. He made another sound, and then their gazes connected when he looked up at her and took her nipple into his mouth. Claire perhaps lost consciousness for a couple of seconds when the pleasure shot through her.

"I want you naked," Riley insisted.

An excellent plan. She'd worn her good panties, too, but this time it was going to be a mutual stripping off because she got a great deal of pleasure from seeing him naked. That's why she went after his shirt, but she was mindful of the injury. In fact, she tried not to even look at it...too late. She looked.

"You're sure you're up to this?" she asked.

Without breaking the nipple kisses, he latched on to her hand and put it to the front of his jeans where she felt him not only "up" but rock hard.

"Ha-ha." Except she was moaning when she said it so it didn't sound like a fake laugh.

Still, Riley had proven his point. And she got to feel that proof when he made his way back up from her breasts to her mouth. At first Claire couldn't figure out why he was backtracking, but then she realized it was because it put him in a better position to yank off her top.

She did some yanking, too. His shirt came off. So did her bra, and when he sent it sailing, it landed in the baby potatoes. *Oh, well.* A cream-sauced bra was a casualty of the hot need that was making them both a little crazy and affecting their aim.

His shirt went in the recycling bin.

Riley turned her so fast that she nearly lost her balance, but he was right there to steady her. He leaned against the wall so he could go after her skirt next. She wasn't sure where it landed, but her panties soon followed, and Claire realized she was stark naked in her kitchen.

It occurred to her that she should suggest going to the bedroom. Where she'd put out some candles and washed the sheets. But then Riley did a trail of tongue kisses back down her body, and she knew the candles and clean sheets would have to wait.

He lifted her leg, putting her knee on his good shoulder, and he gave her more of those kisses and nibbles that would bring her to a really fast orgasm if she didn't do something about it. Not that she would have balked too much about a fast orgasm from Riley's mouth, but this time she wanted to make it the main course and not an appetizer.

"I've got condoms, and we're going to use them," she mumbled.

She caught on to his hair, pulled him back up, and in the same motion, Claire went after his jeans.

"How many condoms?" he asked.

A whole box. "Three," she said instead. A whole-box confession would make her seem slutty instead of just frugal. The box had been on sale.

"Good. I brought two with me," he said. "I lied about that earlier."

All right, so they had fifteen counting the one Lucky had left. Claire wouldn't mention that one, either. Fifteen condoms had to be more than enough to quell this raging heat. Riley unzipped his jeans, came back to her for another kiss while they got them off him. Not easily. She was all thumbs and crazy now. She blamed that on the kisses he kept dropping on various parts of her body.

So Claire turned the tables on him.

Literally. She pushed him against the table, anchoring him in place so she could kiss his neck. His chest. And because she felt that she owed him a little payback, she went down on her knees, too. She took him into her mouth.

He cursed.

But she thought that was a good thing. However, he didn't let those bubblegumming kisses go on for long. Still cursing, he fumbled through his pocket, located a condom and somehow managed to get it on despite the fact she was *helping*.

More payback for driving her crazy and allowing her

to go years and years without having him. Claire intended to make up for some of those years in the bed.

Or on the table.

Riley turned her, leaning her against the table and stepping between her legs. Of course, he didn't wait long before thrusting inside her.

Good gravy.

The pleasure just sort of burst through her head to toe and especially to the parts in between. Big and hard wasn't overrated. At all.

Despite being on the table and sticking her hand in the key lime pie, it was somehow perfect. Riley found just the right rhythm, the right everything down to the sweet kiss he gave her that sent her flying. He flew, too, and then he landed against her, their bodies slick with sweat.

Parts of their dinner, too.

It took him a few seconds to get back to earth, and when he did, he licked the key lime from her hand.

"Hungry?" she asked when she finally caught her breath.

"Yeah, but not for that yet." Riley scooped her up and headed for the bedroom.

"How's your shoulder?" Claire asked. She leaned in to have a look for herself.

Riley wasn't exactly comfortable having her examine the scar. It was still raw and ugly. Maybe it always would be. But thankfully Claire didn't have the same horrified expression as she had the first time she'd seen it.

"It's fine." No lie this time. The muscles still twinged and pulled when he moved it, but sex hadn't aggravated it, and even if it had, Riley doubted he would have noticed.

He wasn't noticing now, either.

He was admiring the view. Riley was sure he'd never

had dinner in bed and certainly not while he was naked. While Claire was naked, too. And while they were still wearing some of that food.

"I could heat up the roast," Claire offered, kissing him.

Riley shook his head. That would only require her to get up again, and while he'd have a good show of her coming and going, it really wasn't necessary. The food was just to stave off starvation.

In addition to the key lime pie that Claire had gotten on her hands, Riley had somehow managed to get potatoes on him. That was probably why sex should never happen on the dinner table, but at the time it'd seemed like his only option. He'd had to have Claire right then, right there. And he had managed to do just that. However, with the heat temporarily sated and his stomach getting there, as well, he had to wonder.

What now?

She smiled at him around a forkful of key lime. A smile that seemed genuine, maybe even a little giddy, but he knew Claire well enough to know that there could be nerves behind it, too.

Yeah, Claire had offered him no-strings-attached sex, but he wondered if she'd even thought it through. He certainly hadn't, but Riley was certain he'd be doing a lot of thinking about it in the days to come.

There was a crashing sound, and Claire practically tossed the rest of her pie on the nightstand, flung back the covers and was out of the bed before Riley could get up. He seriously doubted it was a burglar. And it wasn't.

It was the kitten.

It had somehow managed to topple a basket filled with Ethan's toy cars. Riley certainly hadn't forgotten about the gift from his brother. A gift he'd discuss with Lucky first chance he got. Lucky had something up his sleeve.

Claire scooped up the kitten, redirected it to its own toys. No doubt gifts from Lucky, too, and she dumped some of the kitten food into the bowl. While she was doing that, Riley set up the litter box. All while they were stark naked. She noticed him naked, too. He noticed her naked. And all that noticing began to feel a little like foreplay. He wasn't sure he was up for another round so soon.

Yes, he was.

He was always ready for Claire even if his shoulder disagreed.

But Claire no longer seemed ready. That's because her attention landed on that damn journal again.

Riley huffed. "I wish you'd let me burn that thing for you."

She made a sound that could have meant anything, and she kept looking at it. Not as if it were a coiled rattler ready to strike but as if it were a new pie that she wasn't sure she'd like or even wanted to try.

"I think I should read it," she said.

"Shit. Sugar," he automatically corrected even though Ethan wasn't around. "Why would you want to do that?"

Claire looked at him, and he knew why. Because it was there. It was from her sorry excuse for a mother, and Claire needed to know what the woman had written.

Part of Riley got that. If he were in her shoes—or in this case, her naked body—he would want to read it, too. But he also wanted to protect Claire from the woman's venom.

"Tomorrow," she said. "I can read it when Ethan's napping."

"No way. If you're going to read it, do it while I'm here." Riley didn't have to think about that.

She shook her head. "It's not fair to you. You came

over for a night of dinner and sex. You don't need to have a course of old baggage to go with all that."

Actually, he'd come over just for dinner. Hadn't had a clue about the sex course. And while old baggage wouldn't be nearly as tasty a dessert as Claire or the key lime pie, if those long-ago written words caused her to fall apart, and they almost certainly would, Riley wanted to be there to pick up the pieces.

And despite the fact there would be pieces, Riley didn't stop her when she went to the mantel and picked up the journal.

For some stupid reason it didn't feel right reading the journal while she was naked. Maybe because she already felt exposed just by holding it in her hands. Claire grabbed a T-shirt and put it on despite Riley grumbling something about losing a great view. That caused her to smile.

Which was probably why he'd said it.

He put on his shirt and boxers, and after losing that view, Claire was rethinking her decision. This wouldn't just put a damper on the evening; it could ruin it. But the wounds inside her seemed to keep festering with each passing minute that the journal stayed around. She needed to think of it as a bandage that should be ripped off so the old wounds could finally heal.

Not that she expected to find anything healing on those pages.

No, she had no hopes of that whatsoever. But if she dealt with them all at once, the pain wouldn't be piecemeal.

"You want me to read it first?" Riley offered.

It was such a sweet gesture that Claire paused to kiss him. Of course, she hadn't needed a sweet gesture as an excuse. She planned to kiss him a lot throughout the night in case this was the last chance she got to do that. For now, they were still basking in the aftermath of the sex glow, but in the morning light, Riley might decide to turn down any future sessions of casual sex.

But she'd deal with that later, too.

Claire took the journal back to bed. Riley joined her, of course, not sitting so close that he was reading over her shoulder but close enough to be there if she needed him. Then, he handed her the fork that he'd used to eat the roast beef.

"I want you to use it to stab the page whenever you read something hurtful," he instructed. "That probably means multiple stabs on every page."

She smiled, took the fork and yes, kissed him again. "Do you remember ever seeing her?"

He shook his head. "But I remember a picture of her. Your grandmother used to have it on the mantel."

Claire remembered that picture, as well, but wasn't sure where it was. Maybe with the mystery letter that she hadn't been able to find.

"Deep breath," Riley coached. "And get the fork ready."

She did. Claire leaned her back against the headboard and flipped past the first couple of pages that she'd already read. Still, she took a moment to stab them. It felt surprisingly good even if it did leave a little au jus on the old pages.

When she got to an unread page, the first thing that jumped out at her was the profanity. She had so few memories of her mom, but she hadn't remembered her using profanity every other word. Claire could almost feel the anger jumping off the page.

So she stabbed it.

"How bad?" Riley asked.

Claire shrugged. "More bitching about being pregnant

and Rocky leaving her. I don't think she ever figured out she was better off without a man who ran out on her."

Even though Riley hadn't moved, she thought maybe he went still. No doubt because he thought Ethan's father had done the same to her. He hadn't. But she didn't want to get into that, not with the emotional powder keg in her hands.

The next pages were filled with comments about doctor's appointments, gaining weight, swollen ankles and the boring homework she'd been given by the school so she could graduate. Claire wasn't sure if her mother had ostracized herself or if the school had had a policy back then of not allowing pregnant students to attend.

"Remember, you can stop at any time," Riley reminded her.

She nodded, thanked him for his concern and kept turning the pages. Thankfully, after a while the profanity-laced entries became numbing, and it occurred to Claire that she had done plenty of whining in her own diary. But she'd had the good sense to destroy it before she headed off for college so that no one would ever see it.

The next date was one she instantly recognized because it was Claire's birthday. One word took up half the first page.

Hell.

That was just the beginning of her mother's profanity. Since Claire had gone through childbirth, as well, she knew it was painful. However, so were the words her mother had put in bold block letters:

I thought that fucking kid would never come out. My poor body won't ever be the same. Neither will my fucking life.

Claire stabbed the page twice with a fork and nearly bolted from the room. She needed to hold Ethan. She needed to tell him that she loved him.

She needed to breathe.

But Riley caught on to her and pulled her back into his arms. It was the right thing to do. Claire didn't bolt but stayed put in his arms. "Why couldn't I find the letter instead of this?" she mumbled.

Did Riley go still again? No. He was probably just trying not to remind her that she'd been wrong to read this.

"My question is why didn't your grandmother just throw away the journal?" he asked.

"I know the answer to that one. Gran didn't throw away much of anything. The proof is in all the boxes and drawers. There were over a hundred twisty ties from bread bags. It was as if she was prepping for doomsday and a twisty-tie shortage."

Riley chuckled, kissed her head again. "Now can you throw the journal away? With those fork marks on it, the next page would be hard to read anyway."

True. She'd stabbed it so hard, the tines had gone straight through the paper. Still… "There isn't much more of it."

He grunted, and it had a hint of disapproval to it, but Claire turned the page. The date was the day after she was born.

Mom put Claire Marie on the kid's birth certificate. The nurses kept bugging me about a name so I said Clover Lane, but Mom said she was going to put Claire Marie, and I told her I didn't give a shit, that she could name the kid whatever she wanted. The nurses are giving me shit about not holding the kid, too. I told them they're getting paid to hold her, I'm not.

That hurt, too, so she stabbed it. *Clover Lane?* That sounded like a 1960s rock band or a stripper. "I spent months picking out Ethan's name. Months decorating his nursery. I held Ethan the moment he was born and didn't want to let go of him. She didn't do any of those things."

"But your grandmother did," Riley pointed out.

She nodded. It wasn't as if she hadn't felt loved. She had. However, Claire could never understand why her mother had felt this way, especially after seeing or holding her child. Of course, she hadn't held Claire, so maybe that was at the core of this latest page filled with bile.

"Gran didn't talk much about it, but my mom left Spring Hill with me when I was four and a half. But there aren't enough pages left in the journal for her to get into that."

"You don't have any memories of those six months or so you were away from here?" he asked.

"Some. I remember a man, but I don't know his name. I guess he was her boyfriend because they slept in the same bed. They yelled a lot." Thankfully, there were only bits and pieces of that, like the car accident that'd taken Riley's parents.

"Did either of them ever hurt you?" A muscle flickered in his jaw.

"No. No physical abuse." But her mother had indeed hurt her.

He paused a long time. "You think it'll help if you know the reason your mother left town with you and then came back?"

She nodded. "I think it would."

Another long pause, and Claire could practically see

the debate he was having with himself. "Lucky remembers Della and Stella talking about it. Your mother met some man in San Antonio, took you and ran off with him. Take this with a grain of salt, but they say he was wanted by the law."

Well, that would explain why her mother had left. Of course, it was just as likely that six months of motherhood had been more than enough. So, her mother had come running back to Spring Hill in order to dump Claire and take off again.

She reached to turn the page, the last one, she realized, but Riley put his hand over hers. "Let me read it to you."

Claire was instantly suspicious. "I don't want you to sugarcoat it. After the other pages, I can take one more." She hoped.

"No sugarcoating."

She believed him, but it still took Claire a couple of long moments to let go. Riley took it. And the fork.

"Last page," he verified. "It was two days after you were born." He took a deep breath. "'Finally got out of that hellhole hospital and am home. It sucks but not as much as the hospital. Those nurse bitches! They made me hold the kid before I could leave. Blackmail! So, I held her—Claire—not a bad name, I guess. It suits her.'"

He stopped, looked at her. "Are you okay?"

Dang it. There were tears in her eyes and all because her mother called her by her name. Such a simple thing. But she held on to the half compliment as if it were a lifeline.

"I'm fine," Claire insisted. "Keep going."

Riley read ahead, silently, and she saw some sort of emotion in his eyes. What exactly, she wasn't sure, but he didn't look ready to stab the page. Instead, he handed it to her.

"You should finish this," he said.

All right, so it must not be too bad for him to offer that. Still, her heart was racing. Her mind, too. And while Claire wanted to finish it and put it behind her once and for all, finishing it also meant they'd come to the last link she had with her mother. After learning that her mother had considered ending the pregnancy and then wishing her dead, she only hoped there wasn't anything else so painful.

Claire did take the journal, but she also took the fork back, just in case. Not much was left at all, just a few sentences, and before she read them, she had a horrible thought. This was literally the last page in this particular journal, but what if there were others? That was a stomach-churning thought.

"Deep breath," Riley reminded her.

She took two of them and started reading.

Claire doesn't look like Rocky. She looks like Mom and me. That's good. Looking at her won't remind me of him. I don't want to think about him ever again. I just want to get on with my life. That means getting on with my life with Claire. God, she'll never know how scared I am. I'm so going to screw this up.

There it was. The end. Ironic, since it had been the beginning. And her mother hadn't sounded bitter but rather scared. Claire had felt the same way about Ethan. She'd desperately wanted and loved him, but she'd been terrified, too. It was strange to know her mother had felt the same way.

Riley slipped his arm around her, pulled her close.

"What do you want to do with the journal now?" he asked.

That required more deep breaths. Ninety-nine percent of the journal was filled with anger and profanity—most of it directed at Claire and Rocky. There was no way Claire wanted to go back through that again.

But she tore out the last page.

This one she'd keep.

She got up and took the rest of it to the fireplace. It was a good night to put some things in her past to rest.

RILEY COULD SMELL the fire in his dream. But it wasn't an ordinary fire. It was from the explosion. From the IED. He'd heard IEDs go off before. Never this close, though.

Never.

Get the hell out now!

He had to get out of there. Sixty-forty. That had been the kid's odds. Good odds. But that was before the last IED. Before Riley had felt the blood and the pain. Before the extraction had become a kid in his arms.

The kid moaned. Still alive. Riley held him even tighter, hoping the pressure would stop the bleeding—both his and the kid's. Hoping he'd get back in time to the Pave Hawk. Hell, hoping he'd find the damn thing and that it hadn't been blown to bits.

The fire and smoke were all around him now. Blobs of fiery debris left over from the IED. God, he couldn't hear. The blast was still ringing in his ears.

Couldn't see, either, because of the sand.

But he could think, and he went through all the things he'd learned in his training. Hadn't it been about this anyway? Needing to take evasive measures. Doing whatever it took to finish the mission.

Sixty-forty.

Get the hell out now!

Riley forced himself to move, one foot ahead of the other, and he made the mistake of looking down. He was leaving a trail of blood on the sand. His own blood.

There was too much of it.

But since he was moving, his odds were better than the kid's. Riley's blood type was on his name tag. If the medic was still alive, he'd see it and would be able to give him whatever he needed to stay alive.

The kid was a different matter.

Kids didn't wear their blood types on their clothes. Sure as fuck-hell shouldn't have been in this place, and Riley couldn't let him die here, either.

Sixty-forty.

One step ahead of the other.

He thought of his brothers. Of Claire. Why had she popped into his mind? He wasn't sure, but it was a welcome memory. Of Claire in the marching band on the football field of Spring Hill High School. Her stiff blue uniform that made her look like a soldier. The memory of her, the sound of the clarinet she was playing was weaving in and out of the sand so Riley marched with her.

Get the hell out now!

Claire said his name. Except he hadn't remembered her doing that that day of the extraction. In the memory, she'd been playing her clarinet. No talking. She certainly hadn't called out to him. Nor had she touched him. But she was doing that now.

"Riley?" she said. Claire was shaking his good arm. "You're having another nightmare."

His eyes flew open, and it took a moment to pull himself from the dream and figure out where he was. Hell. He was still in Claire's bed, which would have been a good thing if he hadn't had the nightmare. She'd already seen him have one on the porch swing and the flashback at the pub. Two experiences too many. Riley didn't want her seeing any more of that.

Too late.

He saw the worry in her eyes. Easy to see it since the sunlight was already streaming through the window. Riley sat up, scrubbed his hand over his face.

"Sixty-forty?" she asked.

Mercy, he'd obviously talked in his sleep again. His breath was still gusting, and it took him a moment to gather himself. "What else did I say?"

"My name." Claire paused. "Was sixty-forty your odds of getting out of there alive?"

"No." That was all he was considering saying, so why he said more, Riley didn't know. "Mine were better."

"Those were the *kid's* odds," she said on a rise of breath.

"Yeah." At least they had been before the last IED. Riley wasn't sure what they were after that.

He could see the question in her eyes—she wanted to know if the kid made it—and Riley considered using a personal evasive measure. After all, Claire and he were practically naked in her bed, and if he just started kissing her, she wouldn't be able to talk.

But that didn't seem right.

It didn't matter that Riley wanted to protect her from this, because he couldn't. Claire had already heard too much. Had also seen too much with the scars on his body.

"Two of the crew and an airman didn't make it," Riley said. "But the kid did."

The tears were in her eyes, and she didn't even try to blink them back. "He's alive because of you."

It hadn't all been because of him. Riley had just gotten him out, had given him a fighting chance. The medic

and then the doctors had done the rest. But the bottom
line here for him was something that'd gotten lost in all
the pain and the flashbacks.

The kid had made it.

All those steps through the sand. All the blood he'd
left behind. The pain. The loss of the other crew mem-
bers. All of it had brought him to this one realization.

The kid had made it.

And so had he.

It was somehow that journal all over again. Tough to
take and with an ending that wouldn't necessarily make
everything right. And Riley decided to do what Claire
had done.

He mentally tore out the last page—*the kid had made
it*—and pitched the rest of the nightmare into the fire.

CHAPTER TWENTY

SMILE, CLAIRE REMINDED HERSELF.

If she didn't do that Livvy would think something was wrong. Too late. One step outside her car, and Livvy's attention zoomed straight past the weak smile and to Claire's eyes. Livvy didn't exactly look crestfallen, but she didn't look so eager to ask for juicy details of Claire's night with Riley.

"I didn't bring wine," Livvy called out, "but I brought something better." She scooped up a giggling Ethan like a football and ran with him to the porch.

Since Livvy was teetering on mile-high heels again and wobbling, to Ethan it must have felt a little like being on a carnival ride.

"How'd he do last night?" Claire asked.

"Good as beans." Whatever that meant. "But I bought him some pull-ups."

Despite the fact Ethan was still tucked under Livvy's arms, he pulled down the waist of his jeans for her to see. "Ull-ups."

He seemed very proud, though Claire couldn't imagine what'd prompted Livvy to buy them. Or how the heck she'd found them in the store. Livvy wasn't exactly a pro at buying baby supplies. Once Claire had asked her to buy wipes, and Livvy had come back with eye-makeup remover pads.

"He kept peeing on the fake rubber tree I have in the

living room," Livvy explained. "And each time he undid
his diaper to do that, I couldn't get the tape to stick so I
took him to the store and asked one of the moms I saw
shopping what I should get."

Good choice. These had smiling toy cars on them.
Ethan's selection no doubt. Though Claire would need
to scold him for peeing on the rubber plant. Later, she'd
sit him down and talk to him about that.

Claire took him from Livvy the second they made it
to the porch, and she managed to steal some kisses before Ethan wiggled out of her arms. That's because he
saw the kitten on the other side of the screen door, and
he scrambled to get inside.

"Van Gogh," he said with perfect clarity. Though
Claire had no idea why until she realized the kitten did
indeed look like one of the gold-star blobs in the painting that she'd been showing him for weeks.

"Is it a gift from Riley?" Livvy asked, following Claire
inside.

"From Lucky. He brought it over before Riley got here
last night."

"No. I mean that." Smiling and winking, Livvy
touched the spot on Claire's neck.

The very spot that was doused with every drop of
concealer that Claire had been able to squeeze from the
tube. Between the bruise from the pub brawl and the love
bite, she'd gone through more concealer in a week than
she had in the past six years.

"That was an accident," Claire explained.

But she was sorry she'd even offered that small bit of
an explanation. Because now Livvy would want more.
And Claire had no intention of sharing. But the "accident" had involved her learning that the spot on her neck

was very sensitive and whenever Riley kissed her there, she was within a heartbeat of having an orgasm.

So he'd kissed her there.

A lot.

And when coupled with "other things" he'd done to her, the orgasm did indeed happen.

"Van Gogh, van Gogh," Ethan repeated. He sat on the floor, and the kitten crawled into his lap. It was instant love. She could see it all over her boy's face.

Claire sighed. Because it meant they were keeping the kitten. Now, she was feeding the gray tabby and Whoa, and if she included the one Riley had reserved for her at the pound, she was well on her way to being a crazy cat lady.

With a hickey.

Ethan couldn't take his eyes off van Gogh and Livvy wouldn't take her eyes off Claire's neck. "I'll tell you about my date if you'll tell me about yours," Livvy said.

"You didn't have a date. Ethan stayed at your place last night."

"I meant the date the night before. The one with Lucky."

"That wasn't a date." Claire leaned in to whisper the rest. "That was hot monkey sex. Wasn't it?"

"Always is with Lucky. But, no, there's nothing serious between us. Not like with Riley and you."

Of course, Ethan latched on to that. "Riley?"

"He's not here, baby," Claire answered.

Ethan looked disappointed, and Claire knew exactly how he felt. It'd been hard for her to see Riley fully dressed and walking out her door. Hard because she might not get a night like that with him again. Yes, she'd offered him no-strings-attached sex, but after the mixed bag of stuff that'd gone on, he might decide sex with her could never be string-less.

"It is serious now between you two, right?" Livvy asked.

"No. Of course not. Last night wasn't about getting serious. It was about, well…" She might as well just call it what it was. "Fudging."

"Well, fudging can become serious. With the right person," Livvy added. "And I'm pretty sure R-i-l-e-y is the right person."

Claire wasn't sure of that at all. "It takes two people for it to be right." And Riley wasn't on board for anything that would take him away from the military. "He saved a kid when he was over there. That's how he got hurt."

"That's what you talked about last night?" Judging from her tone and the face Livvy made, she guessed that had been a real mood killer.

And in a way, it had been when it came to the sex. But in other ways, it'd been incredible. She had watched Riley's mind heal right in front of her eyes.

"His body's healing, too," Claire continued. "I was amazed at what he could do."

Livvy grinned. "Do tell."

"I didn't mean s-e-x-u-a-l-l-y." Not completely anyway, though he had been especially good at all that. "He lifted me up like I weighed nothing, and after all that apology ice cream I've been eating, you know that couldn't be farther from the truth."

Livvy made a sound of agreement, patted her stomach. She'd been eating some bowls of Riley's I'm-sorry offerings, too.

"I think he might have had some pain a time or two," Claire went on, "but it was nothing like it was when he first got home."

Livvy studied her a moment. "You don't exactly sound happy about that."

"No. I am." Claire couldn't say that quickly enough or mean it more. "I hated seeing him in pain." Of course, there was a *but* coming.

One that Livvy had no trouble interpreting. "But it means he'll pass that physical."

Yes. Mercy, that was selfish of Claire to even think otherwise. She wanted Riley to pass the physical, wanted him to be happy and free from those horrible flashbacks, and she wanted that even if it meant she couldn't have him.

"I think the old adage applies here," Claire said. "I made my bed, and I can sleep in it." *Alone.*

She didn't say the alone part aloud, but Livvy had no trouble picking up on it. Her hug tightened around Claire. "But at least you had a great night with him," Livvy reminded her. "And you have a kitten. The place is looking better every time I come over. Soon, it'll be ready to go on the market."

Yes, soon, and for some reason that caused her stomach to churn. "I still want to find the letter, though."

"And what about that sugary journal from your sugary mother?" Livvy asked.

Claire tipped her head to the ashes in the fireplace. "Gone. Well, gone except for the one good part. I kept that."

"Good. Because it's time for your mind to heal, too."

Yes, it was, and Claire was certain she was almost there. Almost. But she wasn't exactly doing a victory dance. Because even if all the final pieces fell into place—selling the house, finding the letter and having some peace that her mother maybe hadn't hated her with every fiber of her being—it all suddenly seemed a little hollow.

Because she'd have none of those things with Riley.

RILEY TOOK HIS TIME walking through the pasture. Why, he didn't know. It was too hot. He was tired after helping the new cutter with the horses. Considering he'd gotten less than an hour of sleep, he should be hurrying to catch a nap before dinner. Still, he didn't rush.

He'd seen his father do this a hundred times, stroll through the pasture as if soaking it all in. Riley supposed that's what he was doing now. His mind had slowed down enough for him to be alone with his own thoughts and not be sickened by what was in his head.

The kid was alive.

That would replace "Jingle Bells" if the flashbacks threatened again. Everything he needed to remember about what had happened in that wall of sand was that he'd done his job. The kid was alive.

He tested the shoulder. Stiff and sore. But considering the workout he'd given it the night before with Claire, he was surprised it felt as good as it did. Ditto for him. Sex with Claire had been everything he'd thought it would be, but he hadn't managed to keep the regrets at bay.

Yes, he was already having regrets.

Without the night of sex, leaving Ethan and her would have been hard, but now he'd taken hard to a whole new level. Which had pretty much described his dick most of the night.

Hard-dick thoughts aside, Riley wasn't sure how this was all going to work out with Claire, but he didn't see a white picket fence in their future. Still, that didn't mean he wasn't going to enjoy the short time they had together. That's what Claire wanted.

Or rather what she'd said she wanted.

While that might have been wishful thinking on her part, Riley was feeling too at peace, too content, too happy to question it. By damn, he was putting on a pair of rose-colored glasses for a while, and he whistled on the walk back to the house. Only the horses and Crazy Dog were around to notice that he was acting like a giddy fool.

Lucky, too, he realized when Riley saw his brother coming out of the house.

Riley stopped whistling when he spotted him. For one thing he didn't want Lucky picking up on his good mood and asking him about how his night had gone with Claire, and for another Lucky's own mood seemed to be several steps past the riled stage. Lucky cursed, threw his hat on the porch and picked it up only to throw it again.

"Should I ask?" Riley offered as he approached him.

"No."

With that, Lucky started to pace. It only lasted a couple of seconds. Lucky wasn't known for doing long stretches of anything, and it was the same this time. He headed off the porch and in the direction of his truck.

Riley huffed, followed him. "Did something happen between Logan and you?"

It wasn't exactly a guess. Lucky's fits of temper were rare. For the most part, Lucky was a lover. However, his occasional clashes were usually with Logan.

"He's three minutes older than me," Lucky snarled.

Yeah, definitely Logan. "He's decades older than you, than both of us," Riley pointed out.

Lucky opened his truck door, but he didn't get in. "Is that some kind of an old soul reference? Because an old asshole would be a better label for it. No matter what I do, it's not enough. Well, you know what? I don't want to do enough to make it enough. Understand?"

Maybe. Riley thought he had mentally worked his way through all those *enough*s. "Does this have to do with the other horse trainer who'll be coming in?"

"You bet it does. I called in a friend for that job, and Logan fired him on the spot. Well, if he didn't trust my judgment, why ask me to do it in the first place?"

Riley didn't have an answer for that, but it did bother him that Logan had fired the guy. They had nearly fifty horses thanks to the deal he'd made with the Army Ranger and only one trainer.

"You know what Logan wants?" Lucky continued, but he decided to answer his own question. "He wants me to train them. He wants me to drop everything I'm doing and work a program I was against from the beginning."

Riley hadn't been around for those *discussions* about the cutting-horse program between Lucky and Logan. Riley's first reaction was that it was a good thing. That was his usual reaction anyway. Stay uninvolved. Hear about all the spats after the fact and not give a damn about any of it.

But the breakthrough he'd had about those flashbacks must have softened his brain because Riley had a new thought. If he had been around for those discussions, he could have soothed them over. A stupid thought because it wasn't his place to do that.

He frowned.

Of course it was his place. These were his brothers, and while more times than not, he wanted to punch them in their faces, it was still his place to smooth things over. *Hell.*

He wasn't sure he liked all these revelations.

Lucky's fit of temper seemed to leave him as quickly as it had come. "Dixie Mae's sick," Lucky threw out there, and judging from the way he dodged Riley's gaze, that admission was at the heart of his anger. Not the run-in with Logan.

Riley knew Dixie Mae, of course. Lucky and she were rodeo promoters together. But Dixie Mae was old. *Really* old. Like maybe past ninety. Riley would have been more surprised if Lucky had said the woman was in stellar health.

"Is there anything I can do?" Riley asked.

Lucky looked at him then, the corner of his mouth lifting in what Riley had heard some women say was Lucky's panty-dropping smile. "Not a thing, but thanks for offering."

Lucky moved again as if to get into his truck, but he apparently had something else to discuss with Riley because he kept his boots on the ground. "You're spending more time with Claire."

Ah, that. "So are you. You gave her a cat."

"One that was on death row. Maybe it wasn't right at the moment, but if no one had adopted it within the next three months, it would have gone on death row."

"There was a waiting list to adopt it and the other two in the litter," Riley pointed out.

But Lucky just shrugged. "I thought her boy would like it."

Riley was sure Ethan would. In fact, that was why he was so anxious to get back over to Claire's—to see Ethan's reaction. One of the reasons anyway.

"I know you stayed with Claire last night," Lucky went on.

Riley felt a lecture coming on. Lucky was protective when it came to Claire, and he was looking at Riley as if he'd just defiled her. He hadn't. Well, that depended on Lucky's definition of defiled, but he hadn't done anything that Claire hadn't wanted him to do.

Multiple times.

"Daniel still wants to marry her," Lucky went on. So, no lecture after all. "He told Maude Kreppner that when he was checking out at the grocery store."

If Daniel had told Maude, then he wanted it to get around town since Maude was the top spiller of gossip.

But why had Daniel done that?

Riley had to shake his head. "Claire turned down his proposal."

"This time, yeah. But Daniel's thinking that once you're out of the picture—and you will be soon—that he'll be there to help Claire finally get over you for good."

Riley wanted to believe that wouldn't happen, but he had to be realistic. Claire was an attractive young woman. Great in bed. She wouldn't live like a nun just because he was back in uniform. And she did want a home, a family. Daniel just might end up wearing her down with the lure of giving her those things.

"Something to think about, huh?" Lucky said.

No, it wasn't something Riley wanted to think about at all. He definitely didn't want any images in his head of Daniel and Claire.

Too late.

They were there, and he might have found a new use for "Jingle Bells."

Lucky took out a piece of folded paper from his pocket. "Before I go, Claire asked me to ask around about a guy named Rocky."

"Her father," Riley said.

Lucky nodded. "Anyway, I asked Maude since she seems to remember every dribble of gossip and news that's ever spread through town. We don't need archives with Maude around. She remembered his last name and the rest of the stuff I jotted down there." He paused.

"You can decide whether or not it's a good idea to give to Claire."

Shit.

If it was good, Lucky would have no doubt done the honors himself, and after the journal experience, Riley wasn't sure she was ready for anything bad.

"It wouldn't be right to keep it from her," Lucky added, and this time he did get in the truck. That's when Riley noticed he already had his bag inside. Packed. It was stuffed to the point of bulging.

Riley couldn't argue with Lucky about it not being right, but it might not be right to put her through another emotional wringer, either.

"One more thing." Lucky started the engine, shut the door and finished what he was saying through the open window. "If you break Claire's heart, I'll have to punch you, hard. Like, right in the nuts."

Yes, he knew that. Lucky would consider it his duty to punch him.

And Riley would let him.

"You do know I will hunt you down if you hurt Claire," Livvy said.

For Riley it was a déjà vu moment because Livvy's threatening call had come less than an hour after Lucky's nuts-punch-threatening goodbye. At first Riley hadn't been certain why the woman was calling him, but Livvy hadn't wasted even a greeting before she'd launched right into the reason.

"I don't want her hurt," Riley assured her.

"Wanting and making sure it doesn't happen are two different things. Claire's vulnerable right now."

"I know. But unless she's told you something different, she wants to be with me. No strings attached."

"Bullocks. She'd take those strings in a second if you offered them to her. And, no, I know you can't, but you can do this the right way."

"Then tell me what the right way is." Riley was serious, too. He'd never thought he'd ask for love advice from Livvy, but he was open to suggestions.

"Offer her an out. She won't take it, but it'll remind her that you're worried about how deep this shit is you're both stepping in and tracking all over her life."

An out? Instead of asking Livvy to tell him the right way, maybe he should have said he was open to *good* suggestions. That didn't sound like a good one since Claire had been the one to put this sex pact together. If he offered her an out now, she might interpret that as his thinking she sucked in bed.

And she didn't.

Nor did she suck on the kitchen table.

"If you hurt her," Livvy went on, "I'm coming after you with a set of rusty pliers, and I won't be using them on your teeth."

Riley couldn't help it. He winced. But thankfully he didn't have to listen to the details of what Livvy planned to do with those pliers because she hung up, leaving Riley to sit there and wonder if every single human being on the planet knew he'd slept with Claire.

And that latest threat wasn't the end to the unpleasant parts of what had otherwise been a pleasant day. Riley had some manning up to do. He needed to talk to Daniel about Claire, but the question was—how should he do that?

He'd have to do this face-to-face, which was the reason Riley had stopped in town when he'd seen Daniel's car in front of his real estate office. He'd parked up the block, though, to give himself a few minutes to figure how to work this out. It was getting late, well past eight, so it was possible Daniel was in there doing paperwork and not with a client. Riley hoped so anyway. This wasn't something he wanted to discuss in front of an audience.

There wasn't a man-rule about manning up, but Riley didn't need a rule to let him know that he had to own up to having slept with Claire without actually saying he'd slept with her. Something like that was Claire's to tell, but Riley also knew he'd have to let Daniel know the other man-rule had been broken.

Don't take anything that wasn't his.

Claire hadn't been his, but then she hadn't exactly been Daniel's, either. Not after turning down his proposal.

"Need a drink before you go in there?" someone asked. Trisha.

Hell. With all his special ops training, Riley should have heard a woman in high heels walking up to his car. He needed to get back to par with his observation skills because if he had heard, he could have avoided this conversation with Trisha by going straight into the office.

Riley lowered the window and hoped this would be a short conversation. But Trisha leaned against his car. Thankfully, that wasn't a come-and-get-me look in her eye. More like sympathy.

Great.

That meant she'd likely heard about Riley staying the night with Claire. Maybe she even knew about both times. Of course, he hadn't expected something like that to stay quiet. Anyone driving by Claire's house would have seen his car. Or Daniel's for the first overnight stay.

"Daniel's upset, you know," Trisha said. "I probably should be, too. After all, I thought you were with Jodi.

Jodi thought you were with her, too, but it turns out we were both wrong."

And she waited for Riley to verify something he had no intention of verifying. Instead, he got out of the car.

"I'll be seeing you, Trisha," he said.

But she trailed along beside him. "You should probably wait a day or two before talking to Daniel. I heard from Maude that he wasn't taking this well. He especially didn't take it well when he found out Claire had bought that deluxe box of condoms on sale at the convenience store."

Riley didn't stop walking, but that slowed him down a bit. Claire hadn't mentioned the box of condoms, probably because he'd brought one, but damn it, just the thought of her doing such a thing nearly gave him a hard-on.

Coupled with Lucky's threat to punch him, his own threat to punch himself if he did indeed break her heart, Riley wasn't sure what the hell he was going to do. Have sex with her again and then beat himself up? Sadly, that was the best solution he could think of because he wasn't going to be the one to end the sex pact with Claire. She would have to do that.

"The clerk said he'd never seen Claire buy condoms before," Trisha added. She paused, but Riley stayed mum.

"If you don't mind, I think I should talk to Daniel alone," Riley told her.

"You're sure? I mean, if it comes to blows, I could be there to stop it. I don't want you to hurt your shoulder."

Neither did he, but if Daniel started throwing his fists, Riley didn't want an audience for that. Especially an audience who would blab it to Claire before Riley could even make it to her house.

"I'm sure," Riley insisted, and he waited for Trisha to leave before he finished walking to Daniel's door.

The building was an old midcentury glass front so it was easy to see inside through the wall of windows. There was a desk where it looked as if a receptionist would usually be. No receptionist now, though, but there was an office just behind the desk. Riley went inside and headed there. Since the door wasn't fully closed, he pushed it open.

And got a big eyeful.

Earful, too.

Daniel shrieked, a very unmanly sound, probably because his bare ass was facing the door. Probably, too, because there was a naked woman beneath him on the desk. She didn't shriek, but she did curse, and it was both a profanity and a voice that Riley recognized.

Jodi.

Daniel got up, scrambling to get dressed. Jodi didn't scramble. Despite the fact that she was naked, too, she got up off the desk as if doing a leisurely stroll in the park.

"You should have knocked," Daniel growled.

Riley gave him a flat look. "You should have locked the door. Or at least closed it all the way."

However, Riley could see how this had all played out because something similar had played out between Claire and him the night before. He'd taken her on the kitchen table, which wasn't that much different from a desk.

Huffing and puffing enough to blow a house down, Daniel got dressed and then took Riley by the arm to lead him back into the reception area. He shut the door between them and Jodi.

"What happened in there wasn't planned," Daniel said, removing his hand from Riley so he could fling it back toward the office where he'd left a naked Jodi. "Jodi came by to comfort me because I was upset."

"About Claire and me. I heard. That's why I came, too.

To tell you in person that the man-rule had been broken. But now it appears it's been doubly broken."

"How can you say that? Jodi and you broke up."

"So did Claire and you," Riley reminded him.

"That's temporary."

"What if it's temporary between Jodi and me?" It wasn't, but Riley was making a point here.

Point taken judging from the way Daniel's face got red and sweaty. Of course, that could have been from the sex on the desk.

"So, we're at a stalemate," Daniel concluded.

Were they? Riley had enough unresolved situations without continuing this one with Daniel. So, no, it wasn't a stalemate.

"The man-pact is null and void because I'm seeing Claire again," he told Daniel, and he spoke slowly enough so that neither Daniel nor Jodi would miss a word. Jodi was almost certainly listening at the door. "And I'll continue seeing Claire as long as she wants. Or until I leave, whichever comes first. In fact, I'm headed to her place now."

"To use all those condoms she bought at the convenience store." Daniel's face got redder. "I'll bet she didn't tell you they were on sale."

Riley wasn't sure what that had to do with anything and was afraid to ask. It was time for him to get out of there.

"You'll just break her heart," Daniel said as he was walking away.

"So I've heard," Riley mumbled.

"And you know what I'll do to you if that happens."

Riley did know. He'd just punch him, but Daniel would apparently have to wait in line to do that—behind

Lucky's fist and Livvy's pliers. God knew how many people were ready and willing to maim him for Claire's sake.

Finally, Riley started back toward his car, and that meant he'd see Claire in just a matter of minutes. However, the thought alone must have tempted fate because his phone rang. He glanced at the screen and cursed.

Hell.

What now?

WELL, THIS WAS not what Claire had in mind when she'd offered Riley sex. She'd expected him to take her up on the offer, and he had. For one night anyway. Two if she counted the no-condom night before the offer. But she hadn't heard a peep from him since he'd left that morning.

Of course she thought the worst.

But in her mind, there were several worsts, including but not limited to that he was dead in a ditch somewhere. She wasn't certain why her mind always paired unexplained absences with ditches and death, but she did.

Ditches and worst-case scenarios aside, she had another problem. One that she hadn't actually thought through when she'd started this affair with Riley—if one and a half times could be considered an affair, that is. And what she hadn't thought through were the logistics of having hot sex with a toddler in the house. Certainly, parents had figured out a way to accomplish an orgasm or two, but they must have adjusted.

Definitely no sex on the kitchen table.

Probably minimal moaning, too. Claire hadn't realized until she'd been with Riley that she was a moaner.

"Riley?" Ethan asked.

Had she said Riley's name aloud again? If so, she needed to watch that. Because now that Riley was paired with sex in her mind, Claire didn't want any naughty words tumbling out of her mouth when Ethan was around.

"I don't think Riley's coming tonight," she answered, and Ethan seemed to understand that. He frowned, kept playing his newly created game of chase van Gogh—or just Gogh as he was now calling the kitty—with a toy van while he chanted, "Go, go, go."

Claire was sure she frowned, too, and nearly broke her hand reaching for the phone when it rang. Not Riley. Livvy. Claire moaned again, but this time there was nothing orgasmic about it.

"Has he called yet?" Livvy asked.

Livvy didn't have to clarify the *he* or the *yet* because this was Livvy's third call of the evening to see if Riley had shown. Something was up, and while Claire had been too preoccupied with her ditch-and-death fears, she hadn't noticed that Livvy was on edge. But she noticed it now.

"All right, what's up?" Claire demanded.

Silence. Never a good thing with two-year-olds, kittens or best friends.

"I might have scared Riley off earlier," Livvy finally answered.

Her stomach went to her kneecaps. "You did what?"

More silence. "I called him and told him he'd better not break your heart. I might have implied a threat."

Claire groaned. "Not the rusty pliers again." It was one of Livvy's favorite threats when a guy dumped her. She'd never go through with it, of course, but it couldn't have been fun for Riley to hear. But it was just a threat. "That alone wouldn't have scared Riley off," Claire insisted.

"No, but I'm pretty sure Lucky threatened him, too. And maybe Daniel."

Sheez. Lucky she understood. It was a brotherly thing to do. But Daniel? "When did Daniel see Riley?"

More silence. "Uh, how much gossip do you want to hear?"

Claire wasn't sure. "Is the gossip related to Riley?"

"Yes."

She debated it. Gossip rarely left her feeling good, and her mood already sucked. "All right, spill it but only if it really relates to Riley. I don't want to hear any sidelines like bad wax jobs or crabs."

"Crabs?" Livvy latched right on to that. "Who has crabs?"

According to the gas station attendant, apparently one of the Nederlands did, but Livvy had already missed the point. "That's not related to Riley or me. Or you."

Another round of silence, but Claire figured that was because Livvy was only trying to pick through whatever it was she'd heard. There was a lot of gossip floating around at the moment.

"According to Trisha," Livvy finally continued, "Riley caught Daniel fudging Jodi in his office. On his desk."

Her heart nearly tumbled out of her chest. That was definitely relevant gossip. "Did they get in a fight? Is Riley hurt?" And better yet, was Riley crushed that he'd caught Jodi with another man?

That was really the key point here. The next key point was that Claire was having trouble picturing Daniel and Jodi together that way... *Nope.* She pictured it, and she wished she hadn't. Not because she cared if Daniel had sex with Jodi, but because she didn't want the naked image in her head of them having sex on a desk.

And here Daniel usually kept his desk neat as a pin.

She'd never be able to look at that desk again, or his office, without that image popping up.

"There was no fight that Trisha could tell, but she was watching from a distance. Maybe even through binoculars since she said she couldn't tell what they were saying because she doesn't lip read."

Claire nearly asked for more as to how Trisha knew all of this, but she already had too many details to sort through. "So, if there was no fight, then what happened?"

"Trisha said Daniel and Riley talked, or rather they argued. She said Daniel's face got all red, and after they talked for a while longer, Riley stormed out."

Stormed? That meant he was upset. Maybe upset about Jodi having sex with Daniel. Maybe upset about whatever Daniel had said to him. For the first time since she'd become aware of the gossip epidemic in Spring Hill, Claire wished Trisha had gotten more info.

"What was Jodi doing during all of this?" Claire asked.

"Getting dressed. Trisha said she didn't come out and talk to Riley after he found Daniel and her bare-assed naked."

Poor Riley. Even though he had broken off things with Jodi, that would have given him a jolt. Ditto for the argument he would have no doubt had with Daniel. No wonder he'd stormed off.

"Are you okay?" Livvy asked. "Want me to come over?"

"No. I'm fine."

"You're sure? Because I can cancel my date with the actor."

Despite her own troubles, Claire caught that last word. "You have a date with an actor?"

"A wannabe actor," she clarified. "It's a match from the dating site. But I can cancel it—"

"No. Go on your date and have fun. I'm fine. Bye,

Livvy." And she hit the end call button before Livvy could keep arguing.

Livvy would know that she wasn't fine and just might show up anyway. Too bad because Claire thought it would make her feel a smidge better if one of them wasn't miserable. Thankfully, Ethan hadn't noticed that his mommy was in the miserable mode. He kept playing the go game with Gogh.

Claire stared at her phone, wondering if she should just call Riley and ask him about his encounter with Daniel and Jodi. Of course, then she'd have to mention the gossip she'd heard, and he would feel obligated to talk about it. If they'd been in a real relationship, that would have been okay. But with a relationship based purely on no-commitment sex, he probably wouldn't want to discuss finding his ex with another man.

Especially since Jodi might not stay his ex.

She had to be realistic about this. If Riley went back overseas, he'd likely run into Jodi again. Hadn't he said something about them being together for years and that their paths crossed often? Their paths would cross again when they were back to their normal lives.

When Claire wasn't in the picture.

And that ex status might go right out the door of the helicopter. Claire knew Daniel was banking on that, too. He'd chatted up the store clerk about how he still wanted to marry her. She doubted Daniel was thinking about that when he was fudging Jodi on his desk.

Maybe the cosmos was actually tuned in to her tonight because Claire stared at her phone so long that it dinged. A text message.

From Riley.

Before she'd heard the sex-on-the-desk gossip, she would have jumped to look at the text, but she took her time, and a few deep breaths, before she touched her phone screen so she could read it.

It didn't take long.

Something's come up, Riley texted. Will call you to-morrow.

Oh, no. That definitely didn't sound like good news. Still, she kept her reply short.

OK, she texted back.

But it wasn't okay. Claire felt as if an elephant and a dozen of his biggest friends had just sat on her heart.

CHAPTER TWENTY-ONE

IF LIVVY KEPT UP her ice-cream therapy, Claire was going to have to buy some bigger clothes. Still, it was hard to fault something that worked. She no longer felt as if she had elephants sitting on her heart; they were now on her stomach.

Just as Claire had thought, Livvy had ditched her date and dropped by the night before, and she'd brought lots of sugary goodies and wine with her. After a pint of Ben & Jerry's Karamel Sutra and a wine so sweet and cheap that it was only one step above Kool-Aid, she and Livvy had collapsed into a sugar coma.

When her alarm had gone off the following morning— the alarm being Ethan calling out for her—Claire had felt like jumping right out of bed. The sugar coma hadn't left her wrung out and bloated. Claire had gotten up ready to finish sorting through the rest of the boxes.

Therapy to keep her mind off Riley.

Livvy knew that, of course. Thankfully, Ethan didn't. While Claire sorted and fought off the bad thoughts, her son was teaching Gogh to color.

On the van Gogh painting.

Since Claire had decided to cut her losses and toss the Baby Genius packet, she figured Ethan might as well get to do something FUN! with them. And he was. Gogh, too. Ethan added more gold blob stars to the painting while Gogh batted the crayons around like elongated soccer balls.

Livvy wasn't quite into the coloring activities, the crayon batting or the box sorting. She hadn't dodged the sugar-coma bullet. She was on her back on the floor, her body stretched out like a corpse, and she had a washcloth on her face. She occasionally mumbled something about drinking the Kool-Aid.

What Livvy hadn't brought up was Riley.

But Trisha had.

Apparently, Trisha thought she hadn't spread the story of Daniel and Jodi to enough people because at 8:01 a.m., she'd called Claire to offer her *sympathies*. Or so Trisha had said. Claire wouldn't have minded the call if Trisha had managed to give her any useful information about Riley, but the only revelation Claire had gotten from the woman was that Jodi had skedaddled—and yes, Trisha had used that particular word—shortly after Riley left. It was possible that Jodi was going after him.

That information wasn't useful.

It only added to the gloom and doom Claire already felt. Thankfully, the contents of the boxes were giving her short distractions. A ball of rubber bands. Some old construction paper. And a stack of valentine's cards that Claire had gotten when she was in third grade. They were the kinds of cards that came twenty-five to a pack. One was from Riley—it had combat robot–looking things on it. There were four from Daniel. All of those had kittens and hearts.

She hoped the number ratio wasn't some kind of omen for her future, that Daniel cared for her four times more than Riley did.

Claire moved on to another box. It was the next to the last, and while she went through that one—more Valentine and Christmas cards—Ethan finished his coloring project and decided to help. He tipped the final box on its side, spilling the contents on the floor and on Gogh. Gogh treated that like an adventure, too, and started batting everything including her own tail.

Then Claire saw it.

The cigar box. It'd been her "treasure" box from her childhood, and she'd painted it purple and had glued sequins on it. The sequins had long fallen off, but she could still see the glue bits. Could also see where she'd written her name and *keep out* in permanent marker.

Claire shoved the other things aside to get to the cigar box, and all that shoving alerted Livvy because she sat up. "Did you find something?"

"Maybe."

With Ethan and Livvy both watching her, Claire opened the cigar box, and the first thing she saw was a picture. It was of Daniel, Riley and her. With her in the middle, of course. Riley's mother had snapped the shot while they were at the county fair and had had an extra print made for Claire. It was the very photo Claire had studied years later as she'd chosen between the two.

And, yes, Riley was hot.

Not just in that picture but also the ones beneath it. There were six photos in all. One was of them eating watermelon on the Fourth of July. Another was of them at the Christmas parade, all bundled up with knit caps and heavy coats. Claire hadn't even remembered putting the pictures in the box, but she was glad she had. It was like a little time capsule.

She rummaged through the box and found other treasures. The cheap heart-shaped necklace Daniel had given her in fifth grade. A pretty blue river rock that Riley had found one time when his dad had taken them all fishing. A dried flower she'd picked on that trip.

Claire worked her way through all the bits and pieces and nearly missed the white envelope. That's because at first it looked like the bottom of the cigar box. It wasn't.

"Is that what I think it is?" Livvy asked. "*The* letter?"

"Maybe." She certainly didn't remember putting a letter in the box, mainly because she'd never gotten a letter. And maybe she still hadn't. Because this one wasn't addressed to her.

But rather to her grandmother.

However, her gran had put a sticky note over the top of her own name and had written three words: "Keep for Claire."

"Is it from your mother?" Livvy didn't scoot closer, but she was volleying glances between the envelope and Claire.

Claire shook her head. "It's not the same handwriting as the journal." Which meant this could be from her father.

Oh, God.

Was she ready for this? Especially since it might be another rant about the pregnancy, and therefore a rant about Claire herself.

"Want me to read it for you?" Livvy volunteered.

Did she? Claire was still debating that when she heard the knock at the door. *Riley.* And despite the fact that she had just found the very thing she'd been searching for, seeing Riley felt a lot more important.

Claire hurried to the door, threw it open and wished she'd checked out the window first. She still would have opened the door, but she would have steeled herself up first.

Because it was Jodi.

"Punch me," Jodi greeted her, outstretching her arms.

Claire glanced around the porch to see if the woman was alone. She was. Then Claire looked at her to try to figure out what the heck was going on.

"Go ahead," Jodi prompted. "Punch me."

Claire actually considered it. For a very brief moment anyway. But only because she was still jealous about that earlier thought of Jodi and Riley getting back together. However, it was a fleeting notion that Claire resisted. She'd already been in a pub brawl and didn't want to add a fistfight to the list of her life regrets.

Livvy hurried into the room. "I'll punch her for you," she volunteered.

But Claire waved her off. "Can you make sure Ethan doesn't get into anything in those boxes?"

Livvy hesitated, but Claire knew in the end that watching Ethan would win out when it came to punching Jodi's face. *Barely.* Livvy might still try a face punch later, though. Unlike Claire, Livvy didn't mind adding such things to her own life experiences.

"I was with Daniel," Jodi said, her arms still outstretched and waiting for that punch.

"I heard." Claire pushed down the woman's arms because she didn't want to hear the kind of gossip that it would create if anyone saw her. Trisha could be out there somewhere with her binoculars.

"Then you know you have every right to punch me," Jodi concluded.

"Uh, no. Daniel's free to have sex with whomever he wants."

Jodi frowned, pulled back her shoulders. "You're sure about that? Daniel said you two were probably getting back together."

At least Daniel had remembered to include the *probably*. "We're not getting back together."

And the fates aligned again to remind Claire—and hopefully Jodi, too—as to why that wasn't happening. Riley pulled his car into the driveway.

Claire immediately saw the concern on his face, and he didn't exactly run to the porch, but it was close.

"Everything okay?" he asked.

Claire nodded. "Jodi was just here so I could punch her for sleeping with Daniel. I declined," she added.

Maybe Riley heard what she said, but if he did, he didn't show it. Instead, he hooked his arm around Claire, pulled her to him and kissed her into the middle of next week.

RILEY HADN'T PLANNED on kissing Claire at the door. He'd planned on doing that later. But he realized this was his chance to clarify to Jodi how things were.

Or at least how Riley hoped they were.

He'd missed Claire, and even though their relationship was temporary, it was best for Jodi to understand that he was with Claire, not her. And Jodi got it all right. When Riley finally broke the lip-lock with Claire, he saw the thunderstruck look in Jodi's eyes. Maybe because he'd never kissed her like that. Heck, he'd never kissed any woman like that. Claire was looking a little thunderstruck, too.

"Um, I just came to apologize to Claire," Jodi said, "but I'll be going." She didn't just go, though. She stared at them, and while still staring, she made her way down the steps. Walking backward so that she kept her eyes on them the whole time.

Riley didn't wait to watch her drive away. That kiss with Claire had been so good that he pulled her inside for another one. A much shorter one this time because Livvy, Ethan and the kitten were there, all staring at Claire and him.

"Riley!" Ethan squealed, and he raced toward them. Riley broke his grip on Claire so he could scoop him up. And so he could give him the toy car in his pocket. A 1967 yellow Firebird that was the same color as the kitten. The moment Riley had spotted it online, he'd ordered it with rush delivery.

Ethan rattled off his version of thank you, smacked a kiss on Riley's cheek and then took off running the moment Riley set his feet back on the floor. No doubt to add the car to his stash.

"I'll just check on him," Livvy said, going off after Ethan. With all the gossip that was no doubt going around about Daniel and Jodi, Livvy probably thought Claire and he needed to talk privately. But what he really wanted to do was just kiss Claire again.

So, he did.

Oh, man. She tasted good, like birthday cake and Christmas candy all rolled into one. She looked just as good, too. Well, with the exception of some dust in her hair and a bit of concern in her eyes. Concern no doubt caused by how he was reacting to the gossip.

"I can't stay long. I have something I need to do for Logan. But I wanted to tell you that I'm over Jodi," he let her know right off. Although he and Jodi had never been serious enough for him to have to get over.

She nodded. Whether she actually believed him was anyone's guess. "Trisha saw what happened, and she's been spreading the *news.*"

Of course. Riley should have guessed that Trisha would have hung around, waiting to see how things played out between Daniel and him, and that glass front

on Daniel's office building would have given her a good
view. Heck, Trisha might have even seen Jodi and Daniel go in before Riley arrived, and then stood back and
waited for the chaos to begin. And she'd likely been disappointed that there hadn't actually been any chaos.

"What about you?" he asked. "How are you handling
this?"

She kissed him. It was such a great way of communicating, and Riley wished he had time to deepen this
communication in bed. That wouldn't happen with Livvy
and Ethan around. Plus, the new cutter would be arriv-
ing at the ranch soon, and Riley needed to be there to
show him around.

Claire paused the kiss, looked up at him. While standing really close to him. Like with her body right against
his. "I was worried when you didn't come by last night.
I thought maybe Daniel and you had gotten into a fight."

"No fight. I've been at the hospital all night with
Lucky."

The concern in her eyes quadrupled. So did the body
contact. She went right into his arms.

"Lucky's okay," Riley explained. "His business partner had a heart attack, and Lucky was shaken up. He
called and asked me to stay with him. Dixie Mae's out
of the woods. The doctor's pulled her through."

Some of that concern turned to relief. "I'll call Lucky
later and see if there's anything I can do."

That was Claire. Kind, thoughtful. Soft. Her breasts
were right against his chest so he could feel two good
examples of that softness.

"So, what have you been doing all morning?" he
asked. "Other than kissing me and getting visits from
Jodi?"

He expected her to say something sexual. Something

naughty, even. Because if she didn't, Riley certainly intended to do that. Not that he could do any of those naughty things. He had fifteen minutes at most, and that wasn't enough time to drag Claire off somewhere. But the new look she got in her eyes wasn't remotely naughty, and she pulled back to make eye contact with him.

"I found the letter," she said.

The letter. The one that hadn't been on Riley's radar because he was too busy building a sex fantasy with Claire.

"I haven't read it yet," Claire continued, "but I'm positive it's the one Gran mentioned on the calendar."

So was he, and he wanted to come clean. Not just about the letter but also the note Lucky had given him about her father. But that would have to keep. And, no, it wasn't because it would ruin what was left of the sexual fantasy. It was because after they talked about those things, Claire would likely fall apart.

Fifteen minutes wasn't enough time to fix that.

"Any chance I can cook you dinner?" he asked. And talk to her. And sleep with her. "It's Della and Stella's night off. Lucky will be at the hospital, and Logan will be at his loft in town. You and Ethan could maybe even stay the night."

Yes, he was blatantly offering her sex along with that package deal. Just in case she didn't pick up on that, he kissed her again.

Message received.

At least it was until Livvy cleared her throat. "I'm taking Ethan out for ice cream."

Ethan clapped. "Ice cream!"

"How about just going to the farmer's market for some fruits and veggies instead?" Claire said.

Ethan wasn't enthusiastic about that at all.

Livvy nodded. "Veggies first and then a small cone. How does that sound?"

Ethan clapped again. Livvy grabbed her purse, Ethan's hand and headed out the door.

Later, Riley would thank Livvy, but for now, he didn't want to waste a single moment of those remaining fifteen minutes. Or waste a footstep. He shut the door, locked it, and with Claire and he already grappling to get closer, Riley pulled her to the living room floor.

CHAPTER TWENTY-TWO

OTHER THAN THE rug burns on her butt, there was a lot to be said for quickie sex.

A lot not to be said for it, too.

No cuddling, and since the quickie had taken nearly twenty minutes, that meant Riley had been late for his appointment with the horse trainer. He'd dressed and hurried out of the house, leaving her with a smile but also wanting a whole lot more.

Like maybe a second orgasm for starters.

Plus, they hadn't really had a chance to talk about the letter. She'd wanted his advice about whether or not she should read it. She hadn't wanted to turn her feelings about reading it into how she felt after reading most of her mother's journal. But if it was bad, then why would Gran have made a note to give it to her?

Of course, Gran hadn't actually given it to her, and maybe she had done that because she'd known it would upset her.

And it still might.

However, while Livvy was off with Ethan on their ice-cream run—which might or might not include veggies—Claire decided to woman-up and read it. If it caused her to crumble, then so be it, but the quickie sex hadn't just given her an amazing orgasm, it had also apparently made her fearless.

She went back to the sorting room/nursery and picked up the letter. Her fearlessness took a little dip when she actually had it in her hands, but she opened it anyway. One page. Handwritten. Not her mother's handwriting. Probably not her father's, either. This was a child's scrawl so her attention zoomed to the signature on the bottom on the page.

Riley McCord.

Riley had written the letter? Riley? Like Claire, he would have been just ten years old at the time, so why had he written Gran a letter? Riley and Gran saw each other almost daily. Anything he wanted to say, he could have said to her in person.

Couldn't he?

Claire's fearlessness turned to shock, and she sank down on the floor to read it.

Dear Mrs. Davidson,
I feel real bad about Claire not having any folks. I know she loves you, but it's not the same as having a mom and dad, like me. So, I talked to my mom and dad, and we all think they could be Claire's mom and dad too.

Oh.
The tears came. So did the warm feeling that blanketed her from head to toe. Claire certainly hadn't seen this coming, and she kept reading, eating up each word that Riley had written two decades ago.

If you don't mind and if you think Claire would like that, I want her to be part of my family. What do you think? Check yes or no.

The tears had filled her eyes, but Claire could see that Riley had drawn four sets of square boxes. Each set had a yes and no box. The first set was for him.

Which he had checked yes.

The second set was for his mom and dad. Another yes check.

The third was for Gran. And she had checked yes, too.

The last set of boxes was for Claire. It was empty and waiting for her.

There was only one more line at the bottom after Riley's signature.

PS: Don't give this to Claire until her birthday.

But Gran hadn't given it to her. Why? Had she simply forgotten about it?

No.

It was a lifetime ago, but Claire's mind went back to that birthday. That was around the time Daniel's parents had started including her in more of their family gatherings. In fact, his parents had given her a tenth birthday party. Since Riley had gone to that party, maybe he'd thought the offer of his parents was no longer necessary. Too bad. Because that would have been an incredible birthday present.

Still was.

Riley had obviously cared for her a long time. Of course, as a child she hadn't been able to see it, but she could certainly see it now.

She tucked the letter in her pocket and went to the door when she heard Livvy and Ethan coming up the steps of the porch. Judging from the volume and intensity of the giggling, no veggies had been consumed today. But that didn't matter. Smiling, Claire walked to the door, not in a hurry, but rather taking her time to look at the wallpaper-free walls. The floors that she'd finished. The fresh coats of paint.

The house itself.

People had always said the house had good bones, and it did. But it had a whole lot more than that.

Livvy opened the door cautiously as if concerned Ethan and she would walk in on a naked mommy and Riley. No nakedness. Just Claire smiling. Her smile must have looked a little off balance, though, because Livvy looked concerned.

"He only had one scoop," Livvy said, motioning toward the smears of chocolate ice cream around Ethan's mouth. Ethan took off running after Gogh.

"It's okay." Claire couldn't help it. She kept smiling. It felt as if everything had suddenly become crystal clear.

"Well?" Livvy asked, bobbling her eyebrows.

Normally, Claire didn't like to spill any sex details to Livvy, but she'd make a small exception this time. "It was great."

Perfect in fact. Despite her butt burns, those twenty minutes had been amazing. Better yet, she was going to get more than twenty minutes of amazing tonight when she went to Riley's for dinner.

Claire wasn't sure how long their sex agreement would last, and she decided not to worry about it. She couldn't hog-tie Riley and make him stay, but now that she knew just how much he cared about her, how much he'd always cared, she would just enjoy every minute she had with him.

"That's a big smile," Livvy observed. "Did something else happen? Like maybe a marriage proposal?"

Claire waved that off. "I read the letter."

That got rid of some of the joy and speculation on

Livvy's face. "You what? You did that while Riley was here?"

"No. After he left. But it's okay, Livvy. Everything's okay." Claire looked around and knew exactly what she wanted to do. "I've decided not to sell the house. I'm moving back home."

THERE WAS ONE last thing Riley needed to do before his hot date with Claire, and it wasn't something he especially wanted to do. However, he had to give Claire the note from Lucky, and Riley didn't want to wait and have her have to deal with it during dinner. Best to clear it out of the way rather than risk having it spoil the entire evening. Of course, she'd be surprised to see him so soon after their sex-by-the-door encounter. Even more surprised when she read the note. But Riley hadn't imagined there'd be a surprised look on his own face when he arrived at her place.

Surprise from seeing Daniel's car in front of her house.

Not now. He'd already had too many doses of Daniel in the past couple of weeks.

Riley spotted his old friend right away because Daniel was on the porch. Claire, in the doorway. Well, it didn't appear to be another proposal unless Claire was signing a prenup. Or maybe a restraining order. Judging from the glare Daniel gave him, it was the latter.

"She's not selling the house," Daniel snarled, and he took the clipboard of papers from her and hurried off the porch.

"I'd done some initial paperwork with him for the listing," Claire explained, motioning toward a fleeing Daniel. "I had to cancel it, and that required my signature. Or so he said."

Ah. Maybe Daniel had tried to use it as an excuse to sneak in another proposal after all.

"You're really not selling?" Riley asked at the same moment that Claire asked, "What are you doing here?"

"I just dropped by to give you something," he answered. "But you're really not selling the place?" Riley repeated.

"Nope." And she seemed pretty happy and sure about that, too. *Good.* Then Riley was happy for her, as well.

"What about your business, though?"

"Not a problem. I can run it from here just as well as San Antonio. Ethan's not here," Claire added when Riley looked around. "Livvy took him and the kitten home with her."

"Again?" Riley hated to sound so disappointed, and then he remembered he was cooking dinner for Claire at his place so this was a good thing. She opened her mouth to say something, but he kissed her. This was really shaping up to be a great day, and Riley hated to ruin it, but this was something she needed to know.

"Lucky asked me to give you this," he said, taking the note from his pocket.

He didn't have to clarify. Claire took one look at the note, another look at his expression, and any trace of her smile disappeared. "It's about Rocky, my father."

Riley nodded. "Lucky said you wanted him to ask around. He did, and that's what he found."

"It's bad?" she asked, studying his eyes.

He lifted his shoulder. Nodded.

She handed him back the note. "Just tell me what it says, then."

All right. Riley wished there was a good way to say this. There wasn't. "Maude remembered Rocky. She thought his last name was Lambert, but Lucky did some checking, and it was Landrum. Rocky Landrum. He had cousins in the county but never lived here."

"Was, had, lived," she repeated. She paused, gathered her breath. "He's dead?"

"Yeah." Riley gave her a moment to let that sink in. "But there's some good news in this. Possibly good," he amended. "Rocky got a job working on an offshore oil rig when he found out your mother was pregnant." Riley had to pause. "He was killed his first week out there in a freak accident. No one told your mother because she wasn't listed as his next of kin."

Claire stayed quiet a moment. "That's why he never came back."

Yes, and all her mother's anger over being abandoned was for nothing. Because Rocky hadn't abandoned her, or Claire, after all. In fact, it appeared Rocky had gotten the job so he could support Claire and her mother. Riley hoped she would see the silver lining in that, but the bottom line was her father was dead.

She tried to smile, stepped back and held up her finger in a give-me-a-second gesture. "I'm okay," she insisted. "Knowing is better."

In a day or two, she might actually believe that.

Riley was about to try to hug her again and to ask if she needed a rain check on their dinner plans but his phone rang, and he fished it from his pocket. His heart stopped a moment when he looked at the screen, and he saw the number for Colonel Becker.

"I'd better take this on the porch," Riley said, and he went outside. "Captain McCord," he answered.

"Just got a call from your new commanding officer, Colonel Hagan. You need to report to the base at fifteen thirty today for a physical."

Fifteen thirty? That was three thirty civilian time and

just two hours from now. "The physical was scheduled for next week," Riley reminded him. Eight more days. Eight more days that Riley needed to get ready.

"Sorry, but there was a change in plans. Someone put the wrong date on your medical leave. The flight surgeon will do the physical, and if you pass it, be ready to report to duty ASAP."

The colonel didn't say good luck or any other farewell. He just hung up, leaving Riley to stand there, stunned, with the phone still pressed to his ear.

He finally turned, ready to tell Claire the news, but she was in the doorway, her hands bracketed on each side of the jamb. She wasn't crying, but it seemed to him that she was blinking awfully fast, maybe to stave off some tears. Maybe because she just didn't know how else to react.

"I heard," Claire said.

CHAPTER TWENTY-THREE

THERE WERE PLENTY of thoughts going through Riley's head. The physical that he'd just taken. The results that were in a computer file, a file that he'd know all about as soon as Colonel Hagan briefed him.

Whenever that would be.

It was already past normal duty hours, but the colonel was apparently still tied up with meetings. His exec officer had told Riley to wait in the outer office, that the colonel would see him as soon as he was free.

There were so many questions about his future. So much riding on what was going to happen in the next half hour or so. But the one thing that Riley consistently kept seeing was the look on Claire's face when she'd overheard his phone call. In a way her overhearing it had made it a little easier.

Because Riley hadn't had to say the words aloud.

Hadn't had to answer her questions, either, because she hadn't asked any. Claire had simply kissed him goodbye and asked him to call her when he had any news. It was a polite, no-pressure kind of comment.

Sort of like their sex pact.

But Riley figured she had started crying the moment he left. Hopefully she'd called Livvy to bring Ethan home, too. Riley really didn't want her being alone right now. He was, and he knew that sucked.

He had considered calling Lucky, but he was still at

the hospital with Dixie Mae. He hadn't bothered trying to get in touch with Logan, but Riley had told Della and Stella where he was going. Of course, they'd guessed, too, when he'd come out of his bedroom wearing his uniform.

His phone dinged with a text, a reminder for him to turn it off, but he checked the message first. It was from Logan. Anything yet?

So, Della and Stella had already told him. Riley didn't answer because the colonel's door finally opened, and the exec—a young captain—ushered him in. The colonel wasn't alone. Colonel Becker was there. The hospital commander, as well.

Hell. This couldn't be good. It felt more like a firing squad than a meeting.

Riley reported in, and Colonel Hagan immediately asked him to sit. Only Hagan had papers in front of him, which meant the other two had likely been briefed already as to what was going on.

"You didn't pass the physical, Captain," Hagan said. Without any warning or fanfare.

Oh, man. Hearing that nearly knocked the breath right out of him. Riley fought to gather what breath he needed just so he could speak.

"I can retake it," Riley insisted.

The trio mumbled some variation of no. *No*s that went straight to his gut. "The PT and the flight surgeon don't believe you're going to regain the mobility necessary for you to remain a Combat Rescue Officer," Hagan informed him.

There was a term in the Air Force, military bearing, that meant maintaining an outward appearance of being professional, being a serviceman in uniform. Usually it wasn't a big deal to keep his military bearing, but Riley was sure struggling with it now. It took everything he could muster up just to stay seated and not shout out how wrong this was.

"We've already discussed some of this," Becker continued. "It would endanger your crew if you didn't have the mobility needed for your job."

"My experience could make up for it," Riley argued. "And the mobility issue is temporary. I've been working out. The exercises are helping."

"This isn't up for discussion," Hagan snapped. But then his expression softened. "Look, we know this isn't the news you want to hear. We didn't want to hear it, either, but we can't keep you in the Air Force as a Combat Rescue Officer."

The flashbacks came. Probably because his pulse was galloping and his breathing was too fast. But Riley fought them back.

The kid was alive.

Because of him, the kid was alive.

"You have options," Hagan went on, the words droning in Riley's head. "You've fulfilled your active duty service commitment so you can get out, of course. We hope you won't do that. As you said, you have experience you can pass on to others, and that's where the options come in."

Riley didn't want options. He wanted to be a CRO with a shoulder the way it'd been before that damn IED. Because that was repeating in his head now, too, Riley missed the first part of what Hagan said. He didn't miss the second part though.

"You can become an instructor."

There it was. One of those soul-crushing *options*. The Air Force's version of putting him out to pasture.

"Of course, you'd have to continue your physical therapy," the hospital commander said. "You'd still have to pass the standard fitness tests."

"I don't want to instruct," Riley said.

Hagan hardly reacted. Maybe because he'd anticipated it. Maybe because he just didn't give a shit. Riley wondered how the colonel would feel if someone had just told him to give up being what he was.

If someone told him he'd have to be ordinary again.

"There are other career fields," Becker said. "With your aptitude scores and security clearances, you could choose whatever you want."

No, he couldn't. Riley didn't go into the broken record mode and repeat himself, but there was no other job he wanted. No other job that wouldn't feel ordinary after being a CRO.

"Another option would be for you to transfer to the reserves," Becker continued. "You couldn't be a CRO, of course, but you could stay in the local area where I understand you have family."

Weekend Warrior. No, thanks. It was still a huge step down from what he'd been doing.

"We can give you some time to think about it," Hagan said a moment later. "But not much. We'll need to have your decision in the next twenty-four hours."

Somehow Riley nodded. And got to his feet. Somehow he saluted Colonel Hagan and made it to the door.

Keep your military bearing.

He was succeeding, for the most part, until he opened the door and saw Lucky there. Lounging as usual, and he was chatting up a blonde lieutenant who quickly excused herself when she took one look at Riley's face.

"Wanna go get drunk and raise some hell?" Lucky asked, getting to his feet.

"No." There was only one place Riley wanted to be right now, only one person he wanted to see.

Claire.

CLAIRE FORCED HERSELF not to pace while she waited for news. Besides, it wasn't as if she didn't have things to do. The last of the boxes had been sorted, and she needed to find places for the stuff she was keeping. The rest she had to haul to the curb for trash pickup. All in all, it felt like the same thing she'd been doing with her life.

Daniel was out forever.

She was keeping Gran's house, except it'd be her house now. Ethan's and her home. She'd come to a peaceful place with her mom and dad. Not a perfect place. Never would be. But it didn't cut and gnaw at her as it'd done in the past.

In short, things were perfect.

Except for Riley.

She was the one who'd invited him in to her head and bed, and Claire had known right from the start that this day would come. Riley wanted to be back in uniform, and he would be. That would leave her to pick up the pieces of her heart—something she would do.

Somehow.

And that somehow was coming sooner rather than later, she realized, when she saw Riley's car coming up the road to her house. Claire put the box she'd been carrying on the curb and watched him as he got closer and closer. One look at his face, and she knew the physical hadn't gone as he'd wanted.

He parked, got out and walked to her. Without saying a word, he slipped his arm around her waist and got her moving back into the house.

"They want me to retrain into a different career field or become an instructor," he said, looking her straight in the eyes. "Or get out." He paused, his jaw muscles stirring. "I have until tomorrow to make a decision."

Claire only saw this playing out one way. Just one. "You've already made your decision."

He didn't look surprised. Didn't argue. Because it was true. One of the first two things would happen—he'd stay in uniform and become something else. But he wouldn't get out. And that meant he'd be leaving.

Soon.

Riley pulled her closer, brushed a chaste kiss on her forehead. "I'm sorry."

Claire did know he was sorry—for hurting her. But not for the decision he'd made.

"You were up-front with me and everyone else right from the start," she reminded him. "I knew this day would come."

She just hadn't known that it would hurt this much. God, someone had clamped a fist around her heart and wouldn't let go. Still, she had only a matter of hours to spend with Riley, and she didn't want to be crying, moping and aching from the heart crushing.

That would come later. And possibly last a really long time.

"Is Ethan still at Livvy's?" he asked.

Claire nodded. She'd considered having Livvy bring him and Gogh back, but Claire figured if she was going to have a breakdown, she didn't want anyone around to witness it. Or say I told you so. Livvy wouldn't have actually said the words, but it would have been in her friend's eyes.

"Can you stay for a while?" she asked. "Or do you need to tell your family?"

"Lucky knows. He'll tell the others. I have until morning." He gave her another chaste kiss. "But I didn't come here for this to be a drive-by sex call."

Claire tried to be brave. Not that she had an alternative other than that. If she fell apart, Riley would leave knowing he'd done that to her. She preferred him leaving with much better memories. Which meant she'd have some memories to hold on to, as well.

She locked the door. Forced a smile. "Too bad. I've never had a drive-by sex call and was looking forward to it."

Riley shook his head, no doubt ready to tell her that this didn't feel right. Or some other such nonsense. Of course, it didn't feel right. But it soon would. Sex with Riley could make everything feel all right. For a while anyway.

Before he could say anything, Claire slid her hand around his neck and pulled him to her for a kiss. One touch of his mouth, and things were instantly better. A little better anyway. So she kept kissing him until she felt the stiffness ease from his muscles. Until she felt some of her own dark thoughts turn warm and dreamy.

Riley could do that. With just some kisses.

Heck, he could do that by breathing.

She felt the exact moment that he surrendered. Mainly because he took charge of the kissing. He snapped her to him, deepening the kiss until Claire almost expected him to lower her to the floor again.

He didn't.

She and Riley stood there while he lowered the kisses to her neck. *Oh, yes.* To that spot that made her crazy. Maybe that's why he'd put a love bite on it, so he wouldn't have any trouble finding it again.

No more just warm and dreamy. Claire wanted him in her bed. Maybe she even said it aloud because Riley picked her up, and without breaking the neck-kissing assault, he headed there.

"You're sure?" he asked, easing her onto the mattress.

She took out the deluxe box of condoms and slapped them on the nightstand. "I'm sure."

It got the exact reaction she wanted. A smile. Perhaps a little fear.

Claire could have relieved that possible fear by telling him she didn't expect them to go through the whole box, but he kissed her again, and she was beyond something as complex as human speech. The only thing she could do was feel.

And Riley made sure she did plenty of feeling.

This was their fourth time together, and he'd learned all her good spots, not just the one on her neck. He kissed her in each one of them until she could take no more. She almost hated the frenzy inside her as much as she loved it because the frenzy—the need—made her want to rip off their clothes and end this all too fast. Of course, anything, even a snail's pace, would have been too fast.

Because it was the last.

Claire pushed that dismal thought aside. It wasn't hard to do because Riley took off her top and delivered some of those kisses to the very spots he'd kissed seconds earlier through her clothes.

Without the clothes, it was better.

But it built more of that frenzy until Claire couldn't help herself. She got rid of his shirt. Went after his jeans, too, and through it all she tried to grasp on to each memory. The way he looked.

Amazing, by the way.

The way he felt in her arms. His taste. Amazing, too.

She wanted to keep all of that, but at the same time her body was begging for release.

Riley knew what to do about that release thing. He got her naked. One of Claire's favorite parts, and despite what had to be a frenzy in him, too, he slowed down, sliding off her jeans inch by inch, and admiring the view along the way.

Maybe he was trying to hang on to this, as well.

And drive her insane.

Because despite the jumbo box of condoms, he pushed her legs apart and kissed her in the very spot that would indeed make this end too soon. He flicked his tongue in her, causing Claire to curse him. Pull her hair. And try to hold on for the ride. Just when she thought he would finish her this way, Riley surprised her again by stopping and getting one of those condoms.

Thankfully, he was fast at putting it on because Claire no longer wanted to hang on. Or so she thought. When he pushed inside her, she changed her mind for just a second. She did want it to last for more than the couple of seconds that her body was urging her to last. Too bad she couldn't bottle this sensation and then she could walk around with a goofy look on her face all the time.

Too bad she couldn't bottle Riley.

He kissed her when he moved inside her. Slowly at first. No urgency. As if they had years to finish this. Of course, slow was still effective, and the urgency came. Riley made sure of that with those maddening strokes, his erection hitting her in the exact spot she needed to fly.

So that's what she did.

Claire tried to cling to it. Failed. But instead she held on to Riley. For now, she was his, and he was hers.

For now.

And that's when she allowed herself to admit something she'd known for most of her life.

That she was in love with the man who'd just given her that orgasm.

RILEY KNEW IT was time for him to go. Claire was already up, fixing him breakfast. And Livvy was on the way to drop off Ethan before she started work for the day. He didn't want Ethan to find him naked in his mommy's bed, so Riley used that to get him up and start gathering his clothes.

He tried not to think of each step as the last time. The last time he'd be naked in Claire's bed. The last time he'd get dressed here at her house. Or have a love bite that she'd put on his chest near his scar. He was going to have fun explaining that to the physical therapist.

Was going to have fun remembering it, too.

But in the back of his mind he couldn't help wondering if he should have just turned down this sex pact. It would have certainly made this goodbye a whole lot easier. Then again, Riley had never chosen the easy path.

And he wouldn't now.

He'd say goodbye to Claire and Ethan. Kiss them. And report to the base to begin the process for his retraining. It wasn't the job he wanted, not by a long shot, but it's the job he'd take to keep him in uniform. There was even a small consolation prize. Even though he could no longer be a CRO, he could always wear the badge on his uniform since he'd earned it.

That gave him an uneasy jolt.

It was sort of like those has-been high school football stars who continued to wear their letter jackets.

With that gloomy thought on his mind, he took a quick shower, dressed and went into the kitchen. The smell of coffee lured him there, and while he was desperate for a cup, he took a moment to admire the view.

Claire wearing those cutoff shorts. Maybe the same ones she'd worn the morning after he'd first arrived home with his bum shoulder, full of flashbacks and a bad attitude. The flashbacks were gone. The shoulder, not so bum. The attitude, not so bad. But he didn't get that giddy feeling this time when he saw her hips swaying as she scrambled some eggs.

Hell.

This was hard.

She turned, looking at him over her shoulder. Smiling. It didn't look like a fake smile, either, but Riley bet she had to remind herself to do it. He sure had. He went to her, kissed her. Not one of those deep French kinds that was the start of foreplay. A morning kiss.

"Hungry?" she asked.

"Starved," he lied.

He helped himself to a cup of coffee as she dished up a plate of eggs. She didn't pause even a second when she put the plate on the table. Claire headed to the fridge and took out the OJ.

That's when Riley stopped her by taking hold of her arms.

That's when he made another mistake, too. He kissed her. Really kissed her. Not one of those morning deals, either. This one had goodbye written all over it, and Claire knew it, too, because when Riley finally pulled away from her, he saw the tears in her eyes.

"I'm not gonna cry," she insisted. Maybe trying to convince him. Or convince herself.

Her attempt to blink back those tears would have likely failed if she hadn't heard the quick knock on the front door, followed by someone opening it. Followed then by Ethan's giggle and hurried footsteps. Ethan bolted into the kitchen—where did the kid get all that energy this time of morning?—and he made a beeline for Claire.

She scooped him up and showered some kisses on his smiling face. Riley was betting Ethan hadn't had to remind himself to smile because it was the real deal.

The moment Claire set him down, Ethan ran to Riley,

and the whole process repeated itself. Riley got some kisses, too, and a big hug from Ethan.

Something he definitely wouldn't be getting from Livvy.

Livvy came into the kitchen, and she volleyed some uneasy glances between all three of them. Maybe Claire had already told her friend that he was leaving, or perhaps Livvy just picked up on the vibe in the room. Either way, she gave Riley a scowl, and he looked to make sure she didn't have those rusty pliers in her hand.

"Sorry, but I gotta run," Livvy said. "Got an appointment in under an hour. But I can come back later if you want."

"I'll be fine," Claire assured her. She put Ethan at the table, busied herself with dishing him up some eggs. "Really," she added when Livvy didn't budge.

"I'll come back later," Livvy insisted, giving Riley another glare. That glare was the last he saw of her as Livvy left.

Ethan gave them some uneasy glances, too, even after Claire set the plate of eggs in front of him. The kid was only two, but Riley figured there was a lot going on in that little head.

"It's okay if you don't eat," Claire said, and it took Riley a moment to realize she was talking to him not Ethan. Probably because Riley hadn't even picked up his fork.

He did eat some, but not too much since anything, including the coffee, was causing his stomach to churn.

"You need to say goodbye to Riley," Claire prompted Ethan. She turned back toward the stove, and Riley hoped she wasn't crying. He already felt like an asshole, and tears would only make him feel worse.

But Ethan didn't say goodbye. He bolted from the

chair, heading toward the living room, and a few seconds later, he came back with a toy. It was another of those defender action figures. This one looked a little like Cher on steroids.

"For you," Ethan said. Or rather he said something similar to that.

Riley considered telling him to keep it, especially since it was a toy that Ethan played with often. But Riley wanted it. He wanted to be able to look at it and think of Ethan. Not that he didn't already have enough memories in his head.

Enough memories of Claire, too.

"And I have something for you, as well," Claire said. She handed him a five-by-seven envelope. "Don't open it yet. Go through it in a day or two."

When he'd be gone from Spring Hill.

Riley nodded. Since it was probably a goodbye letter, he wasn't sure he wanted to read it just yet anyway.

"It's the day for gifts, I guess," Riley told her. "Well, it's not really a gift, more like a project. But it's not ready yet. Summer Starkley will be bringing it by when it's finished."

Maybe the project/gift would cause Claire to smile. A real one.

He kissed the top of Ethan's head. Kissed Claire one more time because he couldn't stop himself. And before Riley could say or do something that would only make this worse, he headed for the door.

CHAPTER TWENTY-FOUR

RILEY FINISHED DRESSING and checked himself in the mirror. It'd been a while since he had worn his full dress blues, but he was glad he'd brought them with him. Everything fit and was aligned the way they should be. All his medals, his Combat Rescue Officer badge and his name tag.

This one didn't have his blood type on it. Only his last name.

That would have to be enough.

He checked the time. Nearly noon. He'd already said all his goodbyes so there was no reason to hang around the house. Lucky had already left for Abilene. Logan was at the office. Claire and Ethan were at their place. Della and Stella were around, but they were so accustomed to saying goodbye to him that they weren't even upset. Ditto for Logan and Lucky.

Even though he'd already done it once—okay, twice—he went through his duffel again to make sure he had everything. He did. Including the envelope that Claire had given him. The one she'd said not to open for a day or two. Vague instructions for something that might not be so vague because it was almost certainly a goodbye letter. Maybe one where she poured out her heart. Or maybe she would just let him know that it was all right for him to head out again.

It was probably the latter, he decided.

Claire wouldn't make this harder on him even if in doing so, it made it harder on herself.

Riley opened it.

And a picture fell out.

Not a recent one, either. This was a shot of Claire, him and his parents on a fishing trip. Lucky was behind Claire and had lifted up her ponytail so that it looked like a blond palm tree on her head. However, Claire wasn't paying any attention to Lucky. She was looking at Riley. All four of them were smiling. And it made Riley smile, too.

So did the next one. It was a shot of Daniel, Claire and him at a picnic. She was looking at him in that picture, too. And smiling. They must have been ten or so, long before she'd chosen Daniel and set that man-rule into motion. Long before Riley had had sex with her and broken her heart.

Since that was such an unsettling thought, he moved on to the final thing in the envelope. Not another photo but rather another envelope.

One that he recognized.

Because it was the one he'd sent Claire's Gran more than two decades ago.

Of course, Claire had said she'd found it, but they hadn't discussed it. Probably because there hadn't been anything to discuss. Heck, it was possible that she'd been disappointed when she had finally found it because Claire had believed it would be from her father or mother. Not from some ten-year-old kid with a silly notion of how to make her happy.

Riley turned the envelope to open it and saw that Claire had written something on the back.

Thank you for sharing your family with me.

Maybe she hadn't been completely disappointed after all.

He opened it, though, like the contents of his duffel, Riley already knew what was inside. It had taken him nearly a week to write and rewrite that letter, and the words were permanently stuck in his head. Still, he groaned when he saw what his ten-year-old self had produced.

Not his best effort.

So, I talked to my mom and dad, and we all think they could be Claire's mom and dad too. If you don't mind and if you think Claire would like that, I want her to be part of my family. What do you think? Check yes or no.

Below the letter were the boxes for everyone to check yes or no. Not exactly original, but he saw some new additions to the letter. Her gran had checked the yes box.

And so had Claire.

It was just a little check mark, like the others. His, his parents', her gran's and now hers. Riley had to smile. Then shrug. Since his parents were long gone, he hadn't expected her to check no.

Actually, he hadn't expected her to check anything.

He looked through the letter again, wishing that Claire had added a note here instead of just on the envelope. Something he could read and reread when he started missing her.

Like now.

Too bad she hadn't put something in that theoretical note that would let him know just how she felt about him leaving. How she felt about *him*.

Of course, Claire wouldn't have done that because she wouldn't have wanted to say or do anything that would make him feel guilty about going. Again, that was Claire. Always thinking about others' feelings.

Even though the minutes were ticking off, Riley kept looking at that check mark. Maybe that was her version of a note. Her way of saying something she didn't really need to say.

Because it was all there.

In those pictures. The way she had been looking at him. *Hell.* The way she still looked at him.

Claire was in love with him.

Oh, man. That hit him like a punch to the gut. How could he have missed it all this time?

And better yet—what was he going to do about it?

"Riley pee-pee," Ethan said.

That got Claire's attention, and she hurried to the living room where Ethan was playing to make sure he wasn't trying to get outside to pee again. But he wasn't at the door but rather the window, and he was pointing at something.

"Riley pee-pee," he repeated.

She couldn't imagine what had prompted Ethan to say that, but she sincerely hoped no one was outside peeing.

Claire rushed to the window, nearly tripping over Gogh and the car menagerie on the floor, and she saw something she darn sure hadn't expected to see.

A man carrying a toilet.

And he was walking toward her house.

She couldn't see the man's face because of the way he was holding the toilet, but at first she thought it might be Lucky. But not Lucky.

Riley.

Why was he here? They'd already said their goodbyes. But it was indeed Riley, wearing a blue uniform, and he was apparently bringing her a toilet.

Maybe it was some kind of weird goodbye gift, but if so she wasn't sure she was up to the gift or another goodbye. The last one had left her wrung out, and the crying jag afterward had only made it worse. Besides, she didn't want Riley to see her with her face all puffy and red like this.

Ethan tried to open the door, and Claire helped, though she did wonder if Riley had intended just to leave the "gift"—hopefully, with a note explaining why he'd chosen it—and then he could have just taken off. Again. After all, the minutes to his twenty-four-hour deadline were ticking away.

Keep it light, Claire.

But she wasn't sure she could deal with ripping open wounds that hadn't even had a chance to heal.

"I took a chance you'd be home," Riley said, smiling. He made it sound as if that explained everything. It didn't.

"And you walked here with that?" She tipped her head to the toilet.

"It wouldn't fit in the car. It's for Ethan."

That obviously wasn't enough explanation, either. Well, it wasn't until Riley set it down in the foyer for her to see inside the toilet bowl.

There was a painted tree inside. Similar to the peeing tree in the backyard at Riley's house.

Ethan giggled, clapped his hands and would have dropped his pants and peed in it right then, right there if Claire hadn't stopped him. Clearly, he'd picked up on the abstract concept right away. But Claire was still dealing with her own abstract concept of why Riley had brought it over. And why he wasn't at the base.

"When I found out she was an art student, I hired Summer Starkley to do it," Riley added. "She was supposed to bring it by, but she got sick, and I decided to do it."

So it was a goodbye gift. An amazing one. "Ethan loves it. So do I. The neighbors, too, I'm sure. It'll stop him from peeing on the tree out back and Livvy's fake plants."

"Then it's well timed." He took out a piece of paper from his pocket. "When you want it installed, just call that number and make an appointment with the plumber. It's already paid for. All you have to do is let him know a good time for you."

She nodded, tried to think of something clever and funny to say. She failed.

Claire burst out crying.

Ethan looked stunned. Riley, even more stunned. Claire was mortified.

This was the last thing she wanted. Heck, she would have taken Ethan peeing in the unconnected toilet over this. And the sudden unstoppable string of words that started coming out of her mouth.

"I used artificial insemination to get pregnant with Ethan. And the reason he looks so much like you is because I chose a donor who looks like you." God, she couldn't stop. It was like a seizure or something. "Your hair, eye color, height, weight. I saw a picture of him, and he even had your smile."

Even though there was no way Ethan could have understood that, he continued to look stunned. Riley continued to look even more stunned. And the mortification on her part went up a huge notch.

And the blasted verbal lava flow just kept on coming. "I just thought you should know that I've never believed you were ordinary, and I wanted my son to look, and be, just like you."

Mission accomplished. Seeing them side by side, gaping at her, Ethan was a little version of Riley.

But that wasn't the end of her word eruption. "I kept it a secret because I didn't want you to know. Because I thought maybe it would make you feel…I don't know… obligated or responsible or something. You might have also thought I was obsessed with you."

Riley finally did something to stop the babbling. He kissed her. Probably just to shut her up, but it worked.

"Are you…obsessed with me?" he asked.

There was no smart answer to this. If she said yes, it might cause him to say that goodbye even faster. Of course, the same could happen if she said no. So, for the first time in the past two minutes, she went silent.

Ethan broke that silence. "Pee-pee now?" he asked, and he was dancing around while holding his crotch.

Since that was his way of letting her know he had to go potty, Claire scooped him up and hurried toward the bathroom. It wasn't a tree-toilet, but he lifted the plain white lid, shoved down his jeans and pull-up, and took care of business.

"Good boy," she praised, but her attention was on Riley. This was hardly the moment or the situation for her to answer his question, but Riley was apparently waiting for an answer.

Claire went with a question of her own. "How much time do you have?" she asked. "When do you have to leave for the base?"

Riley walked closer, took her hand. "I asked first."

Indeed he had, and even though she'd had a couple of long moments and a potty break to give her time to come up with an answer, Claire still didn't know what to say. She decided to go with another lava approach. She opened her mouth and waited to see what would come out.

"Yes," she admitted. *Oh, no.* Now, she had to explain. Or else she could just get angry with herself for the confession. She went with the second option. "I am obsessed with you. There. Satisfied?"

Riley frowned. "Well, I was until you got pissed. Angry," he corrected for Ethan's ears. But Ethan wasn't listening. Triumphant from his accomplishment, he hurried back into the living room, not washing his hands and also leaving the toilet lid up.

That was clearly something they'd have to work on.

But Riley was working on something, too. He pulled a piece of paper from his pocket. Paper that she recognized.

The letter.

"I didn't want you to see that until after you were gone," she reminded him.

"Yeah. And I'm guessing that's because you didn't want to discuss it with me. Well, we're discussing it."

He unfolded the letter, pointed to the box at the bottom. "If you don't mind and if you think Claire would like that, I want her to be part of my family," he read. "You checked yes. Did you mean it?"

Well, that wasn't a question she'd seen coming. "Uh, of course. Your parents treated me like I was one of their own kids."

"No. Did you mean it?" he repeated.

Claire studied his expression, trying to figure out what was going on here, but she was either dense or Riley was. "Of course?" she repeated, this time adding a different inflection. "What's this all about, Riley?"

He certainly didn't develop a case of verbal lava. Riley stood there, staring, breathing too fast and generally looking as if he might lose his lunch instead of his mind.

"Because I want you to be part of my family," he finally said.

"All right. It won't be much of a stretch. I'm over there a lot so Ethan can play with Crazy Dog, and Lucky drops by whenever he's in town—"

That obviously wasn't the right answer because Riley

took hold of her, snapped her to him and kissed her. This wasn't one of those goodbye pecks he'd given her earlier in the kitchen. This was the real deal. The kind of kiss that would have made her think about carting him off to bed if Ethan hadn't been in the house.

The kiss went on for a while. Too long and too short at the same time, and when he finally let go of her, Claire immediately felt the loss, or something. It was as if she was in the wrong place with him standing there and not touching or kissing her.

"I'm not leaving," Riley said.

Claire nodded, figuring he meant he was staying until they talked this out. Whatever it was they had to talk out. But it was obvious that Riley had something on his mind.

"I mean, I'm not leaving," he repeated.

Maybe it was the look in his eyes or the addition of his own inflection, but Claire thought she knew what he meant. But he couldn't mean that.

Could he?

"You're not leaving?" she clarified. "But what about being in the Air Force? What about being ordinary?"

He shrugged. "I'm leaving the service. I'm staying here in Spring Hill."

She checked his eyes to make sure he meant it. He did. But she shook her head. "I don't want you doing this for me."

"Nope. I'm doing it for me. My mind's already made up."

"Are you sure? What about—"

"You said you never believed I was ordinary," he interrupted. "And that you believed that so much that you wanted Ethan to look and be just like me. Was that true?"

"Absolutely." She couldn't say it quickly enough.

Riley gave a crisp nod. "Along with that checked box on the letter, there's only one thing missing."

Since he kissed her after that, Claire couldn't imagine anything was missing. Until Riley spoke again.

"I'm in love with you," he said.

There it was. Magic words indeed. Words that she had held in her heart for so long that they slipped right out of her mouth.

Claire gave those right back to Riley. And ditto for the kiss.

* * * * *

Look for more books in
USA TODAY *bestselling author Delores Fossen's*
THE McCORD BROTHERS
when LONE STAR NIGHTS goes on sale in June 2016.
And be sure to check out her Harlequin Intrigue books.
TROUBLE WITH A BADGE goes on sale in April 2016
and is available wherever books
and ebooks are sold!

WHAT HAPPENS ON THE RANCH

CHAPTER ONE

ANNA MCCORD FIGURED she had committed a couple of sins, maybe even broken a few laws, just by looking at the guy in the bed. He was naked, so it was hard not to have dirty thoughts about him.

Drool, too.

Mercy, he was hot.

Thick blond hair all tousled and bedroomy. Lean and muscled. At least what she could see of him was muscled anyway. He was sprawled out on his stomach, his face cocooned in the fluffy feather pillows of the guest bed. He reminded her of a Viking just back from a good pillaging, minus the bed and feather pillows, of course.

But who was he?

Even though she should have bolted out of there the moment she opened the guest room door and saw a partially exposed butt cheek, Anna stayed put. Someone had obviously glued her feet to the floor. Glued her eyeballs to the hot guy, too.

She glanced around the room and spotted a clue as to who he was. There was a military uniform draped over the back of a chair and a duffel bag on the floor near the bed.

Anna didn't actually need more clues to know he was an Air Force officer and likely a friend that her brother Riley had brought home. But she also saw the dog tags. The ball chain holding them was still around the hot guy's neck, but the tags themselves were lying askew on the bed like smashed nickels.

Maybe he sensed she was there, because he opened an eye, and the seconds trickled by before it must have registered in his mind that he had a woman ogling him.

He made a grunting sound mixed with some profanity and rolled over, no doubt because that was the fastest way he could reach the sheet to cover himself. However, the rolling over gave her a view of his front side.

Definitely more dirty thoughts.

"Sorry, I didn't know anyone was in here," Anna said, as if that explained the gawking. The drool. The long, heated look that she was giving him.

But both the heated stuff and the drool came to a quick halt when Anna got a better look at his face. "Heath?"

He blinked. "Anna?"

Good gravy. It was Heath Moore, all right. Well, a grown-up Heath anyway. The last time she'd seen him had been nine and a half years ago when he was barely eighteen, but he had filled out a lot since then.

Oh, the memories she had of him came flooding back.

He'd been naked then, too—for part of those memories anyway, since she'd lost her virginity to him. Though she certainly hadn't seen as much of him during that encounter in the hayloft as she'd just witnessed. He had filled out *everywhere*.

He sat up, dragging the sheet over his filled-out parts, and still blinking, he yawned and scrubbed his hand over his face. More memories came. Of his memorable mouth. The equally memorable way he'd kissed her.

She fanned herself like a menopausal woman with hot flashes.

"Why are you here?" she asked at the same moment that Heath asked, "Why are you here?"

Anna figured he was going to have a lot better explanation than she did. "I thought I might have left a book in here," she told him.

A total lie. She had been in search of a book that the housekeeper, Della, had said she'd left in her room on the nightstand. But when Anna had seen the guest room door slightly ajar, she'd opened it and had a look.

She made a show of glancing around for a book that had zero chance of being there since it was all the way at the end of the hall.

"This is your room now?" Heath asked.

"No. But I come in here sometimes. For the view." Anna motioned to the massive bay window. She wouldn't mention that every bedroom on the second floor had similar windows, similar views. As did her own room on the first floor.

Heath glanced in the direction of the bay window as if he might get up to sample that view, but his next glance was at his body. Considering he was naked under the sheet, he probably didn't want to get up until she'd left, and that was her cue to leave. First though, she wanted an answer to her question.

"Why are you here?" she repeated.

"Riley. He saw me at the base in San Antonio and said I needed some…R & R before I left on assignment. He was headed back here to the ranch to finish out his leave, and he asked me to come."

All of that made sense because Riley, too, was an Air Force officer and had indeed been at the base the day before. Yes, it made sense except for Heath's hesitation before R & R.

"You weren't here last night when I went to bed." She would have noticed Heath, that's for sure.

"We stopped for a bite to eat, then to visit some mutual

friends, and we didn't get in until late. We didn't want to wake anyone up so Riley just sent me here to the guest room." Heath paused. "Riley's my boss."

Uh-oh. That wouldn't play well with Riley if he found out about her lustful thoughts over his subordinate. It wouldn't play well with Heath, either, since he probably didn't want to do or think anything—or have *her* do or think anything—that would cause his boss to hit him upside the head with a shovel.

A threat that Riley had first rattled off nine and a half years ago when he thought a romance was brewing between Heath and her.

If Riley had known what had gone on in the hayloft, he might not have actually carried through on the shovel threat, but Anna would have never heard the end of it.

And there was that whole underage-sex thing.

When Heath had first started working at the ranch, he'd been eighteen. But she'd been only seventeen. Riley and her other brothers had made a big deal about the attraction they'd sensed going on between Heath and her.

The term *jail bait* had been thrown around.

Since Heath had been making a big deal of his own about going into the military, it was an issue. Heath wanted to go into special ops, which would have required a lengthy background check for a top-secret clearance, and Riley had brought up her age for the sole purpose of scaring Heath into keeping his jeans zipped.

It had worked. Until the day Anna turned eighteen, that is. After that, she'd made the trip to the hayloft with Heath, and she had the memories of the orgasm to prove it.

Heath smiled at her, but it felt as if he'd had to rummage it up just to be polite. Again, the nudity was probably driving that. But the nudity didn't stop him from looking at her with those sizzling blue eyes. Also bed-roomy like his hair. He slid his gaze from her head to her toes, lingering in the middle. Lingering especially on her breasts. Perhaps because she was wearing a T-shirt and no bra.

"Riley didn't mention you'd be here at the ranch," Heath said.

"Oh? Well, usually I leave the day after Thanksgiving, but I decided to stay a little longer." Since it was already two days after Thanksgiving, she probably hadn't needed to add that last part. "I'm in law school at University of Texas, but I finished my courses early this semester. I'm also planning a transfer. I need a change of scenery…or something."

And a life.

And perhaps sex, but she'd only gotten that idea when she'd seen Heath naked.

"Yeah, a change of scenery," he repeated, as if he were aware of what she meant by the *or something.*

"So, how long will you be here?" Anna tried to keep her eyes directed just at his face, but her gaze kept drifting a bit to that incredibly toned chest. Either he'd gotten very good with contouring body paints or the man had a six-pack.

"Until the cows come home," he said.

That's when she realized both her eyes and her mind had seriously drifted off, and she didn't have a clue what he'd been talking about before that.

The corner of his mouth lifted. A dreamy smile, and he hadn't had to rummage up this one. It was the real deal.

"I'll be here about two weeks," he said. Probably repeated information. "How about you?"

"Two weeks. More or less. I was going to stay until the final exams were over and the campus was less busy.

Then, the plan was to talk to my advisor about the transfer."

"For that change of scenery or something?" Heath made it sound like a question.

Anna pretended not to hear it. No need to get into all that. Instead, she glanced at his left hand, the one part of his body she'd failed to look at during her gawking. No ring.

"I'm not married," Heath volunteered. "Never have been." He looked at her left hand, too, where she was still wearing the opal ring her Granny Ethel had left her.

Anna shook her head. "No I-do's for me, either." Close, though, but best not to get into that after her change-of-scenery slip. "So, catch me up on what you've been doing."

"Maybe I can do that after I've put on some clothes? Or we can talk like this?" Another smile.

He was flirting with her, a ploy she knew all too well since she'd been on the receiving end of his flirting that summer. Well, she could flirt, too.

"I guess I can restrain myself for a quick catch-up," she joked. "A *quick catch-up*," she emphasized. "What are you doing these days? I mean, other than sleeping naked, that is. How's the job going?"

The smile faded, and she was sorry she'd taken the conversation in that direction. Of course, it was something a normal nondrooling woman would have asked the man who had been her first.

Even though it was a dumb-as-dirt thing to do, she went closer. Much closer. And she sat down on the bed. Not right next to him, though, because she didn't want to move into the dumber-than-dirt category, but it was still too near him. Six miles would have been too near.

"Sorry," she added. "Didn't mean to hit a nerve. And

I should have known better because Riley doesn't like to talk about his assignments, either. I think he believes it'll worry me, but whether he talks about it or not, I still worry."

"You shouldn't. Riley's been on plenty of deployments and hasn't gotten a scratch. Some guys are just bullet-proof, and Riley's one of them."

Maybe. But Anna had a bad feeling about this deployment coming up. A bad feeling she definitely didn't want to discuss with Heath. Or Riley. If she didn't mention it aloud, maybe the feeling would go away. Maybe the danger would as well, and her brother would come back with his bulletproof label intact.

"You okay?" Heath asked.

That was a reminder to push aside her fears and get on with this catch-up conversation. "Riley always says if he tells me about his job, he'll have to hit me with a shovel afterwards. Riley really likes that shovel threat."

"I remember." Heath took a deep breath, causing the muscles in his chest and that six-pack to respond. "Well, shovels aside, I can tell you that I just finished up a deployment in a classified location where there was a lot of sand, followed by eight months in Germany where there was a lot of paperwork. That's where Riley became my boss. Small world, huh?"

Yes. Too small, maybe. "Riley and you are in the same career field?"

"For now." The short answer came out so fast. As did his hand. He brushed his fingers over the ends of her hair. Even though he didn't actually touch skin or anything, it was enough of a distraction. "Your hair is longer," he said.

"Yours is shorter." And yes, she achieved dumber-than-dirt status by touching his hair, as well. Since it was on the short side, she also touched some skin.

She felt everything go still, and even though Anna was pulling back her hand, it seemed to be in slow motion. The only thing that was in the revving-up mode was this flamethrower attraction that had always been between Heath and her.

"Yeah," he drawled. No other words were necessary. They were on the same proverbial page along with being on the same actual bed. The flamethrower had had a go at him, too.

"I, uh…" Anna stuttered around with a few more words and syllables before she managed to say something coherent. "This could be trouble."

"Already is." He drawled that, too. Hitched up another smile.

The past nine and a half years just vanished. Suddenly, Anna was eighteen again and was thinking about kissing him. Of course, she hadn't needed vanishing years for that to happen, but it was as if they were back in that hayloft. On all that warm, soft hay. Heath had taken things so slow. Long kisses. His hand skimming over various parts of her body.

Then, into her jeans.

That had been the best part, and it'd all started with a heated look like the one he was giving her now.

Even though they didn't move, the foreplay was in full swing. His gaze lingered on her mouth. She picked up the rhythm of his breathing—which was too fast. Ditto for her heartbeat. Everything was moving in sync.

"Anna, we're playing with fire," he whispered. It was a drawl, too.

She was near enough to him now that his breath hit against her mouth like a kiss. "Yes," she admitted, but she was in the "fire pretty" mindset right now, and she inched closer, her drifting gaze sliding from his mouth to his abs.

"Is it real?" she asked, but was in the wrong mindset to wait for an answer. She touched that six-pack.

Oh, yes. Definitely real.

It probably would have been a good time to snatch back her hand and be outraged that she'd done something so bold, but she kept it there a moment and saw and heard Heath's reaction. He cursed under his breath, and beneath the sheet his filled-out part reacted, as well.

He cursed some more, but it was all aimed at himself. "I really do need you to leave now so I can get dressed. Once I can walk, that is. Maybe you can shut the door behind you, too."

That caused the past nine and a half years to unvanish. Heath was putting a stop to this. As he should.

Anna was about to help with that stopping by getting to her feet and doing something that Heath clearly would have trouble doing right now—walking. But before she could budge an inch, she saw the movement in the doorway.

And saw the source of that movement.

Riley.

His eyes were so narrowed that it looked as if his eyelashes were stuck together.

"What the hell's going on here?" Riley growled. He opened his eyes enough to look at her. Then at Heath. Then at the other *thing* that was going on. "And what are you doing with my sister?"

No way was Heath going to be able to explain with the bulge of his filled-out part beneath the sheet. And neither could Anna.

CHAPTER TWO

WELL, HELL IN A big-assed handbasket. This visit was off to a good start.

Heath had known it wasn't a smart idea to come to the McCord Ranch, and he was getting a full reminder of why it'd been bad, what with Riley glaring at him.

"Get dressed," Riley ordered, and yeah, it was an order all right. "And we'll talk." Then he turned that ordering glare on his sister.

But Anna obviously wasn't as affected by it as Heath was, even though Riley was in uniform and looked thirty steps past the intimidation stage. Still, Anna matched Riley's glare with a scowl and waltzed out.

Thankfully, Riley did some waltzing as well and left, shutting the door behind him. Though it was more of a slam than a shut. Still, he was gone, and that gave Heath some time to take a very uncomfortable walk to the adjoining bathroom for a shower. Cold. Just the way he hated his showers. And if he stayed on the ranch, there'd be more of them in his near future.

It was time for a change of plans.

Not that he actually had plans other than passing time and moping. Yeah, moping was a definite possibility. At least it had been until Anna had shown up in the doorway. Difficult to mope in his current state.

Regardless, Anna was off-limits, of course.

He repeated that while the cold shower cooled down

his body. Repeated it some more while he dressed. Kept repeating it when he went down the stairs to apologize to Riley and tell him that he'd remembered some place he needed to be. Riley would see right through the lie, but after what he had witnessed in the guest room, he'd be glad to get Heath off the ranch.

Heath made his way downstairs, meandering through the sprawling house. Since he was hoping for some coffee to go along with the butt-chewing he would get from Riley, he headed toward the kitchen.

He heard women's voices but not Anna's. He was pretty sure they belonged to Della and Stella, sisters and the McCords' longtime housekeeper and cook. Yep. And Heath got a glimpse of them and the coffeepot, too, before Riley stepped into the archway, blocking his path.

"I know," Heath volunteered. "You want to hit me on the head with a shovel."

"Hit who with a shovel?" Della asked, and when she spotted Heath, she flung the dish towel she was holding. Actually, she popped Riley on the butt with it and went to Heath to gather him into her arms for a hug. "It's good to see you, boy."

Heath hadn't even been sure the woman would remember him after all this time, but clearly she did. Or else she thought he was someone else.

"Nobody's gonna get hit with a shovel in this house," Della warned Riley, and then she added to Heath, "Have you seen Anna yet?"

"Earlier," Heath settled for saying.

"Well, I hope you'll be seeing a lot more of her while you're here. Never could understand why you two didn't just sneak up to the hayloft or somewhere."

Heath choked on his own breath. Not a very manly reaction, but neither was the way Riley screwed up his face. Della didn't seem to notice or she might have used the dish towel on him again.

"Have a seat at the table, and I'll fix you some breakfast," Della offered.

"Heath and I have to talk first," Riley insisted.

"Pshaw. A man's gotta have at least some coffee before he carries on a conversation. Where are your manners, Riley?"

"I think I left them upstairs."

Della laughed as if it were a joke and, God bless her, she poured Heath a cup of coffee. He had a couple of long sips, figuring he was going to need them.

"Thanks. I'll be right back," Heath said to Della, and he followed Riley out of the kitchen and into the sunroom.

No shovels in sight, but Riley had gone back to glaring again, and he got right in Heath's face. "Keep your hands off Anna, or I'll make your life a living hell."

Heath had no doubts about that. He didn't mind the living hell for himself so much, but he didn't want any more of Riley's anger aimed at Anna. "I'll get my things together and head out."

Riley's glare turned to a snarl. "And then Anna, Della and Stella will think I've run you off."

Heath had some more coffee, cocked his head to the side in an "if the shoe fits" kind of way. Because in a manner of speaking, Riley was indeed running him off. Except that Heath had already decided it was a good idea, too. Still, he didn't acknowledge that. He was getting some perverse pleasure out of watching Riley squirm a little.

"I'm guessing Anna, Della and Stella will make your life a living hell if they think you've run me off?" Heath asked. And he said it with a straight face.

Riley opened his mouth. Closed it. Then he did a wash, rinse, repeat of that a couple more times before he finally cursed. "Stay. For now. And we'll discuss it later. I've got to do some more paperwork at the base. Just keep your hands off Anna while I'm gone. Afterwards, too."

His hands were the least of Riley's worries, but Heath kept that to himself. Besides, Riley didn't give him a chance to say anything else. He lit out of there while growling out another "Stay" order.

Heath would stay. For the morning anyway. But it was best if he put some distance between Anna and all those parts of him that could get him in trouble.

He went back into the kitchen, got a hug and warm greeting from Stella this time, and the woman practically put him in one of the chairs at the table.

"How do you like your eggs?" Della asked.

"Any way you fix them." Heath added a wink because he figured it would make her smile. It did.

"Tell us what you've been doing with yourself for the past nine years or so," Della said as she got to work at the stove. "I seem to recall when you left here that summer you were headed to boot camp."

Heath nodded, took a bite of the toast that Stella set in front of him. "I enlisted in the Air Force, became a para-rescuer and took college classes online. When I finished my degree, I got my commission and became a combat rescue officer."

"Like Riley," Stella said.

"Yeah, but he outranks me."

"How is that? Didn't you go in the Air Force before Riley did?"

Heath nodded again. "Only a couple months earlier, though. We've been in the service about the same amount of time, but for most of that I was enlisted. I've only been an officer for three and a half years now. And Riley's my boss. Well, until the rest of my paperwork has cleared. That should be about the time Riley leaves for his assignment in two weeks."

Della stopped scrambling the eggs to look at him. "You won't be going with him?"

There it was. That twist to the gut. Heath tried to ease it with some more toast and coffee, but that was asking a lot of mere food products. And Della and Stella noticed all right. He'd gotten their full attention.

"No, I won't be going with Riley this time," Heath said.

He still had their attention, and judging from their stares, the women wanted more. Heath gave them the sanitized version. "The Air Force feels it's time for me to have a stateside assignment. It's standard procedure. A way of making sure I don't burn out."

His mouth was still moving and words were coming out, but Heath could no longer hear what he was saying. That's because Anna walked in. Or maybe it was just a Mack Truck that looked like Anna because he suddenly felt as if someone had knocked him senseless.

She'd changed out of her sweats and T-shirt. Had put on a bra, too. And was now wearing jeans and a red sweater. Heath tried not to notice the way the clothes hugged her body. Tried not to notice her curves. Her face.

Hell, he gave up and noticed.

Not that he could have done otherwise. Especially when Anna poured herself a cup of coffee, sat down next to him and glanced at his crotch.

"Back to normal?" she whispered. Then she gave him a smile that could have dissolved multiple layers of rust on old patio furniture. Dissolved a few of his brain cells, too. "So, did Riley try to give you your marching orders?"

Since Della and Stella got very, very quiet, Heath figured they were hanging on every word, so he chose his own words carefully and spoke loud enough for the women to hear. "Something came up—"

Anna glanced at his crotch again and laughed. Obviously, a reaction she hadn't planned because she clamped her teeth onto her bottom lip after adding "I'm sorry." Too late, though. Because Della and Stella weren't just hanging on every word but every ill-timed giggle, too.

"Well, I'm sure whatever came up—" Della paused "—you can work it out so you can stay here for at least a couple of days. That way, Anna and you have time to visit."

"Especially since Anna needs some cheering up," Stella added.

Anna certainly didn't laugh that time. She got a deer-about-to-be-smashed-by-a-car look. "I'm fine, really," Anna mumbled.

Which only confirmed to Heath that she did indeed need some cheering up. Maybe this had to do with the "change of scenery or something" she'd mentioned upstairs.

Well, hell.

There went his fast exit, and no, that wasn't the wrong part of his body talking, either. If Anna was down, he wanted to help lift her up.

Stella dished up two plates of eggs for Anna and him, and she smiled at them when she set them on the table. "You two were as thick as thieves back in the day." She snapped her fingers as if recalling something. "Anna, Heath even gave you that heart necklace you used to wear all the time. It had your and his pictures in it."

Hard to forget that. Heath referred to it as the great engraved debacle. He'd spent all his money buying Anna that silver heart locket as a going-away gift. Something to remember him by after he left Spring Hill and the McCord Ranch. It was supposed to be engraved with the words *Be Mine*.

The engraver had screwed up and had put *Be My* instead.

Since Heath hadn't had the time to get it fixed, he'd given it to Anna anyway, but he hadn't figured she would actually wear it. Not with that confusing, incomplete *sentiment*.

"Where is that necklace?" Della asked.

"I'm not sure," Anna answered, and she got serious about eating her breakfast. Fast. Like someone who'd just entered a breakfast-eating contest with a reprieve from a death sentence waiting for the winner.

Della made a sound that could have meant anything, but it had a sneaky edge to it. "I think Heath needs some cheering up, too," Della went on. "And not because Riley was going on about that shovel. That boy needs to get a new threat, by the way," she added to her sister before looking at Anna again. "I get the feeling Heath could use somebody to talk to."

Heath suddenly got very serious about eating his breakfast, as well. Either Della had ESP, or Heath sucked at covering up what was going on in his head.

Anna finished gulping down her breakfast just a bite ahead of him, gulped down some coffee, too, and she probably would have headed out if Stella hadn't taken her empty breakfast plate and given her a plate of cookies instead.

"I need you to take these cookies over to Claire Davidson at her grandmother's house."

"Claire's back in town?" Anna asked, sounding concerned.

Heath knew Claire. She'd been around a lot that summer he'd worked at the McCord Ranch, and if he wasn't mistaken Claire had a thing for Riley. And vice versa.

"Her grandmother's sickly again. Thought they could use some cheering up, too." Della shifted her attention to Heath. "And you can go with Anna. Then maybe she could show you around town."

"Spring Hill hasn't changed in nine and a half years," Anna quickly pointed out.

"Pshaw. That's not true. The bakery closed for one thing. And Logan bought that building and turned it into a fancy-schmancy office. It has a fancy-schmancy sign that says McCord Cattle Brokers. You can't miss it."

Logan—one of Anna's other brothers who ran the family business and probably also owned a shovel. Ditto for Logan's twin, Lucky. At least the two of them didn't stay at the ranch very often, so Heath might not even run into them. Well, he wouldn't as long as he avoided the fancy-schmancy office and any of the local rodeos since Lucky was a bull rider.

"I thought I'd go out and see if the ranch hands needed any help," Heath suggested.

That earned him a blank stare from the women. "You don't have to work for your keep while you're here," Stella said. "You're a guest."

"I know, but I like working with my hands. I miss it." He did. Not as much as he'd miss other things—like having the job he really wanted—but grading on a curve here, ranch work was missable.

"All right, then," Della finally conceded. "At least walk Anna to the truck. There might be some ice on the steps. We had a cold spell move in."

"Now, go," Stella said, shooing them out. "Della and I need to clean up, and we can't do that with y'all in here."

This wasn't about cleaning. This was about match-making. Still, Heath grabbed his coat so he could make sure Anna didn't slip on any ice. He only hoped Anna didn't ask why he needed cheering up, and he would return the favor and not ask her the same thing.

"So, why do you need cheering up?" Anna asked the moment they were outside.

He groaned, not just at the question but also because it was at least fifty degrees with zero chance of ice.

"Is it personal or business?" she added.

"Is yours personal or business?" he countered.

She stayed quiet a moment and instead of heading toward one of the trucks parked on the side of the house, she sat down in the porch swing. "Both. You?"

"Both," he repeated. But then he stopped and thought about her answer. "Yours is personal, as in guy troubles?"

For some reason that made him feel as if he'd been hit by the Anna-truck again. Which was stupid. Because of course she had men in her life. Heath just wasn't sure he wanted to hear about them.

She nodded to verify that it was indeed guy trouble.

No, he didn't want to hear this, so he blurted out the first thing that popped into his head. He probably should have waited for the second or third thing, though.

"I had a girl break up with me once because I kept calling her your name," he said.

"*My* name?" She didn't seem to know how to react to that.

"Uh, no. I kept saying *your name* because I couldn't remember her name." And he added a wink that usually charmed women.

But, of course, it'd been Anna's name. The way stuff about her often popped into his head, her name had a way of just popping out of his mouth.

"Any other confessions you want to get off your chest and/or six-pack?" she asked. And she winked at him.

Man, that's what he'd always liked about Anna. She gave as good as she got. "Let me see. I don't wear boxers or briefs. I like mayo and pepper on my French fries. And my mother's in jail again."

All right, so that last one just sort of fell from his brain into his mouth.

Anna didn't question the *again* part. Maybe because she remembered the reason he'd ended up at the McCord Ranch all those years ago was that his mother had been in jail then, as well.

In jail only after she'd stolen and spent every penny of the money that Heath had scrimped and saved for college. She'd also burned down their rental house with all his clothes and stuff still in it.

Heath had snapped up Riley's offer of a job and a place to stay—since at the time Heath had had neither. His father hadn't been in his life since he was in kindergarten, and what with him being broke and homeless, he'd had few places to turn.

If it hadn't been for his jailbird mom, he would have never met Anna. So, in a way he owed her.

In a very roundabout way.

"Want to talk about why your mom's in jail?" Anna asked.

Well, since he'd opened this box, Heath emptied the contents for her. "Shoplifting Victoria's Secret panties. She'd stuffed about fifty pairs in her purse—guess they don't take up much room—and when the security guard tried to stop her, she kicked him where it hurts. Then she did the same to the manager of the store next door. Then to the off-duty cop who tried to stop her. My mom can be a real butt-kicker when it comes to high-end underwear."

Anna smiled, a quiet kind of smile. "I do that, too, sometimes."

"What?" And Heath hoped this wasn't about butt-kicking or stealing panties.

"Defuse the pain with humor. I'm not very good at it, either. Pain sucks."

Yeah, it did, and he thought he knew exactly what she was talking about. "You lost your parents when you were a teenager."

"Yes, they were killed in a car accident before you and I met. I was fourteen, and I thought my world was over. That was still the worst of the *world's over* moments, but I've had others since."

"Is that why you need cheering up?" he asked.

She didn't answer. Anna stood. "I should deliver these cookies before the ice gets to them."

Heath put his hands in his pockets so he wouldn't touch her as she walked away. Not that he would have had a chance to do any touching. Because someone pulled up in a truck. Not a work truck, either. This was a silver one that Della would have labeled as fancy schmancy. It went well with the cowboy who stepped from it.

Logan McCord.

The top dog at the McCord Ranch and the CEO of Mc-Cord Cattle Brokers. He made a beeline for the porch, passing Anna along the way. She said something to him, something Heath couldn't hear, but it put a deep scowl on Logan's face.

"Smart-ass," he grumbled. "She threatened to hit me with Riley's shovel if I didn't make you feel welcome. So—welcome."

Warm and fuzzy it wasn't, but at least it wasn't a threat. Not yet anyway.

"Riley called," Logan continued. "He said I was to come over here and convince you to stay."

"Because of Anna, Della and Stella."

Logan certainly didn't deny that, and his gaze drifted to Anna as she drove away before his attention turned back to Heath. "You're only going to be here two weeks at most, and then you'll leave, right?"

Since that pretty much summed it up, Heath nodded.

"Well, the last time you did that, it took Anna a long time to get over you. *Months*," Logan emphasized. "We all had to watch her cry her eyes out."

Hell. Crying? Months? This was the first Heath was hearing about this, but then he hadn't been around to see those tears. He'd been off at basic training at Lackland Air Force Base. He'd written her, of course. In the beginning at least. She'd written back to him, too, but she damn sure hadn't mentioned tears.

Logan took a step closer, got in his face. So close that Heath was able to determine that he used mint mouthwash and flossed regularly. "You won't hurt my kid sister like that again."

"The shovel threat?" Heath asked, aiming to make this sound as light as a confrontation with Logan could be. Heath wasn't sure friendly bones in a person's body actually existed, but if they did, Logan didn't have any.

"Worse. I'll tell Della and Stella what you've done and let them have a go at you. If you piss them off, the shovel will be the least of your worries."

Heath didn't doubt that. In fact, the whole McCord clan would come after him if he left Anna crying again. And that meant Anna was way off-limits.

He'd survived months in hostile territory. But Heath thought that might be a picnic compared to the next two weeks with Anna and the McCord brothers.

CHAPTER THREE

HEATH HAD BEEN avoiding her for the past three days. Anna was certain of it. And she was fed up with it, partly because if Heath avoided her, it was like letting her knot-headed brothers win.

The other *partly* was that she couldn't get him off her mind, and she didn't know what riled her more—her brothers' winning or her own body whining and begging for something it shouldn't get.

Shouldn't.

Because another fling with Heath would only complicate her life and possibly get her heart stomped on again. That was the logical, big-girl panties argument, but the illogical, no-underwear girl wanted Heath in the hayloft again.

And the hayloft was exactly where she spotted him.

He was standing in the loft, tossing down bales of hay onto a flatbed truck that was parked just beneath. He was all cowboy today: jeans, a blue work shirt, Stetson, boots. Oh, and he was sweaty despite the chillier temps.

She wasn't sure why the sweat appealed to her, but then she didn't see a single thing about him that didn't fall into the appeal category.

Anna stood there ogling him, as she'd done in the bedroom, and she kept on doing it until his attention landed on her. Since she should at least make an attempt at not throwing herself at him, she went to the nearby corral and looked at the horses that'd been delivered earlier. It wasn't exactly the right day for horse ogling, though, because the wind had a bite to it.

An eternity later, which was possibly only a couple of minutes, the ranch hands drove off with the hay, and Heath made his way down the loft ladder. Then he made his way toward her.

"You've been avoiding me," she said. All right, she should have rehearsed this or something. For a soon-to-be lawyer, she was seriously lacking in verbal finesse when it came to Heath.

"Yeah," he admitted in that hot drawl of his. And he admitted the reason, too. "Your brothers are right. I'm not here for long, and they said you cried a lot the last time I left."

Her mouth dropped open, and the outrage didn't allow her to snap out a comeback. But her brothers were dead meat. Dead. Meat.

"They told you that?" She didn't wait for an answer. "I didn't cry. That much," Anna added.

Heath lifted his eyebrow, went to her side and put his forearms on the corral fence. "The fact that you cried at all tells me that I should keep avoiding you."

"Should?" she challenged.

He cursed, looked away from her. "You know I'm attracted to you. You saw proof of that in the bedroom."

She had, indeed. "And you know I'm attracted to you."

There, she'd thrown down the sexual gauntlet. But it caused him to curse again.

"I don't want to hurt you," he said.

"And I don't want to get hurt—"

A commotion in the corral nipped off the rest of what she was about to say. And it wasn't a very timely commotion.

Sex.

Specifically horse sex.

It went on a lot at the ranch. So often in fact that Anna rarely noticed, but because Heath was right next to her, she noticed it now. And he noticed that she noticed.

With all that noticing going on, it was amazing that she remembered how to turn around, but she finally managed it. She took hold of Heath's arm and got him moving away from the corral and toward the pasture.

Where she immediately saw cow-and-bull sex.

Dang it. Was everything going at it today?

Heath chuckled. "The Angus bull was getting restless, trying to break fence, so the hands brought in some company for him."

The ranch's version of Match.com. And the icy wind definitely didn't put a damper on things. Not for the bull anyway, but it did for Anna. She shivered and wished she'd opted for a warmer coat instead of the one that she thought looked better on her. It was hard to look your best with chattering teeth and a red nose.

"In here," Heath said. He put his hand on her back and maneuvered her into the barn.

"The scene of the crime," Anna mumbled. She'd fantasized about getting Heath back in here, but not like this. Not when she needed a tissue.

He glanced up at the hayloft, his attention lingering there a moment before coming back to her. The lingering lasted more than a moment though, and he took out a handkerchief and handed it to her.

"I should probably take you back to the house so you can warm up," he offered.

She considered it just so she could blow her nose. It was tempting, but Riley was inside. Della and Stella, too. So Anna touched the handkerchief to her nose and hoped that did the trick. In case it didn't, she went for what Riley would have called a tactical diversion.

"I'm surprised you're not off somewhere enjoying some *company* like that bull before you leave for your deployment," she said.

Anna figured that would get Heath to smile. It didn't. And she saw it again—the look on his face to remind her that he needed to be cheered up about something. Apparently, it had something to do with his assignment.

"Unless a miracle happens, I won't be deploying," he finally answered. The strewn hay on the floor was suddenly riveting because he stared at it. "The Air Force wants me to take an instructor job in Florida."

With the hay-staring and the gloomy look, Anna had braced herself for something a lot worse. "You make it sound as if you're being banished to Pluto."

"In a way, it is like that for me. I trained to be a combat rescue officer, like Riley. I didn't go through all of that to work behind a desk."

Anna wasn't sure how far she should push this so she just waited him out. Waited out the profanity he muttered under his breath. Waited out more hay-staring.

"I feel washed up," he added.

Ah, she got it then. "But the instructor job is temporary, right? You'll go back to being a combat rescue officer?"

"In three years."

She got that, too. It was an eternity for someone like Heath or Riley.

Anna touched his arm, rubbed gently. "The three years will fly by. Look how fast the past nine and a half years went."

The hay finally lost its allure for him, and he looked at her. "Yeah." Not so much of a sexy drawl this time.

The hurt was still there. Time to pull out the big guns and do a little soul-baring.

"Remember when I told you I needed a change of scenery? Well, what I really need is to get away from my exboyfriend," Anna confessed. "We had a bad breakup."

Evidently, Heath didn't like this soul-baring so much because he frowned. "Are you telling me this is rebound flirting you've been doing with me?"

"No. The breakup happened two years ago, but he's getting married to one of my classmates. And they're having a baby. Twins, actually. The classmate is a former Miss Texas beauty pageant winner."

He nodded, made an "I got it" sound. "You're still in love with him."

"No!" And she couldn't say that fast or loud enough. "He's a lying, cheating weasel. My need for a change of scenery isn't because I still care for him but because I'm sick and tired of everybody walking on eggshells around me."

Her voice had gotten louder with each word, and she couldn't stop the confessions now that the floodgates were open.

"Poor pitiful Anna McCord got dumped for the beauty queen," she blathered on. "It reminds me of the stuff my brothers pull on me, and I'm tired of it. Tired of being treated like someone who needs to be handled with kid gloves."

She probably would have just kept on blathering, too, if Heath hadn't slid his hand around the back of her neck, hauled her to him and kissed her.

All in all, it was the perfect way to shut her up, and Anna didn't object one bit. In fact, she would have cheered, but her mouth was otherwise occupied, and besides, cheering would have put an end to this kiss.

She didn't want it to end.

Apparently, neither did Heath, because he put that clever mouth to good use and made the kiss French. And deep. And long.

All the makings of a good kiss even if Anna's lungs started to ache for air.

Heath broke the kiss just long enough for them to take in some much needed oxygen, and he went in for another assault. Anna was no longer shivering, could no longer feel her nose, but the rest of her was hyperaware of what was happening. The heat zoomed from her mouth to her toes, but it especially fired up in her orgasm-zone.

Soon, very soon, the kiss just wasn't enough, and they started to grapple for position. Trying to get closer and closer to each other. Heath was a lot better at grappling than she was because he dropped his hands to her butt and gave her a push against the front of his jeans.

Anna saw stars. Maybe the moon, too. And she darn near had an orgasm right then, right there while they were fully clothed.

Her heart was pounding now. Her breath, thin. She was melting. And there was a roaring sound in her head. That roaring sound was probably the reason she hadn't heard the other sounds until it was too late. Not horse or bull sex this time.

Footsteps.

"Interrupting anything?" someone asked.

Not Riley or Logan. Her brother Lucky.

And he was standing in the barn doorway with a shovel gripped in his hand.

ONCE AGAIN HEATH was facing a McCord brother when he was aroused. Hardly the right bargaining tool for dealing with Anna's older siblings who were hell-bent on protecting their sister.

Anna stepped in front of him as if she were his protector, but Heath remedied that. He stepped in front of her. But that only prompted her to attempt another stepping in front of him, and Heath put a stop to it. He dropped a kiss on her mouth, a chaste one this time hoping it would get her to cooperate.

"I need to talk to your brother alone," Heath told her.

"No way. He's here to browbeat you, and he's got a shovel."

Lucky shrugged. Propped the shovel against the wall. "Riley said I should bring it and do my part to remind Heath that he should keep his jeans zipped around you." He shrugged again when he glanced at the front of Heath's jeans. "The zipper's still up, so my work here is done."

Lucky turned to walk away.

"That's really all you've got to say?" Anna asked.

Her brother stopped, smiled in that lazy way that Lucky had about him. Heath knew Lucky loved his sister, but he'd never been as Attila the Hun as Riley and Logan. Heath suspected that's because Lucky got out all his restless energy by riding rodeo bulls. And having lots of sex.

"Should I ask you two to stay away from each other?" Lucky didn't wait for an answer though. "Wouldn't work. You two have the hots for each other, and there's only one way to cool that down." His gaze drifted to the hayloft before he turned again to leave.

Was Lucky really giving them his approval?

No.

This had to be some kind of trick.

Heath went after Lucky. Anna, too, and they caught

up with him by the porch steps. However, before Heath could say anything else, the door opened, and Della stuck her head out.

"Anna, you got a call on the house phone. It's Claire."

Anna volleyed glances between Heath and her brother and then huffed. "Don't you dare say anything important before I get back."

She hurried inside. So did Lucky and Heath, but they stopped in the sunroom.

"Zippers and haylofts aside," Lucky said. "I don't want Anna hurt again. She sort of fell apart the last time you left."

"Yes. I heard about the crying from Logan." Heath paused. "Define *fell apart*."

"It wasn't just the crying." Lucky paused, too. "It was the pregnancy scare."

Heath felt as if all the air had just been sucked out of his lungs. Out of the entire planet. And if there was air on Pluto, it was also gone.

"Anna doesn't know that I know," Lucky went on. "No one does, and I'd like to keep it from my brothers. If Riley and Logan find out, they'd want to kick your ass. And mine since I didn't tell them. Then I'd have to kick theirs. If you don't mind, I'd rather not have to go through an ass-kicking free-for-all."

"Pregnancy?" Heath managed to ask. Considering there was still no air, he was doing good to get out that one word.

Lucky nodded. "A couple of weeks after you left, I went into Anna's bathroom to get some eye drops, and I saw the box for the pregnancy test in her trash can. She'd torn up the box, but I was able to piece it together to figure out what it was."

Heath managed another word. "Damn."

"Yeah. Two words for you—safe sex."

"I used a condom."

Lucky shrugged again. "Then, it must have worked because when I found the pee stick—it was in the way bottom of the trash can, by the way—it had a negative sign on it."

Heath heard the words. Felt the relief at that negative sign. Then managed another word.

"Hell."

Anna had gone through a scare like that, and she hadn't even told him.

"The only reason I dragged this up now was so that you'd understand why I'm protective of her," Lucky went on. "Now, go find her. Confront her about all of this. Then use a condom when you have makeup sex."

There'd be no makeup sex. Because Heath wasn't touching her again. Hell. She could have had his kid.

Heath went looking for Anna, and when he didn't find her in the kitchen or any of the living areas, he went to her bedroom. Of course she was there. The one room in the house where he shouldn't be alone with her. The door was open, and she was still on the phone, but she motioned for him to come in. He did, but only because he wanted answers and didn't want to wait for them.

But he had to wait anyway.

He listened to Anna talk niceties with Claire. Several "you're welcomes" later, she finally ended the call and looked at him. The smile that was forming froze on her mouth though when she saw his expression.

Heath shut the door just as he blurted out, "You had a pee stick in the bottom of your trash can."

Anna gave him a blank look.

"The pregnancy test from nine and a half years ago,"

he clarified. "Lucky found it and just told me about it. I'm wondering why I had to hear it from him."

She laughed. Hardly the reaction he'd expected. "It wasn't my pee on that stick. It belonged to Kristy Welker. I bought it for her so her folks wouldn't find out, and she did the test here."

Heath had vague memories of this Kristy. Anna and she had been friends, and Kristy had come over a couple of times that summer.

Anna's laughter quickly stopped. "What the heck was Lucky doing in my bathroom?"

She was using her sister voice now, and it wouldn't have surprised Heath if she'd gone running out of there to confront her brother about it. She might have done that if Heath hadn't done something so unmanly as having to catch on to the wall to steady himself.

"Whoa. Are you all right?" She slipped her arm around his waist, led him to the bed.

Heath didn't even try to say he didn't need to sit down. He did. "I thought… Well, I thought…"

"Trust me, if you had knocked me up, I would have told you about it."

Of course she would have. But it might take a year or two for his heart rate to settle down.

She gave his arm another rub like the one she had in the barn. "Relax. You were my first, but I wasn't totally clueless." She stopped, paused. "I wasn't your first though, and that's why you knew to bring a condom to the hayloft."

Even though Heath was still coming down from the shock-relief whammy, he heard her loud and clear. She'd given him something that a girl could only give once. Her virginity. That upped the encounter a significant notch, and maybe she was looking for some kind of assurance that she'd given it to the right guy.

"You were the first one that mattered," he said. "I risked being hit by a shovel to be with you. That should have told you something."

No smile. No more arm rub, either. "And yet you left."

He nodded, tried to ignore the sting of that reminder. "I was leaving for basic training, and you were barely eighteen."

Anna waved that off. "I know where this is going. We were too young for it to have been real love."

"No, we weren't too young."

Okay, he hadn't meant to say that, and it was another opened box with contents that Anna was clearly waiting to be spilled.

"What I felt for you was real," Heath said. And strong.

He hadn't cried as Anna had done, but leaving her had left a hole in his heart. Best not to mention that, especially since he would be leaving again soon.

"I knew I couldn't give you a good life," he added. "Not when I was still trying to figure out my own life."

She stayed quiet a couple of seconds. "Fair enough. And if you'd stayed, you would have resented me because you gave up your dream of being in the military. Your wanderlust and need for an adrenaline fix would have come into play. We would have fought, broken up, and all these years later we would have cursed the mere mention of each other's names."

Heath frowned. He didn't like that version of what could have been, but she was probably right. Probably. Now he was cursing her name for a different reason. Because it reminded him of how much he wanted her.

"I still have the need for that adrenaline fix," he admitted. "The need to be...something. Somewhere. It's easier if I stay on the move."

"I get it." She motioned around the room. "That's why it's hard for me to be at the ranch sometimes."

He was pretty sure they were talking about her parents now, about the hole in her heart that their deaths had no doubt left. "Are the memories of your folks harder to deal with while you're here?"

"Every now and then. But sometimes it's hard no matter where I am. Sometimes, I wake up, and I can't remember what they looked like. That sends me into a panic. So I run to grab one of the photo albums just to remember their faces."

"It's your way of keeping them in your life," Heath said around the lump in his throat.

"Yes. The past has a way of staying with you like that." Anna took a deep breath, then sighed. "And you can't run away from your past. I know, I've tried. It's like that little mole I have on my right butt cheek. It just goes with me everywhere." She looked at him. "I know what you're thinking."

Because he thought they could use some levity, Heath asked, "You have a little mole on your butt cheek?"

"All right, I didn't know what you were thinking after all. I thought you might be wondering if I was trying to outrun my past by transferring colleges."

That hadn't even crossed his mind, mainly because he wondered why he hadn't noticed that mole on her butt cheek. He was also wanting to see that mole. Clearly, he had a one-track mind here.

He shook his head. "I didn't think the transfer was about running, more like ulcer prevention. No need for you to have to face a daily dose of Mr. Wrong and his new family."

"Exactly." She smiled in a triumphant *I didn't think you'd get that* kind of way.

Heath got it all right. He got a lot of things when it came to Anna. A lot of things because of her, too. Like that tug below his belly that nudged him to kiss her again. That was his red-flag warning to get moving, and he would have done just that if he hadn't spotted the silver heart locket on her nightstand.

When she saw that he'd spotted it, she tried to put it in the drawer, but Heath took hold of her hand to stop her.

Yes, it was the locket he'd given her all right.

"After Della asked about it, I found it in my old jewelry box," she said. Then, she frowned. "All right, I wear it sometimes. Okay?"

She didn't sound especially happy about that, but it pleased Heath that she still had it. Pleased him even more than she occasionally wore it. What didn't please him was the reminder of the two words engraved on it.

"Be my." Anna ran her fingertips over it. "I wasn't sure what you were saying—be my heart, be my locket. Be my lay in the hay." She chuckled, poked him with her elbow.

"It was a fill-in-the-blank kind of thing," he joked, poking her back with his elbow.

"It sounds to me as if you didn't know what you wanted to say." No elbow poke that time.

"I was eighteen. I didn't know."

"And now?" she asked.

For two little words, it was a mighty big question. One that he didn't have to answer because there was a knock at the door, and the knocker didn't wait for an invitation to come in. The door opened.

Riley.

Well, at least Anna and he weren't in a butt-grabbing

lip-lock as they'd been in the barn when Lucky had found them.

"I need to talk to you," Riley said, looking at Heath. Then his gaze swung to his sister. "And no, this isn't about you. It's business."

Damn it. That didn't sound good.

Anna must have thought so, too, because she gave Heath a sympathetic look as Riley and he headed out. They didn't go far, just into the foyer.

"I just found out that you're still trying to get out of your instructor assignment, that you put in a request to go on another deployment," Riley threw out there.

Heath cursed. He wasn't exactly keeping it from Riley. Okay, he was, but he didn't want to justify what he was trying to do.

"You've already had two back-to-back deployments as an officer," Riley reminded him. "Before that, you had back-to-back-to-backs as a pararescuer."

"You're going on another one," Heath reminded him just as fast.

"I've had breaks in between. In the past ten years, the only time you've been stateside is for leave and training." He put his hand on Heath's shoulder. "You don't have anything to prove."

"No disrespect, *sir*, but I have everything to prove. To myself anyway."

Riley huffed. "You can prove it by being the best Air Force instructor you can be."

"That sounds like a recruitment pitch."

"It is." Riley took his hand from Heath's shoulder, and his index finger landed against Heath's chest. "And here's some more advice—sometimes life gives you crap, and you just have to make crappy lemonade out of it."

Heath frowned, thinking he might never again want

another glass of lemonade. Or another lecture from Riley. Of course, there wouldn't be any more Riley lectures if Heath got stuck with that instructor job he didn't want. Then Riley would no longer be his boss.

Frowning, too, possibly over that bad lemonade analogy, Riley walked away. Heath would have, as well. He would have headed back to the pasture to do something, anything, to burn off some of this restless energy inside him.

Yeah, he needed an adrenaline fix *bad*.

He figured in that moment that his thought must have tempted fate, because his phone dinged with a text message. There was that old saying about when the gods wanted to punish you, they gave you what you wanted. Well, it wasn't from the gods.

It was from Anna.

And the text flashed like neon on his phone screen. A sort of warning from the gods out to punish him.

Meet me in the hayloft in one hour.

CHAPTER FOUR

ANNA FIGURED SHE wasn't just going to be able to sneak out of the house without anyone seeing her.

And she was right.

As she was cutting through the sunroom, Della spotted her. Anna smiled, tried to look as if she weren't up to something, but that was sort of hard to do considering she had a six-pack of beer in a plastic grocery bag. A six-pack Anna had just scrounged from the fridge.

Della glanced at the bag and its distinctive shape. Then gave Anna no more than a mere glance.

"What are you up to?" Della asked.

Anna shrugged. "I'm considering playing with some fire. Running with scissors. Taking candy from some guy I don't know."

Falling hard for an old flame she shouldn't fall hard for was something Anna could add to that list of no-no's.

"So, you're going to the barn again with Heath," Della said. It wasn't a question.

"No. Yes," she admitted when Della gave her that liar-liar-pants-on-fire look. Anna huffed. "Don't give me a hard time about this. I'm tired of everyone babying me."

"They do that because you're the baby."

"*Was* the baby," Anna corrected. "I'm a grown woman now, but none of them can seem to accept it."

"They love you," Della pointed out.

"And I love them, but I want the key to my own chastity belt."

Della smiled that sly little smile of hers which meant she could be up to something. But she only kissed Anna on the cheek. "Honey, you've had that key for a long time now. Might be time to see if it works the way you want it to work."

Anna opened her mouth to respond, but she had nothing to say. Not a word. Instead, she returned the cheek kiss, tucked the beer under her arm so the bottles wouldn't jiggle and clang, and headed out the back.

No brothers in sight. No ranch hands, either.

But she also didn't see Heath.

Since it was—Anna checked the time on her phone—three minutes to rendezvous, she'd hoped she would see him waiting for her. He better not have blown her off. Except Heath wouldn't do that. Well, he might have done it with a text, call or chat, but he wouldn't do an unannounced blowing-off.

And he hadn't.

The moment she stepped in the barn, she saw him. Not in the hayloft, but standing by the steps that led up to the loft.

"You came," she said.

"Of course I came. I'm a guy and I'm not stupid. All right, maybe I am stupid, but the guy part's still true, and I've got the junk to prove it."

She smiled, chuckled. All nerves, and she hated the nerves because they didn't go well with this blistering attraction. "Yes, I got a glimpse of your junk. You're definitely a guy."

He smiled, too. "Beer?" he asked, tipping his head to the bag.

"I thought you might be thirsty. It was either this, milk or a questionable green smoothie."

"You made the right choice. I've already had my quota of milk and questionable green smoothies for a while."

He reached out, took her by the fingertips. That was it. The only part of her he touched. It was like being hit by a really big dose of pure, undiluted lust.

"You may have made the right choice with the beer," he added a heartbeat later. "But asking me to meet you here might fall into the stupid category."

"Might?" she repeated. Well, it was better than an out-and-out "this ain't gonna happen."

"Is this going to happen?" Anna came out and asked.

With only that teeny grip on her fingertips, he inched her closer. So close that when she breathed, she drew in his scent. Mixed with the hay and the crisp November air, it gave her another dose of lust.

"It shouldn't happen," Heath said. "I've tried to talk myself out of it."

"And?" She was still breathing, through her mouth now. Still taking in that scent. Still feeling him play with her fingers. "I hope you're really lousy at talking yourself out of things."

He closed his eyes a moment. Groaned. And, as if he were fighting—and losing—a fierce battle, he brought her another inch closer. She figured if the lust doses kept coming that she was going to launch herself into his arms.

"I'm leaving soon," he reminded her. "And I'm trying to do the right thing here."

She wanted to point out that unless he was leaving within the hour, then this could indeed happen, but that would just make her sound needy. Which she was. So very, very needy.

He let go of her fingertips, and she figured this was it.

Heath would send her on her way. But he took the beer from her, and as if he had all the time in the world, he set the bag next to a hay bale.

"So, what now?" she asked.

Heath didn't answer her. Not with words. He reached out, and just when she thought she was going to get more fingertip foreplay, he took hold of her, snapped her to him and kissed the living daylights out of her.

Anna forgot all about the stupid argument that he was leaving soon. She forgot how to breathe. But other feelings took over, too. Probably because Heath didn't just kiss.

He touched.

He slipped his hand between them and ran his fingers over her right breast. Nice, but he double-whammied it with a neck kiss, and Anna felt herself moving. At first she thought it was just her body melting, but nope, she and Heath were walking.

"What are we doing?" she asked.

"Complicating the hell out of things."

"Good. I like complications." At the moment she would have agreed to a lobotomy.

Heath kept kissing her, kept moving. Not up the steps of the hayloft but rather toward the tack room. Maybe because it had a door. Maybe because it didn't require the coordination of step climbing with an erection. Maybe because it was just closer.

It was the erection thing, she decided, and since she could feel it against her stomach, Anna added some touching of her own. She worked her hand over his zipper and would have gotten that zipper down if Heath hadn't stopped her.

She heard herself make a whiny sound of protest, but then he put her against the back of the door that he'd just shut, and he lifted her. Until his hard junk was against her soft junk. Everything lined up just right to create a mind-blowing sensation.

"Let's play a game," he said. And yeah, he drawled.

Anna nodded. She would have agreed to a second lobotomy.

"On a scale of one to ten, rate the kisses, and then I'll know which parts to concentrate on."

She wasn't sure she could count to ten, much less rate kisses, but Heath jumped right into the game. He kissed her mouth.

"A ten," she said after he left her gasping for air and reaching for his zipper again.

He put his hand over hers to stop her, but Anna just used the pressure of his hand to add pressure to his erection.

"We'll play that particular game later," he promised.

Heath moved on to the next kiss. He placed one in the little area just below her ear, and he must have remembered that was a hot spot for her because it didn't seem like a lucky guess.

"Fifty," she blurted out. If Heath hadn't held her in place with his body, she would have dropped like a rock. There were no muscles in her legs, and her feet had perhaps disappeared.

"I'll definitely put that on my playlist," he said and added a flick of his tongue in that very hot spot that needed no such licking to further arouse it.

She went after his zipper for a third time, and the only reason she failed, again, was because he pushed up her sweater, pushed down her bra and did that tongue-flicking thing over her nipples.

"A seventy," she managed to say.

"Scale of one to ten," he corrected.

"Ten plus sixty."

He chuckled, which made for some very interesting sensations since he still had his mouth on her nipple.

"And this one?" he asked. He went lower, kissed her stomach.

"Ten," she admitted, and she was about to pull him back to her to breast and neck.

Then he went down a few more inches.

Heath clearly had some experience in zipper lowering. *Fast* zipper lowering. He slid down, unzipping her and dragging her jeans just low enough so that he could plant the next kiss on her panties.

Anna threw back her head, hitting it against the door and perhaps giving herself a concussion. She didn't care if she did. That's because the only thing that mattered now was the pleasure. Such a puny word for the incredible things Heath was doing with his mouth.

"Your rating?" he asked, and mercy, he added some breath with that question.

"Six million," she managed to say.

He laughed.

"One more kiss," he said. "Then it'll be your turn."

Oh, she wanted a turn all right. Wanted it badly. Until he shimmied down her panties, put her knee on his shoulder and kissed her again. A special kiss.

Tongue flicks included.

After a couple of those flicks, Anna went into forget mode again. The thought of taking her turn went right out of her head. Everything vanished. Except for the feeling that she was about to shatter. And fall. And shatter some more.

Heath made sure he gave her the *more* she needed for shattering. One last well-placed kiss. An equally well-placed tongue flick. And all she could do was fist her hand in his hair and let him shatter her.

She had to take a moment to gather her breath. Another moment to keep gathering it. But even with the ripples of the climax tingling through her, she wanted to get started on her turn. And she was going to torture the hell out of Heath and his junk.

"Damn," Heath growled.

It took her a moment to realize that he was reacting to something he heard.

A knock at the tack room door.

"Heath?" Riley called out.

Hell.

"Uh, Heath, I need to talk to you," Riley added. "It's important."

Unless the world was about to end and Heath could stop it, then it wasn't that important, but Anna conceded that was the lust talking.

"How important?" Heath asked.

"Very."

Heath and she both cursed.

"Anna's in here with me," Heath volunteered.

It took Riley several snail-crawling seconds to respond to that. "Yes, I figured that out. Didn't think you'd go into the tack room alone and close the door. But this isn't about Anna. It's about your assignment."

Heath groaned, stood back up, helping her fix her jeans and panties. "You can wait in here if you want," he offered.

"Not a chance," Anna argued. "Riley knows what we've been doing. Or rather what we started doing, and the assignment thing could be a ruse to draw us out so he can ambush you with a shovel."

He brushed a kiss on her mouth. "You've got a very

active imagination." Though she knew there might be a grain of truth in her theory.

Heath went out ahead of her, and Riley was indeed right there. He was sitting on a hay bale, drinking one of the beers. She braced herself for him to say something snarky like had she been trying to get Heath drunk or why did she have this thing for barn sex?

He didn't.

Riley did give her a look that only a big brother could have managed, but it had some, well, sympathy mixed in with the brotherly snark. A strange combination.

"I just came from the base," Riley said to Heath. "They want to see you about your deployment request."

"Deployment request?" Anna repeated. "I thought Heath was going to Florida."

Riley remained quiet, clearly waiting for Heath to explain.

"I asked to be diverted from the instructor job to another deployment," Heath said.

Riley's arrival had been a killjoy in the sexual-pleasure department, but hearing about Heath's request was a different kind of killjoy. Although obviously not for Heath since this was something he wanted.

Very much.

After all, he'd told her that the instructor job made him feel washed up, and maybe now he wouldn't have to feel that way because he could go back to one of those classified sandy locations. Where people shot at him and where he could be hurt or killed.

Mercy.

That felt as if she'd been slammed with a truckload of bricks. And there was no reason for it, because this was Heath's job. No logical reason anyway. But Anna wasn't feeling very logical at the moment.

"They want to see you out at the base right away," Riley added.

Heath nodded, looked at her as if he needed to say something, but Anna let him off the hook. She smiled, brushed a kiss on his cheek.

"Go," she insisted, trying to keep that smile in place. "We can talk when you get back."

Heath hesitated, gave another nod and then walked toward the house. Anna managed to keep her smile in place until he was out of sight. Riley opened a bottle of beer and handed it to her.

"Will he get to come back here to the ranch if the deployment is approved?" Anna asked, though she was afraid to hear the answer. "Or will they send him out right away?"

"Hard to say."

Or maybe not. The next thing Anna saw was Heath leaving the house, carrying his gear. He put it in his rental car and drove off. Obviously, he was prepared to go.

Anna took a long swig of that beer and wished it was something a whole lot stronger.

"Best to forget him," Riley said as they watched Heath drive away. "Heath isn't the settling-down type."

If only that weren't true.

"It's just a fling," Riley added. "That's what it was nine and a half years ago, and that's what it is now."

If only that were *true.*

CHAPTER FIVE

THE MCCORD BROTHERS were waiting for Heath when he got back from the base, and they didn't even try to make it look like a friendly, casual meeting. They were in the living room just off the foyer, and the moment Heath stepped inside, they stood.

No shovels. Not physical ones anyway.

"Where's Anna?" Heath asked. "You didn't lock her in her room, did you?"

The joke didn't go over so well, but Heath didn't care. He was tired, frustrated and wanted to talk to Anna, not the kid-sister police.

"Anna's Christmas shopping in San Antonio," Logan answered. "She'll be back any minute now."

Good. Well, sort of good. Heath definitely wanted to see her even if she probably hadn't liked his news. Hell, he hadn't liked it much, either.

"My request for deployment was denied," Heath explained. "The Air Force wants me to report to the base in Florida day after tomorrow so I'll have to cut my visit here short."

He expected them to jump for joy. Or at least smile. They didn't.

Riley immediately shook his head. "I didn't have anything to do with that."

Heath nearly snapped out "Right," but he knew in his gut that Riley was telling the truth. He wouldn't do anything like that even if it meant saving his sister from having sex with a guy Riley didn't think was right for her.

And Riley was spot-on.

Heath wasn't right for her. End of subject.

"I'll leave tomorrow," Heath added. "I just want a chance to say goodbye to Anna first."

None of the brothers objected, and Heath wouldn't have cared if they did. Yeah, it was the pissed-off mood again, but he had to get something off his chest.

"I know you think I'm a jerk, that I'm here only to try to seduce Anna, but I do care about her. Always have. If I hadn't cared, I would have never had sex in the hayloft with her nine and a half years ago."

There. He'd said it. But they weren't saying anything back to him. Maybe because Riley and Logan hadn't known about the sex. Lucky had, of course, because of the pee stick discovery, but even Lucky might have been stunned to silence to hear the de-virgining had taken place in the barn.

"Anna cares about you, too," Lucky finally said.

"She'll cry a lot again when you leave," Logan added.

"She'll be hurt," Riley piped in.

Maybe. Probably, Heath silently amended. Yeah, he was a jerk all right, but he was a jerk on orders, and that meant leaving whether he wanted to or not.

And he did want to leave, Heath assured himself.

He did.

Silently repeating that, Heath went to the guest room so he could finish packing.

HER BROTHERS WERE waiting for Anna when she got home. Hard to miss them since they were on the sofa in the living room.

She so didn't have the energy to deal with them now.

"You're all grounded," Anna said, going on the offensive. "Now, go to your rooms."

Of course, they didn't budge. Well, except to stand, and judging from the somber looks on their faces they had something serious to tell her. But she had something to say, too.

"I already know about Heath's deployment being denied. He texted me right after he got the news. He was at the base and couldn't talk, but he wanted to let me know that he's leaving tomorrow."

They stared at her as if expecting her to sprout an extra nose or something. Then Riley's hawkeyed gaze moved to the Victoria's Secret bag she was holding.

"Yes, I bought it for Heath," Anna admitted. "For me to wear for Heath," she amended when their stares turned blank. "It's red and slutty, and if you don't quit staring at me like that, I'll give you lots of details about what I want Heath to do to me while I'm wearing it."

Logan's eyes narrowed. Riley's jaw tightened. Lucky shrugged and went to her. He pulled her into his arms despite the fact she was as stiff as a statue from the mini hissy fit she'd just thrown.

"I've got two words for you," Lucky whispered to her. "Condom."

She pulled back, looked at him. "That's one word."

"If you wear what's in that bag, you'll need two condoms. Three if you skip what's in the bag all together and just show up in your birthday suit. Either way, condoms."

In that moment he was her favorite brother. Lucky had always been her champion and not judgmental. Most of the time anyway. Plus, he was the only brother who talked safe sex with her. Or any kind of sex for that matter. He wasn't just her brother, he was her friend.

Anna kissed his cheek. "Thanks."

He shrugged in that lazy but cool way that only Lucky or a Greek god could manage. It was as if he drawled his shrugs. And his life.

Lucky returned the cheek kiss and apparently considered his brotherly/friendly duties done because he strolled toward the door and headed out. Logan went to her next.

"I love you," Logan said. "And no matter what happens, I'll be here for you. You can cry on my shoulder all you need. Or if you prefer, I can kick Heath's ass for you. Your choice."

She had to fight a smile, but she didn't have to fight it too hard because the nonsmiling emotions were just below the surface. "I don't want his ass kicked, but I might need the shoulder."

Logan tapped first one shoulder, then the other. "Any time. They're reserved just for you, and I swear *I told you so* will never cross my lips or my mind. You're a grown woman, and if you want to wear what's in that bag, then you have my blessing."

In that moment she loved Logan best. Logan had been her father more than her brother, mainly because he'd been the one to step up after their folks died. He'd been the one to bust her chops when she needed it and had been a whiz helping with her math homework.

Logan would walk through fire for her and not once complain. Well, maybe he would complain, but he'd still do it.

He kissed her forehead and headed off, not out the door but to his old room. Since he lived in town and no longer spent many nights at the ranch, Logan must have wanted his shoulders to be nearby in the event of an impending crying spell.

Uh-oh.

It was Riley's turn.

"If Heath makes you cry again, I'm hitting him with the shovel," Riley growled. "And wear a robe with whatever's in that bag."

Anna sighed. The support of two out of three wasn't bad.

Riley sighed as well, and he pulled her into his arms. "FYI, Heath did some crying, too, after he left here that summer."

Anna wiggled out of his grip so she could see if he was serious or not. He was.

"I don't mean he actually shed tears," Riley went on, "but he cried in his own man kind of way."

"How do you know that?" she asked.

"Because I'm the one who drove him to his basic training." A muscle flickered in his jaw. A sign that he was remembering that day as unfondly as she was. Some of the anger returned. "Heath asked me to make sure you were okay. Can you believe it?"

"The bastard," Anna joked.

"He said it as if I needed to be reminded of it. I didn't. Not then, not now. If you need someone to make sure you're okay, I'll do it. As long as I don't have to hear any sex details. Or see what's in that bag. And I'll do that— minus the exceptions—because you're my sister."

Anna blinked back tears. In that moment, she loved Riley best. Yes, he was hardheaded, and they had a history of sibling squabbles. Plus, there was the time when he'd ruined all her dolls with camo paint and duct-tape combat boots, but still she loved every stubborn, camo-painting ounce of him.

Riley wasn't her father or her friend. He was her brother.

And sometimes, like now, that was exactly what a sister needed.

CHAPTER SIX

HEATH PACED. CURSED. He figured this much debate hadn't gone into some battle plans, but a battle plan would have been easier than trying to figure out what to do about Anna.

Or better yet what to do *with* Anna.

If he went to her room, sex would happen. Then tomorrow he would leave—just as he'd done nine and a half years ago. That hadn't turned out so well, what with all the crying and her brothers wanting to shovel him.

If he didn't go to her room, sex wouldn't happen. But then he would have to leave things unsettled between them—again—as he'd apparently done before.

He was screwed either way, so Heath decided he might as well go for it. He threw open the door and nearly smacked right into some idiot wearing a hoodie and an army-green vinyl poncho.

Except this was no idiot. It was Anna, and in addition to the garb, she was also carrying a blue sock.

She practically pushed him back into his room and shut the door. "Shhh," she said. "Della and Stella's book club is meeting tonight."

He was still wrapping his mind around the fact that Anna was there, that she had come to him, and maybe that's why Heath couldn't quite wrap his mind around the book club or the poncho.

"There are six of them in the living room, and I had

to sneak past them," Anna added when he gave her a blank look.

When Heath kept that blank look, Anna pulled off the poncho, and he saw the hoodie. No pants. No shoes.

Just a pair of really tiny devil-red panties.

He was sure his blank look disappeared because his mouth dropped open. This was the best kind of surprise.

"I didn't have a robe here at the ranch, and the plastic poncho felt sticky against my skin so I put on the hoodie," she explained. Then she unzipped it.

No top. No bra. Just the Be My heart locket dangling between her breasts. Heath thought maybe his tongue was doing some dangling, too.

"And the sock?" he asked.

She smiled and emptied the contents onto the bed. Condoms. At least a dozen of them.

"I took them from Lucky's bathroom," Anna explained. She was still whispering, but it had a giddiness to it. "The poncho and hoodie didn't have pockets so I put them in the sock. I only brought the normal-looking ones. Some had pictures on them and some were glow in the dark." Anna looked at him. "Why would a man need that?"

Heath didn't have a clue. He didn't need any illumination to find anything on Anna's body. His most vital organ agreed. In fact, it wanted to go on that particular search mission right now.

But there was a problem.

"You got my text saying I was leaving, right?" he asked.

She nodded. "Tomorrow. That's why I didn't want to wait until after the book club left. Sometimes they hang around until midnight if Della breaks out the tequila, and we don't have much time."

Not if they were planning on using all those condoms, they didn't, but Heath had to make sure that Anna was sure. She stripped off the hoodie, and he was sure she was sure.

At least he wanted her to be.

He wanted that even more when she slipped into his arms and kissed him. Heath was stupid and weak so it took him a moment to break the kiss.

"Anna, I don't want you hurt," he said.

She frowned. "I think that ship's sailed. I'll be hurt, but I'll get over it. And tonight you'll give me some really good memories to help me get over it, right?"

Yeah.

Whether they had sex or not, Anna would be hurt. Or at least she would be sad to see him go. Ditto for him being sad to leave her. But at least this way they'd have new memories, and they didn't need glow-in-the-dark condoms to do it.

Now that he had a clearly defined mission, Heath pulled her back to him to kiss her. One of those kisses that reached scorch level pretty darn fast. But Anna was aiming for fast, too, and not with just the kisses. She was already going after his zipper.

"We're going to play that scale-of-one-to-ten game," she insisted.

Maybe. But the way she was tugging at his zipper, it was possible she was also trying to finish this all way too fast. Tonight, he didn't want the kissing game, and he didn't want fast.

Heath stopped what she was doing by catching on to her wrists and putting her against the wall. He liked walls because it gave him some control...

Damn.

He had no control. Anna ground herself against him,

sliding her leg up the outside of his so that the millimeter of red lace was right against his crotch. Apparently, the orgasm she'd had earlier in the barn hadn't done anything to take the edge off because she was going for another one very quickly.

Again, Heath tried to slow things down. With her leg still cradling his, he turned her, intending to put her against the dresser, but he tripped over the poncho and fell onto the bed.

With Anna on top of him.

"Let's play a game," she said. Definitely not a virginal tone or look. "I'll use just my tongue to find all your special spots. You don't have to give it a number rating. Just a grunt for pleasure. A groan for find another special spot that's more special."

"Men only have one special spot," he told her. Heath took her hand and put it over his sex.

She laughed. Not a humor kind of laugh but the sound of a woman who'd come to play. Or maybe give a little payback for the things he'd done to her in the tack room. Well, Heath wanted to play, too. After all, he had a nearly naked Anna straddling him, and her breasts were making his mouth water.

He managed a quick sample of her left nipple before she moved away. Anna didn't waste any time. With her hand still on his special spot, she went in search of others. His earlobe.

He grunted, but Heath didn't know if that was because, at the same time, she started lowering his zipper.

"That wasn't a loud enough grunt," she said and went after his neck.

Heath grunted. Again, mainly because she lowered the zipper, and when she did that, her breasts got closer to his mouth again. She didn't grunt when he kissed her there, but she did make that silky sound of pleasure that Heath would never tire of hearing.

He would have kept on kissing her breasts, but apparently it was special-spot search time again because she scooted lower and ran her tongue over his own left nipple.

Oh, yeah. He grunted.

Grunted some more when she circled his navel with her tongue. All that tonguing and circling though didn't stop her from getting his zipper all the way down, and as he had done to her earlier, she shimmied his jeans lower.

"You really do go commando," she said.

"Yep—"

He might have added more. Something clever or at least coherent, but her hands were on him. The condom, too. Heath wasn't sure when she'd opened one of the packets. Nor did he care. The woman had clever hands after all—

Hell.

He grunted loud enough to trigger an earthquake when she dropped down onto him. That's when he figured out really, really fast that the panties were crotchless and that he was in her warm and tight special place all the way to the hilt.

"That's not your tongue," he said through the grunts.

"So, I cheated."

The woman was evil. And damn good. Heath usually liked to be the alpha when it came to sex, but even more than that, he liked taking turns with Anna. Apparently, she was going to make the most of her turn, too. She had the whole *ride 'em, cowgirl* motion going on. So fast that Heath knew this would all end too soon.

Of course, sixteen hours was going to be too soon.

As if she'd read his mind, she slowed. Anna put her

palm on his chest and, still moving against his erection, leaned down and kissed him.

"After this," she said, "I want you all the way naked."

Heath thought that was a stellar idea. He wanted those panties off her, too, even though they fell into the *why bother* category of women's undergarments.

The locket whacked him in the face, but even that didn't put a damper on the moment. Heath just pushed the locket aside, gathered her close and let his cowgirl screw his brains out.

CHAPTER SEVEN

Anna wished there were some kind of anticry shot she could take. Even one that worked for just an hour or so would do. She figured she'd do plenty of crying after Heath had left, but she didn't want any tears shed in front of him.

Or in front of her brothers.

She wanted Heath to remember her smiling. Or maybe naked, since that's how he'd seen her for a good portion of the night. It was certainly how she wanted to remember him.

With that reminder/pep talk still fresh in her mind, Anna left her bedroom and went in search of Heath so she could give him that smiling goodbye she'd practiced in the mirror. But he wasn't in his bedroom. Or the living room. Or the kitchen. In fact no one was, and she figured they'd all cleared out to give her a chance to have a private goodbye with Heath.

Or maybe they'd cleared out because Heath was already gone. She had several moments of panic when she sprinted to the back porch to make sure his rental car was still there.

It was.

And so was Heath.

He was at the fence pasture, looking at some cows that'd been delivered that morning. He made a picture standing there with his foot on the bottom rung of the fence, his cream-colored cowboy hat slung low on his face.

He must have heard her approaching because he turned, smiling. It looked about as genuine as the one she was trying to keep on her face. Until he reached out, pulled her to him and kissed her.

Then the smiles were real.

"How soon before you leave?" she asked.

"Soon."

That reminder made her smile waver. Anna wasn't sure how far to push this part of the conversation, but there was something she had to know. "Are you feeling any better about the instructor job?"

"I've accepted it. Sometimes, that's the best you can do with crappy lemonade. Sorry," Heath added when she frowned. "It was just something Riley said. An analogy of sorts."

Riley not only needed a new threat, he needed new analogies, as well.

Since their time together was about to end, Anna reached into her pocket and took out the "gift" she'd gotten him on her shopping trip the day before. She hadn't wanted it to be a big gift because that would have made this goodbye seem, well, big.

Which it was.

But she didn't want it to feel big to him.

She took his hand and dropped the smashed penny in it. "It reminded me of your dog tags, and it's supposed to be good luck."

He stared at it, gave a slight smile. "Thanks."

"I was going to give you the red panties," she added, "but I thought it would look strange if the TSA went through your luggage."

Now she got the reaction she wanted. A bigger smile. A bigger kiss, too.

"I have something for you," he said. He took out a silver heart locket. It was similar to the other one he'd given her nine and a half years ago. Very similar.

Right down to the Be My engraving.

Anna checked to make sure she had on the original one. She did. And she was shaking her head until Heath opened it, and she saw what was inside. Not pictures of him and her.

But of her parents. Her dad on one side of the heart. Her mother on the other.

"Della got the pictures for me," he explained. "You said sometimes you forget their faces, and this way you won't forget."

Oh, God.

She was going to cry.

No matter how hard she blinked, the tears came, and they just kept coming.

"I'm sorry." Heath pulled her back in his arms. "I didn't know it would upset you."

"It doesn't," she said, sobbing. "It's a good kind of upset." Still sobbing. "Thank you, Heath, thank you."

He held her while she sobbed, and it took Anna several long moments to stop.

"I got you something else," he added.

Anna couldn't imagine getting anything better than the second locket. It was even more precious to her than the first one. But Heath must have thought "the more the better" because he took out a wad of lockets from his coat pocket.

"I went to the jewelry store this morning and bought every locket they had."

She had no doubts about that—none. There was another silver one, one gold and another in the shape of a cat's head.

"They're, uh, beautiful." Though she couldn't imagine needing that many lockets. Or the ugly one with the cat's head.

"I had them engraved," he added, "and this time I watched to make sure they did it right. You can choose which one you want."

It took her a second to realize he'd finished his sentence. Not "which one you want *to wear*." Not "which one you want *to keep*." Not "which one you want *to remember me by*."

Heath turned over one of the silver ones, and she saw the engraving there. One word.

Lover.

He put the Be My locket next to it, and she got the message then. Be my lover.

She laughed. "Does this mean you want to see more of me?"

"Well, I've already seen more, but I'd like to see more of you more often."

That dried any remnants of her tears, and she blurted out an idea she'd been toying with for days. "I could look into transferring to a law school in Florida." And she held her breath.

No smile from him. "I don't want you to sacrifice going to a school that maybe doesn't have as good of a reputation as the one you're in now."

"No sacrifice. There are a couple of really good ones. And besides, I was transferring anyway. Might as well transfer so you can—" she held up the two lockets to finish that thought "—Be My Lover."

Anna tested his neck again with a kiss. And her tongue.

"Keep that up, and you'll be my lover again right now," he grumbled.

"If that's supposed to make me behave, then it won't work. Not with the hayloft so close. How much time do you have before you need to leave for your flight?"

"Not enough time for the hayloft."

She kissed him again, and he seemed to change his mind about that. He started leading her in that direction.

"Not enough time for the hayloft unless we hurry," Heath amended.

Good. The kisses were working.

Since she'd already put her heart on the line, Anna put the rest of herself out there, too. "I don't want a fling."

"Good. Flings are overrated." He kissed her again. "And temporary."

She released the breath she didn't even know she'd been holding. Heath didn't want temporary. Nor a fling. He wanted sex.

That was a solid start since she wanted that, too.

"I'm not done," he said. "Remember, you pick the locket you want." He held up the next one, the gold one, and it also had a single word engraved on it.

Woman.

As in Be My Woman.

Yes, they were so going to that hayloft, and then she was going to the university to start that transfer to Florida.

"Can I wear both the *Lover* and *Woman*?" she asked. Because she wanted both.

"You haven't seen the third one yet."

And she probably couldn't see it before the next kiss crossed her eyes. Along with singeing her eyelashes.

Still, he put the locket in her hand just as her butt landed against the ladder. Anna backed up one step at a time, which wasn't easy to do with Heath kissing her like that. And he kept on kissing her until they made it all the way to the top of the hayloft.

But Anna froze when she saw what was engraved on the tacky cat's head locket.

Love.

"Be My Love," she said, putting the words together.

Putting *everything* together.

"The *L* word?" she asked.

Heath nodded. "Sometimes it's the only word that works. What about you? Does the *L* word work for you?"

Anna had to catch her breath just so she could speak. "It works perfectly for me." She kissed him. "Does this mean we're going steady?"

"Oh, yeah," Heath confirmed. "That, and a whole lot more."